"Oh, my G[...] [...]ked a handsom[...] [...]ht orange Jet Sk[...] [...]idn't see you. What are you doing floating all the way out here by yourself?"

Ayana glanced around the vast body of water and didn't see the beach. She had drifted out farther than anticipated. "I hadn't planned on floating this far—guess the waves carried me away," she said, treading water.

He reached out his hand to her. "Get on. I'll take you back to shore, so you don't have to swim so far."

She brushed her hair out of her face, rubbed the salt water out of her eyes and looked up into his face. She couldn't believe her eyes. Behind a pair of dark aviator shades was Brandon. "Uh...sure." She took hold of his hand, climbed out of the water and settled on the back of the Jet Ski. Ayana wrapped her arms around his bare chest and held on tight as he sped off.

"Where are you staying?" he yelled.

With the Jet Ski creating a cascade of waves and the roar of the motor, she could barely hear him. "What'd you say?"

"I said where are you staying?" he asked more loudly.

"Just keep straight," she responded, finally hearing him.

He doesn't know it's me.

Books by Velvet Carter

Harlequin Kimani Romance

Blissfully Yours

VELVET CARTER

is not just the name of a luxurious fabric, but it's also the name of one of the world's leading writers of "exotica." She's a prolific novelist, who paints pictures with her words. Velvet has her finger on the pulse and knows how to make your heart race with her tantalizing stories filled with romance and seduction. Her novels have been translated into German, and released in London to critical acclaim. Velvet uses the world as her muse, traveling the globe for provocative inspiration.

Blissfully Yours

VELVET CARTER

HARLEQUIN® KIMANI™ ROMANCE

To those who found bliss when they least expected,
and to those who are still joyfully looking!

Recycling programs
for this product may
not exist in your area.

ISBN-13: 978-0-373-86337-2

BLISSFULLY YOURS

Copyright © 2014 by Danita Carter

HARLEQUIN®

Printed in U.S.A.

™ www.Harlequin.com

Dear Reader,

I'd like to thank you for purchasing *Blissfully Yours,* my first of many novels under the Harlequin Kimani imprint. I had an absolute ball writing *Blissfully Yours.* The characters I created seemed more like close friends than fictional people….

You might notice a piece of yourself in Ayana, who is multifaceted, resourceful and fiercely independent. Brandon is such a strong yet sweet man that I wanted to immerse myself in the novel and date him! Since that wasn't possible, I left the dating to Ayana, who does a fantastic job of showing Brandon around her native island of Jamaica. They party on the beach, have romantic picnics in the Blue Mountains and make love with the sounds of the ocean as a soundtrack. I hope that *Blissfully Yours* transports you to a romantic state of relaxation.

Velvet

Chapter 1

Ayana awoke to a gentle breeze flowing through the screened French doors of her parents' Jamaican hillside home. The delicious smell of ackee and saltfish tickled her nose as she stirred underneath the white cotton sheet. She yawned wide and stretched her long limbs before climbing out of bed. Today was her last full day in Negril and she planned to make the most of her time before heading back to her hectic New York life.

She showered and dressed in cutoff blue jean shorts, a T-shirt and flip-flops. Ana—as she was known in Jamaica—pulled her long raven hair into a ponytail before trotting down the small back staircase that led to the kitchen.

"Hmm, something sure smells good," Ana said to her mother, who was laboring over the stove.

"I made ya favorite—ackee and saltfish, callaloo

and johnnycakes," her mother answered in a thick Jamaican accent.

Ayana looked at the plate of food that her mother had dished up. "Ma, I can't eat all of that." Having lived in New York for more than ten years, Ayana had adjusted her eating habits and now ate mostly salads, fish and very few carbs.

"Ya too skinny, gurl. Gotta fatten ya up." Mrs. Tosh was a traditional Jamaican mother who believed in eating heartily at every meal.

"I'm not skinny, Ma. I still have plenty of thighs and a butt," she said, looking over her shoulder at her full rear end.

"Yeah, ya are. Don't argue wit me, gurl. Sit down and eat."

Ayana didn't say another word. There was no use in debating. Her domineering mother always got the last word, so Ayana sat at the wooden kitchen table and ate every morsel. She then polished off her mega breakfast with a cup of Jamaican Blue Mountain coffee. She had to admit that eating some of her favorite childhood dishes felt good and satisfying.

"Ma, do you wanna go with me over to New Beginnings?" New Beginnings was a local women's and children's shelter that Ayana helped support with generous donations of her time and money.

"Me got no time to go to the shelter today. Got too much housework to do," she said, taking Ayana's plate and rinsing it off.

"Ma, I bought you a dishwasher so you wouldn't have to stand there and hand wash every dish. Where is the dishwasher, anyway?"

"Why ya waste ya money?"

Ayana just shook her head. She never stopped trying to spoil her parents, but they were simple people and didn't want the modern gifts she bought. "I don't consider buying my parents gifts a waste of money. Ma, you and Dad struggled for so long. Now that I'm in a position to make your lives a little easier, that's what I'm going to do." Ayana had her own stubborn streak, a trait she'd inherited from her mother.

"Go on, gurl." Her mother waved her away and continued washing dishes.

Ayana kissed her mother goodbye, went to the living room, grabbed her sunglasses and keys off the parson's table near the front door and left. She hopped on her canary-yellow Vespa and took off down the winding road. The lush hillside, dotted with hibiscus and white bougainvillea, whizzed by. Ayana loved jetting around Negril on her scooter. She had driven one ever since she was a teenager. The open air was refreshing and helped to clear her mind. This was where she'd fled to two years ago after her nasty, well-publicized divorce. Ayana thought back to that time.

"If you walk out on me, you're not getting one red cent!" Those were the last words her ex-husband, millionaire Benjamin Lewis, the founder and CEO of BL Industries, had said as Ayana left their sprawling Long Island mansion. The estate was set on three manicured acres, complete with a pool, tennis court and guest house.

Although Benjamin ran one of the world's leading electronic manufacturing companies, making millions in the process, he was a tightwad. After three years of marriage, Ayana had become sick and tired of adhering to his strict budget. He had given her a weekly allowance of two hundred dollars, much less than she had made when she was his secretary. He only increased her allowance when he wanted her to buy expensive outfits for their black-tie affairs. Benjamin loved parading her around. To him she had been nothing more than a trophy wife.

Ayana had become tired of being treated like one of his prized possessions. She couldn't take any more of his selfish ways and filed for divorce, citing cruel and unusual punishment. While the proceedings wore on, Ayana had spent her days in a tiny studio apartment on the Lower East Side, sparsely furnished with a futon, throw rug and nine-inch television.

A few days after she'd moved there, the phone rang, startling her out of her sleep. She'd reached for the cell and pressed Talk. "Hello?"

"You are still asleep? It's eleven-thirty," Reese, Ayana's best friend, had said.

"What's up?"

"You need to get out of that apartment. It's a beautiful sunny day, so let's go to lunch at that new restaurant in the Village."

"I don't have money to waste on lunch. All my cash is going toward attorney fees."

"What happened to all that jewelry Ben gave you?"

"I have a few pieces here. But the rest is in my safe-deposit box. Why do you ask?"

"You need money, right?"

"Of course I need money. You of all people know how stingy Ben was," Ayana had said, sounding irritated.

"Instead of sounding like a wounded victim, you should sell some of that ice."

"I'm not selling my jewelry. That's the one thing Ben did right. He may have been a frugal SOB as far as giving me cash, but he didn't hesitate giving Tiffany, Cartier and Harry Winston his plastic. He loved telling his business associates how much he spent on my jewelry. It was like a competition to see which man could spend the most on their wives."

"Girl, you have a fortune sitting in the bank collecting dust."

"Like I said before—I'm not selling anything. I like my jewelry."

"Have you ever heard of paste?"

"No. What's paste?"

"Basically, paste is leaded glass made to look like diamonds and colored stones. I know a place where you can take your jewelry, have it copied and then sell the originals." Reese had once worked in the Diamond District as a sales clerk, and she still had connections on Forty-Seventh Street.

"I don't know, Reese. This jewelry is the only thing of value I have left. If I sell it, then what?"

"You'll be able to pay your bills and not have to wait for the divorce settlement to get some much-needed cash."

Ayana had digested her friend's words. Reese made perfect sense. Ayana thought about the five-carat diamond engagement ring, set in platinum and sitting in the safe-deposit box. The ring that she had once treasured and wore with pride had little meaning now that her marriage was over. "I guess you do have a good point."

"I have an excellent point. Besides, you'll still have the same jewelry designs to wear—they just won't be the real thing. This jeweler is so good that no one will be able to tell the difference."

"Okay. I could actually sell my wedding set and a few other pieces. That should hold me over until the divorce is final."

That afternoon, Ayana had gone to the bank and taken her five-carat engagement ring, diamond-encrusted wedding band and sapphire necklace out of the safe-deposit box, then met Reese at the jeweler's shop on Forty-Seventh Street. A week later, she'd picked up the pastes and couldn't believe how authentic the pieces looked. She'd sold the originals, making enough money to sustain herself for the duration of the proceedings.

"Ana! Ana!" yelled the children from the shelter when they saw the yellow scooter pull into the yard.

New Beginnings was near and dear to Ayana's heart. The small, privately run shelter relied on donations from generous patrons, and Ayana was at the top of that list. She didn't have any children of her own and considered the kids at the shelter her babies.

"Hey, guys! What's happening?" Ayana hopped off the scooter, gathered as many children into her arms as she could hold and gave them all a huge hug.

"Now, now, chilrin, leave Ms. Lewis be. Go now and do yo work," Marigold, the shelter's administrator, said as she came into the yard waving her hands and shooing the children away.

"Did you get the shipment yet?"

"All dose big boxes come, and me didn't know what to do wit all dose clothes." She smiled. "We thank ya."

"You're welcome. It was no problem. All I did was

collect clothes from friends of mine who were purging their closets."

"Ya do more than send clothes. Ya send checks too, and dey help keep dis place going."

Ayana looked a bit embarrassed; she didn't like when Marigold praised her for helping. The shelter needed assistance, and she was just glad that she was now in a position to help.

"And dat stuff you send look brand-new. Some of dem tings still had da tags on 'em."

"Yeah, I know. I only select clothes that are gently worn, if not new. Did you see the note attached to that blue dress? It's for you."

"I saw it, but dat dress is too fancy fo me."

"It's only a sundress."

"Yeah, a sundress by Ralph, uh…uh…"

"Lauren. Ralph Lauren."

"Where me gonna wear some designer dress to? After me husband die, I don't go out much."

"Well, you never know what life has in store. Maybe you'll get invited to a party or asked out on a date. It's always good to have a go-to dress in your closet."

"I no want no date. James was de love of me life and after he die, a piece of me died too."

"Marigold, you're still a good-looking woman, and I'm sure James wouldn't want you to be alone for the rest of your life." Ayana sympathized with her friend but always tried to be encouraging.

"James did tell me not to pine away for him for too long," she said with a sorrowful look in her eyes.

"See what I mean. James wouldn't want you spending every night home alone."

"Okay, okay, me keep Mista Lauren. Ya wanna come

in fo some lunch? Me make kingfish stew and coco bread."

"No, thanks. I already ate. I have to go back home and pack. I just came by to see if you got the clothes and to see you and the kids."

"We hate to see ya go." Marigold gave Ayana a warm hug.

"I hate to go, but duty calls."

The truth was, Ayana wasn't looking forward to returning to New York, but her hiatus was over. The reality show that she starred in was resuming filming in a few days. She had spent two glorious months in Jamaica, eating her mother's home cooking, taking long walks on the beach and meditating at her favorite place high in the Blue Mountains. The serenity and beauty of the island, and being surrounded by people who loved her, had rejuvenated her soul. Now Ayana was ready to resume her hot-blooded persona and tackle another season of *Divorced Divas*.

Chapter 2

"We'll be starting our descent in the New York area shortly, so please return to your seats and fasten your seat belts."

Ayana heard the flight attendant's announcement through the lavatory door. She looked in the mirror and was satisfied with her transformation. Gone was the girlish ponytail, replaced by a long, flowing, platinum-blond lace-front wig. She'd traded in her island uniform of cutoff blue jean shorts, sleeveless T-shirt and flip-flops for a sexy black-and-white Tom Ford pencil skirt that hugged her full hips. The matching chiffon blouse with blouson sleeves was secured around her slim waist with a wide black leather belt dotted with silver studs. Black-and-white layered necklaces and a pair of five-inch strappy platforms completed the high-maintenance look. She applied a double coat of ruby-red lipstick to her perfectly made-up face to add a pop of color. Ayana gathered her belongings and put them back in her Prada tote. She exited the lavatory and returned to her seat in first class.

"Would you like anything else before we land?" asked the attendant.

"I'll have a glass of champagne. Actually, make it two."

After the attendant brought the drinks, Ayana drank the two flutes of bubbly and readied herself for any photographers or reporters who might be waiting for her once she deplaned. *Divorced Divas* led in the ratings due to Ayana's prima-donna persona. The gossip rags were always trying to get dirt on Saturday Knight—Ayana's name on the show—and stalked her on a regular basis. The latest story going around town was that Ayana was the reason Erick Kastell—her love interest on the show—had fled the country.

"Welcome to New York, and thanks for flying with us today. You are now free to use your cell phones," the pilot announced once they'd landed.

As the plane taxied to the gate, Ayana called Reese. "Hey, girl, we just landed. Where are you?"

"In the car, waiting outside of baggage claim."

"Okay. See you in a few."

Once the doors opened, Ayana put on a pair of over-size shades, retrieved her carry-on from the overhead bin and strutted down the pedway, into the terminal and out the door.

"Saturday! Saturday Knight! Look this way!" a photographer yelled, snapping pictures as she strolled past.

"Saturday, is it true you're the reason Moses Michaels left his girlfriend, Lisa?" a reporter shouted.

"Have you read Lisa's tweets? She's calling you a home wrecker," another reporter blurted out.

Ayana didn't even glance in their direction, though that didn't stop them from blurting out questions.

"Is it true that you and Moses Michaels are dating?" another reporter shouted.

Moses Michaels was the hot single moderator of the reality-show circuit. He and Saturday had gone out a few times, but it had not lasted.

She kept walking, looking straight ahead as if they weren't there. She saw Reese's black Benz and concentrated on making it to the car without acknowledging the annoying paparazzi and reporters.

"Hey, girl, welcome home." Reese turned to kiss Ayana on the cheek. "Well, it isn't such a good welcome with the media stalking you and accusing you of breaking up Moses and his girlfriend," Reese said as Ayana settled into the car.

"Their claims are totally untrue. Moses had broken up with his girlfriend before we'd started to date. Anyway, Moses and I are now just friends. The lies remind me of my nasty divorce," she said, remembering the highly publicized proceedings.

During the divorce trial, reporters and photographers had lined the steps of the courthouse, begging for interviews and snapping pictures. Salacious details of their marriage had made interesting headlines. Ayana had been embarrassed to read about their rather unorthodox love life.

Benjamin had leaked photos of Ayana dressed as a dominatrix, beating him with a whip. He'd accused her of dominating him against his will. It had incensed her. The entire bondage and sadomasochism idea had been his. Benjamin had bought her the black latex cat-suit, platform boots and whip, and he'd even made her watch an instructional DVD to teach her the nuances of BDSM. Ayana had resisted at first, but Benjamin had insisted. He'd said it was the ultimate thrill to have her beat him. But he'd backpedaled in court, playing the victim. He'd even produced pictures of bruises on his back.

In addition to the accusations of sexual abuse, Benjamin had accused Ayana of spousal abandonment, saying that she spent months in Jamaica. On the stand, Ayana did admit to visiting her parents. However, it was Benjamin who'd insisted that she extend her stay, saying that since they didn't have children, there was no need for her to rush back home to New York.

His team of highly paid attorneys had earned every dime of their retainer, working overtime to paint a negative picture of Ayana. Her attorney had presented her case, stating to the court that Benjamin willingly withheld funds from her, making her practically lead a destitute life, except for the times when they were out together. Her case was weak in comparison to Benjamin's. And as the weeks had dragged on, Ayana became worn out. With her funds dwindling and her emotional state deteriorating, Ayana had agreed to settle. Initially, she had been seeking half of the money he'd made while they were together but then realized that Benjamin was willing to fight dirty in order to keep from paying Ayana her share. To put an end to the spectacle and move on with her life, she'd settled for a fraction of the estate, signed the divorce papers and never looked back.

Although the proceedings had been emotionally draining, one good thing had come out of the ordeal—a job.

Little did Ayana know that tracking her divorce proceedings was show creator Ed Levine, who had struck
gold with his string of reality TV shows. He had been
looking to staff *Divorced Divas,* his latest undertaking
about divorced women of millionaires seeking a second
chance at love. He had seen Ayana on the news and in
the papers and had become taken with her. Ayana was
tall, attractive, stylish and well-spoken—all the ingredients of a television star. He'd contacted her attorney
and set up a meeting.

However, Ayana had had no interest in exposing her
life on camera. Being in the media during the divorce
was enough, so she'd turned down the meeting. Ayana's
post-divorce plan was to reenter corporate America. The
only problem was her limited experience. Her last job
had been as Benjamin's administrative assistant. She'd
dusted off her résumé, made calls and tried to set up
interviews to no avail. Her skill set wasn't the problem;
being the former Mrs. Benjamin Lewis was. Apparently,
he had put the word out and blacklisted her.

In need of an income, Ayana had asked her attorney
to contact the producers. Their initial meeting had gone
well, except for one glitch. Ed had wanted Ayana to play
the role of the good girl, but he had filled that role after
she had turned him down. The only slot left to fill was
that of the "diva." Ayana had been reluctant but was in
dire straits and needed money badly, so she'd accepted
the role along with the stage name. A year later, Saturday Knight was a household name. Luckily, the show
wasn't broadcasted in Jamaica. Ayana couldn't stand
the thought of her family knowing that she degraded

herself on camera for a living. She hated her job but was determined to make it work. Ayana read about reality stars branding themselves, launching clothing, perfume and cosmetics lines and even going on to co-star in prime-time network series and movies. Some of them were making millions, and that was exactly what she planned to do.

"So are you well rested and ready for another season of *Divorced Divas?*" Reese asked as they drove along the FDR.

"I am rested, but the thought of another unnecessary catfight makes my stomach churn."

"Girl, what's up with that? Why do people love to see grown women acting like teenagers, fighting and yelling at each other?"

Ayana hunched her shoulders. "Wish I knew. Seems the more controversy on the show, the higher the ratings."

"Does the creator of the show even know your true personality? You're the nicest person anyone could ever meet."

"Yeah, he knows, but for Ed, it's all about ratings."

"Then have a meeting and ask him to change your role so that the viewers can see who you really are."

"Last season, a director made some show suggestions and he was fired."

"I thought reality television was all about depicting people in their true form."

"Reese, the *reality* is that reality television is a money-making machine. The creators of these shows will go to any length to ensure ratings, even if they have to fudge the truth and stage scenes."

"What an oxymoron."

"That's an understatement. After losing nearly everything in the divorce, my focus is on building a solid financial future so that I won't have to rely on a man ever again."

"You may not need a man for money, but what about for sex?"

"Girl, sex is the furthest thing from my mind."

"When was the last time you had any?"

"Any what?"

"Stop playing. You know what I mean."

"I haven't had sex in months."

"I couldn't go a week without Joey."

"Well, consider yourself one of the lucky ones. You and Joey have a happy, healthy relationship." Reese and her husband, Joey, had met in the Diamond District.

"Yes, we do, but it didn't happen overnight. In the beginning Joey traveled to South Africa a lot on business, and the distance was hard on our relationship. It's taken years for us to get to a good place. One day you'll find your Mr. Right. What about Moses Michaels? You two went out a few times. Maybe he's the one. He sure is one good-looking man."

"No, he's not *the one* for me. I can't handle the ladies'-man type. The problem is he's *too* good-looking. Women throw themselves at him all the time, and he loves the attention. He told me in no uncertain terms that he was only interested in sex—not a relationship."

"He said that?" Reese asked, astounded.

"Yep, he sure did."

"Well…maybe you should have at least tried him on for size. He looks like he'd be a good lover."

Ayana lightly pushed Reese on the shoulder. "Ohhh, I can't believe you're saying that!"

"Why?" She smiled sheepishly.

"Because you are happily married to Joey, that's why."

"I'm married, not dead, and you would have to be dead not to notice Moses Michaels."

"Guess you have a point, and I was soooo tempted to take him up on his offer. I just didn't want to become another one of his many conquests."

"I understand that, but did you at least kiss the man?"

"Yes, we kissed."

"So was he a good kisser?"

"Aren't you the nosy one?"

"Well…curious minds want to know."

"Yes, he's a great kisser. Are you satisfied? Now can we change the subject, please?"

"Okay, okay. Forget about the players of the world. Plenty of men out there want a committed relationship. What about that guy from Switzerland who was on the show?"

"You mean Erick?"

"Yes, that's him. From the episodes I watched, you two appeared to have mad chemistry."

"We did. The producers sent us on several romantic dates and we were getting along really well until he had to go back to Switzerland and take care of some issues regarding his work papers to stay in the U.S."

"That's too bad. Don't worry. You'll find Mr. Right," Reese reiterated.

"I'm not worried, and I'm not waiting either." Ayana looked out the window for a moment, digesting her friend's words. She didn't want to admit it, since she had talked so much about getting her financial house in order, but she silently hoped for a true love of her own.

"Oh, I forgot to tell you that Joey and I are going to South Africa and then we're heading over to Antwerp, Belgium, for a diamond-buying trip. After our business is done, we're taking a holiday in Capri. We'll be gone for at least a month. I'll call you when we get back."

"That sounds like a fun trip."

"It should be. I can't wait."

Listening to Reese expound about her overseas trip with her husband, Ayana couldn't help but be a little jealous. The thought of spending time away with the man you loved was not in Ayana's near future and that reality saddened her.

Chapter 3

"Man, have you heard from Jaclene?"

"No, not since I moved back."

Brandon Gilliam was at home talking on the phone with his best friend, Jon. Brandon had recently moved back to New York from California. Luckily, he had sublet his apartment in Tribeca and was able to make a smooth transition without having to search for months for a place to live.

"What happened between you guys? I thought you were in love."

"I thought so too. Jaclene, the wannabe starlet, was into me when she thought I was going to be a Hollywood director and cast her in a movie. When I wasn't able to land a major gig, she wasted no time dumping me. Last I heard, she was involved with some studio executive."

Brandon prided himself on his stellar career. Over

the course of ten years at a major television network in New York, he had earned five Emmys for outstanding directing of a newsmagazine show. Brandon's dream was to parlay his television skills into directing movies. Feeling that he'd done his time at the station, he'd quit, packed up his awards and moved to Hollywood. But breaking into the movie business wasn't as easy as he had envisioned. The only thing he had to show after being on the West Coast for a year was a failed relationship with a starlet and a list of contacts who would no longer accept his calls. Frustrated and tired of the endless sunshine, as well as the fake people, he'd moved back to New York as soon as his sublease agreement was over.

"Don't worry. When you become a famous director, your casting couch will have a waiting list of women begging to have sex with you."

Brandon chuckled. "Man, I'm not interested in women who want to use me to advance their career."

"Hey, as long as I'm using them back, I don't have a problem with it. Use my body, just don't abuse it." Jon laughed.

"I guess we differ in that way. I want a woman who loves me for me and not for what I can offer professionally."

"Oh, listen to you sounding like a soap opera. You were always the soft-hearted one of the group." Jon and Brandon had grown up together in Queens. They, along with three other boys, were a tight-knit bunch. Jon and Brandon were now the only two guys still single with no kids.

"Soft, my ass."

"Don't try to sound hard now. Remember that time

when we were sixteen and fine-ass Lisa McCoy came crying to you because her boyfriend left her?"

"Yeah, I remember. What about it?"

"She wanted to have sex with you to make her ex jealous. Instead of taking the panties, you talked to her on the phone all night. Now, if that ain't soft, I don't know what is."

"I didn't want to take advantage of her situation. She was clearly upset over being dumped and needed a friend."

"See, that's what I'm talking about. Even at sixteen you had a conscience."

"All men aren't dogs like you, my brother." Brandon was always a one-woman man. He had never dated multiple women at the same time, like most of his friends had.

"I prefer the term *ladies' man.*"

"Whatever, Mr. Ladies' Man. Enough of memory lane. I gotta get off the phone. I have an early call in the morning."

"That's right—you start your new gig tomorrow."

After moving back to New York, Brandon had landed a job right away. However, the position wasn't on another newsmagazine show. He was the new director of *Divorced Divas.* Though he wasn't thrilled about directing a cheesy reality show, after being out of work for a year and exhausting his savings, he had to take what he could get and that was the only show hiring.

"Unfortunately," Brandon said, sounding disgusted.

"Why do you say that?"

"Don't get me wrong. I'm grateful to be among the working class again, but directing a bunch of catty women isn't what I call good television. I can't believe this reality genre is still going strong."

"Personally, I love reality TV—the cattier the better. Seeing them chicks fling their boobs and fake hair is a turn-on. Those chicks on *Divorced Divas* are all fine, especially that Saturday Knight. I'd love to get that beautiful body of hers into my bed and show her a few tricks."

"I'll bet you would."

"You gotta hook a brother up."

"I don't think so."

"Come on, Brandon. I'm serious. Hook me up."

"I know you're serious, but I'm not there to make friends or play matchmaker. I've seen clips of the show and those chicks are cutthroat, *especially* Saturday Knight. She's the worst of them all. If I didn't need the money, I would've turned down the job. The last thing I want to do is spend my day directing a train wreck."

"Don't worry. With your smooth-as-butter nature, I'm sure you'll calm them down when they get out of hand."

"See, that's where you're wrong. I'm not going on set tomorrow playing mediator or trying to talk sense into those wildcats. I'm leaving Mr. Nice Guy at home. Tomorrow, I'm Mr. Hard Nose. I refuse to let those chicks run all over me. They'll never see my, as you say, 'soft' side."

"I can't believe you pick now to be a hard-ass, when I need you to score a number or two from the divas."

"The only thing I plan to score are high ratings while I'm working on the show, and, hopefully, once my contract is over after this season, there'll be an opening back in news." Brandon had had his agent negotiate a

one-season deal in the hopes of him returning to a reputable newsmagazine show like *60 Minutes*. He wanted
to work on a television show that he could be proud of.

He laughed inwardly. He hadn't even started the
new job, yet he was already planning his exit strategy.
Thankfully *Divorced Divas* only ran half a season, so
he wouldn't be subjected to the lunacy that was reality
television for too long.

Chapter 4

Ayana was getting her hair and makeup done in the dressing room she used while taping the show. She looked at her reflection in the huge mirror and barely recognized herself. Her face had three layers of makeup—foundation, powder and blush. Her naturally long eyelashes were glued with two sets of extended lashes, giving her eyes a dramatic look, and her lips were painted a bright glossy orange. Covering Ayana's real hair was a platinum-blond wig with natural curls that cascaded midway down her back.

"You're all set," the makeup artist said, giving Ayana's face one last swipe of the sable brush.

"Thanks, Denise."

Ayana rose from her chair and walked to the rack of clothing the wardrobe stylist had selected for the day. She looked at the first outfit and shook her head in disgust. "Do they really expect me to wear this?" she muttered to herself.

As she stood there looking at the neon orange micromini shorts and matching midriff top, Ed Levine, the creator of the show, walked in.

"Hey, Saturday, are you ready for another great season?" Ed waved his chiffon scarf in the air. He was full of enthusiasm and wore a wide grin that spread across his face. Ed had every reason to be happy: *Divorced Divas* was now the number one reality show in the country.

"Ed, why do I have to wear this whorish-looking getup?" she said, cutting right to the point and ignoring his question.

"Saturday…"

"Can you please call me Ayana when we're off set?"

He folded his arms and said, "Ayana, when I approached you about doing the show, I pulled no punches. I told you that the nice-girl role was already taken and you were being hired to play the bad, malicious girl."

"Bad girl, not slut. Look at this trash," she said, pulling the orange two-piece violently off the rack.

"Why do we have to go through this every season? Last season you complained about the hair and makeup, so we toned it down. Now you're complaining about the clothes. You should be used to the Saturday Knight persona by now."

It was Ed himself who had created the outlandish character in the first place. Years ago, before becoming a successful show creator, he'd worked as a female impersonator under the name Saturday Knight. He'd worn heavy makeup, flashy clothes, towering heels and waist-length wigs. When he'd conceived *Divorced*

Divas, he'd jumped at the chance to see his alter ego come to life on camera.

"I'll never get used to dressing like a slut and acting like a wild banshee."

"I could always release you from your contract if you're tired of playing the role. I have a list of divorced wives of millionaires waiting in the wings to take your place. Give me the word, and I'll tear up your contract and you can walk away, free and clear, before the season starts. No hard feelings. But once we start production, you'll have to honor your contract and stay for the duration of this season."

Ayana plopped down on the sofa, tossing the outfit to the side, and exhaled. She wasn't in a position to quit. She hadn't amassed enough money to secure her financial future, nor had she made inroads into the licensing business so that she could brand herself. As much as Ayana hated the charade, she hated being poor more. She wasn't going to leave the show until all of her ducks were lined up. She was determined to make the most out of being on the show, even if that meant portraying herself as a loudmouthed troublemaker. "No, Ed, I don't want to be released from my contract, but can we come to a compromise?"

"And what might that be?"

"Let me choose my clothes. The stylist isn't quite getting my look right."

"I guess you can do that. Just don't come on set in anything conservative."

"Thanks. I won't," she said with a broad smile spreading across her face.

"Don't get too happy. I came in here to tell you about the new director."

"What about him?"

"We didn't tell him that Saturday Knight is a fake persona. He doesn't know your real name is Ayana Lewis, and I want to keep it that way."

"Why is that?"

"We want to maintain a sense of reality, and the less he knows about your real personality, the better he can direct you as a wildcat."

"So you're telling me that he doesn't realize my role on the show is an act?"

"No, he doesn't. As you know, the rest of the cast doesn't know either. Remember the confidentiality clause in your contract binding you to keep quiet about your true identity."

"Of course I remember."

"So you'll keep up the act?"

"Yes, but I refuse to be tacky."

"Deal. On another note, I've been introducing the new director to the cast individually before we start shooting. He's meeting with Trista now and will be in to meet you shortly."

"No problem."

As they were talking, in walked the new director. Ayana looked at the handsome man and nearly gasped. He was tall—well over six feet—with broad shoulders and an athlete's build. His head was shaven, giving off a slight glisten. His eyes were warm, the color of chestnuts, and his skin looked as if it had been dipped in milk chocolate. The white cotton shirt he wore seemed to glow against his dark skin. He was handsome in a rugged urban-cowboy-type way. In fact, he was exactly her type. If they were in another setting, she could envision the two of them sitting down and having a friendly chat over a cup of coffee. However, she had a job to do and wasn't going to let his good looks distract her.

"Brandon, perfect timing," Ed said, turning toward the door. "Let me introduce you to Saturday Knight, the show's hot-blooded diva."

Ayana took a step backward and went into character. She sucked her lips, put her hand on her hip and rolled her eyes in his direction.

"Hello." Brandon extended his hand.

Ayana looked down at his hand. "Whatever."

"Ed, I'll be on set," Brandon said, turning his back to Ayana, ignoring her rude behavior and directing his comment to the creator of the show.

"Okay, sounds good."

Brandon walked out without giving her a second look. Once he was gone, Ed closed the door. "Nice work. You did a damn good job of showing him how nasty you can be."

"That was nothing. Wait until I get in front of the camera. Then I'm going to really cut up."

"Perfect. That's what I want to hear. *Divorced Divas* is leading in the ratings and I want to keep it that way."

"Don't worry, Ed. You can count on me to do my part."

"See you on set, Ayana."

When Ed left the room, Ayana closed the door and walked back to the clothing rack. As she was looking for another outfit, she thought about how rude she had been to the new director and began feeling guilty. He didn't deserve to be disregarded, but as long as she was under contract, she wasn't going to do anything to jeopardize her future.

Ayana changed into a pair of white skinny jeans and

a sheer black blouse with a deep V-neck that showcased her ample cleavage. She completed the casual outfit with a pair of four-inch cork platforms. The shoes added to her height, making her a towering figure of six feet.

Ayana left the dressing room, and as she walked down the long hallway, she took a series of deep breaths. With each step, she dreaded the beginning of another season of lies. To make her job tolerable, Ayana tried to find something to focus on. Last season, she'd concentrated on the shelter in Jamaica. The thought of helping the women and children in her homeland had gotten her through the catfights, backstabbing and blind dates gone awry. This season, she hadn't picked a focal point, until meeting the director. Although she had treated him like dirt on the bottom of her designer shoes, she found him extremely sexy and attractive. Even if she couldn't have him personally, she could at least fantasize about his muscular body being pressed against hers. That thought alone would sustain her for at least a few episodes.

Chapter 5

I must admit, Jon was right. Saturday Knight is one pretty woman. Her body is made by Frederick's of Hollywood, but her attitude is made by Freddy Krueger. Her ugly interior totally cancels out her gorgeous exterior, Brandon thought as he walked down the hallway toward the set. The first scene of the day was being shot in a sprawling Central Park West penthouse that the show leased for taping. Brandon was the first on set. He sat in his director's chair and waited for the ladies— Trista, the Good Girl; Petra, the Russian; Brooke, the Flirt; and Saturday, the Bad Girl—to arrive.

The beginning of the day's show centered on Saturday's blind-date follow-up. Last season had ended with her being set up with three seriously wealthy men. Now the audience would find out if she picked one of the three. If not, her search for love would continue.

Trista was the first to enter the room. She had once been married to a strict CFO of a finance company. He detested tardiness and was always the first to arrive and the first to leave. His mantra was that time was money, so he waited on no one. His punctuality had rubbed off on Trista. They would still be married if he hadn't gotten caught embezzling millions from the company. After he was sent to prison for ten years, Trista instituted his mantra and didn't waste any time filing for divorce. She wasn't going to waste ten whole years waiting around for him.

Brandon looked at the petite redhead with a pixie haircut. She was soft-spoken and had a girlish quality. She looked more befitted for a family with two kids and a dog than a cutthroat reality show. But for contrast, Ed had Trista going on dates with rocker types who wore leather, torn jeans and tattoos—the opposite of her sweet personality.

As Brandon was reading over the show notes one last time, he heard footsteps and commotion coming down the hall in the form of two loud voices.

"I'ma do you a favor, and let you have first pickings over the men that I turn down."

"I no want you damn leftover!" a voice with a Russian accent bellowed.

"If I didn't give you my throwbacks, you wouldn't have any dates at all."

Brandon turned toward the entry of the living room as the two women marched in. *I should have known it was Saturday arguing with someone.*

"No true. I have entee man I want," Petra responded.

Petra Kazakova was a Russian immigrant and former model who'd married the head of a cosmetics conglomerate. The two had divorced when he was caught wearing lipstick in a compromising situation with his business partner. Petra's dates for the show ran the gamut from European millionaires looking for trophy wives to taxi drivers. The broken English spoken by Petra and her dates often had to be accompanied by subtitles, which Ed loved because he thought it made his show unique.

"You should want some English lessons. It's not *entee*.... The word is *any*. And you also need to learn to pluralize your words," Saturday spouted.

"And you need lesson on how to be nice person."

"Nice ain't never got me nowhere. I prefer to tell it straight with no chaser. I can't help it if you can't take the truth."

"I take truth. You bully. How is that for truth?"

Saturday walked close to Petra and got in her face. "I got your bully."

Ed watched their exchange from the sideline, where he sat along with the executive producer, Steve. While Ed looked on in admiration at the way Saturday was performing, Steve watched in disgust.

"That Saturday is some piece of work. She should give poor Petra a break," Steve whispered to Ed.

"She's perfect just the way she is. Everyone on the show can't be Mary Poppins, or the show would be a bore," Ed said, coming to Saturday's defense.

"Well, I guess you're right. But at least she could wait until the director says 'action' before giving Petra hell."

"I'm sure this is her way of warming up before we start taping," Ed said.

Saturday continued to go at Petra, insulting her broken English and pointing her finger in Petra's face.

"Hey, you two, save the bickering for the camera," Brandon said, breaking up the spat. He had seen enough.

Petra stomped over to the huge picture window, folded her arms and muttered under her breath.

"What is all this chatter going on? I could hear you two all the way in my room, *and* the door was shut. This is not a barroom brawl. We're in an elegant penthouse and should act accordingly," Brooke said in a chastising voice as she entered the room.

Brooke Windsor had once had it all. Born with a platinum spoon in her pretty mouth and raised on the Upper East Side, her great-grandparents were blue bloods who'd made their fortune in the railroad industry. Rumors had it that she and her ex-husband were first cousins, which wasn't unusual for people of their stature. What was unusual was for a family with old money to lose their fortune within a generation. And that was exactly what Brooke's husband did when he invested all of their money with a shifty investment adviser who swindled them in a Ponzi scheme. Distraught over losing his family's fortune, her husband fled to Europe, leaving his wife to fend for herself. With no marketable skills, Brooke jumped at the chance to star on *Divorced Divas*. The only problem was that Brooke had an air of superiority and thought she was better than the other divas. Also, in her quest to find her next meal ticket, Brooke flirted with just about any man with earning potential. Brooke, who had grown up with the best of everything, had now lost everything. She still had her family's name, but that didn't keep her in designer clothes or pay for lavish vacations. Ed thrust Brooke in the world of athletes when choosing her dates, setting her up with basketball players, football players, hockey players and the like. Most of the guys had no problem being seen on camera with the beautiful Brooke. And she had no problem dating these men earning seven-figure salaries.

"Don't worry about how loud we are. Worry about finding another cousin to marry," Saturday shot back.

Brooke rolled her eyes, swung her long blond hair and whipped her slim body around, giving Saturday her back.

"Girls, girls, save all the backbiting for the camera," Brandon repeated.

Saturday started in again. "First of all, we're not girls. Second…"

"Second, I'm the director and this is now my show, so when I say save it, I mean save it," Brandon interrupted her. "I assume everyone has read the show notes for the day, so let's get started. Saturday, I want you sitting on the sofa next to Trista. You two are discussing Saturday's latest blind date. When the bell rings, Saturday, I want you to answer the door."

"Wait a minute—isn't the maid supposed to answer the door?" Brooke interrupted.

Brandon shot her a look. He turned back to Saturday and continued. "Like I said, when the bell rings, answer the door. Got it? Good."

Saturday went over and sat beside Trista. Brooke and Petra were seated in the background at a table set for high tea.

Once everyone was in position, Brandon yelled, "Action!"

The set lights came on, and the cameras began rolling. Saturday and Trista starting chatting as if they were best friends. Saturday recalled her past dates, a mix of businessmen, athletes, rockers and Europeans. Ed wanted her dating base to span the range so Saturday could swoop in at any given time and steal a cast member's date, bringing high drama to the show.

"That guy Anthony you went to dinner with seems nice. Are you excited to see him again?" Trista asked.

"He's the one who should be excited."

"And why is that?"

"Hello, have we met? Look at me." Saturday stood up and twirled around. "Who wouldn't want to see me again?"

Damn, that chick has no shame, Brandon thought, sitting in his director's chair and staring at Saturday.

As they were talking, the bell rang. Saturday strutted over to the door, paused and opened it. Standing before her was a portly Italian man who looked as if he had eaten too many meatballs. He was dressed in a navy business suit, wore rectangle glasses and carried a black briefcase. He looked like a public defender heading to court instead of someone standing on the set of a reality show.

"Hey there, how are ya? You're looking fine as ever," he said nervously.

"Hello, Anthony," Saturday answered drily.

"Cut!"

"What? Why'd you yell cut?" Saturday asked. "We just got started."

"I want you to show some enthusiasm. Act like you're happy to see him. Take two. Action."

Saturday leaned in and gave the man a hug with a friendly pat on the back. Obviously there was no chemistry between them. She towered over him and they looked mismatched, like complete opposites.

"Cut!"

"What now?" Saturday rolled her eyes and put her hand on her hip.

"When I said show some enthusiasm I meant give him a hello kiss. Take three. Action."

Saturday leaned down and gave him a quick peck on the lips.

"Cut! Cut!" Brandon was getting frustrated. He walked over and got in Saturday's face. "What's wrong with you? Why did you kiss him like he's your brother?"

"I didn't kiss him like a brother."

"You sure didn't kiss him with any passion."

"That's because I don't feel any passion toward him," she said as if the man weren't even standing there.

"Look, the viewers want to see chemistry. Not some lukewarm peck on the lips. Now try it again." Brandon went back to his director's chair and yelled, "Take four! Action!" Saturday kissed Anthony again, and again Brandon cut the scene.

"What the hell do you want?" she hissed, rolling her eyes.

Brandon got up, went over to Saturday, took her firmly by the shoulders and gave her a long juicy kiss. He could feel himself responding to her; his crotch was getting heated with every passing second. "That's what I want," he said, releasing her before he had a full-blown erection.

Saturday was speechless. "Got it," she said once she recovered from the surprise kiss.

When Brandon returned to the director's chair and yelled "action" again, he didn't have any more problems. She kissed Anthony as if he were her long-lost lover. As Brandon watched the scene play out, he could still feel the warmth of her lips against his. Her lips were soft and he could envision kissing and making love to her all night. His mind momentarily drifted into a fantasy where their naked bodies were intertwined in a heated embrace and their tongues were doing a sensuous, synchronized dance. Brandon shook his head, trying to rid himself of the image. He was there to work, not fantasize. Besides, divas were not his type, and Saturday was beyond your typical diva. After being dumped by an actress, he wanted nothing more to do with the entertainment types. He wanted a down-to-earth woman with traditional family values, and Saturday Knight certainly didn't fit that description.

Chapter 6

The first day of taping had been long and drawn out. By the time Ayana returned home, she was exhausted. After showering and putting on her favorite pink Hello Kitty pajamas, she climbed into bed. She then pulled the comforter up to her chin and shut her eyes. An hour later, she was still wide-awake, sleep eluding her. Ayana tossed and turned, switching from her left side to the right, in an effort to get comfortable, but it wasn't working. Ayana sat up and attacked the pillows, punching them with her fist, trying to soften them. Satisfied that she had loosened the down feathers sufficiently, she laid her head back on the creased pillows. The moment she closed her eyes, visions of Brandon appeared. Ayana could see him walking toward her with a sexy strut. Her body's memory could still feel his strong hands taking hold of her shoulders, pressing her against his body and giving her a sensuous kiss.

His lips touching hers had been a welcome surprise. The last thing Ayana expected was to be lip-locking with the new director. She could tell from the way he introduced his lips to hers—purposeful, yet gentle—that he was an experienced lover. He had turned her on with only one brief kiss, and now her body craved more of his touch.

Ayana bolted straight up. "Get that man out of your mind," she said quietly, underneath her breath, in the darkened room. She inhaled several times, fast at first and then slowly in a Zen-like effort to calm herself. As Ayana was going through the breathing exercises, her cell phone rang. She froze, and her heart started beating fast. Her mind instantly flashed to Brandon. *I wonder if that's him calling?* A phone list with all the cast and crew's home and cell numbers had been passed out before rehearsals began, so it wasn't unlikely that he could be calling.

She turned over, looked at the nightstand and saw her cell glowing in the dark. As Ayana reached for the phone she glanced down and was disappointed to see Reese's name on the screen. Ayana didn't really feel like talking. She wanted to focus on going to sleep, but she knew if she didn't answer, Reese would only call back in a few minutes. Reese didn't leave messages; she was a repeat caller, and she hit Redial until she got an answer.

"Hey," Ayana said without an ounce of enthusiasm in her voice.

"Are you asleep already? It's only nine o'clock," Reese said, full of energy.

"No, not really. I'm just lying here."

"What's wrong? You sound agitated."

"Nothing."

"Come on, now. I know you better than that. Something must have happened on the shoot today if you can't sleep." Reese and Ayana had known each other since high school, and they were adept at reading each other, much like an old married couple.

"Well, something out of the ordinary did happen, but it was no big deal." Ayana was reluctant to tell Reese what had happened because she didn't want her friend blowing the incident out of proportion, trying to make a love connection like she had done so many times in the past.

"Do tell. I like hearing about the action on the set. It's like watching the show before it airs. Did you get into another catfight with Petra? Or did Brooke piss you off with her hoity-toity attitude?" Reese knew the antics of each cast member as if she were part of the show.

"No, it had nothing to do with either of them. It's the new director. He kissed me today."

"What! Are you kidding? Why did he kiss you?"

"He was demonstrating how I should've kissed one of my dates," Ayana said, as if kissing the director was an everyday occurrence.

"Why do you sound so matter-of-fact about it? Was he a bad kisser?"

Ayana closed her eyes, reminiscing. "On the contrary— the kiss was awesome. I can't stop thinking about him," she said, unable to hide her feelings any longer.

"Girl, you sound like you have a crush on him!"

"You see, this is why I didn't want to say anything. I knew you were going to blow the whole thing up. I'm not in high school, and I don't have a crush. I was just surprised at his bold demonstration, that's all." Ayana had said enough and didn't want to fully admit how much the kiss had affected her, so much so that Brandon and his lips were on repeat in her mind, playing over and over.

"Yeah, right."

"I'm serious. I don't have time to get involved with anybody, let alone someone I work with. I'm concentrating all of my energy on the next phase of my life. I don't plan to be on *Divorced Divas* forever. My focus is on branding myself, not on romance," she said, redirecting the conversation.

"That's a good speech, but what's wrong with having a relationship and working on your career at the same time? I'm working on my gemology certification and taking care of my husband at the same time."

"Well, that might work for you, but for me romance is often a distraction. Remember when I started working for Benjamin? My plan was to climb the corporate ladder at BL Industries. Instead, I ended up dating and then marrying the boss. Look how that turned out. I don't plan on making the same mistake twice. I'm not getting any younger, and I need to secure my financial future while I can."

"My point exactly. You're not getting younger and you need to find a man so you won't grow old alone. Don't get me wrong—I understand your financial concerns, but love is important too. Money won't hug you around the waist at night and keep you warm."

Ayana sighed. She was tired and ready to end the conversation. She had heard Reese's speech on finding true romance more than she could count on two hands. "Love will just have to wait. Look, Reese, I need to get to sleep. I have an early day tomorrow."

"Okay, but maybe you need to give that director a second look. He might be the *one*."

Ayana sighed into the phone.

"I'm not preaching. I only want you to be happy like Joey and me."

"Everybody isn't as lucky as you guys. Maybe finding a soul mate isn't in the cards for me."

"I don't believe that, and I'm sure you don't either."

"Having a significant other would be the icing on the cake, but at this point in my life, I'm not going to hold my breath for my soul mate to come along. I'll just take the cake and forget about the icing."

"All I'm saying is just don't close yourself off to an opportunity that presents itself. You never know when love will come knocking."

"I hear you, Reese. I hate to cut our conversation short, but I really have to get to sleep. Talk to you later."

"Okay, good night."

After Ayana ended the call and put the phone back on the nightstand, she thought about Reese's advice. Although she had made a point of saying that true love wasn't in her future, Reese was right about finding someone to grow old with. Ayana didn't want to be alone the rest of her life, but for now, her search would have to wait.

Chapter 7

Barneys New York, the swanky department store on Madison Avenue, was the site of the day's shoot. The cast was scheduled to come in and comb through the designer racks in search of outfits for their upcoming dates. Viewers loved seeing the ladies buy five-thousand-dollar shoes without blinking an eyelash and adding their names to the waitlist for designer purses that cost as much as a small house in some cities. The producers were adamant about portraying the ritzy world of glitz and glamour, and Barneys, with its multiple floors of designer swag, was the perfect venue.

Brandon was scheduled for a brief meeting with Ed before the cast arrived to discuss blocking for the shoot. The lighting and audio teams had already set up and were waiting patiently for the show to begin. Ed had arrived ahead of Brandon. He was dressed in teal-blue skinny jeans, a yellow silk camp shirt, a pair of pink platform sneakers, a monogrammed Louis Vuitton messenger bag strapped across his chest and his signature chiffon scarf—this one in multicolored shades of teal, yellow and pink. He strutted through the store looking like a designer-clad peacock.

"Hey, Ed, how's it going?" Brandon said, entering the cordoned-off shoe section the store had reserved for the shoot.

"Other than a little heartburn, I'm good. Guess I shouldn't have had a second helping of lasagna and tiramisu last night." His protruding belly was indication of his love for fattening Italian food.

"Why don't you send the PA to Duane Reade to pick up some Pepto?"

"Good idea." Ed took his cell phone out of his messenger bag. "Hey, Gabby, can you run to the drugstore and buy a large bottle of Pepto-Bismol? Thanks."

"Where do you want the first scene to start?" Brandon asked as Ed completed the call.

Ed crossed the room and stood next to a display of designer pumps. "Here is fine. I want the girls to ogle over these beauties."

"No problem." Brandon picked up a shoe to inspect it. "Are they serious with these prices?" he asked, holding a red, leather-bottomed pump.

"Those are Louboutins. What do you expect?"

"Lou Who?"

"Christian Louboutin. Don't tell me you've never heard of him. Everyone is familiar with his signature red bottoms," Saturday said in a snarky tone as she walked up behind him.

Brandon put the shoe back on the display. "Not everyone is as consumed with material possessions as you ladies seem to be," he said, looking her dead in the eyes.

For a few moments they stood face-to-face without saying a word. Brandon could feel himself being drawn to her. His eyes scanned her body up and down. She wore a slinky, red, ankle-length dress that fitted her curvaceous body like a second skin. Saturday oozed sensuality, and there was no doubt that he was attracted to her. Brandon shook off the feeling. Although Saturday was beautiful, her personality was offensive and he couldn't imagine spending his life with such an abrasive woman.

"Whatever." Saturday twisted her lips, flipped her long wig and turned her back to him. "So, Ed, what's wrong with you? You look pale as a ghost. Are you okay?"

"I'm fine, just a little heartburn. Let me sit down until Gabby gets here with the medicine." He sat in one of the cushy chairs and continued talking. "Now, about today's shoot, Saturday. I want you and Petra to really go at it. Get in her face and don't back down until the director says 'cut.'"

"I don't have a problem with that, but you need to tell Petra this is your idea. I'm tired of her thinking that I'm always picking on her."

"I'll have a chat with her when she gets here."

As they were talking, Gabby, the production assistant, came in with the pharmacy bag. "Here you go, Ed."

"Thanks." He took the medicine out of the bag, opened the bottle and tilted it up to his mouth, guzzling the pink liquid as if it were a refreshing beverage.

"What is that you drink?" Petra asked as she entered the shoe section.

"The word isn't *you,* it's *you're,* and it's *drinking,* not *drink,*" Saturday said, ribbing Petra on her broken English.

"I so tired of you teasing about way I talk."

Saturday started laughing. "You just can't get your tenses right. Ed, why don't you get Petra a speech coach?"

"I no need coach. I need you to shut up and leave me alone." Petra crossed her arms tightly across her chest.

Ed stood up. "Petra, can I speak to you for a minute?"

While Ed and Petra talked near the edge of the room, Brooke and Trista entered the set. Neither woman acknowledged Saturday, but they did glance at her as she sat in a nearby chair holding an iPad in her hands.

"So, Brandon, what's your story?" Brooke asked, coming closer to him.

"Excuse me?" Brandon asked, taking a step back.

She flipped her golden-blond tresses. "I mean, are you married? Have a girlfriend? Have a boyfriend? What's your status?" Brooke spoke as if he were required to answer her questions.

"First of all, we're not friends and my personal life is none of your business, and second, we are all here to do a job, so I suggest you read over today's notes before we start shooting."

She moved closer to him, smiled and put her hand on his arm. "Oh, sweetie, I was just trying to make conversation."

Brandon stepped back, allowing her hand to drop from his arm. "My personal life isn't up for general conversation," he said sternly.

Saturday glanced up and smiled, obviously pleased that he had put the snooty flirt in her place.

Brooke huffed, flipped her hair again and strutted

away, her charms totally lost on the director. Trista then sat down next to Saturday. "Good morning. How are you?"

"I'm good," Saturday said without glancing up.

Trista looked over at Saturday's iPad. "What are you doing? Playing a game?"

Saturday flipped the gadget over. "I don't like people looking over my shoulder. It's irritating," she said, putting the tablet in her purse and standing up.

"Okay, ladies, let's get started," Ed announced after his brief meeting with Petra. "Saturday, I want you and Petra over here near the Louboutins, gushing over the shoes and then arguing about who's going to buy the last pair of silver pumps. Saturday, after about five minutes of verbal sparring, I want you to throw the shoe at Petra, but be careful not to hit her—just make it look deliberate."

"Why she throw at me? Why I not throw at her?"

"She'll throw the first shoe, and then you can throw the next one. I want you guys to have a shoe fight."

This show is such a joke. I can't wait to get out of here, Brandon thought as he stood there listening to the creator's stage directions.

"Why not let the action flow organically?" Brandon knew the former director had been fired for being too opinionated. He had been committed to keeping quiet, doing his job, completing the contract and hightailing it back to a major network, but this staging was ridiculous and he couldn't hold his tongue any longer.

"I know you're the director, but this is my show, and to keep the ratings high, I want to ensure there's plenty of drama," Ed responded.

"Don't you think there's enough drama between the

ladies without you orchestrating it? Isn't this supposed to be reality television?" Brandon countered.

"What's with all the questions? When you came on board, you knew what type of show you were going to be working on," Ed replied, slightly raising his voice.

"Of course I knew what I was signing up for. However, I don't think forced conflicts are the way to go."

Saturday watched the exchange in silence. Outwardly she showed no emotion, but inside she was doing somersaults. Brandon was expressing exactly how she felt. Saturday found herself being drawn to him as he stood his ground against Ed.

"Look, Brandon, this discussion is over. I don't feel like arguing with you. Just shoot the scene like I requested." Ed inhaled deeply and plopped down in a chair.

Brandon backed down. He couldn't afford to lose this job. If the creator of the show wanted a train wreck, then that was exactly what he would direct. "Ladies, we're going to start shooting in five. Saturday and Petra, I'm going to need you two over here by these Louboutins. Brooke and Trista, you guys aren't in the frame yet. I want you off camera. Walk in once the shoes start flying. Understood?"

"I want to throw first shoe," Petra said.

"Sorry, hon, that's not going to happen. Ed said that I'm throwing the first shoe," Saturday said with her hand on her hip.

"Why you throw first? I throw you."

"You're not throwing me. You're throwing a shoe."

Petra huffed. "You know how I mean."

"It's *what I meant*."

"Ladies, again I'm going to tell you to save it for

the camera." Brandon interrupted their ongoing spat. "Okay, places, please. Cue lights and sound."

The shoe salon brightened up and everyone—actors, cameramen, soundmen—took their respective places. Saturday and Petra positioned themselves near the designer shoes. Brooke and Trista waited on the sidelines until their turn to enter.

"Take one. Action!" Brandon announced.

"What are you wearing tonight for your date?" Saturday asked Petra.

Petra picked up a silver metallic platform shoe off the display and held it in her right hand. "Platinum minidress and this shoe. It perfect together."

Saturday walked up and snatched the shoe out of Petra's hand. "Actually, it goes perfectly with my fuchsia-and-silver pantsuit. I'm going to buy them."

Petra snatched the shoe back. "No! Mine!"

"How dare you take something out of my hand!"

"You take from me first," Petra said, holding on tightly to the shoe.

Saturday stepped closer and tried to take the shoe back, but Petra had a firm grip and she couldn't pry it out of Petra's hand. "Give me the shoe!"

"No! Mine!" Petra held the shoe to her chest.

"Cut!" Ed yelled, getting up and walking onto the set. "I said I wanted a shoe fight, not a tug-of-war. Petra, hand me the shoe so I can demonstrate what I'm talking about." Ed raised the shoe in the air and hurled it across the room with such force that he fell forward, landing on the carpet.

After a few seconds, Ed was still on the floor. He hadn't made any attempt to get up.

"Hey, man, are you okay?" Brandon asked. When Ed

didn't move or speak, Brandon came over and knelt beside him. He shook him softly. "Ed, Ed, are you okay?" Still no answer.

Saturday knelt next to Brandon, reached down and felt Ed's pulse, but there was no rhythmic beating. She immediately started doing CPR, pressing on his chest and blowing air into his mouth.

"Somebody call nine-one-one!" Brandon yelled.

The cast and crew looked on as Saturday repeated the CPR routine over and over until the paramedics arrived. They quickly checked Ed's vitals. He now had a faint pulse, thanks to Saturday's emergency CPR. They placed an oxygen mask around his nose and mouth, loaded him on a gurney and rolled him out of the store and into a waiting ambulance.

Brandon grabbed Saturday and they quickly hopped into an approaching taxi and followed the ambulance as it wove in and out of traffic. They rode to the hospital in silence, each with pensive looks on their faces. The shoot had begun with an orchestrated frivolous scene, but it had ended with a real life-and-death drama.

Chapter 8

The bright rays of the midday Caribbean sun kissed Ayana's brown skin as she lounged on the sandy Negril beach in a snow-white two-piece swimsuit. She looked up from the romance novel she was reading and stared off into the calm turquoise waters. Looking out into the ocean, Ayana took a moment to reflect on the recent events that had shifted her life momentarily.

The past week had been a traumatic whirlwind. It all began with Ed's unexpected heart attack. He barely escaped death that day on the shoot when he collapsed. His condition was critical, rendering him bedridden, hooked up to intravenous drips and monitors in the intensive-care unit. Steve, the executive producer, had told the cast and crew that because Ed was the visionary for the show, he had no other choice but to halt production until Ed made a full recovery. And, based on the cardiologist's grim prognosis, that wouldn't be anytime soon.

During the same week, Ayana's father had had a mild stroke. Her mother's tone had been cool and calm when she called to tell her the news. She had told Ayana that everything was under control and that she didn't need to rush home. But with the show on hold indefinitely, Ayana booked a flight to Jamaica and was at her father's bedside two days later. Luckily, his stoke hadn't caused any major paralysis. He was back to his old self, piddling around in the garden, in less than two weeks. Although her father was back to normal, Ayana was sticking around to monitor his condition. She wasn't taking any chances.

With her father's health under control, she used her time on the island like a holiday. After dealing with fake confrontations and staged fights, and acting like an out-of-control hyena, Ayana welcomed the downtime.

The more she gazed at the aqua-blue waters, the more inviting they seemed. Growing up on an island and spending her summers at the beach, she was an avid swimmer. She stood up, took off the oversize, floppy straw hat, tossed it on her towel and padded through the warm sand toward the ocean. She then dipped her toes in the water and splashed around a bit before wading in farther. This secluded spot along Seven Mile Beach was off the beaten track where tourists didn't tread.

Ayana slowly waded in until the water was waist high. The ocean was so warm that it felt like bathwater. She cupped her hands, taking in the salt water and splashing it on her face. Gone was the heavy makeup, long, flowing wig, false eyelashes and ugly personality. Ayana dipped down into the clear waters, submerging her entire body. She held her breath and said a silent prayer of gratitude. Even though she hated her job, she was grateful for the opportunity to make a living and not have to rely on a man for her financial security. She was also grateful for her father's speedy recovery and for the CPR efforts that had saved Ed's life. When she reemerged, she felt renewed, as if she had been through a much-needed baptism. Ayana lay on the water, arched her back and floated. She felt free and closed her eyes, savoring the feeling of being carried away by the gentle waves. Her body drifted effortlessly, and her mind was clear of any negative thoughts. With her head tilted back and ears partially submerged, she could hear only muffled sounds. Ayana felt as if she were in a safe cocoon and continued floating without a care.

The tranquillity of her solitude came to an abrupt halt when she heard the roar of a motor. Before she knew it, she was flipped over and submerged by a series of violent waves. Her eyes popped open underwater, and she kicked her legs quickly until she was back on the surface.

"Oh my God, are you all right?" asked a handsome man straddling a bright orange Jet Ski. "I'm so sorry, but I didn't see you. What are you doing floating all the way out here by yourself?"

Ayana glanced around the vast body of water and didn't see the beach. She had drifted out farther than anticipated. "I hadn't planned on floating this far. Guess the waves carried me away," she said, treading water.

He reached out his hand to her. "Get on. I'll take you back to shore."

She brushed her hair out of her face, rubbed the salt water out of her eyes and looked up into his face. She couldn't believe her eyes. Behind a pair of dark aviator shades was Brandon. "Uh…sure." She took hold of his hand, climbed out of the water and settled on the back of the Jet Ski. Ayana wrapped her arms around his bare chest and held on tight as he sped off.

"Where are you staying?" he yelled.

With the Jet Ski creating a cascade of waves and the roar of the motor, she could barely hear him. "What'd you say?"

"I said, where are you staying?" he repeated more loudly.

"Just keep straight," she responded, finally hearing him.

He doesn't know it's me. Ayana held him a little tighter, enjoying the anonymity of the moment. She thought back on his unexpected kiss and smiled. She could see the beach coming closer and closer and wondered what Brandon would say once he learned who was hitching a ride with him. It was no secret they bumped heads on the set and that Saturday gave him a hard time whenever she could. Her heart began beating faster and faster in anticipation of the reveal. *Might as well enjoy the moment.* As the Jet Ski cut through the water, she took in the sights. She spotted a bright yellow banana boat filled with tourists. A catamaran was heading farther out into the ocean, probably taking people snorkeling. Waves crashed against the Jet Ski, and the spray of water in her face was refreshing. Being a native of the island, Ayana had never bothered renting a Jet Ski; that was something tourists did. This was her first time on one and she found the ride exhilarating.

"Is this it?" he yelled, approaching the sand.

"Yeah."

Brandon turned off the engine and slid the Jet Ski into the shore with the precision of a race-car driver. He hopped off first and then helped her.

"Thanks for the ride," Ayana said, keeping her head down. She was enjoying his kindness and wasn't ready to be outed.

"No problem," he said, secretly admiring her toned, bikini-clad body from behind his shades. She was au naturel and beautiful—wet hair and all. The more he stared, the more familiar she seemed. He took off the dark glasses to get a better look. "Saturday?"

Ayana hung her head even farther, trying to bury her chin in her chest. Realizing there was no use attempting to hide her identity, she inhaled deeply, exhaled and said, "Yes, it's me."

He stood there seemingly in shock. "What are *you* doing here?"

"I grew up in the area. I'm here visiting my parents."

"Wow! *You're* Jamaican?"

"Yes, I am. Why are you saying it like that?"

"Most Jamaican women I know are sweethearts, but…"

"Stop right there. You really don't know me like you think you do."

"I know enough."

Ayana knew the impression she made on Brandon as Saturday Knight wasn't a positive one, and that was putting it mildly. Standing there in front of him stripped of that persona, she was embarrassed about the way she portrayed herself on the show and how badly she had treated him. She looked into his eyes and could see judgment. She wanted to tell him the real reason for the fake persona, but what was the use? His impression of her had already been sealed in his mind. She couldn't take his critical stares any longer; she had to get out of there. She reached down, grabbed her hat, plopped it on her head and put her beach towel and novel in her tote. "'Bye, Brandon," she called behind her as she walked away as quickly as the sand would allow.

Brandon stood there in shock and watched her scurry away. He was speechless. The last person he'd expected to see was *the* diva of *Divorced Divas*. He also couldn't believe that Saturday was a beach person, floating in the water and actually getting her hair wet. Nor in his wildest dreams did he think that she was Jamaican. She seemed to have been born and bred on Madison Avenue among the multitude of designer boutiques. He watched as she disappeared over the cliff, and then he returned to his Jet Ski. Riding back to his hotel, he wondered if he would bump into Saturday again. She had thrown him a curveball, and now he was intrigued and wanted to know more.

Chapter 9

It had been two days since Brandon scooped Saturday out of the ocean. He still couldn't believe how different she looked without the heavy makeup, wig and designer clothes. With the water splashing against her face, he didn't recognize her as she recovered from being flipped over by the waves created from his Jet Ski. She had a vulnerable quality as she stood in front of him on the beach clad only in her bikini. He had quickly dismissed that thought and reminded himself that she was the same person who demeaned the cast members on a regular basis. Be that as it may, Brandon couldn't help but wonder where she was staying. She had fled so fast that he didn't get a chance to ask where her parents lived—not that it mattered because he wasn't planning on visiting. Seeing her in New York on the set was more than enough.

The reason for Brandon's trip to Jamaica was two-fold. He was there to unwind after the untimely hiatus from the show and to check on his sister-in-law. His brother, James, had married a Jamaican woman, and they'd had one of the best relationships that Brandon had ever seen. Even after ten years of marriage, they were still inseparable. The vows "till death do we part" fitted them. They were together until the day James died of cancer two years ago. Before he'd passed away, James made Brandon promise to look in on his wife from time to time. Marigold was such a sweetheart that Brandon didn't have a problem flying to Jamaica whenever he had the chance.

"Marigold, I don't know how you do it," Brandon said. He was having lunch in the industrial-sized kitchen of the shelter that his sister-in-law ran.

"Whatcha mean, mon?"

"I mean, dealing with all these kids on a daily basis is so much work."

"T'is no problem a'tall. Most of dem mommas is here wit dem. And da ones wit no momma are da sweetest, so I don't mind givin' dem extra attention." Marigold ran a private shelter for women and children. She and James had never had any children, so she treated every child at the shelter as if they were her own.

"No, Marigold, you're the sweetest. Not many women would give of themselves like you do." Brandon thought back to the cast of *Divorced Divas*. They were some of the most selfish women he had ever seen.

"Go on now wit dat," she said, getting up from the table and waving her hand. "You want more goat stew?"

"No, I'm full, but I will have another glass of your famous pink lemonade."

"Comin' right up." Marigold took his bowl, put it in the sink, then went to the double-door refrigerator and took out the pitcher of homemade lemonade.

"Is that my favorite drink?"

Brandon's back was to the door, so he turned around to see who had come into the kitchen. His mouth flew open as he stared at Saturday coming toward Marigold. She was looking directly at his sister-in-law and didn't see him sitting at the long communal table. Being unnoticed gave him the opportunity to check her out before she spotted him. She wore a simple yellow cotton sundress with matching yellow flip-flops. Her hair was pulled back in a ponytail, and again her face was makeup free. Her toned-down look gave her an innocent quality, which he found very attractive. He sat there in silence and watched their exchange.

"Oh, me Lord!" Marigold gave Saturday a big bear hug, released her and asked, "Whatcha doin' here, chile?" Her voice was full of excitement.

"My dad had a mild stroke so I came to check on him."

"Oh, no! He okay?"

"Yes, thank God. It wasn't major and my mom got him to the hospital quickly, which is so critical when someone has a stroke. He doesn't have any paralysis. He's even back planting in the yard. I keep telling him to take it easy, but he won't listen. You know how stubborn most men are."

"Yeah, me do." Marigold poured two glasses of lemonade and handed one to Saturday. "Come, chile, let me introduce ya to me brother-in-law." Marigold walked over to the table with Ayana following behind.

When Marigold stepped to the side to make the introductions, Ayana instantly began to perspire. One, she hadn't expected to see Brandon. Two, he was related to her friend, and three, she wondered if he would unknowingly divulge her secret. No one on the island knew she worked on a reality television show, and for obvious reasons she wanted to keep it that way.

"Ayana, this here is Brandon, me late husband's brother," Marigold said, handing Brandon his glass of lemonade.

"Nice to meet you," she said quickly before he had a chance to say that they already knew each other. Based on the look registered on his face—mouth agape and eyes slightly bulged—he was just as shocked as she.

"Ayana, huh?"

"Yes, but we call her Ana 'round here. She a gem. Without she pitchin' in and helpin', we wouldn't have enough clothes and shoes for da women and chilrin. Ya know most residents come here wit only da clothes on dey backs. She ships boxes and boxes of stuff on a regular basis. And she even send checks, which we need so much." Marigold gave Ayana another hug. "Me couldn't get along witout she."

"Is that right?" Brandon remarked in a shocked tone.

"Yep, dat's right. I'm surprised ya don't know her since ya both live in Manhattan."

Saturday—Ayana—and Brandon glanced at each other. She quickly spoke first before he could respond. "New York isn't like a small village where everyone knows each other." She evaded Marigold's comment with a generalized response, probably because she didn't want to outright lie to her friend, but she wasn't prepared to tell her the truth either.

Before Marigold was able to ask any questions or

make any more comments, her assistant came into the kitchen. "Excuse me, Marigold, but ya have a phone call in da office."

"Me be right back."

When Marigold was gone, Ayana exhaled. She smoothed down the front of her dress and then ran her hand over her hair. She seemed to be a ball of nerves and didn't know what to say or do.

"So, Marigold is your sister-in-law? Small world," she said, sitting across the table from him. Ayana took a long sip of lemonade and exhaled.

"Yep."

He'd answered with an edge to his voice, still viewing her as the troublemaker on the show.

"Brandon, I'm sure you have a ton of questions."

"Yep, I sure do."

"First of all, my real name is Ayana Lewis. Saturday Knight is a name that Ed created."

"Did he create your wicked personality too?"

She cast her eyes down in shame, stared in her lap for a few moments, then looked in his eyes and said, "As a matter of fact, he did."

"And you're okay with demeaning yourself? If what you're telling me is true, I would have told him to take a hike, as any other person with decency would."

"I wish I could have, but I wasn't in the position financially to turn down the job. I was recently divorced and my bank account was running on fumes."

Brandon hadn't expected her to be so open. He'd automatically assumed, based on her Saturday Knight persona, that she would get defensive and come up with a ton of lies. Upon hearing the truth, his resolve began to soften. He more than understood her financial situation. He had been in the same predicament after moving to Los Angeles trying to become a Hollywood director, exhausting his savings in the process. "Why didn't you ask him to cast you as the good girl of the show?"

"I did, but that role was already taken. When Ed initially approached me, he wanted me to play Trista's role, but I turned him down. I had no interest in acting on a reality show. To be honest, I think the entire reality genre has become one big joke." Her eyes were welling up. She looked down in her lap and said softly, "And now, unfortunately, I'm the headliner."

Brandon studied her face and could see she was on the verge of tears. He reached across the table and patted her hand. "Don't cry. It's not that bad," he offered, surprising himself.

Ayana seemed to try to fight back the tears, but they fell anyway. She sniffled and wiped her face with the back of her hand. Brandon gave her a napkin and she blew her nose. "I'm sorry for being such a crybaby," she said with a slight smile, trying to lighten the mood.

"No problem. I've been where you are, so I completely understand. Actually, the reason I'm working on the show is because I also exhausted all my savings."

Ayana stared at him inquisitively.

"I quit my job with a major network, moved to L.A. and tried to break into the movie business. I pounded the pavement for a year with no luck. My living expenses, as well as trying to schmooze and network in La-La Land, devoured my savings quickly. When I moved back to New York, the only show hiring was *Divorced Divas*. I had no choice but to take the job. I already have my agent contacting the networks so I can get back to 'real'—" he put his fingers in the air and made quotation marks "—television, once my contract is over."

"I have an exit strategy myself. I don't plan on being a *Diva* forever. Acting the way I do on the set is so out of my comfort zone. You have no idea how bad I feel every time I insult Petra. The poor girl doesn't deserve my constant brutal tongue-lashings."

Brandon was both pleased and surprised to hear her confess. His judgment of her had been all wrong. "So what should I call you?"

"Ayana or Ana. My family and friends here don't know about the show or my fake Saturday Knight persona, and I'd like to keep it that way. My parents would have a fit if they knew I degraded myself for money. If they had known about my financial hardship after the divorce settlement ran out, they would have tried to scrape up and send me whatever money they could. I think grown children should provide financial support to their elderly parents, not the other way around."

"I totally agree."

The more they talked, the more Brandon admired her. Not only did she do good deeds for the shelter, but she also took care of her parents. She was exactly the type of woman he could see having a future with. "Don't worry. Your secret is safe with me."

"Thanks. I'm relieved that you now know the truth. I saw the way you looked at me on the set every time I acted out."

"Honestly, I couldn't stand you. I'm glad you told me the truth. I must confess you are a really good actress. The way you portray Saturday Knight, no one would ever guess that isn't the real you."

"It's really hard to pull off, but for now I have no choice."

"Have you ever thought about acting as a career?"

"You mean in the movies?"

"Yes, or television. You're acting anyway, so you might as well put your talent to good use."

Ayana was silent for a moment, digesting his words. "You know, I never thought about it that way, but you're absolutely right. I portray a character on the set every day, and the audience thinks that's the real me. Thanks for the idea. I will definitely look into it."

"What ya two over dere gabbin' about?" Marigold asked, coming back into the kitchen.

"Nothing much. Just getting to know each other," Brandon said, smiling at Ayana.

"So, are ya goin' to da dance tonight?"

"What dance?" Ayana and Brandon asked in unison.

"Da Reggae Fest down at da pier. Dey gonna have a live band, plenty of food and barrels of rum punch."

"Sounds like fun. Ayana, would you like to go?"

Her eyes perked up. "Sure," she answered with a huge smile, exposing her pearly bright teeth.

"Where are you staying? I can pick you up."

She gave him her parents' address. "Do you know how to get there?"

"Yes. I'm familiar with the island. I've been here enough times. Marigold, what time does it start?"

"Eight o'clock."

"How about I pick you up at seven-thirty?"

Marigold looked at her brother-in-law and then back at Ayana, watching their conversation. She smiled.

"Sounds good. Let me dash. I have a few errands to run. Marigold, I'll talk to you later."

"Okay, me love."

Brandon watched her leave and couldn't believe the sudden change of events. He had totally misjudged the woman he knew as Saturday Knight. Now he couldn't wait to get to know Ayana Lewis.

Chapter 10

A cover band was wailing "Buffalo Soldier" when Brandon and Ayana walked into the open-air concert. The crowd was thick with both islanders and tourists, shoulder to shoulder, grooving to the music and drinking rum punch, Guinness Stout or Red Stripe beers. The smell of jerk chicken permeated the balmy night air. The mood of the crowd was happy and carefree, conducive to dancing the night away.

"I'm so glad Marigold told us about this. I haven't been to a Reggae Fest in a while," Ayana said over the music. Cameramen had been present at her last date, observing her every move. Being there with Brandon on a real date was a welcome change of pace.

"Me either."

"Is Marigold coming out tonight?" Ayana asked.

"She had planned on being here, but a mother and

her two children came to the shelter as Marigold was
leaving and she wanted to make sure they settled in
comfortably."

"I'm not surprised. I know how dedicated Marigold
is to the shelter."

"She's amazing. My brother was a lucky man to find
such a good woman." Brandon looked into Ayana's eyes,
paused for a moment and then said, "Some people are
just meant to be together."

Listening to his words and peering back into his
eyes, Ayana could feel herself being drawn to him and
subconsciously took a step closer. "Do you believe in
fate?"

"Never really thought about it much until now, but
life has a way of throwing you a curveball when you
least expect it."

"That's true." Brandon was the last person on earth
that Ayana thought she'd be spending time with. The
possibility of them getting even closer was now ever
present in her mind. She tried to shrug it off. They were
just beginning to get to know each other and she didn't
want to push the envelope. In an effort to dismiss her
growing desire, she looked around, spotted the food
vendors and changed the subject. "Do you want something to eat?"

"No, thanks. I had dinner earlier. Are you hungry?"

"No. My mother cooked a small feast and made me
eat before I left. She thinks I'm too thin."

"That's sweet. I wish my mother was still alive to
fuss over me. She died five years ago from lung cancer, which was weird because she never smoked a day
in her life."

"I'm sorry to hear that. I'm also sorry about the loss of your brother. He was such a nice guy."

"Thanks." He didn't want to dwell on the matter, so he quickly switched the subject. "How about a drink?"

"A stout would be great."

"Guinness?

"Yep."

"Wow, I would've never imagined you as a dark-beer drinker."

"And why is that?" she asked, putting her hand on her hip.

"Remember, I've only seen you on the set all dolled up, and you look like a girl who only drinks dainty pink cocktails that are served in chilled martini glasses."

"Well, looks are deceiving."

Brandon raised his eyebrow. "They surely are." He took Ayana's hand and led the way through the throng of people toward the drink stand. Once there, he ordered two cold beers.

"To new friendships," she said, tapping her bottle to his.

"I'll drink to that."

"Yo, Ana!" a voice behind them yelled.

She turned around and saw her friend Cedella cutting through the crowd. Cedella and Ayana had grown up together and remained close even after Ayana had moved to the States years ago. The two friends hugged, happy to see each other.

"Me moms told me ya were here," Cedella said. As she spoke she checked Brandon out from head to toe. Cedella was a serial flirt with no shame in her game. "And who is dis fine bro'her? Is dis yo man?"

Ayana looked over at Brandon and had to admit that

he looked sexy in his baby-blue polo shirt that complemented his milk-chocolate skin, straight-leg jeans that
hugged his muscular thighs and a pair of sandals. She
loved men who were confident enough to show their
feet. *I wish he were my man,* she thought. "No, he's just
a friend from New York."

"Ya two look good together. Ya should be a couple.
If ya don't want him, maybe me'll have a chance," she
said as if Brandon weren't standing there.

"CeDe, you still haven't learned to keep your thoughts
to yourself."

"Ya know me'll never change," she said, laughing.
"So, ya gonna introduce me or what?"

"Brandon, this is my friend Cedella. We were next-
door neighbors growing up."

"Nice to meet you, Cedella."

"Call me CeDe," she said, making googly eyes at
him. "So ya married, Brandon?"

"No, I'm not. CeDe, would you like a drink?" he
asked.

She raised a plastic cup filled with a ruby-colored
liquid. "No, thanks. Me already have a rum punch. Me
meeting some friends up front near da stage. Ya wanna
join us? We have a good spot."

"No, thanks. We're good," Ayana said before Brandon could answer. She and Brandon had melted the ice-
berg between them, and she wanted to continue their
getting-to-know-you session without CeDe interrupting or trying to hit on him.

"Suit yourself. Be sure to call me before ya leave
town," Cedella said as she gave Ayana a hug goodbye,
then disappeared back into the crowd.

"Tell me something—why don't you talk with an accent?"

"Me can talk wit da Jamaican accent if me want to," she said in a sassy tone. "When me interviewed for da show, Ed didn't want me to use me accent. Me worked wit a vocal coach to perfect me U.S. accent. So whacha tink of me talk now, mon?"

Brandon started to blush. "Your accent is sassy. It suits you."

The band was now singing "No Woman, No Cry." Ayana turned the beer up to her mouth, drained the bottle and tossed it into the garbage can. Brandon followed suit.

"Com on, mon. Let's dance," she said.

They walked hand in hand through the masses and joined the concertgoers dancing to the music. Brandon wrapped his arms around Ayana's waist and gently held her close.

The old-school reggae was soothing, transporting Ayana to a state of total awareness. She could feel her body molding into his as they swayed to the beat. Ayana closed her eyes and rested her head against his broad chest. She was so accustomed to being on the defensive that it felt good to let her guard down. Being in his arms felt comfortable, as if they were a couple that had been together for years instead of coworkers getting to know each other.

When the song ended, the band switched gears to an up-tempo beat, but Ayana and Brandon continued clinging to each other, seemingly in their own world, oblivious to the change. Brandon spun her around so that her backside was to him. He grabbed her hips and moved them to match his steps. Ayana looked over her shoulder, surprised that he was adept at a traditional reggae dance.

"I see you've got skills," she said, turning to face him.

"You haven't seen nuthin', mon," Brandon responded, using his own Jamaican accent.

They began doing a sensuous butterfly dance, spreading their legs in and out with their hands on their hips. Ayana hiked up her skirt, exposing her long legs. She bent her knees and squatted low near the ground. Brandon kept pace with her, placing his legs against hers. Together their waving limbs resembled a butterfly in heat. One song blended into another as they continued their hedonistic moves.

Brandon put his hands on his knees, easing his long, lean body lower and lower. Their legs were now intertwined, moving in sync. Brandon then wrapped one hand around her waist, pulling her close. He put his other hand on her exposed thigh, rubbing her smooth brown skin. Sweat was pouring off their bodies, dampening their clothes. The cotton gauze material of her top stuck to Ayana's skin, accentuating her breasts. Brandon licked his lips as he stared at her sexy body. He wiped beads of perspiration off his brow.

The combination of the humidity and the heat emanating from within was igniting a passion for Brandon that she was finding hard to resist. The feel of his hands on her body was driving Ayana crazy inside. One hand was clinching her waist, while his other hand was moving slowly up her thigh, getting closer and closer to her forbidden fruit. She was wet with perspiration and desire. Ayana was craving him sexually, but she didn't dare make the first move. She firmly believed that if a man wanted you, nothing could hold him back. And then, as if he were reading her thoughts, he leaned down and whispered in her ear.

"Come on. Let's get out of here." Brandon took Ayana's hand and led her off the dance floor.

No words were spoken as they wove through the crowd toward the exit. The intensity of the moment spoke volumes. Their sensuous dance moves were a prelude for a much-anticipated night of passion.

Chapter 11

Longing and lust filled the beach bungalow where Brandon had taken Ayana. She hadn't objected when he took her by the hand and led her out of the concert to his rented Fiat. When they reached the bungalow, Brandon didn't turn on any lights. Moonlight bathed the small cottage, creating a romantic glow. He closed the door and pulled her to him. They stood face-to-face, looking deeply into each other's eyes without saying a word. He took her face in his hands and rubbed her smooth cheeks. He leaned down and touched his lips to hers. The soft kiss slowly intensified, turning passionate, their tongues dancing harmoniously together, hungry for one another.

Brandon released her face, slipped his hands underneath her top and gently touched her nipples through her mesh bra. He rubbed the surface of the material, teasing her with each touch. Ayana covered his hands with hers and guided him toward the front snap closure of the bra. He took the hint, unsnapped the bra, unleashed her ample breasts and gently touched her erect nipples. He held her breasts in his hands and sensuously massaged them until he heard her moan.

"Hmm, that feels so good."

"That's just the beginning," he whispered and then licked the inside of her ear.

She gasped.

Brandon abandoned her breasts momentarily and unhooked her skirt, allowing it to slip to the floor. He roamed the soft surface of her skin, looking for delicious treasures. He moved his hand down her taut stomach and fingered the edge of her panties. Brandon was a patient man and didn't plan on rushing their first time together. He was going to savor every moment. He inched his hand into her panties. He could feel coarse hairs as he rubbed her neat bush, moving his fingers one at a time, and applied a little pressure with his index finger directly above her clit.

She gasped.

He leaned down and scooped Ayana up into his arms and carried her across the living room and into the bedroom. The room had floor-to-ceiling windows that looked out over the ocean. The windows were open and a soft breeze blew through the sheer curtains into the room. He laid her on top of the crisp white sheets, took off her wedge-heeled sandals, reached up and slid off her black lace panties. Brandon stood at the edge of the bed and admired her curvaceous body. She was well proportioned. Thick in all the right places—thighs, hips and butt. He licked his lips.

"Like what you see?"

He nodded. "Yes."

Brandon didn't take his eyes off her as he unbuckled his belt, unbuttoned his pants and slipped off his shirt, exposing his muscular chest.

Ayana's eyes were glued to him. Standing there bare-chested, with his jeans hanging off his hips, he looked like a sexy male model.

"Like what you see?" he asked, tossing the question back at her.

"So far, so good." She reached out and tugged at his belt.

He stepped back.

"Come here," she said, crooking her finger.

"Let's not rush. Do you have to get back home?"

"No."

"Good. We have all night, then."

Brandon kicked off his sandals and slowly stepped out of his jeans, one leg at a time. He stood in his boxer briefs with his legs slightly apart. She could see his broad shoulders and firm pecs by the moonlight.

Ayana bit her bottom lip as she gazed up at his sculpted body. The sight of him made her squirm with desire. She wanted him to devour her. She wanted to take her time as much as he did, but the anticipation of lovemaking was getting to be too much to bear. Ayana reached for him again. This time he didn't step back. She touched the imprint of his mound of manhood, which was nice and firm.

"Take them off," she said in a low, seductive tone as she tugged at the band of his briefs.

Brandon peeled off his underwear in slow motion. First, he fingered the elastic waistband suggestively and then eased the boxer briefs past his pubic area and down over his semierect penis.

She gasped.

He took hold of himself and began stroking the shaft of his penis, going all the way to the tip and back, causing his penis to grow with each stroke.

Ayana watched intently and could feel herself getting moister and moister. She put her hand between her legs, found her clit and started pleasuring herself too.

Watching her masturbate brought Brandon's penis to a fully erect state. His body was now aching for her, but he wasn't going to rush the moment. "Here, let me do that," he said, kneeling on the bed.

She spread her legs wider. "Be my guest."

He placed his massive hands on her knees and trailed his tongue from the inside of her right thigh, circling around to her left thigh, and back again, stopping at her exposed clit. He tasted her erogenous zone with the tip of his tongue before wrapping his lips around her clit. He alternated between sucking softly and firmly.

Ayana closed her eyes, grabbed the sheets with both fists and arched her back in ecstasy. "Ohhh, don't stop."

Brandon increased the pace, saliva dripping from his chin as he made love to her clit. He was a selfless lover and always wanted to please his partner first. But her oral climax was just the beginning. He reached for his jeans and retrieved a condom from his pocket, tore the foil package and rolled it onto his manhood. Brandon wedged himself between her legs and eased the tip of his penis into her ready vagina.

She gasped.

Ayana was wet and tight—a perfect combination. He wrapped her up in his arms and worked his rod, inch by inch, into her deep canal. The muscles of her vagina gripped his dick, causing him to pump faster, flexing his butt with each move. She held on to him with both hands and they rode the motion of lovemaking, pumping, pushing and panting. This was the first of many explosive climaxes.

After recovering, they changed positions. Now Ayana was on top, positioning herself near his manhood. She rolled the used condom off and replaced it with her mouth. She leaned down, wrapped her lips around his substantial manhood and went to work sucking in a rapid motion. She stopped and trailed her tongue up and down the sides of his shaft before using her tongue to tease the tip of his penis. She could taste his essence. Ayana covered him with her mouth again, and again went to work sucking and licking his penis as if it were a delicious chocolate-covered banana.

Brandon could feel himself coming. He moved her to the side, retrieved a fresh condom and rolled it on. "Get back on top."

Ayana did as instructed. This time, she squatted down over his erection and didn't stop until he was all the way inside. With her knees pressed close to his sides, she bounced up and down on his penis, crying out in ecstasy with each decadent move.

"You feel so good inside of me."

He held tightly on to her waist, thrusting upward, matching her moves with his own. "Being inside of you feels so right." He then flipped her over in one smooth motion. Now he was on top. Sweat dripped off Brandon's forehead as he increased his pace. The swiftness of his moves knocked the headboard back and forth against the wall. The noise of the bed coupled with their moans created the soundtrack of their first night together.

"Are you coming yet?" he panted.

"Almost."

Brandon reached underneath Ayana, grabbed her butt cheeks and pressed them toward his crotch, bringing her closer to him. He was on the verge of climax but wanted to ensure she was on the same page. "Tell me when you're ready."

"Okay, just don't stop."

He slowed down long enough to move his hands down her legs, grab her ankles and hold them high in the air, positioning himself deep inside of her V.

She gasped.

He ramped up the pace again and again. They each gave some more until their bodies gave in to yet another scrumptious, addictive climax.

Chapter 12

Ayana began to stir underneath the crisp white sheets as the sound of waves washing against the sand brought her out of a restful sleep. With her eyes still closed, she took a deep breath, inhaling the fresh ocean air. She stretched her arms, touching the bed and pillow next to her, but all she felt was the coolness of the sheet. She expected Brandon to be lying there. She opened her eyes to look for him, but he was nowhere in sight. The small bedroom was empty. She glanced at the nightstand, looking for a note from him, but there wasn't one.

Ayana's heart started to beat faster, in a mild panic. *Did he just leave without saying anything?* After sharing an intense night of lovemaking, staying up until the sun rose, she assumed that he would be cuddled up next to her, exhausted and enjoying the aftermath. The thought of him abandoning her didn't sit well. *Maybe I was wrong about our connection. Maybe it was just sex for him. And now that he got what he wanted, he has no further interest in me.* The inner dialogue was making her madder by the second. She began to feel used. The beautiful aftermath of lovemaking quickly evaporated.

"I'll be damned if I just lie here like an idiot and wait for him to show up," she said aloud. Ayana ripped the sheet from around her body, threw her legs over the side of the bed and stood. She looked on the floor for her clothes, but found only her lace panties. She then remembered that their foreplay had begun in the living room, where he had disrobed her. She put on the underwear and marched toward the door, her breasts bouncing with each purposeful step.

"Hey, pretty lady, where are you off to?" Brandon asked, entering the room.

Ayana took one look at him and saw he was holding a breakfast tray complete with a bud vase with a single yellow rose. "Uh, I was looking for my clothes." Admitting what she'd really thought was too embarrassing. Besides, it would make her seem paranoid.

"I folded them and put them over there," he said, motioning his head toward an armchair.

Now Ayana really felt silly. Not only had he brought her breakfast, but he had also picked her clothes off the floor and folded them. "Thanks," she said, walking over to the chair, picking up her top and slipping it on.

"You were sleeping so peacefully that I didn't want to wake you. I'm an early riser. It doesn't matter what time I go to bed, I'm always up between six and six-thirty. As a kid, my mom would wake us up an hour before school so that we could do our morning chores. Guess the habit of waking up early never wore off."

"What were your morning chores?"

"We had to make our beds and feed and walk the dog. Before getting ready for school."

"I always wanted a dog growing up, but my mother was allergic to them. What type of dog did you have?"

"A Siberian husky."

"Oh, a snow dog. I love huskies. The first one I ever saw was on television. As you can imagine, that type of dog is rare around here."

"Yeah, who ever heard of a husky living on an island?" He chuckled. "So, are you hungry?"

"Starving. What do we have?" she asked, peering at the tray.

"Cod fish, ackee, callaloo, johnnycakes and Blue Mountain coffee, of course."

She raised her eyebrow, amazed at his culinary talents. "You cooked all that?"

Brandon started smiling. "Well…no, I didn't. Marigold did."

"Marigold!"

"Yes, this bungalow is on her property. She and my brother bought this place years ago. They used to rent out the bungalow during the high-tourist months. After my brother died, she decided that she didn't want to be bothered dealing with renters, so she just leaves it empty for when I come to town. She lives in the main house."

Ayana was half listening as he spoke. She had something else on her mind. "You told Marigold about last night?" Ayana was totally embarrassed. Although she was a grown woman who could do as she pleased, she didn't want her friend thinking that she slept with men on the first date.

"Don't worry. She thinks it's all for me. She knows

I'm a big eater. Marigold makes me breakfast every day before she leaves for the shelter. She's gone to work already and didn't ask any questions before she left. Our secret is safe." He put the tray on the bed and sat down. "Come on. Let's eat before it gets cold."

Ayana sat next to him, took a fork and dug in. She loved her native cuisine and didn't edit her eating habits when she was home. "So what's on your agenda today?" she asked, in between bites.

"I thought we'd tool around the island. You could show me some of your favorite places—that is, if you're not busy."

It had been years since a man wanted to spend quality time with her and it felt good. "No, I'm not busy. I need to call home first and let my mother know I'm all right."

"That's sweet."

"What?"

"Letting your mother know you're okay, so she won't worry. I can't believe that brassy Saturday Knight has to call home like a teenager with a curfew."

"I really should have called her last night but…" She blushed just thinking about their heated lovemaking session. "I was preoccupied."

"That's an understatement."

Ayana went into the living room, where her purse was, took out her cell phone and made the call.

Brandon could hear her telling her mother a little white lie.

"Hey, Mom. I just wanted to let you know that I stayed at CeDe's last night. Hope you didn't worry too much. We're going to hang out today. I'll be home later. Okay. 'Bye."

When she came back into the room, Brandon said, "I didn't mean to eavesdrop, but didn't your mom see me pick you up last night?"

"No, she wasn't at home. She and my father had gone over to my uncle's for dinner. I don't like lying to her, but my parents are old-fashioned. I would want them to meet you and spend some time with you before I announced that I'm sleeping over at your place."

Brandon looked stunned.

She noticed the strange look on his face. "Don't panic. I'm not saying I want to introduce you to my parents. I'm just saying I'm not going to announce that I slept with a man they don't know. You might find this hard to believe, but they still look at me like I'm their little girl."

"I understand." He picked up his fork and began eating.

Suddenly there was an awkward silence between them. Ayana sipped her coffee and stared out at the ocean. After a few moments, she was the first to speak.

"Actually, I'm going to take a rain check on today. I really need to get back home and check on my dad."

"Oh, okay," he said, sounding a bit disappointed.

"Look, Brandon, I think we might have moved a little too fast. Last night was great, but let's not pretend we're a couple. We don't have to spend the day together. I'm sure you have other things to do," she said, sounding more like Saturday Knight than Ayana. Though she had been looking forward to spending more time with him, she didn't want him to feel obligated. The look on his face when she'd mentioned her parents being old-fashioned and wanting to meet her potential suitor told her that Brandon was uncomfortable with that idea. And she had to admit it was too soon to make any formal introductions, if he even met them at all.

"Aren't you going to finish eating before you leave?" he asked, looking at her half-eaten food.

Ayana had lost her appetite. "No, I'm full. I'm going to get ready to go so I can get out of your way."

"You don't have to rush off. There's no hurry."

She stood up. "I really need to get going." Ayana didn't have anything to rush home to, but she wanted to get out of there and fast. She had given the impression that he *had* to meet her parents, which wasn't true. Ayana was now feeling like one of those needy chicks who force-fed their families to a man on the first date. She was anything but needy, and she wanted to redeem herself. Fleeing the scene would send the message that she wasn't trying to latch on to him.

"I'll drive you back."

"You don't have to do that. I'll call CeDe. My mother will be full of questions if she sees you, and I'm not ready to introduce you," Ayana replied, reiterating her point.

"Ayana, I don't have a problem driving you home, but if you insist…"

"I do. What's the address here?"

He gave her the address, and she walked back into the living room and called her friend.

Then she showered and dressed in less than ten minutes. When she reentered the bedroom, Brandon was standing at the window looking out at the ocean. "I'm leaving now. Thanks for a nice evening."

He turned around. "Come here."

When she got within reaching distance, he pulled her close and covered her in a huge hug. "Can I call you?"

"Don't feel obligated."

"I don't feel obligated. I want to see you again."

Ayana stood still within his embrace. She was confused. One minute they were sharing a tender moment, and the next there was an underlying tension. In New York, Ayana was a brazen city girl, but in her hometown she was a traditional country girl. Blurring the lines had caused friction between them, and now she felt the need to pull back. "Brandon, I'm going to be busy for the next few days."

"Uh, okay."

Standing face-to-face, neither said a word. What had started off as a great morning and a potentially better day had soured into a misunderstanding, with neither really to blame. The sound of a blaring horn broke the silence.

"That's CeDe. See you around," she said and left without a kiss goodbye.

When she was gone, Brandon sat on the edge of the bed. "Damn, what happened?" he said out loud. His plans for the day had quickly fizzled out. Brandon was enjoying Ayana; she was completely different from Saturday Knight. He had been looking forward to getting to know her better but hadn't expected her to drop the parent bomb. Maybe she was right about them moving too fast.

Chapter 13

"Why ya so quiet?" Cedella asked Ayana as they drove along with the windows rolled down and the morning breeze flowing through the compact car.

Ayana didn't answer right away. She was still reeling from the unnecessary exchange with Brandon. She wanted to stay, but the tension between them had made her feel uncomfortable. "I'm not quiet."

"Ya no say more dan two words since ya been in da car. Wat's up? I see ya still have on da clothes from last night, so I guess ya spend da night wit ya boyfriend." CeDe always said exactly what was on her mind.

"Brandon's not my boyfriend," Ayana snapped.

"But ya did spend da night wit him? No?" she said, cutting her eyes at Ayana.

"Yes, I did. So what? We are both consenting adults."

"Since ya got some, ya should be beamin'. Why ya

sounding so mad? What him do? Tell ya to leave once da sheets cooled off?"

"Absolutely not!" Ayana exhaled hard and put her arms across her chest. "If I'd known you'd quiz me all the way to my house, I would have called a taxi. That way I wouldn't have to play twenty questions with you," she said, totally annoyed.

"Calm down. I'm just asking. We used to be able to talk 'bout anyting. Why ya actin' so defensive?"

Ayana looked out the window at the lush landscape and thought about what had transpired with Brandon. Maybe she'd blown the whole thing out of proportion. Maybe she needed another opinion on what had just happened. "I'm sorry for snapping at you. Last night was wonderful, but this morning, when I mentioned how old-fashioned my parents are and said that they like to meet the guys I go out with, his whole attitude changed."

"Oh, me word, chile! Ya know better than ta mention anyting about family ta men, especially in da beginnin'. Dey tink we tryin' ta trap dem in a relationship, or worse...marriage."

Ayana sighed. "You're right. Well, it's not like I straight-out said for him to come and meet my parents."

"Don't matter. Menfolk don't tink like we do."

"True."

"I could tell by da way ya was looking at him last night dat ya really like the man. Dat's why me back off. Oderwise me would've been in him bed last night."

Ayana chuckled. "CeDe, you're too much. But you're right—I do really like him. I haven't been into a guy this much in a long time." Ayana saw no sense in denying the obvious.

"So whatcha gonna do about it, mon?"

"What do you mean?"

"I mean, ya gonna let a little misunderstanding get in da way of ya seeing him again?"

"Well, he did say he wanted to get together, but I told him I was busy."

"Chile, ya need to get unbusy. Dat's one fine man, and if ya don't stake ya claim, dhen some o'her woman will."

Ayana thought about what her friend was saying and knew she was right. Brandon was a catch and probably wouldn't be on the market for long. "I don't want to call him and seem desperate."

CeDe pondered the situation for a few seconds and then said, "Iggy is giving a beach party tonight and everybody's talkin' about it. Maybe he'll be dhere. Dat way ya can see him witout callin' for a date. And if him don't show up, at least ya can get your flirt on. Maybe ya meet someone else. Da party will be filled wit plenty of hot guys."

Iggy was a local event promoter and was known for his legendary beach parties, where the mandatory dress code was some form of beachwear. The women usually wore bikini tops with shorts, swimsuits underneath cover-ups or just swimsuits. Men came in various types of trunks, from traditional boxers, to Speedos, to G-string trunks that showcased their packages. The party was all-inclusive with conch, escovitch and curry goat served, along with plenty of rum punch, dark-and-stormy cocktails and Red Stripe. Live bands and deejays jammed until the break of dawn.

"That's a great idea. I'll definitely go." Ayana's mood

lightened. She didn't like the way she and Brandon had left things and wanted a do-over.

"Ya want me to pick ya up?" CeDe asked once they reached Ayana's parents' house.

"No, I'll drive. Thanks for the ride! See you later."

"Hey, Ma!" Ayana yelled as she entered her quaint childhood home.

"Whatcha doin' home? I thought you and CeDe were spendin' da day t'gether," her mother said, coming into the living room holding a freshly caught kingfish.

"We're going out tonight instead."

"I know CeDe's glad to have ya home. Ya two were thick as thieves growin' up."

"Yeah, we were. CeDe is still the same outspoken person she was when we were little. She says things most people only think."

The truth was, Ayana modeled some of Saturday Knight's characteristics after Cedella. The straight-talking tell-it-like-it-is persona that she displayed on the show was her version of CeDe, coupled with Ed's well-crafted brazen character.

"Yes, that's Cedella a'right. Ya hungry? I'm making kingfish stew."

"No, Ma. I'll be in my room."

Upstairs, her bedroom was still decorated in varying shades of pink and lavender, complete with twin beds and posters of boy bands from back in the day. Ayana rushed into the room and went straight to the closet. She combed through the racks looking for the perfect outfit. Brandon had seen her as two polar opposites—the tempestuous star of *Divorced Divas* and the dutiful Jamaican daughter. Tonight she planned on showing him a hybrid of the two—the sultry, au naturel temptress. After an hour of trying on various outfits, Ayana finally made a decision. Then she climbed into bed. She was exhausted from the night before; she and Brandon had done very little sleeping.

After her nap, Ayana showered and dressed for the evening in a pair of white short-shorts that looked more like panties than shorts and a string bikini top underneath a white T-shirt. She was excited at the possibility of seeing Brandon and was eager to get to the party. She told her parents that she would probably stay the night at CeDe's. Ayana wanted to cover all bases in case she ran into Brandon and they spent the night together again. She didn't want a replay of earlier.

When she reached the beach, the sun was setting, creating a beautiful kaleidoscope of oranges, reds and yellows. Ayana parked in the packed parking lot, got out and made her way to the equally packed beach. The party was filled with scandalously clad bodies gyrating barefoot on the sand to a steel band jamming to a reggae beat. Ayana stood on the raised concrete sidewalk and looked over the sea of red, green and yellow knit caps bobbing up and down to the music, trying to spot Brandon, but she didn't see him. She took off her sandals, put them in her tote bag and made her way onto the sand to get a closer look.

"Hey, Mama, ya lookin' mighty fine tonight. Let's dance," said a buffed, bare-chested man with dreadlocks.

"Uh, sure, why not?" She didn't really want to dance with him, but she did want to get in the middle of the crowd without drawing attention to herself.

He took her hand and they wove their way to the

middle of the dance area, where sweaty bodies were working to the beat. A woman wearing a thong bikini was clapping her butt cheeks to the music. Her dance partner had his phone in the air, taping her. After the song ended, Ayana told Mr. Dreadlocks thanks and left the dance area.

She moseyed through the party, casually searching for Brandon and Cedella, but she didn't run into either of them. She went to the grass-hut bar, ordered a stout and waited, hoping that he would show up. Two beers later, and still no Brandon. She left the bar and moved on. Across from the bar, a wet T-shirt contest was getting under way.

The emcee was on a raised platform with the microphone in his hand and asking for contestants. Several women in the crowd hopped onstage, eager to show their goods. Out of the corner of her eye, Ayana thought she saw Brandon. She slowly turned to her left, and there he was, standing in the crowd. But he didn't see her.

Let me show him what I'm working with, she said to herself. Ayana took a deep breath, swallowed her inhibitions, bolted through the crowd and leaped onstage. She set her purse to the side and joined the other women.

"Okay, ladies, are ya ready?" the emcee asked.

In unison they all said, "Yes!"

Ayana tied a knot in her T-shirt, exposing her taut belly and making her skimpy outfit even more revealing.

"Me gonna need the first tree ladies front and center." When the women stepped forward, the emcee continued. "Where's da Hose Mon?"

A bare-chested man wearing a Speedo appeared at the front of the stage holding a green water hose.

"Ya ready?"

The crowd yelled, "Ya, mon!"

"Okay, Hose Mon, hose dem down."

The man holding the hose turned on the water and sprayed the first three contestants. The women screamed when the ice-cold water hit their bodies. The water assault lasted only a few seconds, but it was long enough to thoroughly drench them.

"Dat's good." The emcee signaled the Hose Man to turn off the water. "Now, ladies, strut yo stuff."

The women went into action, smoothing down their T-shirts and pressing the wet material, showcasing their breasts. The first contestant had a small chest and didn't elicit much response from the crowd. The second woman had on a swimsuit underneath her T-shirt, so nothing was exposed. The third contestant had fake boobs that jutted out from underneath her T-shirt like parking cones. The crowd had a mixed response.

"Lade Numbar Tree, step to da side. Da rest of ya can leave da stage," the emcee said, weeding out the losers. "Now me gonna need da next tree ladies."

Ayana was in this group. She felt nervous. She had never done anything like this before. She looked out over the crowd, making sure that Brandon was still there, and he was. *Showtime,* she said to herself. Ayana was going to work her magic and get their romance back on track.

"Hose Mon, wet 'em down," the emcee announced again.

When the water jetted out, Ayana didn't flinch. She stood there with her hands on her hips like a gladiator ready for battle. When the stream of water stopped, she pressed down on her T-shirt using her hands like a squeegee and stood with her legs spread apart as the water dripped down her thighs. She rubbed the wet material that covered her breasts, but nothing showed through since she was wearing a bikini top.

People started chanting, "Take it off! Take it off!" as they pumped their fists in the air.

The energy emanating from the crowd spurred her on. Ayana reached underneath her wet shirt, untied her bikini top, took it off and tossed it into the crowd. A woman caught it and started swinging the wet top in the air, slinging drips of water with each turn of her wrist. Ayana was in a zone. She closed her eyes and began slowly and sensuously massaging her breasts, focusing on her engorged nipples. The crowd went wild.

She opened her eyes and looked dead into Brandon's handsome face. He had moved from the middle of the crowd and was now standing at the front of the stage. Watching him watch her was making Ayana hot with desire. She kneaded her nipples harder and rotated her hips at the same time, exaggerating her moves like a porn star. The crowd roared!

"Now, dat's what me talkin' 'bout," the emcee said.

The other two contestants were up next, but their performances paled in comparison to Ayana's. When they finished, the emcee told them to step down from the stage, and then he continued. "Lade Numbar Tree, come here." The contestant from the first round stepped up and stood next to Ayana. "When me put me hand above dey head, me want ya to clap. Da lade wit de most claps wins."

He placed his hand above the first woman, and she

received a fair share of claps. He then put his hand over Ayana's head and the crowd started clapping, screaming, yelling and stomping their feet. "I tink we got a winner." He placed a gold tiara on her head. "Congratulations. I crown you Da Queen of Da Wet T-Shirt." She curtsied, blew a few kisses, picked up her bag and left the stage.

Ayana's instant fan club encircled her the second she stepped down, some of the men trying to swipe a feel. She maneuvered out of their grasps, looking for Brandon, but she didn't see him. He was there one second and gone the next.

Damn. Where did he go? Ayana's heart began to sink. Her raunchy display had been to entice him. Obviously, it hadn't worked. He had left and now she felt like a fool. She took the crown off, put it in her tote and slunk through the crowd, feeling defeated even though she had won. As she was walking, someone grabbed her arm from behind. Ayana assumed it was another admirer trying to get her attention. She wasn't in the mood to entertain a stranger. All she wanted to do was go home, get in bed and forget about this night. She'd had enough. If the wet T-shirt contest didn't get Brandon's attention, then nothing would. Ayana swung around to tell whoever was tugging at her to get lost. She turned quickly, breaking the hold the person had on her.

"And where are you going, Queen of the Wet T-Shirts?"

It was Brandon.

Chapter 14

Brandon stood in front of Ayana, staring at the wet T-shirt that was now molded around her breasts, accentuating her nipples. He was finding it hard to keep his eyes focused on her face. As he spoke, his eyes kept darting from her eyes to her chest. Her near nakedness had him mesmerized.

"So, where are you off to in such a hurry?" he asked.

Ayana seemed to notice him staring at her body. She arched her back, suggestively poking her boobs farther out.

"I'm going over to the bar to get something to drink," she replied.

"Mind if I join you?"

"Of course not."

Ayana led the way. Brandon watched her sway her hips from side to side as she moved. He couldn't help but stare at her round rear end in the short-shorts. When they reached the grass-hut bar, people were hanging out, drinking and dancing in the sand.

"Are you having a stout?" he asked.

"Yes, and a shot of rum."

He ordered two shots and two beers. "Here you go," he said, handing her the drinks.

Ayana wasted no time shooting back the rum and chasing it with the beer.

"You want another round?" Brandon asked, looking amazed at how fast she'd drunk the shot and beer.

"Yes, I'd love another round," she said, suggestively licking her lips.

He motioned for the bartender and ordered a second round. "Here you go, Queen of the Wet T-Shirts," he said, handing her the drinks. "Hey, where's your tiara? You deserved to win and should show it off."

Ayana dug the crown out of her bag and placed it on her head, cocking it to the side. "Did you enjoy the contest?"

"Yes, I did. You were amazing. The other contestants didn't stand a chance."

Ayana blushed. "Thanks."

He peered at her shirt again. "Looks like you're drying off."

"Can't let that happen." She bolted back the shot and beer. "Come on—let's go swimming, so I can get wet again." She winked, hoping he'd get the double entendre.

Her words didn't go unnoticed. He smiled, glad that they were on the same page. He didn't like the way things had ended earlier and was eager to start over. "Wet is always good." Brandon wasted no time finishing his drink. He tossed their empty bottles in a trash can, grabbed her hand and led the way through the revelers. They trotted along the shore, down the beach and away from the crowd of people. He wanted to be alone with her without prying eyes watching their every move.

Once they reached a secluded area, he stopped and faced her. He took her face in his hands, looked deeply into her eyes, pulled her to him and said, "I've always wanted to make love to a queen on a beach."

She reached up and wrapped her arms around his neck. "Your wish is my command."

Brandon stepped closer into her embrace and planted his full lips on hers. He slipped his tongue in her mouth and started rotating his hips, grinding his pelvis into hers, intensifying their connection even more.

His manhood rapidly responded, growing inch by inch. He ran his fingers through her hair, bringing her head closer to his. He abandoned her mouth and tenderly kissed her forehead, nose, cheeks and chin. As he covered her face with a series of tender kisses, her crown slipped off.

"Let's go skinny-dipping," she whispered in his ear. "You've got me on fire." Ayana peeled off her T-shirt and shorts and tossed them on the sand.

Brandon untied the string to his trunks and let them slip off, exposing his semierect manhood. "See what you do to me?" he said, stroking himself.

She knelt down on the sand, grabbed the backs of his thighs and brought him closer. Ayana took hold of his penis and kissed the head. She alternated between kissing and licking, flicking her tongue, teasing him with each sensuous stroke.

Brandon closed his eyes and enjoyed her oral talents. After a few minutes of pleasure, he bent down and took her by the elbows, bringing her to her feet. Brandon was on the verge of climaxing but wasn't ready to come yet. He wanted to prolong their foreplay for as long as he could. "Come on."

They raced toward the water, hand in hand, and jumped into the pitch-black ocean, which looked like a Texas oil slick. Ayana splashed the water toward him, creating a rush of waves. Brandon waded in her direction, bobbing and weaving, trying to avoid the onslaught. Once he reached her, he engulfed her in a bear hug and then lifted her high in the air.

Ayana wrapped her legs around his waist, positioning her vagina near his penis. She moved her body rapidly against his, her breasts bouncing up and down with each move.

Brandon took hold of her ass, squeezing her cheeks, bringing her closer. His manhood was like a guiding rod, heading straight to her waiting opening. Entering her sent chills all over his body. His desire for her was stronger than before. He pumped harder and harder, letting the buoyancy of the water aid their synchronized moves. "Oh, baby…you feel like…like…"

"Heaven," she said, completing his sentence.

They rode the waves, holding on and giving in to each other with everything they had. The moon broke through the clouds and beamed a bright ray down on their naked bodies as they each reached a much-anticipated climax.

"That was too good," Ayana said, totally spent.

He held her around her waist, steadying her until she found her balance. "It was better than good."

They held on to each other, ambling arm in arm back

to shore, both weak in the knees. Once they reached the cool sand, they collapsed, consumed from their heated passion. The misunderstanding from earlier was now completely washed away.

Chapter 15

The early-morning sky was pink with shades of lavender streaking through low-hanging clouds as the sun slowly made its appearance. Teal-blue water lapped softy at the shore, creating a melodic rhythm. The beach was serene. Gone were the party revelers from the night before. Brandon was the first to stir. He stretched his long limbs before sitting up. Ayana was still asleep, curled up next to him, looking like a big baby in her birthday suit. He stared at her naked body, admiring her beauty. Her skin was as smooth as satin. Her hair, wet from the ocean, had dried, creating a mass of spiral curls cascading around her head. Their spontaneous romp in the ocean had been both exhilarating and exhausting. They had collapsed on the sand and fallen into a deep sleep before either put on clothes. Brandon's trunks were lying on the sand beside Ayana's clothes and crown. The mere sight of the crown brought a smile to his face. Remembering how brazen Ayana had been onstage, massaging her breasts and showcasing her assets in the wet T-shirt contest, was getting him excited all over again. He could feel his manhood awakening, rising to attention.

Brandon looked around the beach, checking to see if anyone else was wandering about. The strand was deserted with no one in sight. He lay back down and snuggled up close to Ayana, his penis pressing against her bare backside. Brandon reached around, placed his hands on her breasts and began massaging the soft tissue, rubbing her nipples at the same time until they firmed to his touch. He moved her hair out of the way and started sucking her earlobe and then kissing the side of her neck. She began to stir.

Ayana could feel the touch of Brandon in her sleep and thought she was dreaming, but this dream seemed too real. She opened her eyes and saw his hands on her breasts.

"I see somebody has an insatiable appetite," she said, slightly turning her head toward him. She looked over his shoulder to see if anyone was watching them, but no one was within eyesight.

He moved her body closer to his. "You're right. I just can't get enough of you."

With her butt firmly against his crotch, she could feel his thick rod inching between her thighs, making its way to her V-spot, which was getting wetter and wetter by the second. The head of his penis pressed urgently against the lips of her vagina. The feel of him trying to enter her sugar walls made her back arch with desire as they did a sensuous grind, teasing one another with every move.

Brandon turned her over onto her back and moved his body on top of hers, wedging himself between her thighs.

Her toes dug into the sand as she spread her legs apart, allowing him easier access. Ayana wrapped her arms around his back and held on as he made his way into her slippery canal. The sensation of his manhood filling her was exhilarating and sent chills all over her body. She bit her bottom lip to keep from screaming out as she neared orgasm.

He increased his pace, holding on to her, pumping harder and stronger.

As if on cue, the sun broke through the clouds at the precise moment of their dual climax, creating the perfect crescendo to their early-morning loving.

"Now, that was the perfect wake-up call," Ayana said, sitting up and brushing the sand out of her hair.

"Yes, it was." Brandon sat up too and looked down the beach. In the distance, he could see someone walking toward them. "We'd better get out of here." He handed Ayana her clothes. They quickly dressed and made their way back to where the party had been.

"Wait! My crown." Ayana ran as fast as the sand would allow and picked up the golden symbol of her victory. A victory in more than one way—not only had she won the contest, but she'd also won over Brandon. A broad smile spread across her face as she raced back to him.

"Are you hungry?" he asked.

"Yes. I'm starving!"

"I know a great little café not too far from here that serves the best breakfast."

"Sounds good." Ayana wanted to go home first so she could shower and change clothes, but she didn't want to break the momentum. The morning had started off on a good note and she planned on keeping it that way.

"Do you need to…?" He was going to ask if she had to call home before going out, but he caught himself. Brandon didn't want to ruin the day like last time, so he kept his mouth shut.

"What did you say?"

"Uh, I was going to ask if you needed to shower before we have breakfast. If so, we can go back to my place if you want."

"Yes, that sounds good," she said, brushing sand from her arms.

"I drove if you need a ride," he offered.

"I drove too. I'll follow you."

"Okay."

Brandon led the way to the parking lot, where only five cars remained. He walked Ayana to her car, then returned to his rented Fiat, got in and drove off. The ride back to the bungalow was short. He bypassed the main house, where Marigold lived, and pulled around back to the bungalow. He got out, went to Ayana's car, opened the door and helped her out.

Ayana looked around the quiet bungalow. A part of her wondered if Brandon brought other women here. He was such an attractive man who could easily be a player, even though he didn't seem like the type. She casually scanned the room for any evidence of another woman but didn't see anything out of the ordinary. *Stop being paranoid. Obviously he's into you.* Ayana didn't know where these feelings of paranoia were coming from. Probably from the fact that they were bonding really well and she didn't want someone else infringing on her territory.

"You want to shower together?" she asked, walking up close and rubbing her chest against his. Even though they had just made love on the beach less than thirty minutes ago, she was ready for more. Ayana wanted to make sure she was the only woman he craved.

"Hmm, that's a brilliant idea." He lifted her arms over her head and removed her shirt, then leaned down and nibbled on her nipples. "Come on. I'm feeling really dirty," he said, arching his eyebrows.

Ayana took off her shorts and followed him to the bathroom. The previous time she had been there, she had showered in record time, anxious to go home after their disagreement. This morning was completely different. The last thing she wanted was to make a hasty exit.

Brandon turned on the water and then removed his trunks. He stepped in first, the pulsating water beating down on his back as he helped her in. "Turn around."

Ayana moved so that her chest was facing the shower wall. She lifted her arms and put her hands against the pink tiles, slightly spread her legs and waited in heated anticipation for his next move.

Brandon stood and watched as the water dripped down her back and eased between the crack of her butt. "I wish I were that water," he whispered in her ear.

She turned her head over her shoulder and said, "What do you mean?"

He stared intently at her rear end, admiring the view.

"If I were the shower water, I would be dripping all over your body, exploring your hidden treasures."

"You don't have to be water to drip all over me and explore my treasures." She reached for his hand and placed it on her round ass.

Brandon palmed her butt cheeks, caressing them with tenderness. He gently spread them apart, placed his slate-hard cock in between her cheeks and slowly started grinding against her.

Ayana rotated her hips, matching his movements, waiting for him to enter her from behind, but he was taking his time. His slow-motion grind was driving her wild, making her want him badly. She closed her eyes, held on to the shower wall and moaned. "Ohhh…you're making…me…so hot."

He kissed the back of her neck. "Why? We're just taking a shower, that's all." Brandon reached for a bottle in the shower caddy, squirted her back with shower gel and rubbed the substance until it began to lather. He lathered her entire body before putting the bottle back. He slipped his hands over her breasts, down her stomach and in between her legs.

She gasped.

Brandon searched for her clit. Once he found the tiny piece of flesh, he began rubbing his thumb against her pleasure point. He continued rubbing and rubbing and rubbing, increasing the pace until she screamed out.

He bent her forward and began entering her from behind. Even though they had made love earlier, she was still tight, making him work for penetration. Once the tip of his penis was inside her, he pumped slowly, inching himself all the way in. "You feel so good," he said, putting his arms around her waist and pulling her in even closer.

Brandon had been with a fair share of women in his lifetime, but Ayana was by far the best lover he'd ever had. He couldn't get enough of her. Brandon could feel himself falling in love, and it wasn't solely about the sex. Ayana was a good woman. Seeing her outside of New York had shed a new light on the person he knew as Saturday Knight. He tried to hold back, but his body was giving in to her.

They came simultaneously underneath the pulsating water.

"Now, that's what I call a shower," he said.

"I couldn't agree more."

After spending another few minutes showering, they stepped out, toweled off, made their way to the bedroom, fell into bed and passed out. After a few hours of sleep, Brandon made a food run to the main house. Since Marigold was at the shelter, there were no queries to answer while he made two of everything—two jerk-chicken sandwiches on coco bread, two tropical-fruit salads, two slices of rum cake and two ginger beers.

When he got back to the bungalow, Ayana was still curled up underneath the sheet asleep. Brandon didn't wake her. He ate in silence and watched her rest. They never made it out of the bungalow. They spent the rest of the day in bed, eating, sleeping and making love.

Chapter 16

"Of course I'm not dead. I almost checked out, but I had a guardian angel looking out for me. If it weren't for Saturday acting as fast as she did, I would be on the other side, chatting with the Big Guy now." Ed was on the phone talking to Steve, a producer on the show. After two weeks, he was still in the hospital but out of ICU. He had defied the doctor's prognosis and was making a miraculous recovery despite a few setbacks. Once out of ICU, Ed had instructed his assistant to send Saturday three dozen deep pink roses to her apartment as a small token of appreciation for saving his life.

"You can say that again. She jumped into action performing CPR without a second thought. Who knew she'd be the one to resuscitate you? With her bad attitude, I would've thought she was the type of woman to stand by chatting away on her cell phone while someone else did the heavy lifting." Steve had witnessed Saturday's antics up close on the set and wasn't a fan.

Ed didn't say anything right away. He was beginning to feel bad for letting everyone think that the persona he had invented was real. Ayana Lewis was nothing like Saturday Knight. Ayana was sweet and kindhearted, whereas Saturday was just the opposite. He started to tell Steve the truth but didn't want to chance destroying what he had created. The audience loved to hate Saturday, which kept them watching to see what outlandish thing she was going to do or say next. The television business was all about high ratings, and Ed planned to keep his show among the top reality shows for as long as he could.

"Well, you never know who a person really is, now do you?" Ed finally said.

"I guess you're right."

"Mr. Levine, how many times do I have to tell you that cell phones aren't allowed in the hospital?" the nurse said, coming into his private room.

Ed rolled his eyes in her direction. "Steve, I have to go. Nurse Ratched just came in." He disconnected the call and put the phone inside the nightstand.

"I see the heart attack hasn't affected your smart mouth," she shot back.

"Darling Nurse Ratched, I was born with sassiness and will die with sassiness," he said, fingering the pink feather boa that was tied around his neck.

"For the umpteenth time, my name is Nurse Rachel." She walked over to him, flipped back the covers and placed a stethoscope on his chest to listen to his heartbeat.

"Rachel, Ratched, what's the difference?" Ed teased.

Being laid up in the hospital was a bore to him, so he found amusement in ribbing the nurses, and Nurse Rachel—an older, motherly type—was his favorite.

She didn't respond. Most of the time she just ignored him and did her job. She stuck the ends of the stethoscope into her ears and listened.

"How's the old ticker beating?"

"Strong, for someone who had a heart attack less than a month ago and had all the complications that you've had. You're lucky to be alive."

"I was born lucky. So when do I blow this joint?"

She checked his blood pressure, then answered. "Soon, I hope," she said, throwing him a smart line of her own. "But you'll have to discuss that with your doctor."

"When is he coming in? I'm ready to go home. I've had enough of this depressing scene. There are too many sick people in here for my taste."

"This is a hospital. Not that you would notice with all these flowers, balloons and cards everywhere," she said, pointing to the arrangements of roses, gardenias, irises and birds-of-paradise in decorative vases sitting all around the room. Balloons of varying sizes floated on colorful strings, and get-well cards were thumb-tacked to the walls.

"What can I say? I'm well loved by all," he said, with a Cheshire-cat grin.

"Okay, Mr. Well Loved. No more cell phone calls, *especially* business calls. You are still recovering and don't need any added stress, especially if you want to go home."

Ed looked out the window, seemingly ignoring her advice. He felt great, almost 100 percent. He had a show to get back on track and was ready to return to work, even if it only meant calling the shots over the phone.

She snapped her fingers in his direction. "Do you hear me?"

"Of course I hear you. I had a heart attack. I didn't have a cochlear implant for hearing loss," he shot back.

Nurse Rachel shook her head at him as if he were a naughty little boy. "Now open your mouth so I can take your temperature." She stuck the thermometer in his mouth, waited a few moments, took it out and looked at the reading. "All your vitals are normal, so hopefully you'll be out of my hair soon."

"Here's hoping."

"And remember no more cell phone calls. If I see you talking on that thing again, I will have to take it. Understood?"

"Whatever you say, Nurse Ratched."

She rolled her eyes at him and walked out.

Ed waited a few minutes to see if she was going to return. When she didn't come back, he retrieved the phone out of the nightstand, turned his back to the door and made a call. "Hi, it's me again," he said, talking to Steve. "Listen, I want you to call the cast and crew and get them to the penthouse. Since production of the show is on hold momentarily, I want to do a type of reunion show…a special."

"Are you sure? Reunion shows are taped at the end of the season," Steve said.

"I know when they're taped. I want to keep the audience interested in *Divorced Divas,* and running a series of reruns is getting boring. Lying here in this bed, I've been watching the same episodes over and over. If I'm bored with my own show, I'm sure the audience is tuning out. A reunion-type show where we not only focus on this season, but also show some behind-the-scenes clips from last season would pump some energy back into the series. Plus, it's different, and I thrive on being different."

"Now that I think about it, a reunion show would be a good idea."

"Of course it would. We'll call it a *Divorced Divas Divulge* special, not to be confused with the regular reunion show. Now get in touch with the cast and crew and have them report to the penthouse day after tomorrow."

"So soon?"

"Yes. The sooner the better."

"Will you be out of the hospital by then?"

"I plan to be, and if I'm not, I'll leave you with explicit instructions as to how I want the cast to behave." Ed turned back toward the door and saw Nurse Rachel coming down the hall in his direction with a scowl on her face. "I have to go, but be sure to call everyone pronto."

"Okay, you got it," Steve said and hung up.

Ed returned the phone to the nightstand, fluffed up his pillow and laid his head back as if he were resting. He felt better already. Getting *Divorced Divas* back on track was better than any medicine the doctor could prescribe.

Chapter 17

Brandon held on to Ayana's waist as she steered her canary-yellow Vespa through a narrow, tree-lined road. He sat on the back of the scooter with his legs anchored around hers and enjoyed the sights. She was taking him to one of her favorite places—an isolated spot high in the Blue Mountains. As they wove through the secluded mountainside, Brandon gazed up at the trees and spotted one unique-looking bird after another. Some were resting on branches, while others soared through the cloudless blue sky. As many times as he'd been to Jamaica, Brandon had never ventured into these parts before, and he found the journey relaxing.

The day after their indoor lovefest, Ayana had suggested they get out of the house and have a picnic. She had gone home, cooked up a feast, packed it in plastic containers, placed them in the wicker basket on the front of her motorbike, then made her way back to his bungalow. Brandon was surprised to see her zip up the driveway on the scooter, looking carefree with her hair blowing behind her. Initially he was apprehensive about getting on the back because he had never ridden on a motorcycle with a woman before. Not that this was a heavy-duty Harley, but nevertheless, he was hesitant. Ayana assured him that she had been driving a scooter since she was a teenager, which was the best way to get around the island. After some cajoling, he'd agreed and hopped on the back.

"How much longer until we get there?" he asked, looking over her shoulder at the winding road ahead.

"Another few minutes," she answered, slightly turning her head so that he could hear her over the hum of the motor.

"Not that I'm complaining. I like being snuggled close to you," he said, gripping her a little tighter.

Although he couldn't see her face, Ayana was smiling brightly, showing all of her front teeth. She was enjoying being close to him too. Spending the past couple of days with Brandon had been like a vacation within a vacation. They'd been inseparable since the beach party, and she couldn't have been happier. The show's unexpected hiatus had turned into a positive situation for her. Even though it had been only a couple of days, Ayana was falling hard for Brandon. Not only was he an excellent lover, but he also was kind and considerate, a true gentleman. A part of her wanted to pull back and not expose all of her cards, and a part of her wanted to go full throttle and tell him exactly what she was feeling. She knew some men scared easily when confronted with honest emotions, but something told her that Brandon wasn't the squeamish type.

"We're here," she said, pulling over to the side of the road and turning off the motor.

Brandon swung his leg over the scooter, got off, then helped Ayana. He looked around and saw nothing but a mass of trees. "Where exactly are we supposed to have a picnic? I don't see any grass."

"We're gonna climb a tree and eat perched on a branch like squirrels." She laughed.

He came up, tickled the sides of her waist and said, "Oh, I see you think you're funny."

"Stop, stop. I'm ticklish," she said, batting his hands away and laughing.

Brandon went over to the scooter, unhooked the basket and held it in his hand. "So, where are we going?"

"Follow me."

"Are you sure we're not eating in the trees?" he said, looking around at the dense foliage, which resembled a forest preserve.

"No. Come on, silly." Ayana followed a dirt path through the trees, leading the way. She walked a few yards until they reached a clearing. The patch of land looked like a well-manicured grassy knoll surrounded by lush trees.

"What a view," Brandon said, stepping onto the grass and looking out into the distance. From this elevated vantage point, he could see the ocean, which resembled a beautiful, faceted aquamarine, sparkling beneath the midday sun.

"It's amazing, isn't it? This is one of my favorite places on the island."

Brandon put down the picnic basket. "How did you find this place? It's so far off the beaten path."

"I used to come here as a kid with my parents." Ayana went over to the basket, took out a red-green-and-gold-plaid blanket and spread it over the grass. She bent over and untied her beige Timberlands, which she wore with her favorite pair of cutoff blue jean shorts and a pink ribbed tank top, and took them off.

Brandon kicked off his sandals, squatted down on the blanket and flipped open the top of the basket. "What have we here?" he asked, looking inside. He took out four plastic containers and a silver thermos and placed them on the blanket.

Ayana sat next to him and took out two plates, forks and napkins. "I made curry lobster, cabbage with carrots, plantains and beef patties."

"Wow! You made all of this?"

"Yes, I did. Why do you sound so surprised?"

"No offense, but you don't look like the cooking type."

"How many times do I have to tell you that looks are deceiving? I've been cooking ever since I can remember. My mom had me in the kitchen learning how to cook before I started kindergarten. The first dish I ever made was Hawaiian salad."

"Hawaiian salad in Jamaica?"

"Yes, because it's so easy to make, even a five-year-old couldn't mess it up. My parents acted like it was the best thing they'd ever had, and…" Ayana suddenly stopped talking. She realized this was the second mention of her parents, and she didn't want Brandon thinking she was going down the "meet the folks" road again. She didn't want to scare him off.

"And I'm sure it was delicious to them. My parents were the same way. The first time I made them breakfast in bed for their anniversary, I burned the toast and bacon, undercooked the eggs and made watery coffee that looked like tea. I was so proud of myself, and they ate every single bite, like it was brunch at the Four Seasons."

Ayana listened and couldn't believe he was bringing up his parents. *Maybe he's not paranoid about meeting my folks after all,* she thought. Brandon was talking freely. However, she was being cautious, so she just listened as she fixed their plates. "Here you go."

Brandon took the plate and tasted the food. "Hmm, this is delicious."

"Thanks. I'm glad you like it."

He leaned over and kissed her on the lips. "I like it all right."

Ayana could hear her mother's voice in her head. *Da way to a man's heart is thru him stomach. Gurl, if ya wanna land a husband, ya need to learn how to cook.* Looking at the way Brandon was wolfing down her food, Ayana knew her mother was right. "I'm glad," she said, kissing him back.

They polished off lunch and then drank the ice-cold cucumber water she'd made. Brandon stretched out and laid his head in her lap. He looked up at the clear azure sky as a bright green bird with a pinch of crimson streaked across overhead.

"What was that?"

Ayana followed his gaze. "What? I didn't see anything."

"It looked like a parrot but smaller. On the way up here I saw amazing birds."

"You may not know this, but Jamaica is a bird-watcher's paradise. There are more than twenty-eight bird species on the island."

"And how do you know that?" He looked up at her, amazed at her knowledge.

"I was a member of the National Audubon Society. I love bird-watching. It's extremely relaxing."

"You are amazing," he said as he rubbed her leg. "I would have never in a million years thought that Saturday Knight would be a gourmet-cooking bird-watcher. And don't say it—I know, 'Looks are deceiving.'"

They both laughed.

Ayana rubbed his head, and at that moment, she felt close to him. He had shared history about his childhood without any prodding from her. She knew from past experience that when a man opened up freely, it was an indication that he was really into you. Ayana looked up at the sky and said a silent prayer of thanks. She was thankful to finally find a man who valued her as a person. Her ex-husband had wanted a trophy wife that he could control with his money. Brandon, however, seemed genuinely happy just to be in her presence. Again, Ayana contemplated telling Brandon that she was falling in love with him, but it was too soon for true confessions.

"Thanks," Brandon said, looking up into her face.

"For what?"

"For a delicious lunch and sharing your favorite place with me," he said, caressing her leg and snuggling deeper into her lap.

She leaned down and kissed his cheek. "You are more than welcome."

They lounged on the grassy knoll the remainder of

the afternoon until the sun began to set. This had been the perfect day. Good food, a good man and a picturesque view. Life couldn't get much better.

Chapter 18

Brandon was lounging in bed, gazing out the window at the flat calmness of the ocean. The day before, he and Ayana had spent a relaxing afternoon in the mountains, talking and sharing childhood memories. He was feeling closer and closer to her as the days went by. It had been a while since Brandon had been in a committed relationship, and he missed the intimacy that came from bonding with someone. He had thought Jaclene was *the* one, but she turned out to be an opportunist. When she realized that he couldn't help further her career, she dumped him. After that failed relationship, Brandon had focused his attention on work—until now. Although Ayana hadn't mentioned anything about becoming a couple, Brandon could tell by her actions— taking time to cook and giving of herself sexually—that she was becoming attached to him.

Lying in bed alone, with the cool morning breeze blowing through the sheer curtains, Brandon was missing Ayana. She had gone home the night before for a family dinner. She hadn't invited him, and he hadn't invited himself. After being around her and getting to know her better, Brandon was thinking about meeting her parents. As much as she tried not to talk about them, he could tell they were a big part of her life. He knew she shied away from mentioning them because of his initial reaction.

"Maybe I'll call and find out if she has any plans for the day," he said aloud, reaching for the phone.

Brandon looked at the time display on his cell phone; it wasn't even seven o'clock yet. "It's too early. I'm sure she's still asleep."

He put the phone on the bed, closed his eyes and reflected on his time with Ayana. His trip to Jamaica had had a singular purpose—to check on his sister-in-law. Brandon couldn't help but shake his head at the way life threw a curveball when you least expected it. Nearly running into Ayana with his Jet Ski, and her knowing Marigold was indeed fate. Now his Jamaican trip wasn't only about family; it was also about finding an unexpected love. Brandon's cell phone rang, interrupting his thoughts. He quickly picked the tiny gadget off the pillow, thinking it was Ayana.

"Hello?"

"Hey, Brandon, I've been trying to reach you since yesterday," Steve said the second Brandon picked up.

Brandon sat up against the headboard. "Hi, Steve. What's going on? Is Ed okay?" he asked, thinking maybe Ed had had another heart attack.

"Ed is fine. He's almost back to his normal self. He's

still in the hospital but wants everyone back on set to-morrow, so…"

"Tomorrow?" Brandon asked in alarm. Returning to New York was the last thing on his mind. Being in Jamaica with Ayana was exactly where he wanted to be. They were becoming closer and closer every day and he wanted to remain on the island paradise for as long as possible.

"Yes, tomorrow. I left you a message yesterday. You didn't listen to it?"

"No." Brandon hadn't bothered taking his cell phone on the picnic. Since being on the island, he hadn't both-ered much with the phone. It felt liberating to leave it at home, something he could never do in New York. He didn't have any pressing business, so he had only checked his voice mail sporadically.

"Ed is planning a special reunion-type show and wants the cast at the penthouse for rehearsal."

"A reunion show in the middle of the season? Isn't that odd?"

"Well, it's not a reunion show per se. It's a *Divorced Divas Divulge* special taping, and it will focus on this season and never-before-seen scenes from last season. Ed wants to revive the audience's interest in the show. The reruns are bringing the ratings down, so it's a clever idea."

"I guess you're right," Brandon said, sounding less than excited.

"I've been in touch with everyone but Saturday. I'm having a hard time reaching her. I've called and left messages on her cell, but she hasn't called me back yet. She's probably sitting in her dungeon brewing a batch of witches' brew." He laughed.

"I'm sure that's not the case."

"Well, then, maybe she's flying around Manhattan on her broomstick," Steve said, continuing his insults.

"Man, give her a break. Did you ever think that maybe her wickedness is just an act?" Brandon said, coming to her defense.

"I don't think so. Her antics are too realistic to be an act. Anyway, do you know how to get in touch with her? I called Ed to see if he had another number for her, but he hasn't called me back yet."

Brandon thought for a second. He didn't want Steve thinking that he had a direct pipeline to Ayana. With what she had told him earlier about the cast and crew not being aware of her true identity, he didn't want to blow her cover. "I have a list of everyone's cell numbers. I'll give her a call, and maybe I'll get through."

"If you do, tell her she needs to be on the set tomorrow."

"Okay, will do," Brandon said and hung up.

Brandon got out of bed, showered and dressed. He made a cup of Blue Mountain coffee and drank it outside on the patio. It was still early, and he wanted to wait awhile before going over to Ayana's parents' house. He knew where they lived from when he had picked Ayana up for their first date. An hour later, he decided to make the drive.

When Brandon reached Ayana's parents' home, he saw her Vespa was parked out front. Looking at the yellow scooter brought a smile to his face as he thought about cruising through the mountains on the back, holding on to her slim waist. He got out of the car and rang the bell.

"Mornin'," an older, portly-looking woman said as she opened the door.

"Hi, I'm a friend of Sat...uh, I mean Ayana. Is she in?"

"Ya, she in da kitchen makin' breakfast. I'm her muther, Mrs. Tosh. Come in, chile," she said, opening the door wider and stepping aside. "Follow me."

Brandon walked through their quaint home, which was decorated with antiques, overstuffed furniture that was gently worn and traditional Jamaican artwork on the walls. The home was cozy and he got a warm, homey feeling just walking through.

"Ana, someone's here to see ya," her mother said, coming into the small kitchen.

Ayana was standing at the sink with her back to the door. She turned around and nearly dropped the plate she was holding. "Uh...Brandon, what are you doing here?" she asked with a shocked expression on her face.

"Is dat any way to talk to ya friend?" her mother said, scolding her daughter as if she were a five-year-old.

Ayana paused for a moment and took a deep breath. Seeing Brandon standing in her parents' kitchen had caught her totally off guard. While she was collecting her thoughts, her mother chimed in.

"Aren't ya gonna ask him to sit down and have some breakfast? Where ya manners, gurl?"

"Uh...Ma, I'm sure he has better things to do," she managed to say.

"I'd love to have breakfast," he said, pulling out a chair and sitting down at the kitchen table.

Ayana just stood there and looked at him as if he had two heads. *What the hell is he doing here?* She wanted to quiz him, but her mother was standing there watching them both, looking from one to the other.

"Ana, give da young man some coffee."

Ayana followed her mother's instructions and poured Brandon a cup of freshly brewed coffee. She was confused and didn't know what to say. He had gone from acting like a deer in the headlights when she made a mention of her parents to coming to their home unannounced and uninvited. She went about the business of making breakfast until she could think of how to introduce him to her mother. She couldn't say that they worked together because her parents had no idea she worked on a reality television show. She couldn't say he was her boyfriend because technically he wasn't. Ayana didn't like lying to her mother, so she just kept her mouth shut.

"I haven't seen ya 'round here before. So how ya know Ana?" her mother said, sitting across the table from Brandon.

"She knows my sister-in-law, Marigold, and we met at the shelter," he replied.

Good answer! Ayana thought. He hadn't lied, and he hadn't told the entire truth either.

"Oh, me just loves Marigold! She da salt of da earth, helping all thoze battered women and chilren. Me knew her late husband. Him was a good man."

"Thanks. James was my older brother."

"Sorry for your loss. Are ya married too?" Ayana's mother asked, sizing him up.

Ayana swung around. "Ma! Don't start quizzing him."

"It's okay. I don't mind. No, Mrs. Tosh, I'm not married."

"Ya mean, a good-lookin' man like yoself hasn't found a good woman to marry?" She shook her head. "I don't know what's wrong wit ya young people today. Ya tink marriage is a bad ting. Back in me day, we wed as soon as we could and started a family. Don't ya want to get married and have some chilren?" she asked.

Brandon glanced over at Ayana, who had a mortified look on her face, and said, "I'd love nothing more than to marry my soul mate and start a family."

Hearing those words come out of his mouth warmed Ayana's heart, and she smiled. Ayana hadn't known his views on marriage and raising children. Now that she knew he wasn't a man strictly out for a good time, but one who actually had goals, he was becoming more and more attractive. She too wanted a family.

Brandon witnessed Mrs. Tosh glance over at her daughter and smile. He could tell that she was picking up on the fact that they were more than mere friends. Mrs. Tosh had wasted no time asking the important questions.

"Me gonna run some errands. Me be back later. Nice to meet ya, young man."

Brandon stood and shook her hand. "The pleasure was all mine, Mrs. Tosh."

Once she was gone, Ayana went to the kitchen doorway to make sure her mother was out of earshot. Then she walked over to the table and sat down. "So what are you doing here?" she whispered in case her mother was still hanging around.

"Steve has been trying to get in touch with you. He called me early this morning and said Ed wants us to report back to the penthouse tomorrow," he said in a low tone.

"Tomorrow! Why so soon?"

"Ed is feeling better and wants to do a reunion-type show. He's calling it a *Divorced Divas Divulge* special, and he wants to start rehearsals tomorrow."

Ayana hung her head. Being with Brandon the past few days had been a breath of fresh air, and she hadn't given the show or her ugly persona on set a second thought. Sadness began creeping its way into her spirit, and her eyes welled up with tears.

Brandon saw the expression on her face, reached across the table and held her hands. "It's going to be all right."

"How can you say that when you know being back on set is synonymous with me acting like an out-of-control diva?" she said with her face still hanging low.

"Ayana, look at me." He gently raised her chin. "I know the real you now. You're nothing like Saturday Knight. You are a kind, generous person who helps out her family and provides for the shelter. You're a good person."

Hearing his kind words sent tears streaming down her cheeks.

Brandon reached for a napkin in the middle of the table and wiped her tears. "Stop crying. It's going to be fine," he said again, reassuring her. "There's a big difference this time around."

"What do you mean?" she said, blowing her nose.

"This time, while we're taping, your man will be on the set watching your back."

"Are you saying that...?"

He interrupted her. "Yes, I'm saying I'm your man, and you are my woman. Now stop crying and start packing. We have to make reservations and get the next plane back to New York."

Ayana got up, walked over and gave him a tender kiss on the lips. He had soothed her anxiety, and now returning to *Divorced Divas* and reprising her role as Saturday Knight didn't seem so bad. With Brandon in her corner, Ayana knew she could get through just about anything.

Chapter 19

Ayana was able to book a flight from Jamaica to New York with Brandon with no problem. The flight was wide-open with plenty of seats. They sat together in business class, holding hands and enjoying their final hours together before getting back to reality. The time spent in Negril, though brief, had been a dose of paradise. They had become almost inseparable on the island, spending most of their days and nights together. With Ed's grim prognosis before they left New York, returning to the show this soon had been the furthest thing from their minds. As the plane soared through the clouds, getting closer and closer to New York, they sat in silence, mourning their hasty departure from Jamaica. Before leaving, Ayana had called Cedella. They hadn't spoken since the day of the beach party, so Ayana updated her friend on the superb progress she'd made with Brandon and how he had asked her to be his woman. Cedella couldn't have been happier for her and wished her well.

"Would you two care for another cup of coffee?" the flight attendant asked.

"No, thanks. Do you have Guinness Stout?" Ayana asked.

"Yes, we do."

"I'll have a bottle of that and a shot of rum," Ayana replied, wanting to recapture some of their island magic.

"Make that two," Brandon said.

After the flight attendant brought their drinks, Brandon raised his beer bottle and said, "To hot nights on the beach."

"I'll drink to that," Ayana said, tapping her bottle to his. "I still can't believe Ed is well enough to start production again. He was at death's door, barely hanging on, and now he's back in control like nothing happened."

"I guess we can attribute his speedy recovery to modern medicine."

Ayana took a swallow of beer. "I guess."

"Don't sound so sad. Look on the bright side. Ed's heart attack brought us together. If he hadn't gotten sick, the show would have never gone on hiatus, and we wouldn't have been in Jamaica at the same time," he said, sounding optimistic.

"I guess," she responded in the same solemn voice.

"Oh, I hate to hear you sound so glum." He leaned over and kissed her on the cheek. "What can I do to make it better?"

Ayana looked at him and raised her eyebrow. "Uh, I can think of something."

"Name it."

She leaned over and whispered in his ear. "How about joining the Mile High Club?"

"Thought you'd never ask." Brandon peered around the cabin at the other passengers. Some were sleeping, a few were reading, whereas others were entertained by the in-flight movie. "Since there's only one lavatory up here, let's go back to coach, where they have two. You go first, and I'll follow in a few. I'll knock twice so you know it's me."

"Okay!" she said, her mood instantly lightened.

Ayana made her way back to coach, where most passengers were watching the same movie. No one was in line when she reached the lavatories. She opened the door to one, stepped inside and waited. Ayana's heart began to beat faster with anticipation. The thought of getting away with having sex on a plane was thrilling. While she waited for Brandon, she slipped off her jeans and panties, knowing there would be little room to maneuver once he stepped inside the tiny space. No sooner had she folded her jeans and underwear and placed them on the closed toilet lid than the door slid open.

"Hey, sexy," Brandon whispered as he admired her half-naked body before quickly locking the door behind him.

She pulled him by his belt and started unfastening the buckle. "Hey, yourself."

Brandon joined his hands with hers, helping to unfasten his pants more quickly. The expectancy of what was to come had them panting heavily with lust. Once his pants were off, he picked Ayana up and placed her on top of the tiny metal basin.

"Oh, that's cold," she said.

He kissed her on the neck and said, "You won't be cold for long." He then spread her legs apart and wedged himself in between her thighs.

Ayana wrapped her legs around his waist. "You promise?"

"Cross my heart." He reached around, took hold of her butt and brought her closer.

Ayana felt his engorged member pressing alongside the outer lips of her vagina. She wanted to feel the length of him filling her up. "I am so craving you," she whispered in his ear.

Brandon rubbed his growing penis back and forth against her opening, teasing her with each deliberate stroke. "And I want you too."

Ayana opened her legs as wide as the small space would allow, reached down, took hold of his rod and guided him into her wetness. Once he was firmly inside, she hugged him around the neck and held on tight as he thrust deeper and deeper.

"We're…soo…good…together," he whispered in her ear. Brandon picked up the pace, pumping and holding her against him at the same time. Their naughty interlude was fueling his desire for her even more, and he was finding it hard to hold back.

Ayana held on to him with one hand while reaching down and rubbing herself with the other. The dual sensation of her hand and his pulsating penis intensified their lovemaking until she was on the verge of exploding.

They held on tightly to each other in the tiny space and rode the wave of ecstasy to a crescendo, climaxing at the same time. They stayed locked in place, relishing the moment before unwrapping their limbs from around one another. Brandon helped her down from the sink, then reached down, picked her clothes up and handed them to her.

After they dressed, he said, "I'll go out first to make sure the coast is clear. You should wait a few minutes and then come out."

"Okay."

He kissed her tenderly before slipping out the door. Once he was gone, Ayana straightened her clothes and smoothed down her hair. She looked in the mirror and saw that her face was glowing. Brandon had that effect on her. Ayana inhaled deeply and could smell their scent in the air. She smiled and went back to her seat with no one the wiser.

"Feel better now?" he asked, kissing the side of her cheek after she returned beside him.

"Yes, much."

"Membership does have its privileges," he said, winking at her.

"Yes, it sure does." Ayana laid her head on his shoulder, closed her eyes and drifted off to sleep only to be awakened by the sound of the pilot over the intercom.

"Good news, folks. Because of the mild weather, looks like we'll be landing ahead of schedule."

"Well, I guess it's time to make my transformation," Ayana told Brandon.

He looked perplexed. "What do you mean?"

"Say goodbye to Ayana. I have to go and make myself presentable." She stood up, reached into the overhead bin and retrieved her carry-on bag.

"What's wrong with your outfit?" he asked, looking at her jeans and T-shirt. She looked perfectly fine to him.

"I never get off the plane wearing my island clothes. I can't chance reporters and photographers seeing me looking like a country girl. The last time I arrived at the airport, a swarm of reporters and paparazzi were outside, snapping pictures and wanting an interview regarding a scandal I was allegedly involved in. Remember, they are used to seeing the Saturday Knight persona all dolled up, and they know nothing about Ayana Lewis, and I have to keep it that way."

"I understand," Brandon said with sadness in his voice. He wasn't ready for Ayana to turn back into Saturday Knight, but there was nothing he could do about it. He watched her walk into the lavatory, knowing that when she came out she would be a different person, so to speak. Brandon looked down at the cocktail napkin on his tray table, then picked it up.

Fifteen minutes later, Ayana reemerged looking like a celebrity. Gone were the jeans and T-shirt, replaced with a tight black dress that cinched her waist and hips, with black stiletto heels to match. Her hair was no longer in a ponytail—instead, a long platinum-blond wig was cascading loose around her shoulders. She wore dangling earrings that matched a series of necklaces adorning her neck. Her face was made up with bright red lipstick, blush and long false eyelashes.

"Wow, look at you!" he said, having forgotten the glamour of Saturday Knight.

"How's that for a quick transformation?" She put her bag back in the overhead and sat down.

"Here, this is for you," he said, handing her the airline-issued napkin.

Ayana took the napkin out of his hands. "Oh, do I

have lipstick on my teeth?" she asked, assuming he was giving her the napkin to clean her makeup.

"No, read it."

She looked at the white napkin and read the message written in the center. *Blissfully Yours, B.*

"Aww." She touched the napkin to her chest. "That's so sweet. Let me use your pen." She then wrote on the back, *Blissfully Yours, A.* She kissed the napkin, leaving the imprint of her ruby-red lips on the white surface, and handed it back to him.

"I mean it, baby. I am blissfully yours and don't you forget it when we're back in New York on set."

"I promise I won't," she said, snuggling closer to him.

Brandon put the napkin in his pocket and closed his eyes, revisiting their time together in Jamaica. He knew that going back to New York and working on the show as a couple was going to be a challenge, and he wanted to hold on to happy memories for as long as possible.

Chapter 20

Ayana and Brandon went directly to the set from the airport. They arrived at the penthouse on Central Park West together. Riding up in the elevator, Ayana felt her heart sinking. Although she was dressed as Saturday Knight, she wasn't ready to face the cast and morph into character. In her spirit, she was still feeling irie and wanted to return to Jamaica as fast as she could. However, she was under contract and had a job to do.

Standing beside Ayana, holding her hand, Brandon could sense her trepidation. "Are you all right?"

"Yes. I'm fine," she said with coolness to her voice.

"No, you're not. You don't even sound like yourself."

"Brandon, I need to get into character. We'll be on set in a few and I don't want any signs of Ayana showing." She eased her hand out of his. "I didn't mention this before, but I think it's best if we keep our relationship under wraps. It wouldn't look too professional if one of the cast members and the director were dating."

"What difference does it make? We're two consenting adults."

"The difference is, I'm supposed to be single on the show, and going through the dating process to find my next husband."

Brandon exhaled hard. "So, you're telling me, I'm supposed to just sit back and watch—wait, *direct*—my woman with another man? Ayana, I don't like this arrangement one bit."

"Yes, until the show goes on hiatus again. My contract will be up by then, and hopefully I will have found another income."

"Since you have everything figured out, when are we supposed to see each other?" he asked, sounding quite annoyed.

Ayana took hold of his hand again, trying to smooth things over. "When we're not taping you can come over to my place, and I can come over to yours."

Now it was Brandon's turn to remove his hand from hers. "So we have to sneak around like teenagers hiding from their parents."

"No, we're not hiding—just keeping our relationship to ourselves. It's nobody's business what we do after the cameras go off."

He exhaled again. "You told me the truth of why you're on the show back in Jamaica, and I accepted it. I guess I didn't factor in the dating component and the premise of *Divorced Divas*. I'm not going to jeopardize your livelihood, but I'm telling you right now, I don't want you kissing on any of these guys."

Ayana chuckled slightly. "Somebody's jealous."

"It's not funny. I'm serious," he said with a straight face.

"Okay," she said and leaned up and kissed him on the cheek.

The elevator doors opened. Ayana stepped off first and strutted into the penthouse ahead of Brandon. The expansive living room was set up with lights and over-head boom microphones. Two plush white sofas were arranged in a row with a white leather chair positioned in the middle. The walls were adorned with copies of artwork by the masters—Van Gogh, Monet and Renoir. Lead crystal vases with fresh-cut flowers were arranged throughout the room. The scene resembled an old-money Upper East Side matriarch's living room, where high tea and finger sandwiches were served. This room, however, served up juicy gossip and plenty of drama.

"Where have you been?" Steve asked, rushing up to Ayana.

She quickly got into character and gave him one of her demeaning looks, complete with an annoying teeth suck. "I was on a plane. Don't blame me for being late when I only had a day's notice."

"I've been calling you for the past two days," Steve said in his defense.

"Whatever," she responded, flipping her hand. Ayana looked around the room, expecting to see the show's creator, but he wasn't there. "Where's Ed?"

"He won't be here until tomorrow, but he'll be call-ing in throughout the day."

"You're complaining that I'm late, but I don't see anyone else on the set."

"The other ladies are in their dressing rooms wait-ing for you."

"Well, you can go tell those heifers the star has arrived."

Steve didn't say a word. He just looked at her with disdain. Ayana knew he knew better than to get into a verbal sparring match with the infamous Saturday Knight, for surely he would lose.

"Uh, hey, Brandon," Steve said, diverting his attention from her.

"Hi, Steve. How are you doing?" Brandon asked as he walked toward the executive producer. Brandon strolled right past Saturday as if she weren't there, giving no hint that they were a couple. He shook Steve's hand.

"I'm good. No complaints. Just ready to get the show under way."

"When are we going to start with rehearsals?" Brandon asked, also anxious to begin so that he could get out of there and spend time with Ayana.

"Soon. I'm waiting for Ed to call. He left explicit instructions to wait for his call before we began."

"Well, hello, Brandon," Brooke, the blonde flirt of the show, said as she came into the room. She went directly over to him, ignoring Saturday and Steve, and stood so close to Brandon that her surgically enhanced boobs were almost touching his chest.

Brandon took a step back. "Hello, Brooke," he said in a professional tone.

"So, Mr. Director, how was your time off? Too bad we couldn't get together and hang out. I'm sure we would have had a ton of fun," she said with a wink.

Ayana cut her eyes from Brandon to Brooke. She was seething but didn't say anything. She had laid the ground rules but didn't like this game of nondisclosure.

Ayana wanted to let the world know that Brandon was her man, but she was forced to remain silent. She especially wanted to tell Brooke to keep her paws off of him. Instead, she went over to the sofa, sat down, took her phone out of her purse and pretended to play a game, all the while listening to their exchange.

"I don't think my girl would have liked me hanging out with you," he said, giving Brooke the cold shoulder.

Ayana's ears perked up, and she smiled slightly. *That's right, baby. Tell her you're taken.*

"Oh, I didn't know you had a girlfriend," Brooke said, sounding surprised.

"I do and we're extremely happy. So getting together with you isn't even an option." Brandon cut his eyes at Ayana, who was looking down at her phone but had a pleasant expression on her face. From their close proximity, he knew that she was listening to his every word. Although they couldn't reveal their relationship, he wanted to reassure her of how he felt.

"I can be discreet if you can. We could at least have dinner together. Your girlfriend would never have to know," Brooke said, refusing to accept no as an answer.

"Like I said, getting together with you isn't an option."

Yes! Yes! Inside, Ayana was doing a fist pump and happy dance at the same time. Brandon had put Ms. Thing in her place, and she was elated.

Brandon turned his attention back to Steve, totally ignoring Brooke. "I'll be in the production room. Let me know when we're ready to begin."

"Okay, will do. I'm going to get the other ladies so everyone will be on set when Ed calls."

Once Brandon and Steve had left the room, Ayana

put her phone aside, looked up and started in on Brooke. "Tell me something." She stood and walked over to Brooke. "Why are you always trying to push up on somebody's man?"

"What are you talking about?" Brooke asked, flinging her long blond hair, nearly hitting Saturday in the face.

Saturday quickly moved out of the way. "I'm talking about you coming on to Brandon."

"What's it to you?"

"He's here as the director, not your personal boy toy."

"Once again, I'm going to say, what's it to you? Who I flirt with is none of your business," Brooke responded, not backing down.

Saturday stepped closer and pointed her finger in Brooke's face, nearly touching her nose. "I'm going to tell you what it is to me. He's…"

Brooke slapped Saturday's finger out of her face, interrupting her tirade.

"How dare you hit me!" Saturday raised her arms to push Brooke.

"Whoa, whoa, what's going on here?" Brandon said, stepping between them. He had come out of the production room just in time to stop the fight.

"That whore hit me!" Saturday yelled.

"Who are you calling a whore?" Brooke shouted back.

"Did I stutter?" Saturday countered, trying to reach around Brandon and get to Brooke.

"You both need to calm down. This is a production set, not a boxing ring." He took Saturday by the arm and led her over to the huge floor-to-ceiling window. "What's going on? I step out of the room for a few minutes, and when I come back you're arguing with Brooke," he said under his breath.

Saturday looked past him, leering at Brooke. "She thinks she can just come on to you, like you're here for her personal pleasure."

"Are you kidding me? You're getting all riled up because she flirted with me?"

"I needed to put her in her place and let her know that you're not available."

"Ayana—" he looked over his shoulder to make sure no one was listening "—I already did that. Besides, Brooke is just being Brooke. Remember when she flirted with me a while back? I put her in her place then, and you and I weren't even dating."

"Of course I remember. However, that was then. Now you are my man, and I don't want her trying to sink her claws into you."

"I could go over there right now and tell her that we're dating and put an end to her flirting once and for all. Is that what you want?" He peered directly into her eyes.

Saturday folded her arms across her chest, exhaled hard and said, "You know that's not an alternative."

"Well, then, you need to cool your jets."

Saturday didn't say anything. She couldn't believe how upset she had gotten over a little flirtation. *I must really love this man. I've never acted a fool over any guy before,* she thought. Ayana didn't like the vulnerability that came with being in love. She nearly told her own secret and needed to get a grip. If any of these women smelled a whiff of weakness, they would go in for the kill. Saturday was the vixen of the show, and had to stay in character so she wouldn't lose her job.

"Are you all right now?" Brandon asked when she didn't answer.

She exhaled. "Yes, I'm fine." She crossed the room and returned to the sofa, ignoring Brooke, who was still standing in the middle of the room with her arms folded across her chest.

"Looks like we are postponing today's rehearsal. Ed will be here in the flesh tomorrow and we'll start then. I've already told Petra, Trista and the rest of the crew. Tomorrow's call time is eight a.m. See you guys then," Steve said.

Saturday gathered her belongings and made a beeline for the door without giving Brandon a second look. She needed to go home and formulate a better game plan. Ayana realized that pretending she and Brandon were platonic coworkers was going to be harder than she'd initially thought.

Chapter 21

Ayana hadn't been in her own bed in weeks, and it felt good to relax among the myriad of pillows in varying sizes tossed against the headboard. Her body was sandwiched between the six-hundred-count sheets, which were as smooth as silk, and a plush down comforter was folded at her feet. The only illumination in the room was the streetlights streaming through the mini blinds and the light of the muted television. She wanted to quiet the chatter in her head and didn't need any additional noise. Ayana ran through the day's events in her mind and didn't like how she had allowed Brooke to push her buttons. Ayana had nearly blurted out that she and Brandon were dating, which would have defeated her plan to keep their relationship under wraps.

"I really need to keep my emotions in check," she said aloud.

Her cell rang, interrupting her thoughts. Ayana reached for the phone, which was lying on the nightstand. "Hello?"

"It's me! I'm back!"

"Hey, Reese! How was your trip?" Ayana was happy to hear from her friend. She had a lot to tell her.

"It was fabulous. We bought some amazing gems, tooled around Capri and ate and drank ourselves silly. We really needed the time away, so we could reconnect as a couple. The first part of the trip was all business—however, the last leg was all pleasure!"

"Nice!"

"So, how's the show been going? I miss my regular updates."

"The show has been on hold for a while. Ed had a heart attack…"

"What! Is he okay?"

"Yes, he's fine now. Tomorrow, we're taping for the first time since he got out of the hospital."

"How long was he laid up?"

"A few weeks."

"What were you doing all of that time?"

"I was in Jamaica. My dad had a slight stroke."

"What? How is he?"

"He's fine."

"Wow. I can't believe all of that happened while I was away."

"It's not all bad news. Guess what? You were right."

"Right about what?"

"Remember when I told you about the new director of the show kissing me?"

"Of course I remember. Wait a minute… Don't tell me that you guys are dating?"

"Yes, we are!" Ayana said, sounding totally elated.

"That's great—now tell me everything."

Ayana went into detail, telling Reese how Brandon had nearly run her over with his Jet Ski, and how he was related to her friend Marigold. She told Reese that Brandon had been standoffish until she revealed the truth of why she was on the show. Ayana told Reese how she and Brandon had fallen in love while in Jamaica.

"That's fantastic! I couldn't be happier. So how is the cast responding to you guys as a couple?"

"No one knows that we're dating. I have to keep our relationship under wraps until the end of the season."

"Why is that?"

"I can't jeopardize my Saturday Knight persona, and risk losing my job."

"Oh, I see. Hold on for a second."

Ayana could hear Reese talking to someone in the background.

"I'd love to continue our conversation, but Joey has drawn me a candlelit bubble bath."

"Aw, that's so sweet. Okay, talk to you later."

Ayana placed the phone back on the nightstand and wondered if she and Brandon would become a happily married couple like Reese and Joey. Although she was falling deeply in love with Brandon, she couldn't allow her feelings to overshadow her judgment. Ayana already didn't like portraying Saturday, but it had gotten even worse. Now she'd have to conceal two lies. The pressure was already getting to her, and the special taping hadn't even gotten under way.

"I have to get back on my game plan."

The time spent with Brandon in Jamaica had been beyond great but had shifted her focus from finding a way out of reality television into a profession that she could be proud of. Brandon had mentioned that she might try her hand at acting, and she thought that was a great idea. Ayana also had branding ideas in mind, but that would probably take longer to facilitate. Presently, she didn't have a talent agent, but getting one shouldn't be a problem because she was already a television personality.

Ayana reached for her cell phone to call Brandon and ask him about his agent. She didn't want to waste another second. She needed to get the ball rolling.

"Hey, are you asleep?" she asked once he picked up.

"Hey, baby. No, I'm not asleep. I'm just lying here thinking about you."

She smiled. "And what were you thinking?"

"How much I miss you. Why don't you come over?"

"I would, but I'm beat. Traveling and dealing with the show has me wiped out."

"Are you too tired for a little phone action?" he asked seductively.

"Hmm? Are you talking about phone sex?" Brandon's question had taken her totally off guard.

"Yes, I am. So tell me, what are you wearing?" he asked, getting right down to business.

Ayana had on a threadbare Reggae Fest T-shirt that was at least ten years old, panties and a pair of sweat socks—the antithesis of sexy. "Uh…I have on a fire-engine-red lace negligee with a matching red thong tucked between my butt cheeks," she elaborated, playing along and getting in the mood.

"Mmm…that sounds so sexy."

"Trust me, it is. You should see how good my body looks in this negligee. My nipples are peeking through the lace."

"Mmm…nice. I can just envision you lying there looking sexy as hell."

"So tell me…what do you have on?"

"My chocolate birthday suit," he said in a husky voice.

"I just love, love, love big, dark chocolate bars."

"Oh, you do, do you? And tell me, what do you like to do with big…dark…chocolate bars?" he asked, speaking slowly.

Ayana deepened her voice into a come-hither tone. "I like to put them in my mouth and…lick them…and suck them."

"And while you're enjoying your chocolate bar, I'll be softly and ever so gently munching on your pink sweet forbidden fruit like a scrumptious treat."

"Hmm, I like the way that sounds."

"Can you do me a favor?" he asked.

"Yes, anything for you, baby."

"I want you to take off your thong."

"Okay." Ayana reached underneath the sheet and took off her white cotton panties.

"Are they off?"

"Yes."

"Good. Now I want you to spread your legs and put your index finger near your clit but don't touch it, just press firmly above the area."

"Okay." Ayana did what he said and waited for further instruction. This unexpected phone sex was making her hot as she anticipated his next command.

"Now close your eyes. Is your finger still near your clit?"

"Yes."

"Are you pressing firmly?"

"Yes."

"Good. I want you to keep it there while you put the phone on Speaker, then set it on the pillow next to you. You're going to need both of your hands for the next move."

Once again she followed his instructions. "The call is on Speaker. Now what do you want me to do?" she asked eagerly.

"Take your other hand, put your first two fingers in your mouth and get them nice and wet." He waited a few seconds and then said, "Take the hand that's near your clit and expose that delicious pink flesh. Now take your fingers and rub your clit until you get nice and wet."

With her eyes closed, Ayana followed his instructions to perfection, rubbing herself, getting wetter by the second. She began moaning. She was in a zone, and it felt good.

"Listening to your moans is making me harder by the second. If I were there, I would taste your kitty cat."

"And I would lick all over your chocolate bar."

"I'm holding my big chocolate bar right now and thinking about you."

"Good. Now I want you to stroke it up and down and pretend I'm there with you."

"Okay. Are you still pleasuring yourself?"

"Yes, and it feels so good."

They were each enjoying the moment, as evidenced by the panting and moaning coming through the speaker. Brandon had coached her to a climax and she was ready to squirt her juices.

Ayana panted heavily.

"Come with me, baby! Yes, yes!" she yelled.

Brandon let out a series of screeching grunts as

he himself exploded. A few seconds later he said in a breathy tone, "Oh, that was good."

"It sure was."

"But I must apologize," he said.

"For what?" She was puzzled.

"I'm sure you didn't call me to get ambushed into phone sex. I barely let you get the word 'hey' out before I started in."

"Baby, you have nothing to be sorry for. Trust me, I more than enjoyed your ambush. It's just what I needed after this afternoon. However, I did call for a specific reason. Remember when we were in Jamaica and you mentioned that I should think about transitioning into acting?"

"Of course I remember. I think you'd be a great actress."

"Thanks. I hope so. The only problem is that I don't have an agent. My attorney brokered the deal with *Divorced Divas.* I remember you saying that you have an agent. Do you think I can call him or her?"

"Sure. I'll give Mario a call in the morning and let him know to expect your call." He gave her Mario's number.

"Great. Thanks so much. I can't wait to leave the show. I don't know how much more of Saturday Knight I can take."

Brandon wanted to tell her he agreed, but he didn't want to offend her, so he kept quiet. "I'm sure he'll take you on as a client. He's well connected in the industry and will have no problem getting you auditions with some of the heavy hitters."

"Brandon, you don't know how much your vote of confidence means to me." Ayana's ex-husband had wanted a wife with no ambition. Shortly after they'd married, he'd insisted that she stop working.

"Ayana, I only want the best for you."

His kind words nearly brought tears to her eyes. "Brandon, I'm so glad you know the real me. I really hate being a diva on the set. I should have never let Ed talk me into portraying such a malicious villain."

"At the time, you didn't have a choice. Don't worry— you'll be out of there soon enough."

Brandon's reassuring words made Ayana feel much better. She now had a solid exit strategy. It was just a matter of time before she could tell Ed and the show *au revoir*.

Chapter 22

Ed was back and in full form. He flounced throughout the penthouse as if he had springy coils in his orange, high-heeled sneakers. His multicolored chiffon scarf floated in the air as he moved about. Ed appeared to be so happy to be out of the hospital and back at work that he could barely contain himself. All morning, he had been talking to the cast and crew, gesturing at a rapid pace, as if trying to make up for lost time. *Divorced Divas* was losing market share and Ed had devised a plan that would surely get the show back on track.

"I want you ladies sitting on the sofa with Moses Michaels in the middle," Ed ordered the cast, pointing his manicured finger at the custom-made two-piece white couch.

Saturday and her cast mates were all dressed fabulously in black. Saturday had on a one-shoulder dress,

Petra wore a halter dress, Brooke wore a sleeveless dress and Trista had on a peplum-style dress. Ed had informed the stylist that he wanted the ladies in black to make a dramatic contrast against the white sofa. They were also in full hair and makeup. Ed wanted them camera ready.

"Why we all dress up? I thought we no tape show, just rehearse," Petra said with a puzzled expression on her face.

"Mr. Michaels only has today available. He's flying to L.A. tonight and won't be back until next week. I don't want to wait until then. We've lost too much time as it is."

"But how we know who to talk about?" Petra asked.

"You mean 'what' to talk about," Saturday said, correcting her as usual.

"I not talking to you," Petra countered.

"Ladies, let's save the bickering for the camera. Now, Saturday, I want you in the center, sitting next to the moderator. Brooke, you're on the other side of the moderator. Petra, you're next to Brooke, and, Trista, you're sitting next to Saturday," Ed instructed.

"Why I no sit in middle?" Petra whined.

Saturday took her seat, spread her arms across the back of the sofa and said, "Because I'm the star of the show. Therefore, I'm front and center. You're just a sidekick."

"What is sidekick?"

Before Saturday could come back with an insulting remark, Brandon, who had been sitting on the side in his director's chair watching the entire exchange, interrupted. "Petra, why do you always let Saturday get under your skin? Just ignore her."

Saturday shot Brandon a look. She wanted to blurt out, *Why are you taking Petra's side?* His remark had taken her totally by surprise, rendering her momentarily speechless.

"You right. I ignore." Petra took her seat without looking in Saturday's direction.

Once the ladies had taken their places, Ed stood in front of them and said, "While we're waiting for Mr. Michaels to arrive, I want to go over a few key points. Remember this is a reunion-type show, so you guys will be discussing what has happened over the past few episodes. Talk about how you felt about your dates, which men really turned you on and which ones you can't wait to see again. The audience loves to hear about romance. I want you to really spice up the conversation. Any questions?"

"Should we mention your heart attack?" Trista asked.

"OH, ABSOLUTELY NOT!" Ed shouted. "This show isn't about me and my health issues. It's about you ladies and your dating issues. Got it?"

Trista looked sheepish and appeared instantly sorry for asking the question. "Uh…okay."

"And one more thing. I have a surprise planned," Ed announced.

"I detest surprises," Saturday told him.

"Well, I hate to disappoint you, love, but there will definitely be a surprise or two during taping, so be ready for anything."

Saturday didn't like being blindsided. She certainly hoped that Ed wasn't bringing back any of her former dates. It was bad enough that she had to sit next to Moses Michaels. Even though she hadn't slept with the famous moderator, they still had a brief history. Now that she and Brandon were an item, she didn't want to bring her past into her present. Before he came aboard as the director, she had cozied up to several men via Ed's instruction. The thought of Brandon hearing about her exploits made her sick to her stomach, but there was nothing she could do about it now. As Saturday was sitting quietly pondering what Ed's surprise could be, in walked the moderator.

Moses Michaels was known around the reality circuit as the host that brought drama to an already dramatic setting. He was the ultimate pot stirrer, asking probing questions that got members of the cast in one heated debate after another. Moses's shrewdness had him in high demand, commanding top dollar to moderate a litany of reality shows.

Saturday watched Moses greet Ed and couldn't help but admire him. Moses stood less than six feet, but he was well built. He was an immaculate dresser. He wore a black Gucci suit, black shirt, black tie and black Gucci loafers—obviously he had gotten the same dress-code suggestion from Ed. He was clean shaven, making his café-au-lait skin look as smooth as silk. Saturday and Moses had made a striking pair, and she could understand why the tabloids had spread rumors that she had broken up his relationship.

"Hey, Ed, how are you?" Moses asked in his signature baritone voice.

"Couldn't be better," Ed replied, shaking Moses's hand. "Thanks for doing this show at the last minute."

"No problem." Moses smiled, exposing his perfect white teeth and deep dimples.

"Did you get my email with the list of talking points?"

"Yes, I did."

That man is still fine, Saturday thought as she watched him. She hadn't seen Moses since their last date months ago. She turned her eyes away before Brandon caught her staring at the handsome moderator.

"Moses, let me introduce you to our new director," Ed said, leading the way to where Brandon sat in his director's chair.

"Brandon, this is Moses Michaels, the best moderator in the business," Ed gushed.

Moses and Brandon shook hands. "Nice to meet you," Moses said.

Saturday watched them exchange pleasantries and felt a bit nervous. She hadn't told Brandon about dating Moses. Really there was nothing to tell because she and Moses had dated only a few times. They had kissed, as she had told Reese, but it was nothing serious.

"Are you guys ready to get started?" Ed asked.

"Ready as ever," Moses said, heading toward the sofa. He sat down in his designated seat between Saturday and Brooke. Moses leaned over toward Saturday and whispered, "Hey there, lovely. You sure are looking good. I've missed those sweet lips of yours." Moses moved his body a bit closer to her as he spoke.

"Hi, Moses," Saturday said, staring straight ahead, ignoring his comment.

"I'm going to Los Angles tonight. When I come back next week, let's do dinner *and* dessert," he said, licking his lips. Moses was a serial dater and had a reputation in the business of sleeping with the beautiful reality stars he interviewed. His once faithful girlfriend had had enough and had left the handsome moderator to his own devices.

"I don't think so."

Saturday glanced over and saw Brandon watching her and Moses. Brandon had an unpleasant look on his face.

"Ready as ever," Moses said.

"Take one. Action!" Brandon announced.

"Hey, everybody. Moses Michaels here on the set of *Divorced Divas,*" he began, peering into the camera. "I'm here with these lovely ladies for a special divulge-all reunion." He looked at the cast to his right and then to his left. "Okay, ladies, let's get down to business. You know I don't like wasting time."

Here we go, Saturday thought, bracing herself for Moses's direct line of questioning. He was known to go right for the jugular. Her heart began beating faster with anticipation.

"So, Saturday, I will start with you. Last season, you made a love connection with one of your dates, didn't you?"

"I make a connection with all my dates," she said flippantly, determined not to be ambushed.

"Well, this particular connection had a special meaning. Why don't we roll tape and refresh your memory?"

The moment he said "roll tape," a huge HD screen dropped down behind them. The screen showed her with Erick Kastell, a high-powered investment banker. Erick was strikingly handsome with thick blond hair and blue eyes. They had had an instant attraction to each other and had gone out on several successful dates. Their last date, a romantic dinner at Jean Georges, had ended with a carriage ride through Central Park.

Saturday watched the screen as they rode with their arms around each other in the back of the small carriage. A tiny video camera attached inside the carriage had captured their every move—her hand resting comfortably on his knee, his arm draped around her shoulders, nearly touching her breast. She was shocked to see this footage because that episode had never aired. Erick had immigration issues and had had to fly back to Switzerland to straighten them out. At the time, Ed didn't know if Erick was ever going to return to the States, so he decided not to air their last date. She had all but forgotten about Erick until now, as she watched him on-screen.

"You are so beautiful," Erick said, leaning in and kissing her on the lips.

Oh, shit! Saturday thought, watching the scene unfold. She kissed him back.

"I know we haven't known each other for long, but I feel a deep connection to you and I know you feel it too."

"Yes, I do." Saturday had been instructed by Ed to play up the romance, so she had.

"Life is short, wouldn't you agree?"

"Yes, I would agree."

"When the producers approached me to be on the show, I was hesitant until they showed me your picture. From the moment I saw you, I was smitten. I've begun to fall for you over these past few weeks, and every time we are together, I fall deeper and deeper in love."

"Ohhh, that's so sweet."

"It's not sweet—it's the truth." He reached into his pocket and produced an aqua-blue Tiffany's box. He opened the lid, and inside was a five-carat diamond engagement ring.

The camera showed a shocked expression registering on Saturday's face before dramatically shutting off.

Moses turned his head to Saturday and said, "Is your memory refreshed now?"

"What do you think? I'm not blind. I can see my date on the screen, just like everybody else," she replied with attitude in her voice.

"Now, now, let's not get testy. You made a love connection with Erick, and that's great. Isn't finding love what *Divorced Divas* is all about?"

Saturday didn't say anything. She was still reeling from seeing that old footage and embarrassed that Brandon had seen it as well.

"You guys at home are probably wondering why you've never seen this footage. It's because this is our first time airing it. Erick had some issues he had to deal with back in his homeland of Switzerland, but he's back now…. Erick, come on out," Moses announced.

The debonair Swiss banker came strolling onto the set.

Saturday was stunned, alarmed and shocked all at the same time and it showed in her expression. Ed had said there would be a surprise or two during taping, but she'd had no idea he'd bring Erick back.

Erick went directly up to Saturday, knelt down in front of her and took the same aqua-blue box that he had had on-screen out of his jacket pocket. "Saturday, will you marry me?"

Saturday gasped and wanted to walk off the set. She couldn't believe that Ed had blindsided her. She'd known he wanted to breathe new life into the show, but she hadn't known it was going to come at her expense. She wanted to rush over to Brandon and explain, but the cameras were rolling. She glanced in his direction and noticed the pissed expression on his face. No doubt he was upset, and she couldn't blame him. She had to do something and quick. Saturday started coughing uncontrollably and patting her chest as if she couldn't catch her breath.

"Cut!" Brandon yelled. "Let's take five," he said.

Saturday immediately walked off set, made a beeline to her dressing room and slammed the door. A few seconds later, there was a knock. She looked at the door before opening it. She didn't know who was on the other side. She didn't want to see Erick, Ed or Moses. She crossed the room and turned the knob.

Chapter 23

Trepidation took hold of Ayana and wouldn't let go as she slowly turned the doorknob. She held her breath and eased the door open.

"Are you all right?"

Ayana exhaled. "Yes, Gabby, I'm fine. I just need a couple of aspirins and a bottle of water," she said to the production assistant. The drama that had just played out on the set had given her a massive headache.

"Okay, you got it," Gabby said, leaving the room and closing the door behind her.

Ayana crossed the room and sat on the leopard-print chaise lounge, leaned her head back against the wall and closed her eyes. Instantly the image of Erick getting down on one knee and proposing appeared. She quickly blinked her eyes open. Ayana couldn't believe that Ed had arranged for Erick to come back on the show and propose. The whole idea was preposterous. She and Erick had known each other for only a few weeks, not nearly long enough to entertain the notion of marriage. When he'd produced the ring box inside the carriage, she had been taken by surprise. The tape ended right before she'd told him it was entirely too soon for a marriage proposal. She'd told Erick to put the ring back in his pocket, which he had. Of course, Ed had stopped the tape for a dramatic effect, right before she'd told Erick that she wasn't going to marry him.

There was a knock at the door.

"Come in!" she called out to let Gabby know it was okay to enter.

"You can't hide out in here forever. We've got a show to do," Brandon said, standing in the doorway. His face was void of expression. He spoke in a monotone, displaying no emotion. Ayana had never seen him look this way before, and his coldness scared her.

She rose from the chaise and went over to him. "Hey, baby, I'm so sorry about that. I…"

"About what?" he interrupted. "There's nothing to be sorry for. This is the way you wanted things, isn't it?" His tone was more robot than human.

"Brandon, you know I have to go along with whatever Ed has cooked up. He's all about the shock factor. As far as Erick is concerned, I told him that I couldn't marry him, but that conversation wasn't shown," she explained.

"You sure did look cozy, hugged up with him on a romantic carriage ride through the park," he said, giving her a stern look.

Ayana exhaled hard. Brandon was right. She and Erick had been huddled together like two sardines in a can. There was no denying that Ayana had enjoyed Erick's company at that time. He was smart, attentive, attractive and rich—a perfect combination. What was not to like? If Erick hadn't had to abruptly leave the country and return to Switzerland, they would probably legitimately be engaged by now. But Ayana would never admit this to Brandon. Things had changed since then, and Brandon was her man now. She wanted to just forget the past, but the past was alive and well and waiting for her on the set.

"What the clip didn't show was me telling Erick that it was too soon for him to propose."

"So you're basically saying that if you had spent more time with him, you'd be engaged *or* married to the dude," Brandon countered.

"No, no! That's *not* what I'm saying."

"Excuse me. Here's your aspirin and water," Gabby said, appearing in the doorway. "And, uh…" She looked from Ayana to Brandon and seemed to sense the tension in the air. "Ed is waiting for you guys. He's ready to resume taping."

"Thanks, Gabby. We'll be right there," Ayana said. She turned her attention back to Brandon. "Honey, please don't misconstrue what's happening on the set. You know as well as I do that Ed has orchestrated this entire reunion to boost ratings." Ayana hoped her explanation was enough to soothe Brandon's insecurities. She watched him intently, looking for a change in his disposition, but the coldness was still present. Ayana didn't know what else to do. She had explained the clip, but it hadn't made a difference.

"We need to get back on set," Brandon said before turning to leave.

Once he left, Ayana took the aspirin and adjusted her attitude. She didn't need to go on set with the feeling of defeat that was lurking in her spirit. She hadn't swayed Brandon and was feeling horrible that her man had to witness her past exploits. She took a few more sips of water and walked out.

"Okay, ladies, resume your positions," Ed said, standing in the middle of the room and giving directions. "Before the break, Erick proposed." He turned to face Saturday. "Saturday, I'ma need you to express happiness—no, make that total elation—when Erick shows you that gorgeous diamond ring."

"Ed, can I talk to you for a second?" Saturday said.

"Can it wait? We're running behind schedule."

"No, it can't." She walked toward the huge floor-to-ceiling windows, away from the rest of the cast, and motioned for Ed to follow her. Once the two of them were out of earshot, Saturday spoke softly. "Why did you bring Erick back?"

"You two had chemistry, and his return to the show makes perfect sense."

"Okay, that might be true, but it makes no sense for him to propose. We haven't seen each other in months. I know you don't expect me to accept his ridiculous proposal," she said, looking across the room at Brandon, who was sitting in his director's chair and talking on the phone. She wanted to tell Ed that she was in love with Brandon.

"The proposal isn't ridiculous and you will accept his ring. Need I remind you that you are under contract, and…"

"My contract doesn't say I have to be forced into

an arranged marriage," she countered, standing her ground.

"No, it doesn't, and I'm not saying you have to marry Erick, but you will accept the proposal," he said with clenched teeth. "This twist will hike our ratings. Remember, you are under contract, and the contract states that the show makes the final call on all artistic decisions. And this, missy, is an artistic decision that I'm making. Got it?"

"Ed, I can't believe you're treating me like this after I saved your life…literally," she said with tears welling up in her eyes.

"Ayana," he said, using her real name, "I truly appreciate what you did for me, but your administering CPR has nothing to do with the show. It's apples and oranges."

Ayana couldn't believe that Ed was being so indifferent and cold toward her. "So, basically, you're saying it's all about the show, and you'll do anything for high ratings."

"Ayana, stop acting so offended. What's wrong with you? You knew what the show was all about when you signed the contract. I need Saturday Knight to show up and show out. Come on. We've got a scene to finish," he said, walking away, leaving her standing there.

Unfortunately, Ed had total control of the situation. Ayana had no choice but to comply. *I can't wait until this contract is over. I'm leaving the show whether I have a talent agent or not. I can't take this anymore,* she said to herself and reluctantly went back to the set and resumed her persona.

"Before the break, Erick proposed. Let's pick it up from there," Ed said, full of enthusiasm.

Erick got down on his knee again. "Saturday, will you marry me?" He repeated the exact same words he had used before her coughing spasm forced the break.

Saturday looked down at Erick and then glanced over at Brandon, who wore a blank expression. She could see Ed out of the corner of her eye mouthing, "Say yes, say yes." She exhaled, put on a phony smile and said, "Yes, I'll marry you."

Erick took the ring out of the box and slid it on her finger. He stood up and kissed her on the lips.

Saturday wanted to throw up. She felt sick to her stomach as his lips touched hers.

"Let's see that rock," Moses said.

Saturday extended her finger toward the camera.

Moses leaned forward, looking at the other cast members, and said, "See, ladies. Love doesn't have a timeline. With some people, it's love at first sight and they don't need a long, drawn-out courtship. Isn't that right, Saturday?"

"Uh…" She stared at Brandon and said, "You're absolutely right." Ayana only hoped that Brandon knew she was talking about him and not Erick.

"Erick, sit next to your fiancée and tell us if you've made any plans for the big day," Moses said, fueling the fire.

"As a matter of fact, I have." Erick turned to Saturday. "My love, I'd like to marry you at The Plaza in a lavish ceremony. We'll take a horse-drawn carriage ride to the hotel as a reminder of where I proposed." He then turned his attention to the other cast members. "Ladies, we'd love to have you in our wedding."

Brooke, Trista and Petra smiled and nodded their heads. Obviously, Ed had made them play along.

"I would love to stand up for you," Petra chimed in, smiling and grinning at Erick. She was blatantly flirting with him and ignoring Saturday.

"So when is the big day?" Moses asked.

"I'm going to need some time to find the perfect dress. You know I have to be the hottest bride ever," Saturday said, trying to skirt the issue.

Moses directed his attention to the camera. "Well, guys, I hate to leave you hanging, but that's the show for now. Be sure to tune in and follow the ladies as they prepare for Saturday's big day. Moses Michaels signing off. See ya when I see ya."

"Cut!" Brandon yelled.

"Great show, everyone!" Ed said, clapping his hands.

Saturday was getting ready to make her way over to Brandon when Erick stepped in her path.

"Hello, my love. I hope you're not too shocked at all of this, but Ed said you wouldn't mind the surprise. I know we haven't seen each other in a while, but I think we really made a connection, don't you?"

Saturday was only half listening to Erick. She was too busy watching Brandon watch them. And Brandon was giving her the evil eye. She could just imagine what he was thinking. "Erick, I'm going to need to talk to you later."

As Saturday was making her way over to where Brandon stood, Ed approached her. "Now, that was GREAT television! If we keep up this type of drama, we'll be sure to beat the competition."

Saturday barely heard what Ed was saying. Instead, she was focused on Brandon, who gathered his notes and walked off the set. She wanted desperately to talk to him but kept getting waylaid. Their brief conversation in her dressing room hadn't convinced Brandon that she wasn't into Erick, and now she was wearing his ring. She started to go after him but reasoned it was probably better to let Brandon cool off first. *I'll call him later,* she thought as Ed continued to sing her praises.

Chapter 24

Brandon walked the crowded streets of Manhattan in a state of disbelief. He was oblivious to the people swarming around him as he plodded along, his steps much slower than the rest. He was well aware of Ayana's duel persona and had accepted her antics as Saturday sparring with the other cast members. But what he couldn't accept was her being engaged to another man. Brandon didn't care if the entire proposal was staged. In his opinion, she should have straight-out said, *HELL NO, I WON'T MARRY YOU!* But she'd smiled and sat patiently while another man slipped a huge diamond ring on her finger. Brandon probably could have accepted the fake engagement if it hadn't been for the tape. Watching her kiss another man was too much. Not only was she lip-locked with him, but from the looks of it—the way she was hugged up with him—she was enjoying every second of their romantic carriage ride.

As Brandon walked aimlessly down Broadway, his cell buzzed. He dug the phone out of his jeans' pocket and looked at the caller ID. It was Ayana. He thought about answering her call but wasn't ready to talk to her just yet. He was still upset that she had accepted the proposal and needed to wrap his mind around what had happened and what he should do about the situation. He needed time to think. He pressed Ignore and put the phone back in his pocket. Brandon didn't feel like going home and watching mindless television or staring at the walls. Instead, he walked into an Italian restaurant and went directly to the bar.

"Hi, what can I get you to drink?" the bartender asked.

"I'll have a bottle of Apothic Red." Brandon planned on being there awhile and didn't want to bother with ordering one glass of wine after another.

"Coming right up."

While Brandon waited for the bartender to return, he looked around the restaurant. Serafina was packed with the after-theater crowd munching on homemade pizzas, delicious pastas, fresh fish and grilled filet mignon. When the bartender came back, Brandon ordered a thin-crusted margherita pizza to complement the wine.

As Brandon enjoyed a glass of red wine, he heard someone call his name. He swiveled around on the stool.

"Hey, B, where the hell have you been?" his friend Jon asked as he walked up to the bar.

"Hey, Jon, I've been meaning to call you." Brandon hadn't spoken to his friend since the shooting started for *Divorced Divas*.

"Man, you did a vanishing act on a brother. The last time we spoke, you were getting ready for your first day on that reality show with them hot chicks," Jon said, licking his lips as if envisioning the cast. "So, how's it going?"

"What are you doing here? Are you meeting friends?" Brandon asked, ignoring Jon's question. There was so much to tell that Brandon didn't know where to start, so he averted the question.

"Yeah, I'm meeting my new girl, Ashley. I haven't spoken to you since I met her. Man, she's so fine it's ridiculous."

"Sit down and tell me how you guys met. You want a glass of wine?"

When Jon sat down, Brandon motioned for the bartender and asked him to bring another glass.

"Man, she's a dancer and is in the ensemble of *Kinky Boots,* the new Cyndi Lauper and Harvey Fierstein musical. She's so good that she ought to have a starring role," Jon said, gushing. "We met through mutual friends one night after the show."

"Wow, you must really like this woman. I haven't seen you this excited about somebody in a while."

"Well…I wouldn't say all that." Jon was a ladies' man and didn't like admitting that he was hung up on one woman.

"Don't deny it. The way you feel about her is written all over your face."

"Okay, okay." Jon threw up his hands in mock defense. "You got me. It's true—she might be the *one*."

As they were talking, Brandon's cell buzzed. He took the phone out of his pocket and looked at the caller ID.

It was Ayana calling again. He ignored her call and placed his phone back in his pocket.

"The *one?* Wow, I've never heard you say that before."

"That's because I've never felt this way before. Man, we're not getting any younger, and I've been thinking a lot about settling down."

Brandon was floored. Jon, the ladies' man, was actually serious about one woman. Hearing Jon admit his true feelings made Brandon think about Ayana. He had thought that she was the *one,* but now he wasn't so sure.

"So what about you? Have you been dating?" Jon asked.

"Sort of." Brandon didn't feel like baring his soul and confessing that he had fallen in love with the cast member that Jon had gushed over before Brandon started the show. His and Ayana's situation had turned complicated, and it would be difficult explaining that his woman was engaged to another man. Besides, clarifying all the details to Jon would expose Ayana's fake persona, and he wasn't going to jeopardize what she had worked so hard to conceal.

"Oh, I see you're taking a page from my playbook and rotating the ladies," Jon said, smiling.

"Well, I wouldn't say all that."

"Come on, man. Don't be modest. So what if you're dating multiple women? You're single and that's what single men do."

But he wasn't truly single. His heart was with one woman. Even though he was upset with her, he couldn't deny that he was deeply in love with Ayana "Saturday Knight" Lewis.

As they were talking, in walked Jon's girlfriend, Ashley, along with another woman.

"Hey, there's my girl," Jon said, quickly rising from the bar stool and giving Ashley a big hug and kiss. "Man, this is Ashley and her friend Naomi. Ladies, this is my main man, Brandon."

"Hello," the ladies said in unison.

Brandon shook their hands and offered them the two empty bar stools next to him. He had to admit that Jon was right. Ashley was gorgeous, and so was her friend. They both had long, lean dancers' bodies and beautiful faces. Brandon motioned for the bartender and asked him to bring two additional glasses. As he watched the bartender pour the ladies a glass of wine, his phone buzzed. He didn't bother to take his phone out of his pocket this time. He knew it was probably Ayana calling again.

"So, how do you guys know each other?" Ashley asked.

"B and I grew up together in Queens."

"That's ironic. Naomi and I have also known each other since childhood. Ever since we were kids, we both wanted to be dancers. We would put on talent shows in the summer and perform for the neighbors."

Brandon turned his attention to Naomi and asked, "How long have you been dancing on Broadway?"

"This is my first Broadway show. I've been all over Europe and Africa learning different techniques and dancing. I recently came back to the States and landed this gig. So what do you do?"

"I work in television," he said vaguely.

"Oh, really? Where?"

"Brandon is the director for *Divorced Divas*," Jon said, answering for his friend.

"Oh, we love that show!" Ashley and Naomi exclaimed.

"Those women are so sharp. They dress to the nines. I mean, they are put together from head to toe. Do designers donate clothes for the ladies to wear?" Ashley asked.

"I have no idea," Brandon answered.

"So tell me, is Saturday as much of a diva in person as she is on-screen?" Naomi asked.

"Yep," he simply said, not wanting to expound.

He wanted to quickly change the subject. The last person he wanted to talk about was Saturday. So, noticing the bottle of wine was empty, he ordered another bottle and turned to Naomi. "I'd much rather hear about your work."

"There's really not much to talk about. We dance in the chorus line with hopes of one day having a starring role in a show. That's basically it. Your job, however, must be so exciting. I mean, you're the director of a hit TV show. Now, that's something to talk about. Tell me, who's your favorite cast member?" Naomi asked, leaning in closer to him. "Saturday is my favorite. She makes the show interesting. You never know what she's going to say or do. The way she ribs Petra is a hoot. She's always correcting the poor girl's English. Give us a scoop."

"What do you mean? What kind of scoop?"

Naomi moved even closer to Brandon, their bodies nearly touching. "Tell us some juicy insider information. Like which guy out of all Saturday's dates is she going to wind up with? I don't see her with that nerdy-looking guy. And the man she had mad chemistry with, I think his name was Erick, never came back on the show. Do you think he's coming back?"

As Brandon hesitated, he wanted to say, *Her name is Ayana, and she's mine.* But of course he couldn't. As he sat there trying to decide how to steer the conversation away from *Divorced Divas* and Saturday's choice of men, he heard a familiar voice from behind.

"Oh, that's why you couldn't answer any of my calls. You're on a flipping date!"

He spun around and saw Ayana standing there with her hand on her hip, looking from him to Naomi.

"We're not on a…"

"Oh, my God—Saturday Knight! I can't believe it! We were just talking about you," Naomi exclaimed.

Ashley chimed in, "Saturday, is that Erick over there?"

Saturday didn't respond. She stood there and glared at Brandon.

Before Brandon could explain, Ayana turned around and hurried away. He started to go after her, but Ed, Steve and Erick were waiting by the hostess podium. They probably couldn't hear Ayana but they could clearly see her. Brandon watched Ayana as she walked to their table. She had a disappointed expression on her face. He wanted to rush over, take her in his arms and kiss her like he had done in Jamaica. However, one look at Erick, the Swiss banker, and the entire proposal played over in his mind. He got mad all over again. Brandon returned his attention to Naomi. He needed a distraction from his thoughts, and she was the perfect diversion.

Chapter 25

Ayana could barely sit through dinner with Ed, Steve and Erick. She was too busy stealing glances at the bar where Brandon sat with his date. Ed had wanted to go out with his star, her new fiancé and the executive producer to discuss plans for the season finale—Saturday and Erick's lavish wedding.

"You know, I've been thinking. I decided that The Plaza isn't the best venue for the wedding to take place," Ed told the group.

"And why not?" Erick asked.

"Although I love The Plaza, I think it's been done enough. So many celebrities have had their weddings there. I'm envisioning a tropical locale," Ed remarked.

"Like Fiji?" Steve said.

"No, some place closer."

"Like the Bahamas?" Erick asked.

"Actually, I'm thinking Jamaica. It's only a few hours from New York. What do you think, Saturday?" Ed asked.

Although Ayana's body was physically at the table, her mind was elsewhere. She was too busy wondering what Brandon was talking about with the beautiful woman sitting next to him. The woman now had her hand on his arm as she spoke. Ayana was seething. Brandon had all but blasted her about Erick, and now here he was entertaining another woman.

"Saturday, did you hear what I said?" Ed asked when she didn't respond to his question.

Ayana refocused her attention, momentarily taking her eyes off of Brandon and his date. "I'm sorry. What did you say?"

"I said, I think Jamaica would be the perfect locale for the wedding."

"What wedding?" she asked, looking at him strangely.

"Your wedding to Erick," he responded.

"What! Are you kidding? I thought you said the proposal was just for ratings and that I wasn't expected to marry him," Ayana said, slightly raising her voice. She turned to Erick and said, "Sorry, no offense, but we don't know each other well enough to get married."

Erick didn't say anything. He looked at Ed as if deferring the question to the show's creator.

"Don't panic. The wedding will only look real. A marriage license won't be filed. Therefore, you and Erick won't officially be married," he explained.

"Are you sure? I don't want to mistakenly marry a stranger."

"Yes, I'm certain. Your contract is coming up, so

this wedding will be the perfect way for you to exit the show."

Ayana thought about Ed's reasoning for a few moments. "I guess that does make sense."

"I plan to marry off each of you ladies one by one, depending on who wants out of their contract. And then I'll start fresh with a new divorced diva each season. That way the show will remain fresh," Ed explained.

"So you're saying this will be the last antic I'll ever have to enact," Ayana said, warming up to the idea.

"Yes, this wedding will be your final appearance, and then you're off the show—free to do whatever you please."

That was music to Ayana's ears. She could finally see the light at the end of this dreadful tunnel.

"So what do you think about having the wedding in Jamaica?" Ed asked.

"Jamaica!" Ayana shrieked. She had been lost in thought earlier and hadn't heard him mention her homeland.

Steve and Ed, noticing the way she reacted, said at the same time, "What's wrong with Jamaica?"

"Uh…nothing." She couldn't think of a fast answer, short of telling them the truth, which wasn't an option. "Can we shoot in Montego Bay? It's closer than Negril. If we shoot in Mo'Bay, we wouldn't have to transport the cast and crew on a two-hour bus ride into the country." As long as they didn't film the wedding in her hometown of Negril, Ayana didn't feel too anxious about being seen in Jamaica as her alter ego.

"That's a good idea. I want to shoot the wedding as soon as possible. I know Moses said on set that the show will follow you and the girls as you get ready for the wedding, but that's too long to drag this out. The ratings are slipping fast, and this wedding will help salvage our positioning. Steve, can you oversee all of the arrangements?" Ed asked.

"Sure thing. I have contacts at the Grand Palladium, so it won't be a problem to expedite the shoot. The Grand Palladium is a fabulous five-star hotel and will be the perfect venue."

"Excellent!" Ed exclaimed.

As the three men continued to talk about the upcoming wedding, Ayana tuned out again. News of her exit from the show was great, but she still had the fake proposal to deal with *and* the cold shoulder from Brandon. Finding him with another woman had totally caught her off guard. Ayana glanced over at the bar. She watched as another couple sitting next to Brandon raised their wineglasses and toasted with Brandon and his date. It was clear that the four of them were on a double date. Ayana had half a mind to go over there and break up their little party, but she didn't want to cause a scene. Instead, she took out her cell phone and punched in a text to Brandon.

I see you've moved on. So keep on moving. It's over!

She watched and waited for Brandon to acknowledge the text. A few minutes later, she saw him take his phone out of his pocket and look at it. She assumed he was reading her message. He didn't text back—just put the phone back in his pocket and continued his conversation.

Ayana felt hurt and dejected. A part of her—her heart—wanted to keep the relationship going, but another part of her—her pride—wouldn't let her watch Brandon flirt with another woman in front of her face. She thought that after he read her text, he would come over to the table and ask to speak to her, but he didn't. Her sitting there with Erick was probably keeping Brandon from coming over, she reasoned.

The love that she and Brandon had shared in Jamaica seemed like a lifetime ago. Their enchanted time on the island was now nothing more than a distant memory. Ayana was shocked at how quickly everything had changed. She'd thought that Brandon was the *one*. Now he seemed to be the one who was slowly breaking her heart.

Chapter 26

The feel of his muscular arms wrapped around her body, engulfing her in a sensuous full-body hug, felt like a slice of heaven. Every inch of her being craved him. Ayana was hungry for Brandon's touch. He awakened sexuality within her that she hadn't known she possessed.

He nibbled on her earlobe and then whispered, "I've missed you."

"How much?" she asked softly in his ear.

"I can show you better than I can tell you," he said, holding her closer.

Brandon trailed his lips from her earlobe to her neck, where he sucked ever so tenderly, before increasing the pressure, sucking harder and harder.

Ayana closed her eyes and held on to his bald head. "Ohhh…" she moaned.

He didn't stop until his efforts produced a deep crimson spot, branding her with his personalized mark of love. Brandon then trailed his lips to her chest, stopping right between her breasts. He teased her right nipple with his tongue and played with her left nipple until it firmed to his touch. He alternated from one to the other, licking her ample breasts. Brandon continued down her body with his lips, stopping only to tickle her belly button with his tongue.

Ayana lay helpless, enjoying his luscious lips.

He gripped her hips as he slid between her legs, resting his head in the center of her neatly shaven triangle. Brandon eased his tongue between the folds of her vagina and found her clitoris. He positioned his lips around the tiny head and gently sucked.

"Oohh…oohh…"

Brandon was on a mission to bring her to new heights of orgasm. He wanted to ensure she hungered for no other man. He sucked deeper and harder, his wet mouth engulfing her pleasure button. Saliva dripped from his mouth onto his chin and down her thighs as he worked his magic.

Ayana clenched his head tighter as he made love to her clit.

He reached underneath and took hold of her buttocks, bringing her lady lips closer to his mouth. Brandon's deft lips and tongue were working in concert at a rapid pace. Her essence was like sweet cream in his mouth.

Ayana was in a sexual trance and couldn't speak. Her body was doing all the talking. Her head was tilted toward the headboard. Her back was arched and her toes were clenching the sheets as she surrendered to him. She climaxed hard. Her body jerked as she released.

The tension that had been building in her body was now gone.

Suddenly, there was a knock at the door, jolting Ayana out of her delicious dream. She opened her eyes and looked down, half expecting to see Brandon in between her legs, but all she saw was a moistened sheet. The oral encounter with Brandon may have been a dream, but her orgasm had indeed been real. She sighed, frustrated that he wasn't there in the flesh.

"Yes, who is it?" she yelled.

"It's Gabby. Ed wanted me to remind you that rehearsal is in twenty minutes. We're meeting downstairs in the restaurant," she said through the door.

"Okay. Thanks. I'll be right down."

Ayana stretched, climbed out of bed and made her way to the shower. Fifteen minutes later, she was dressed in a white flowing maxi sundress. Her hair was brushed into a ponytail, and her makeup was minimal. Being in Jamaica with the heat and humidity, she didn't feel like putting on the entire Saturday Knight ensemble— wig, heavy makeup, designer duds, jewelry and heels. She would save all of that for the "big day." Ayana put on a pair of oversize sunglasses, took her key card and headed out the door.

When she reached the restaurant with its ocean views and fresh-cut birds-of-paradise, hibiscus and ginger, she felt a sense of home, but that feeling quickly dissipated when Brooke, Trista and Petra came walking into the room. They rolled their eyes in Ayana's direction and went straight to the buffet. Ayana wanted to go over and explain why she had treated them so badly and apologize for her behavior. Unfortunately, she couldn't—not yet. She didn't like being ostracized by the cast and crew, but it was too late now. Ayana walked in the opposite direction, over to the coffee station.

"Where's the groom-to-be?"

Ayana turned around and faced Brandon. She looked through the dark shades into his handsome face and envisioned him making love to her, like he had done in her dream. She wanted to take him by the hand and lead him upstairs to her bed so they could make that dream a reality. They hadn't spoken since that day in New York, and all Ayana wanted to do was make amends. She regretted sending that text when they were at Serafina, but she had gotten upset seeing him talking with another woman and had reacted without thinking it through. The woman at the bar could have just been a casual friend, for all she knew. Being back in Jamaica, where they'd fallen in love, had brought her back to her senses. She truly loved Brandon and didn't want to break up with him. This was all a huge misunderstanding, and she planned on clearing things up and getting their relationship back on track.

She swallowed hard. "Hi, Brandon."

"Look at you in all white." He eyed her from head to toe. "Don't you look like the bride-to-be?" he said with sarcasm in his voice.

"It's not what you think. This wedding isn't…"

Before she could tell Brandon that the marriage was a charade and that she was leaving the show when it was over, Erick came up from behind and hugged her around the waist. "Good morning, sweetheart."

Brandon stood there for a moment, staring at him holding his woman, and then walked away without saying a word.

Ayana saw the disgusted expression on Brandon's

face and knew that he was pissed. She wanted to back out of the arrangement right then and there. This sham wedding was ruining her life. Watching him walk away brought her to tears. Ayana was thankful for the sunglasses so that no one could see her red-rimmed eyes. She wiggled out of Erick's embrace. "Please don't hug me like that again," she told him.

"Why not? We're a happy couple on the eve of our wedding," he said with a huge smile on his face.

"Okay, everyone, finish your breakfast," Ed said, coming into the room with Gabby trailing behind him holding a clipboard. "We'll be heading out to the pool area to rehearse in a few."

Petra rushed over to Ed and said, "Reunion show supposed to be about all of us dating experience, but it the Saturday Knight show. Why she only one get lavish wedding in Jamaica?" she asked in her broken English.

"Cool it," Ed said, waving his floral chiffon scarf in her face. "I plan to marry you off one by one—no worries. You'll get your chance to waltz down the aisle. Now come on, everyone. Down to the pool."

Outside, the pool was enormous and inviting, with crystal clear, ice-blue water. It was the perfect backdrop to the turquoise ocean. A grandiose white-columned gazebo stood at the end of the pool with stunning views of the island.

Ed stepped up on the marble platform of the gazebo. "Saturday and Erick, come up here. You two will stand here with the minister."

Ayana glanced at Brandon, who was standing near the edge of the pool. He was staring into the water, appearing deep in thought.

"Brandon, can you come up here?" Ed called out.

Ayana watched Brandon slowly make his way over. He kept his eyes straight ahead without giving her a second look.

"Stand next to Saturday. I want you to see the vantage point from here. I want a camera at the end of the row of chairs so that it can capture the ocean. A camera will also be in the front to film their faces as the minister conducts the ceremony. Got it?" Ed asked.

"Yep."

As Brandon stood close to her, Ayana became anxious. He still had no idea that the wedding was a sham, and she could see the anger in his eyes as Ed spoke. Ayana was afraid that the longer Brandon went on without knowing the truth, the wider the rift between them would become until it was beyond repair.

"Saturday, I want you looking deeply into Erick's eyes as the minister asks you to recite your vows so that the camera can capture your sincerity," Ed instructed.

The beautiful surroundings were the perfect venue for a wedding. Ayana had always dreamed of having an ocean-side ceremony, but she'd never thought her second wedding would be a sham. Ayana cut her eyes at Brandon and watched his nonexpression as Ed spoke. Brandon looked as though he'd rather be anywhere else but there.

"Excuse me, Ed. Can I talk to you for a second?" she asked.

"Not now, Saturday. I want to run through everything so we'll be ready to shoot tomorrow."

Ayana wanted to tell Ed to ease up and not focus so hard on her reactions during the ceremony. He was talking as if the wedding was going to be the real deal.

The more Ed spoke, the harder it was going to be for her to explain to Brandon the truth about the wedding.

Ayana stepped a bit closer to Brandon so that her arm was touching his. She wanted to convey with body language what she couldn't say with words, but he moved away from her the moment her arm touched his. *What's the use? He's over me.*

The rest of the morning and afternoon was filled with details for the televised nuptials. Ed left nothing to chance. He planned on this being the event of the season. The cast and crew all had their orders, and he expected them to carry out his vision flawlessly. Everyone was excited about the extravaganza except Petra and Saturday. The only thing she could think about was telling Brandon the truth—that the wedding wasn't legal—before she lost him once and for all.

Chapter 27

Ed had hired the best wedding planner on the island, and she arranged everything from ordering the bouquets for the bride and her attendants to selecting the delicious cuisine and champagne for the reception. She even had a designer wedding gown and shoes flown in from New York.

Today was the big day. All the minute details that comprised a wedding were taken care of with all the speed and ease money could buy. To expedite the magical day, Ed used some of his personal funds and told the wedding planner to spare no expense.

Ayana was in her room getting ready to make her grand appearance. She had made up her face expertly, complete with false eyelashes. Hair extensions made her natural hair even longer, giving her a more glamorous look. Ed wanted an attendant to help her dress, but she insisted on being alone. Ayana needed to collect her thoughts before putting on the performance of her life. She stood at the foot of the bed in her underwear and peered down at the pearl-white wedding gown, which was spread out on the bed. There was no denying the dress was beautiful, with its hand-embroidered beading and lace. This was exactly the type of gown she would have chosen if she were marrying Brandon. She sat next to the dress and ran her hand over the duchess silk satin. The feel of the smooth fabric was calming.

Ayana glanced at the clock on the nightstand. "Sixty minutes to showtime," she said out loud and exhaled. A part of her wanted to get the show over with as soon as possible so that she could finally prove to Brandon that the wedding was just for ratings. She planned on showing him that the marriage license was never filed, rendering the union null and void. Ayana reached for the hotel phone. She wanted one last shot at talking to Brandon before he saw her in the wedding dress. The hurt she'd seen in his eyes during rehearsal would be even worse during the actual wedding, and Ayana thought that she could spare him the pain if he knew the truth.

"Hi, may I have Brandon Gilliam's room, please?" she asked the operator.

"Hold on, please." After a few seconds, the operator returned. "I'm sorry, miss, that line is busy. Would you like to call back in a few minutes?"

"Uh…okay, I'll do that." Ayana hung up and thought about calling Brandon on his cell phone, but he would probably ignore the call like he had done in New York. She desperately wanted to talk to him and reasoned that she could get in touch with him if she used the hotel phone. Ayana waited a few minutes and called the operator back.

"Hi, can you try Brandon Gilliam's room again?"

"Sure. Hold on, please."

After a few rings, Brandon picked up. "Hello?"

"Hey, it's me," she said sheepishly.

"Yeah, what do you want?" he asked coldly.

"We need to talk face-to-face before the wedding. What room are you in? I'll come to you," she said, speaking fast.

"You're getting married in an hour. What's there to talk about? This is a done deal. You've made your choice—now live with it. Goodbye, Ayana. Have a good life." Click.

He hung up before she had a chance to explain the situation. Ayana felt like crying. The lie was killing her inside. Ayana had to do something and fast. She considered her options and realized the only thing to do was show Brandon the unauthorized marriage certificate. Maybe once he saw that the document didn't have an official seal, he would believe her once and for all.

Ayana quickly slipped on the gown, zipped it up on the side, stepped into the white satin shoes, grabbed her key card and headed out the door. Ed's suite was on the top floor of the hotel. She made her way down the hall to the elevator and waited impatiently for it to arrive. When the doors opened, she stepped inside. An elderly couple stood near the row of buttons, dressed in matching Hawaiian shirts and khaki shorts and holding souvenir bags.

"Oh, my, what a beautiful bride you are!" the woman said, putting her hand up to her mouth.

"I still remember our wedding day like it was yesterday. You were the most beautiful bride I had ever seen," the man said, turning to his wife and smiling.

"Oh, aren't you the sweetest?"

The husband kissed his wife on the cheek.

"We've been happily married for thirty-seven years. And I wish you and your groom the same type of bliss me and my Walter have found," the lady said, holding on to her husband's arm.

One look at them, and Ayana knew that true happiness was possible. Their love for each other was palpable. Ayana wanted her and Brandon to share that same type of love again. "Thank you. I plan on making that happen."

Once the doors opened, she nearly leaped off the elevator. Ayana picked up the hem of the dress so that she could move faster, and dashed down the hallway. When she reached Ed's suite, a bellhop was wheeling out a white, linen-covered dining cart. She quickly whisked past him. The suite was huge with a long L-shaped entryway. As Ayana was making her way toward the living room, she could hear voices.

"So what are you going to do about the license?"

Ayana stopped in her tracks at the sound of Steve's voice.

"What do you mean?" Ed answered.

"I mean, you told Saturday that the marriage license wouldn't be filed."

"Yes, that was my initial plan, but the officials here said we couldn't have a wedding without an actual license, so I had no choice but to file it."

"The big question is…are you going to tell Saturday and Erick that the marriage is real?" Steve asked.

"I already talked to Erick and he's okay going through

with the wedding. He adores Saturday and would love nothing more than to marry her."

Ayana's knees nearly buckled. She couldn't believe what she was hearing. Her first instinct was to burst into the room and confront Ed, but this was her opportunity to learn what Ed was planning.

"Are you going to tell Saturday the truth?"

Ed started laughing. "Are you kidding? You know as well as I do that she won't go along with this. She didn't want to do a fake wedding, so do you honestly think she'll be okay with an official wedding?"

"I guess you're right."

"Of course I'm right," Ed said with an edge of cockiness to his voice.

And to think I saved his life, she thought, shaking her head. Ayana was hurt and disappointed. She'd thought that Ed was her friend, but the only thing he was loyal to was ratings.

Ed continued, "Besides, if the marriage doesn't work out, they can always get an annulment. People do it every day."

"That's true," Steve agreed.

Ayana had heard enough. She turned around and slowly walked out. As she made her way back to the elevator, she was having a hard time wrapping her mind around the fact that Ed was willing to dupe her into an arranged marriage for the sake of a stupid reality show. At that point, Ayana knew exactly what she had to do.

Chapter 28

The harpist softly strummed her harp strings, playing Bach as the guests arrived. Ed had hired local islanders as extras, so every chair at the ceremony was filled. The outdoor pool area was decorated with white and lavender roses. Large lavender bows were tied to the backs of white chairs and the gazebo was draped with white and lavender chiffon fabric that floated on the midday breeze. The entire scene looked like something out of a fairy tale.

Brandon sat in the last row, taking in the idyllic surroundings. He looked down at the lavender runner and couldn't believe Ayana would be walking down that aisle on her way to marry another man. She had said that the proposal was for ratings and that she had told Erick before that she couldn't marry him. But clearly that was one big lie.

How did things go so wrong? he thought. Brandon reached in his shirt pocket and took out the airline napkin. He gently unfolded it and read the front: *Blissfully Yours, B.* Then he turned it over and read Ayana's writing: *Blissfully Yours, A.* He put the napkin to his lips and kissed the ruby-red lip imprint that she had made. Brandon knew this would be the last time he kissed her lips. His heart ached, but there was nothing he could do about it. Now he wished like hell that he had listened to what she had to say when she'd called his room earlier. She could have been calling to tell him that she wasn't going through with the wedding, but now he would never know. It was too late for should've, would've, could'ves. He refolded the napkin and put it back in his pocket. That memento was all he had left from their time together and he planned on cherishing it forever. As he was sitting there feeling forlorn, his cell phone vibrated. Brandon's heart started racing faster, thinking it might be Ayana. He quickly retrieved the phone from his pocket and looked at the caller ID. His heart stopped racing. It wasn't Ayana; it was his agent.

"Hey, Mario, what's up?"

"Hi, Brandon. My assistant told me you called. Sorry I'm just getting back to you, but I was in Italy on my honeymoon."

Damn! Is everybody getting married but me? "Congratulations, man. I didn't even know you were engaged."

"Well, it wasn't a long engagement. We met at an industry function and had an instant attraction. I just knew she was the woman for me, and I didn't want to wait around and chance somebody else swooping in and stealing my lady."

"Yeah, I know what you mean," Brandon said, looking straight ahead at the altar.

"Well, I didn't call to talk about my honeymoon. I have great news for you."

"Good. I could use some good news right about now," he said.

"It's a good thing you only signed on to work on *Divorced Divas* for one season," Mario said.

"And why is that?"

"I have an awesome deal on the table for you. It's directing a *60 Minutes*–type show for one of the majors. If you want the job, I can start negotiations right away."

"Hell yeah, I want the job! The sooner I leave this train wreck of a show, the better."

"Excellent. I'll contact the executives at the station and get the paperwork going."

"Thanks, Mario, for coming through for me."

"Hey, man, that's why I get paid the big bucks." He laughed and then said, "Oh, I forgot to ask—why did you call?"

Brandon was momentarily so caught up with the news of his new gig that he forgot all about mentioning Ayana to his agent. For a split second he thought about forgetting the favor. Now that she was marrying a rich Swiss banker, she probably wouldn't be interested in pursuing an acting career. However, he had made a promise to her and planned on keeping it.

"Are you taking on any new clients?"

"Yes, I'm always looking for talented people. Why? Do you have someone in mind?"

"As a matter of fact, I do. Saturday Knight is looking for representation. She…"

"Oh, wait right there," Mario said, cutting him off.

"I said I'm looking for talent. I'm not interested in rep-
ping a soiled reality-show diva."

"See, that's where you're wrong." Brandon lowered
his voice and put his hand over his mouth, careful not
to be overheard. "Saturday Knight is a fake persona
that Ayana Lewis puts on for the show."

"What? Who's Ayana Lewis?" Mario asked, confused.

"That's Saturday's real name. Ayana is a sweetheart
and is nothing like the person you see on television."
As Brandon defended his former lover, he realized that
he was still in love with her.

"Wow. So you're telling me that whole routine is
nothing but an act?"

"Yep, Ayana is a natural actress and would be an
asset to your roster," Brandon said, singing her praises.

"I would definitely say so. I really thought that was
her true personality. Man, she had me fooled. Have
her call my assistant and set up an appointment so we
can talk."

"Listen, why don't I just give your assistant Ayana's
number instead?" Brandon suggested. He didn't know
if or when he and Ayana were going to speak again, and
he didn't want to stand in the way of her career.

"That'll be fine. Talk to you later."

"Okay, goodbye." Although he and Ayana were no
longer together, he was happy that he could fulfill at
least that one promise.

"Why are you sitting all the way back here?" Ed
asked, walking up to Brandon.

"What's up, Ed?" he said, looking at the white linen
pants and shirt he wore with a lavender scarf draped

around his neck. Ed looked like a bride himself in his outfit.

"We're ready to get started, and I need you in director mode. I want to start in five."

Brandon exhaled hard. The moment that he had been dreading was finally here. "No problem."

"I'll have Gabby go get the girls," Ed said, turning and scurrying away, his long lavender scarf floating on the breeze behind him.

Brandon went to his designated position, put on his headset and cued the crew, making sure everyone was in place and ready to shoot. From his position near the altar, but out of the camera's frame, Brandon watched Erick and the minister walk onto the gazebo, which was an indication they were ready to begin.

"Okay, everyone. Ready in five, four, three, two, one. Action!" Brandon announced into his microphone.

On cue, out came Trista in a lavender halter dress, carrying a bouquet of white and lavender flowers. Brooke followed behind Trista, also wearing lavender, but her dress was sleeveless. Next was a tiny flower girl also in lavender. She tossed out white rose petals as she walked slowly up the aisle. Petra was a no-show. Brandon figured that she probably didn't want any part in Saturday's wedding.

Once the bridal party had made their way to the altar, the harpist stopped and the bridal march began. Everyone rose to their feet in honor of the bride.

Brandon watched Ayana glide down the aisle in a gorgeous white beaded gown. She looked like a traditional bride with layers of tulle covering her face. His mouth became dry, and his palms began sweating more and more the closer she got to the altar.

Oh, shit, this is really happening. He wanted to voice his objection before the minister had a chance to ask if anyone had "just cause" to stop the wedding. Brandon took a deep breath. But this was Ayana's choice and there was nothing he could do about it.

When she reached the altar, the music stopped and the minister began speaking.

"Ladies and gentlemen, we are gathered here today to witness the marriage between this man and this woman."

Brandon tuned out the minister's words. Once the minister reached the vow part of the ceremony, a few words caught Brandon's attention, bringing him out of his zone and back to reality. He couldn't believe his ears. *This must be some kind of mistake!* Brandon listened as the minister asked them to repeat after him, and he then watched as they slipped platinum bands on each other's fingers.

"…By the power vested in me, I now pronounce you man and wife. You may kiss your bride."

A lump caught in Brandon's throat as he watched Erick lift her veil.

Erick then kissed his new bride, Petra, on the lips, as the audience clapped. The happy couple then turned around and walked arm in arm down the aisle.

Brandon was dumbfounded. A million questions ran through his head, but most important, where was Ayana?

Once Erick and Petra disappeared inside the hotel, Brandon yelled, "Cut!" He took his headset off and raced toward the front of the hotel. He had to find Ayana and fast. He didn't know what had happened, but he planned on finding out.

Chapter 29

Brandon searched the main floor of the hotel but didn't see Ayana anywhere. He hurried to the front desk and asked the clerk to call up to Ayana's room. He tapped his fingers on the counter while he waited.

"Sorry, sir, there was no answer."

"What's her room number? I can go and see if she's upstairs."

"Sorry, sir, we can't give out the room numbers of our guests."

"But it's urgent that I see her," he said with panic in his voice.

"I'm very sorry, but it's against hotel policy to give out room numbers."

Brandon sighed. He took out his cell phone and called Ayana, but his call went to her voice mail. "Hey, it's me. Please call me as soon as you get this message."

He didn't know what else to do. He was dying to talk to Ayana. First, he wanted to make sure she was okay, and second, he wanted to know the reason she hadn't gone through with the wedding.

Since he couldn't find Ayana, he went in search of Ed, who was no doubt behind switching brides at the twelfth hour. Brandon bolted through the doors of the Grand Ballroom, where the reception was being held, and made his way through the throng of people milling about drinking champagne and eating hors d'oeuvres.

"Where the hell have you been?" Ed asked, rushing up to Brandon. "We should have already started taping this reception. I spent good money to have the entire event filmed, not just the wedding."

"Speaking of…what happened to Ayana?" Brandon asked, totally ignoring Ed's comment.

"Ayana?" A shocked expression appeared on Ed's face. "How do you know her real name?"

"Answer my question first. Where is she?"

Ed waved his manicured hand in the air. "I don't have time to waste talking about her. Get your headset on and direct this reception. You are still under contract, remember?"

Brandon really wanted to tell Ed to shove his contract, but he didn't want to walk off the set on the last day of filming. He was a professional and didn't want the word getting out that he had abandoned a show. Brandon turned his back to Ed and went over to the cordoned-off area that was set up for the crew. He put on his headset and went into action.

The reception was a lavish affair, from a Moët & Chandon champagne fountain, to freshly caught seafood, to delicious Jamaican fare. There was a deejay and one of the island's most popular reggae bands. Brandon could hardly concentrate on his job. His mind was intent on finding Ayana. She was somewhere on the island, but where?

"Would you like a glass of champagne?" Brooke asked, walking up to him with two glasses in her hands.

"No, thank you. I'm working."

"So am I," she said, taking a sip.

"Our jobs are totally different. You're paid to party, and I'm paid to direct the party," he said without making eye contact.

"Why are you so mean to me?" she asked, looking wounded.

Brandon turned and looked at her. "Brooke, I'm not trying to be mean. I'm in love with someone else, and I don't want to lead you on."

"I get it. I was in love once, and it's a beautiful thing when two people are on the same page."

Brandon listened to her words and only hoped that Ayana still felt the way he did. A lot had changed since they had left Jamaica. Brandon just hoped it wasn't too late to win her back. "Yes, love can be beautiful."

"Well, I wish you and your lady, whoever she is, good luck," Brooke said and walked away.

"Hey, Brooke," Brandon called after her.

She turned around and came back. "Yes, Brandon?"

"Have you seen Aya…uh…Saturday?"

"I saw her earlier with her bags. She was outside of the hotel getting ready to board a bus. I guess Ed fired her—she left. I don't really know for sure."

"Fired?"

"That's the word going around. I, for one, am glad to see her go."

"Thanks, Brooke," he said, ignoring her last comment.

Shortly after the reception was over, and the cameras had stopped rolling, Ed thanked the cast and crew for a great season. Brandon immediately rushed back to the front desk.

"What time does the last bus leave for Negril?" he asked the clerk. Brandon had a good suspicion that Ayana had gone home. Whatever had happened to prevent her from going through with the wedding must have been serious. He reasoned that she probably wanted to leave Montego Bay for the comfort of her parents' home.

"Sorry, sir, but the last bus left an hour ago."

"Are there any rental-car companies in the area?" Although the road to Negril was long, winding and dark, Brandon was willing to travel during the night to get the woman he loved.

"All of the rental-car places are closed for the evening."

Brandon slumped against the counter. He was out of ideas. The only thing he could do now was wait until morning. He asked what time the first bus to Negril departed in the morning, then thanked the clerk and went to his room.

Sleep escaped Brandon as he tossed and turned. His mind wouldn't let him rest. He kept thinking about Ayana and how he hadn't given her a chance to explain.

Brandon was up with the sun. He quickly packed. It was still too early to go downstairs and board the bus, so he called Ayana, hoping this time she would pick up.

Her cell phone didn't ring. It went right to voice mail.

"Hey, baby, it's me again. Where are you? Please call me back as soon as you get this message." Brandon was really beginning to panic. Maybe Ayana had fallen ill. Brandon sat on the bed and put his head in his hands. He was racked with worry and guilt.

An hour later, he was on the bus headed to Negril. The ride was long and bumpy. The bus driver wove through the winding roads at a breakneck pace, as if the bus were on rails. Brandon was thankful for the accelerated speed. He couldn't get to Negril fast enough. He was a man on a mission. When they finally reached the town, he asked the driver to let him off at the first hotel stop. Brandon then caught a taxi to take him to Ayana's parents' house.

As Brandon sat in the backseat of the taxi, his heart raced. He was moments from possibly seeing Ayana, and he could hardly wait. He had so much to say to her, but most important, he wanted to apologize for acting like a jerk. Had he listened to her in the first place, he wouldn't be racing all over Jamaica trying to find the love of his life. When they reached the house, he asked the driver to wait while he rang the doorbell.

After a few seconds that seemed like hours, the front door opened.

"Hi, Mrs. Tosh. How are you? I'm Brandon, a friend of Ayana's," he said, his words rushing out.

The older lady surveyed Brandon from head to toe and began to smile. "Yes, chile, I remember ya."

"Is Ayana home?"

"No, chile, she not here."

His heart sank. "Do you know where she is?"

"No, chile. Her left here early dis mornin'."

"Oh, okay. Can you tell her I stopped by?"

"Sure."

"Thanks," he said and went back to the taxi. Although she wasn't at home, he was relieved to know that she wasn't lying in bed sick and was at least still on the island. Brandon asked the driver to take him to New Beginnings.

The shelter was busy as usual with children running and playing in the front yard. Brandon walked through the front door and went to Marigold's office. His sister-in-law was behind the desk doing paperwork.

"Hey, sis," he said.

Marigold looked up. "Oh, me word! Whacha doin' here? Me thought ya were back in New York."

He leaned across the desk and gave her a hug. "I'm here for work. Uh…have you seen Ayana?"

"Ana?" She smiled. "No, I haven't seen her. Whacha want wit Ana? Thought ya said ya were here for work. Ya sweet on dat gurl, aren't ya?" Marigold asked, cutting right to the chase.

Brandon nodded his head. "Yes, I am."

"Me knew it! Me could see dat when ya two were here last time. Ya two were lookin' at each other da way me and James used to. Me glad ya finally found da one."

"Me, too." *I just hope it's not too late,* he thought. "Well, if she comes by, can you tell her to call me?"

"No problem. Ya staying at the bungalow?"

"Yes." He planned on staying on the island until he found Ayana.

Brandon kissed his sister-in-law goodbye. He then headed back toward the taxi. Once he got in, he sat and thought for a moment.

"Where to now, mon?" The driver interrupted his thoughts.

Brandon wanted to go to the bungalow and get his brother's car so that he could do a thorough search of the island. He gave the driver the address, then sat back and gazed out the open window. As he looked at the beautiful countryside with its lush landscape, he spotted a yellow Vespa whizzing by on the other side of the road. It was Ayana.

"Hey, turn around and follow that scooter!"

Brandon sat on the edge of the seat as the driver followed his instructions. Brandon's heart was racing as fast as the scooter. He had finally found her. Now he prayed that she would give him a second chance.

Chapter 30

Ayana's long hair blew in the breeze as she sped along the dirt road on the way to her favorite place. She needed the seclusion of the mountains to clear her head and think about her future plans. As Ayana wove through the mountainside, she replayed the past twenty-four hours in her mind.

After sneaking out of Ed's suite, Ayana had gone back to her room and taken off the wedding dress. There was no way she was going through with the wedding after what she had heard. It was one thing to pretend to marry Erick and another thing entirely to actually marry a man she didn't love. She had put the dress back in the garment bag, returned the satin Jimmy Choos to the shoe box and wrapped the jewelry in tissue paper. At the time, Ayana hadn't had a plan. All she knew was that she wasn't going to marry a man she didn't love. She had sat on the side of the bed, trying to devise a strategy. She knew that Ed would be beyond pissed and would probably threaten to sue her for breaching the contract. After all, she had promised to do a final episode. Time was ticking and Ayana had to think fast.

"I've got it!" she said, hopping to her feet.

Ayana quickly dressed in a pair of jeans, T-shirt and flip-flops. She gathered the bridal gear, putting it in bags, and headed out the door. On the elevator ride to Ed's floor, her heart began beating fast. She didn't know how he was going to take the news. When the doors opened, she stepped out and said a silent prayer as she made her way down the hallway. She knocked at his door and waited. A few seconds later, Ed answered.

He took one look at her and said, "What are you still doing in your street clothes?"

"Can I come in? We need to talk." Ayana hadn't waited for him to answer. She'd walked past him into the suite. As she marched down the long hall, she'd flashed back on Ed and Steve's conversation and had gotten mad all over again.

Once she entered the spacious living room, which was decorated in all white with floor-to-ceiling windows and spectacular views of the ocean, she'd relieved her arms of the dress, shoes and jewelry. "Here you go!"

"What the hell are you doing?" Ed had asked, looking at the bags of bridal gear in the chair.

"I should be asking you the same thing" she'd said, putting her hands on her hips.

"What are you talking about?"

"I'm talking about you trying to pull a fast one on me!" Ayana raised her voice.

Again Ed had said, "What are you talking about? Are you drunk or something?" He'd eyed her closely.

"No, I'm not drunk, but you must think I'm stupid."

"What I think is that you'd better pick up this stuff, go back to your room and get dressed. The wedding starts in less than an hour."

"There's only going to be a wedding if you listen to what I have to say."

Ed had exhaled hard. "There's nothing for you to say but 'I do.'"

"Oh, you mean, say 'I do' and get legally married to Erick!"

Ed had opened his mouth but didn't utter a word when he heard her remark. He was shocked that she knew the truth.

Ayana had looked at the expression on his face. "That's right. I know all about your scheme. The marriage license that was supposed to be unofficial is now the real deal, which means that after this wedding Erick and I will be legally married. But of course you don't care about that. All you care about is your stupid ratings. To hell with everything else! Ed, how could you do this to me?" Tears had formed in her eyes. "I saved your life, and this is how you repay me?"

Ed then had flung the lavender scarf around his neck, cleared his throat and said, "It's not personal."

"Are you kidding me? Marrying somebody I don't love is extremely personal! And I'm not going through with it!"

"Oh, yes, you are! You're under contract...remember?"

As they stood there yelling at each other, Ayana took a deep breath. She needed to get through to Ed, and screaming back and forth wasn't doing the trick. "Ed, can we please sit down and talk?" she'd asked in a calm voice.

He didn't move.

"Ed, if my saving your life meant anything at all to you, you'll hear me out." Ayana had been determined to be heard, so she used the only card she had left.

Ed had crossed the room and sat on the sofa. "Okay, what do you have to say? Make it quick."

She sat in one of the leather chairs. "I know that this wedding is important to you, and I've figured out a way for it to still take place. What if Petra marries Erick instead of me?"

"And how is that supposed to work?"

"You have pull at the official's office where you got the license, right?"

"Yes."

"Well, have them take my name off the license and put Petra's name on."

"I guess I could pay them a hefty bonus to come to the hotel and do the paperwork. That way the wedding won't be delayed too long. But what if she doesn't want to marry him?"

"Who wouldn't want to marry Erick? He's handsome, smart and rich. Besides, they are both European and probably have a lot in common. Why don't you run it past both of them? You are a convincing man, and I'm sure you can get them to agree. And you can also tell them, like you told Steve, that they can always get an annulment if it doesn't work out."

Ed had been silent for a moment, and Ayana could see that he was thinking about the idea. She then added, "Besides, this will be the shocker of all shockers. The audience won't see the switch coming. Talk about increasing ratings. And…" She took a breath. "You can use their wedding as a teaser for next season. The promos could focus on how Petra stole Erick from Saturday."

Ed's face had lit up. "Actually, that's a brilliant idea. You two are always going at it, and this would be the perfect way for Petra to get you back—by stealing your man."

"Yes! That's right! To seal the deal with Petra, emphasize that this will put the spotlight on her and make her and Erick's wedding the most talked about event of the season. Tell her that now she's the star of the show."

"I must say, Ayana—you've thought of everything. Let's call them now," he said, getting up and walking over to the phone.

"Now, if it's okay with you, I'm going to leave. I don't want to stick around for the wedding."

"Yes, I think that's best. I don't want Petra irritated. See you back in New York."

She'd turned to walk away.

"Ayana, wait. I am sorry for putting you through all of this, but you know how crazy I get about the show. Sometimes my judgment gets clouded by the ratings. There are a gazillion reality shows, and the competition to stay on top is extremely stiff. I do appreciate you administering CPR when I had the heart attack, and I promise to give you a glowing reference for whatever you want to do in the future."

"Thanks, Ed. I appreciate that."

They said their goodbyes, and Ayana went back to her room and packed. Before leaving the hotel, she had one more thing to do. She called the front desk and asked for Petra's room.

"Hello?" Petra had answered.

"Hi, Petra. It's Saturday."

"What you want?" she'd snapped into the receiver.

"I just want to apologize for always being so hard on you. It wasn't personal—just a job I had to do."

"I no need you apology. I have you man." Click. Petra had hung up in Ayana's ear.

As Ayana left the hotel and boarded the last bus to Negril, she'd looked back and thought about Brandon. She'd wanted to tell him goodbye, but he was probably in work mode by now. *Hopefully I'll see him back in New York,* she'd thought as the bus pulled off.

Ayana had reached her destination. She pulled over to the side of the road and turned off the motor. She climbed off the scooter and cut through the trees until she reached the manicured patch of land. She sat on the grass. She looked out over the trees at the beautiful mountainside and remembered her last time there. She and Brandon had had a perfect afternoon. She sighed. "If only he were here," she said aloud.

"I am here."

Ayana swung around, and standing there was Brandon. She hopped up. "What are you doing here?"

"I came to get my girl."

She ran to him as fast as she could and wrapped her arms around his neck. "I'm so sorry, Brandon. The wedding was Ed's idea."

He put his fingers to her lips. "Hush. You don't have to explain. The mere fact that you didn't marry that guy says it all."

"I would have never married him. I don't love him. I love you."

Brandon passionately kissed her and then said, "And I love you." He took the napkin out of his pocket and gave it to her.

Ayana read his writing. *Blissfully Yours, B.* "And I am always and forever, blissfully yours."

* * * * *

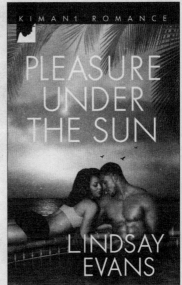

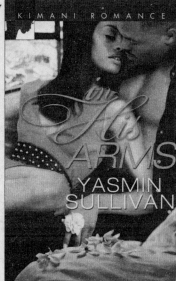

REQUEST YOUR FREE BOOKS!

2 FREE NOVELS
PLUS 2 *FREE GIFTS!*

KIMANI™
ROMANCE

Love's ultimate destination!

YES! Please send me 2 FREE Harlequin® Kimani™ Romance novels and my 2 FREE gifts (gifts are worth about $10). After receiving them, if I don't wish to receive any more books, I can return the shipping statement marked "cancel." If I don't cancel, I will receive 4 brand-new novels every month and be billed just $5.19 per book in the U.S. or $5.74 per book in Canada. That's a savings of at least 20% off the cover price. It's quite a bargain! Shipping and handling is just 50¢ per book in the U.S. and 75¢ per book in Canada.* I understand that accepting the 2 free books and gifts places me under no obligation to buy anything. I can always return a shipment and cancel at any time. Even if I never buy another book, the two free books and gifts are mine to keep forever.

168/368 XDN F4XC

Name	(PLEASE PRINT)	
Address		Apt. #
City	State/Prov.	Zip/Postal Code

Signature (if under 18, a parent or guardian must sign)

Mail to the **Harlequin® Reader Service**:

IN U.S.A.: P.O. Box 1867, Buffalo, NY 14240-1867
IN CANADA: P.O. Box 609, Fort Erie, Ontario L2A 5X3

Want to try two free books from another line?
Call 1-800-873-8635 or visit www.ReaderService.com.

* Terms and prices subject to change without notice. Prices do not include applicable taxes. Sales tax applicable in N.Y. Canadian residents will be charged applicable taxes. Offer not valid in Quebec. This offer is limited to one order per household. Not valid for current subscribers to Harlequin® Kimani™ Romance books. All orders subject to credit approval. Credit or debit balances in a customer's account(s) may be offset by any other outstanding balance owed by or to the customer. Please allow 4 to 6 weeks for delivery. Offer available while quantities last.

Your Privacy—The Harlequin® Reader Service is committed to protecting your privacy. Our Privacy Policy is available online at www.ReaderService.com or upon request from the Harlequin Reader Service.

We make a portion of our mailing list available to reputable third parties that offer products we believe may interest you. If you prefer that we not exchange your name with third parties, or if you wish to clarify or modify your communication preferences, please visit us at www.ReaderService.com/consumerchoice or write to us at Harlequin Reader Service Preference Service, P.O. Box 9062, Buffalo, NY 14269. Include your complete name and address.

KROM13R

National Bestselling Author

ROCHELLE ALERS

PLEASURE SEEKERS

Ilene is a captivatingly beautiful supermodel, Faye is an award-winning advertising executive and Alana is a brilliant editor for today's hottest fashion magazine. From Manhattan to Paris to Southampton, all three women are caught in the whirlwind of the superrich and famous.

Their new worlds are a torrent of sensual delights and unlimited luxuries. But will they ultimately discover that all the money and power in the world means nothing without…love?

"Absolutely wonderful. The characters are deftly crafted, with believable problems and strong personalities. Readers will be absorbed by their stories as they search for love, success and happiness."
—*RT Book Reviews* on *PLEASURE SEEKERS*

Available December 2013 wherever books are sold!

www.Harlequin.com

man's attorney had advised them that I was needed for the reading of the will in a week."

She pulled in a deep breath. "Needless to say, I wasn't happy that my parents had kept such a thing from me all those years. I felt whatever feud was between my father and grandfather was between them and should not have included me. I feel such a sense of loss at not having known Herman Bostwick."

Jason nodded. "He could be quite a character at times, trust me."

For some reason she felt she could trust him…and in fact, that she already did. "Tell me about him. I want to get to know the grandfather I never knew."

He smiled. "There's no way I can tell you everything about him in one day."

She returned the smile. "Then come back again for tea so we can talk. That is, if you don't mind."

She held her breath thinking he probably had a lot more things to do with his time than to sip tea with her. A man like him probably had other things on his mind when he was with someone of the opposite sex.

"No, I don't mind. In fact, I'd rather enjoy it."

She inwardly sighed, suddenly feeling giddy, pleased. Jason Westmoreland was the type of man who could make his way into any woman's hot and wild fantasies, and he'd just agreed to indulge her by sharing tea with her occasionally to talk about the grandfather she'd never known.

"Well, I guess I'd better get back to work."

"And what do you do for a living?" she asked, without thinking about it.

"Several of my cousins and I are partners in a horse breeding and horse training venture. The horse that came in second last year at the Preakness was one of ours."

"Congratulations!"

"Thanks."

She then watched as he eased his body off her sofa to stand. And when he handed the empty teacup back to her, she felt her body tingle with the exchange when their hands touched and knew he'd felt it, as well.

"Thanks for the tea, Bella."

"You're welcome and you have an open invitation to come back for more."

He met her gaze, held it for a moment. "And I will."

Chapter 2

On Tuesday of the following week, Bella was in her car headed to town to purchase new appliances for her kitchen. Buying a stove and refrigerator might not be a big deal to some, but for her it would be a first. She was looking forward to it. Besides, it would get her mind off the phone call she'd gotten from her attorney first thing this morning.

Not wanting to think about the phone call, she thought about her friends back home instead. They had teased her that although she would be living out in the boondocks on a ranch, downtown Denver was half an hour away and that's probably where she would spend most of her time—shopping and attending various plays and parties. But she had discovered she liked being away from city life and hadn't missed it at all. She'd grown up in Savannah, right on the ocean. Her

parents' estate had been minutes from downtown and
was the place where lavish parties were always held.

She had talked to her parents earlier today and found
the conversation totally draining. Her father insisted she
put the ranch up for sale and come home immediately.
When the conversation ended she had been more determined than ever to keep as much distance between
her and Savannah as possible.

She had been on the ranch for only three weeks and
already the taste of freedom, to do whatever she wanted
whenever she wanted, was a luxurious right she refused to give up. Although she missed waking up every
morning to the scent of the ocean, she was becoming
used to the crisp mountain air drenched in the rich fra-
grance of dahlias.

Her thoughts then shifted to something else, or more
precisely, someone else. Jason Westmoreland. Good to
his word he had stopped by a few days ago to join her
for tea. They'd had a pleasant conversation, and he'd
told her more about her grandfather. She could tell Jason
and Herman's relationship had been close. Part of her
was glad that Jason had probably helped relieve Herman's loneliness.

Although her father refused to tell her what had happened to drive him away from home, she hoped to find
out on her own. Her grandfather had kept a number of
journals and she intended to start reading them this
week. The only thing she knew from what Kenneth
Bostwick had told her was that Herman's father, Wil-
liam, had remarried when Herman was in his twenties
and married with a son of his own. That woman had
been Kenneth's mother, which was why he was a lot
younger than her father. In fact, her father and Kenneth

had few memories of each other since David Bostwick had left home for college at the age of seventeen.

Jason had also answered questions about ranching and assured her that the man she'd kept on as foreman had worked for her grandfather for a number of years and knew what he was doing. Jason hadn't stayed long but she'd enjoyed his visit.

She found Jason to be kind and soft-spoken and whenever he talked in that reassuring tone she would feel safe, protected and confident that no matter what decisions she made regarding her life and the ranch, it would be okay. He also gave her the impression that she could and would make mistakes and that would be okay, too, as long as she learned from those mistakes and didn't repeat them.

She had gotten to meet some of his family members, namely the women, when they'd all shown up a couple of days ago with housewarming goodies to welcome her to the community. Pamela, Chloe and Lucia had married into the family, and Megan and Bailey were Westmorelands by birth. They told her about Gemma, who was Megan and Bailey's sister, and how she had gotten married earlier that year, moved with her husband to Australia and was expecting their first child.

Pamela and Chloe had brought their babies and being in their presence only reinforced a desire Bella always had of being a mother. She loved children and hoped to marry and have a houseful one day. And when she did, she intended for her relationship with them to be different than the one she had with her own parents.

The women had invited her to dinner at Pamela's home Friday evening so that she could meet the rest of the family. She thought the invitation to dinner was a nice gesture and downright neighborly on their part. They were surprised she had already met Jason because he hadn't mentioned anything to them about meeting her.

She wasn't sure why he hadn't when all the evidence led her to believe the Westmorelands were a close-knit group. But then she figured men tended to keep their activities private and not share them with anyone. He said he would be dropping by for tea again tomorrow and she looked forward to his visit.

It was obvious there was still an intense attraction between them, yet he always acted honorably in her presence. He would sit across from her with his long legs stretched out in front of him and sip tea while she talked. She tried not to dominate the conversation but found he was someone she could talk to and someone who listened to what she had to say. She could see him now sitting there absorbed in whatever she said while displaying a ruggedness she found totally sexy.

And he had shared some things about himself. She knew he was thirty-four and a graduate of the University of Denver. He also shared with her how his parents and uncle and aunt had been killed in a plane crash when he was eighteen, leaving him and his fourteen siblings and cousins without parents. With admiration laced in his voice he had talked about his older brother Dillon and his cousin Ramsey and how the two men had been determined to keep the family together and how they had.

She couldn't help but compare his large family to her smaller one. Although she loved her parents she couldn't recall a time she and her parents had ever been close. While growing up they had relinquished her care to sitters while they jet-setted all over the country. At times she thought they'd forgotten she existed. When she got older she understood her father's obsession with trying to keep up with his young wife. Eventually she saw that obsession diminish when he found other interests and her mother did, as well.

That was why at times the idea of having a baby without a husband appealed to her, although doing such a thing would send her parents into cardiac arrest. But she couldn't concern herself with how her parents would react if she chose to go that route. Moving here was her first stab at emancipation and whatever she decided to do would be her decision. But for a woman who'd never slept with a man to contemplate having a baby from one was a bit much for her to absorb right now.

She pulled into the parking lot of one of the major appliance stores. When she returned home she would meet with her foreman to see how things were going. Jason had said such meetings were necessary and she should be kept updated on what went on at her ranch.

Moments later as she got out of her car she decided another thing she needed to do was buy a truck. *A truck.* She chuckled, thinking her mother would probably gag at the thought of her driving a truck instead of being chauffeured around in a car. But her parents had to realize and accept her life was changing and the luxurious life she used to have was now gone.

As soon as she entered the store a salesperson was right on her heels and it didn't take long to make the purchases she needed because she knew just what she wanted. She'd always thought stainless steel had a way of enhancing the look of a kitchen and figured sometime next year she would give the kitchen a total makeover with granite countertops and new tile flooring, as well. But she would take things one step at a time.

"Bella?"

She didn't have to turn to know who'd said her name. As far as she was concerned, no one could pronounce it in the same rugged yet sexy tone as Jason. Although she had just seen him a few days ago when he'd joined her for tea, there was something about seeing him now that sent sensations coursing through her.

She turned around and there he stood, dressed in a pair of jeans that hugged his sinewy thighs and long, muscular legs, a blue chambray shirt and a lightweight leather jacket that emphasized the broadness of his shoulders.

She smiled up at him. "Jason, what a pleasant surprise."

It was a pleasant surprise for Jason, as well. He had walked into the store and immediately, like radar, he had picked up on her presence, and all it took was following her scent to find her.

"Same here. I had to come into town to pick up a new hot water heater for the bunkhouse," he said, smiling down at her. He shoved his hands into his pockets; otherwise, he would have been tempted to pull her to him and kiss her. Kissing Bella was something he wanted but hadn't gotten around to doing. He didn't want to rush things and didn't want her to think his interest in her had anything to do with wanting to buy Hercules, because that wasn't the case. His interest in her was definitely one of want and need.

"I met the ladies in your family the other day. They came to pay me a visit," she said.

"Did they?"

"Yes."

He'd known they would eventually get around to doing so. The ladies had discussed a visit to welcome her to the community.

"They're all so nice," she said.

"I think they are nice, too. Did you get whatever you needed?" He wondered if she would join him for lunch if he were to ask.

"Yes, my refrigerator and stove will be delivered by the end of the week. I'm so excited."

He couldn't help but laugh. She was genuinely excited. If she got that excited over appliances he could imagine how she would react over jewelry. "Will you be in town for a while, Bella?"

"Yes. I have a meeting with Marvin later this evening."

He raised a brow. "Is everything all right?"

She nodded, smiling. "Yes. I'm just having a weekly meeting like you suggested."

He was glad she had taken his advice. "How about joining me for lunch? There's a place not far from here that serves several nice dishes."

She smiled up at him. "I'd love that."

Jason knew he would love it just as much. He had been thinking about her a lot, especially at night when he'd found it hard to sleep. She was getting to him. No, she had gotten to him. He didn't know of any other woman that he'd been this attracted to. There was something about her. Something that was drawing him to her on a personal level that he could not control. But then a part of him didn't want to control it. Nor did he want to fight it. He wanted to see how far it would go and where it would stop.

"Do you want me to follow you there, Jason?"

No, he wanted her in the same vehicle with him. "We can ride in my truck. Your car will be fine parked here until we return."

"Okay."

As he escorted her toward the exit, she glanced up at him. "What about your hot water heater?"

"I haven't picked it out yet but that's fine since I know the brand I want."

"All right."

Together they walked out of the store toward his truck. It was a beautiful day in May but when he felt her shiver beside him, he figured a beautiful day in Savannah would be a day in the eighties. Here in Denver if they got sixty-something-degree weather in June they would be ecstatic.

He took his jacket off and placed it around her shoulders. She glanced up at him. "You didn't have to do that."

He smiled. "Yes, I did. I don't want you to get cold on me." She was wearing a pair of black slacks and a light blue cardigan sweater. As always she looked ultrafeminine.

And now she was wearing his jacket. They continued walking and when they reached his truck she glanced up and her gaze connected with his and he could feel electricity sparking to life between them. She looked away quickly, as if she'd been embarrassed that their attraction to each other was so obvious.

"Do you want your jacket back now?" she asked softly.

"No, keep it on. I like seeing you in it."

She blushed again and at that moment he got the most ridiculous notion that perhaps this sort of intense attraction between two people was sort of new to Bella. He wouldn't be surprised to discover that she had several innocent bones in her body; enough to shove him in another direction rather quickly. But for some reason he was staying put.

She nibbled on her bottom lip. "Why do you like seeing me in it?"

"Because I do. And because it's mine and you're in it."

He wasn't sure if what he'd said made much sense or if she was confused even more. But what he *was* sure about was that he was determined to find out just how much Bella Bostwick knew about men. And what she didn't know he was going to make it his business to teach her.

Bella was convinced there was nothing more compelling than the feel of wearing the jacket belonging to a man whose very existence represented true masculinity. It permeated her with his warmth, his scent and his aura in every way. She was filled with an urge to get more, to know more and to feel more of Jason Westmoreland. And as she stared at him through the car's window as he pulled out his cell phone to make arrangements for their lunch, she couldn't help but feel the hot rush of blood in her veins while heat churned deep down inside of her.

And there lay the crux of her problem. As beguiling as the feelings taking over her senses, making ingrained curiosity get the best of her, she knew better than to step

beyond the range of her experience. That range didn't
extend beyond what the nuns at the private Catholic
schools she'd attended most of her life had warned her
about. It was a range good girls just didn't go beyond.

Jason was the type of man women dreamed about.
He was what fantasies were made of. She watched him
ease his phone back into the pocket of his jeans, walk
around the front of his truck to get in. He was the type
of man a woman would love to snuggle up with on a
cold Colorado winter night…especially the kind her
parents and uncle had said she would have to endure.
Just the thought of being with him in front of a roaring fire that blazed in a fireplace would be an unadul-
terated fantasy come true for any woman…. And her
greatest fear.

"You're comfortable?" he asked, placing a wide-
brimmed Stetson on his head.

She glanced over at him and she held his gaze for
a moment and then nodded. "Yes, I'm fine. Thanks."

"You're welcome."

He backed up the truck and then they headed out of
the parking lot in silence, but she was fully aware of
his hands that gripped the steering wheel. They were
large and strong hands and she could imagine those
same hands gripping her. That thought made heat seep
into every cell and pore of her body, percolating her
bones and making her surrender to something she'd
never had before.

Her virginal state had never bothered her before and
it didn't really bother her now except the unknown was
making the naughtiness in her come out. It was making her anticipate things she was better off not getting.

"You've gotten quiet on me, Bella," Jason said.

She glanced over at him and again met his gaze thinking, yes she had. But she figured he didn't want to hear her thoughts out loud and certain things she needed to keep to herself.

"Sorry," she said. "I was thinking about Friday," she decided to say.

"Friday?"

"Yes. Pamela invited me to dinner."

"She did?"

Bella heard the surprise in his voice. "Yes. She said it would be the perfect opportunity to meet everyone. It seems all of my neighbors are Westmorelands. You're just the one living the closest to me."

"And what makes you so preoccupied about Friday?"

"Meeting so many of your family members."

He chuckled. "You'll survive."

"Thanks for the vote of confidence." Then she said, "Tell me about them." He had already told her some but she wanted to hear more. And the ladies who came to visit had also shared some of their family history with her. But she wanted to hear his version just to hear the husky sound of his voice, to feel how it would stir across her skin and tantalize several parts of her body.

"You already met the ones who think they run things, namely the women."

She laughed. "They don't?"

"We let them think that way because we're slowly getting outnumbered. Although Gemma is in Australia she still has a lot to say and whenever we take a vote about anything, of course she sides with the women."

She grinned. "You all actually take votes on stuff?"

"Yes, we believe in democracy. The last time we voted we had to decide where Christmas dinner would be held. Usually we hold everything at Dillon's because he has the main family house, but his kitchen was being renovated so we voted to go to Ramsey's."

"All of you have homes?"

"Yes. When we each turned twenty-five we inherited one hundred acres. It was fun naming my own spread."

"Yours is Jason's Place, right?"

He smiled over at her. "That's right."

While he'd been talking her body had responded to the sound of his voice as if it was on a mission to capture each and every nuance. She inhaled deeply and they began chatting again but this time about her family. He'd been honest about his family so she decided to be honest about hers.

"My parents and I aren't all that close and I can't remember a time that we were. They didn't support my move out here," she said and wondered why she'd wanted to share that little detail.

"Is it true that Kenneth is upset you didn't sell the land to Myers Smith?" he asked.

She nodded slowly. "Yes, he told me himself that he thinks I made a mistake in deciding to move here and is looking forward to the day I fail so he can say, 'I told you so.'"

Jason shook his head, finding it hard to believe this was a family member who was hoping for her failure. "Are he and your father close?"

Bella chuckled softly. "They barely know each other. According to Dad he was already in high school when Kenneth was born, although technically Kenneth is my father's half uncle. My father's grandfather married Kenneth's mother who was twenty-five years his junior."

"Do you have any other family, like cousins?"

She shook her head. "Both my parents were the only children. Of course, Uncle Kenneth has a son and daughter but they haven't spoken to me since the reading of the will. Uncle Kenneth only spoke to me when he thought I'd be selling the ranch and livestock to his friend."

By the time he had brought the truck to a stop in front of a huge building, she had to wipe tears of laughter from her eyes when he'd told her about all the trouble the younger Westmorelands had gotten into.

"I just can't imagine your cousin Bailey—who has such an innocent look about her—being such a hell-raiser while growing up."

Jason laughed. "Hey, don't let the innocent act fool you. The cousins Aidan and Adrian are at Harvard and Bane joined the navy. We talked Bailey into hanging around here to attend college so we could keep an eye on her."

He chuckled and then added, "It turned out to be a mistake when she began keeping an eye on us instead."

When he turned off the truck's engine she glanced through the windshield at the building looming in front of them and raised a brow. "This isn't a restaurant."

He glanced over at her. "No, it's not. It's Blue Ridge Management, a company my father and uncle founded over forty years ago. After they were killed Dillon and Ramsey took over. Ramsey eventually left Dillon in charge to become a sheep rancher and Dillon is currently CEO."

He glanced out the windshield to look up at the forty-story building with a pensive look on his face and moments later added, "My brother Riley holds an upper management position here. My cousins Zane and Derringer, as well as myself, worked for the company after college until last year when we decided to join the Montana Westmorelands in the horse training and breeding business."

He smiled. "I guess you can say that nine-to-five gig was never our forte. Like Ramsey, we prefer being outdoors."

She nodded and followed his gaze to the building. "And we're eating lunch here?"

He glanced over at her. "Yes, I have my office that I still use from time to time to conduct business. I called ahead and Dillon's secretary took care of everything for me."

A few moments later they were walking into the massive lobby of Blue Ridge Land Management and the first thing Bella noticed was the huge, beautifully decorated atrium with a waterfall amidst a replica of mountains complete with blooming flowers and other types of foliage. After stopping at the security guard station they caught an elevator up to the executive floor.

"I remember coming up here a lot with my dad," Jason said softly, reflecting on that time. "Whenever he would work on the weekends, he would gather us all together to get us out of Mom's hair for a while. Once we got up to the fortieth floor we knew he would probably find something for us to do."

He chuckled and then added, "But just in case he didn't, I would always travel with a pack of crayons in my back pocket."

Bella smiled. She could just imagine Jason and his six brothers crowded on the elevator with their father. Although he would be working they would have gotten to spend the day with him nonetheless. She couldn't ever recall a time her father had taken her to work with him. In fact, she hadn't known where the Bostwick Firm had been located until she was well into her teens. Her mother never worked outside the home but was mainly the hostess for the numerous parties her parents would give.

It seemed the ride to the top floor took forever. A few times the elevator stopped to let people either on or off. Some of them recognized Jason and he took the time to inquire about the family members he knew, especially their children or grandchildren.

The moment they stepped off the elevator onto the fortieth floor Bella could tell immediately that this was where all the executive offices were located. The furniture was plush and the carpeting thick and luxurious-looking. She was quickly drawn to huge paintings of couples adorning the walls in the center of the lobby. Intrigued, she moved toward them.

"These are my parents," Jason said, coming to stand by her side. "And the couple in the picture over there is my aunt and uncle. My father and Uncle Thomas were close, barely fourteen months apart in age. And my mother and Aunt Susan got along beautifully and were just as close as sisters."

"And they died together," she whispered softly. It was a statement not a question since he had already told her what had happened when they'd all died in a plane crash. Bella studied the portrait of his parents in detail. Jason favored his father a lot but he definitely had his mother's mouth.

"She was beautiful," she said. "So was your aunt

Susan. I take it Ramsey and Chloe's daughter was named after her?"

Jason nodded. "Yes, and she's going to grow up to be a beauty just like her grandmother."

She glanced over at him. "And what was your mother's name?"

"Clarisse. And my father was Adam." Jason then looked down at his watch. "Come on. Our lunch should have arrived by now."

He surprised her when he took her arm and led her toward a bank of offices and stopped at one in particular with his name on it. She felt her heart racing. Although he hadn't called it as such, she considered this lunch a date.

That thought was reinforced when he opened the door to his office and she saw the table set for lunch. The room was spacious and had a downtown view of Denver. The table, completely set with everything, including a bottle of wine, had been placed by the window so they could enjoy the view while they ate.

"Jason, the table and the view are beautiful. Thanks for inviting me to lunch."

"You're welcome," he said, pulling a chair out for her. "There's a huge restaurant downstairs for the employees but I thought we'd eat in here for privacy."

"That's considerate of you."

And done for purely selfish reasons, Jason thought as he took the chair across from her. He liked having her all to himself. Although he wasn't a tea drinker, he had become one and looked forward to visiting her each week to sit down and converse while drinking tea. He enjoyed her company. He glanced over at her and their gazes connected. Their response to each other always amazed him because it seemed so natural and out of control. He couldn't stop the heat flowing all through his body at that precise moment even if he wanted to.

He doubted she knew she had a dazed look in the depths of her dark eyes or that today everything about her looked soft, feminine but not overly so. Just to the right degree to make a man appreciate being a man.

She slowly broke eye contact with him to lift the lid off the platter and when she glanced back up she was smiling brightly. "Spaghetti."

He couldn't help but return her smile. "Yes. I recall you saying the other day how much you enjoyed Italian food." In fact they had talked about a number of things in the hour he had been there.

"I do love Italian food," she said excitedly, taking ahold of her fork.

He poured wine into their glasses and glanced over and caught her slurping up a single strand of spaghetti through a pair of luscious lips. His gut clenched and when she licked her lips he couldn't help but envy the noodle.

When she caught him staring she blushed, embarrassed at being caught doing something so inelegant. "Sorry. I know that showed bad manners but I couldn't resist." She smiled. "It was the one thing I always wanted to do around my parents whenever we ate spaghetti that I couldn't do."

He chuckled. "No harm done. In fact, you can slurp the rest of it if you'd like. It's just you and me."

She grinned. "Thanks, but I better not." He then watched as she took her fork in her hand, preparing to eat the rest of her spaghetti in the classical and cultured way.

"I take it your parents were strong disciplinarians," he said, taking a sip of his wine.

Her smile slowly faded. "They still are, or at least they try to be. Even now they will stop at nothing to get me back to Savannah so they can keep an eye on me. I got a call from my attorney this morning warning me they've possibly found a loophole in the trust fund my grandparents established for me before they died."

He lifted a brow. "What kind of a loophole?"

"One that says I'm supposed to be married after the first year. If that's true I have less than three months," she said in disgust. "I'm sure they're counting on me returning to Savannah to marry Hugh."

He sipped his wine. "Hugh?"

She met his gaze and he could see the troubled look in hers. "Yes, Hugh Pierce. His family comes from Savannah's old money and my parents have made up their minds that Hugh and I are a perfect match."

He watched her shoulders rise and fall after releasing several sighs. Evidently the thought of becoming Mrs. Hugh Pierce bothered her. Hell, the thought bothered him, as well.

In a way he should be overjoyed, elated, that there was a possibility she was moving back to Savannah. That meant her ranch and Hercules would probably be up for sale. And when they were, he would be ready to make her an offer he hoped she wouldn't refuse. He knew he wasn't the only one wanting the land and no telling how many others wanted Hercules, but he was determined that the prized stallion wouldn't fall into anyone's hands but his.

And yet, he wasn't overjoyed or elated at the thought that she would return to Savannah.

He got the impression her parents were controlling people, or at least they tried to be. He began eating, wondering why her parents wanted to shove this Hugh Pierce down her throat when she evidently wasn't feeling the guy. Would they coerce her to marry someone just because the man came from "old money"?

He forced the thought to the back of his mind, thinking who she ended up marrying was no concern of his. But making sure his name headed the list as a potential buyer for her ranch and livestock was. He glanced over at her. "When will you know what you'll have to do?"

She looked up after taking a sip of her wine. "I'm not sure. I have a good attorney, but I have to admit my parents' attorney is more experienced in such matters. In other words, he's crafty as sin. I'm sure when my grandparents drew up my trust they thought they were looking out for my future because in their social circles, ideally, a young woman married by her twenty-sixth birthday. For her to attend college was just a formality since she was expected to marry a man who had the means to take care of her."

"And your parents have no qualms in forcing you to marry?"

"No, not one iota," she said without pause. "They don't truly care about my happiness. All they care about is that they would be proving once again they control my life and always will."

He heard the trembling in her voice and when she looked down as to study her silverware, he knew her composure was being threatened. At that moment, something inside of him wanted to get up, pull her into his arms and tell her things would be all right. But he couldn't rightly say that. He had no way of knowing they would be for her, given the situation she was in. Actually it was her problem not his. Still another part of him couldn't help regretting that her misfortune could end up being his golden opportunity.

"I thought I'd finally gotten free of my parents' watchful eyes at college, only to discover they had certain people in place, school officials and professors, keeping tabs on me and reporting to them on my behavior," she said, interrupting his thoughts.

"And I thought, I truly believed, the money I'm getting from my trust fund and inheriting the ranch were my way of living my life the way I want and an end to being under my parents' control. I was going to exert my freedom for the first time in my life."

She paused briefly. "Jason. I really love it here. I've been able to live the way I want, do the things I want. It's a freedom I've never had and I don't want to give it up."

They sat staring at each other for what seemed like several mind-numbing moments and then Jason spoke. "Then don't give it up. Fight them for what you want."

Her shoulders slumped again. "Although I plan to try, it's easier said than done. My father is a well-known and powerful man in Savannah and a lot of the judges are his personal friends. For anyone to even try something as archaic as forcing someone to marry is ludicrous. But my parents will do it with their friends' help if it brings me to heel."

Once again Bella fell silent for a moment. "When I received word about Herman and confronted my father as to why he never told me about his life here in Denver, he wouldn't tell me, but I've been reading my grandfather's journals. He claims my father hated living here while growing up. His mother had visited this area from Savannah, met Herman and fell in love and never went back East. Her family disowned her for it. But after college my father moved to Savannah and sought out his maternal grandparents and they were willing to accept him in their good graces but only if he never reminded them of what they saw as their daughter's betrayal, so he didn't."

She then straightened her shoulders and forced a smile to her lips. "Let's change the subject," she suggested. "Thinking about my woes is rather depressing and you've made lunch too nice for me to be depressed about anything."

They enjoyed the rest of their meal conversing about other things. He told her about his horse breeding business and about how he and the Atlanta Westmorelands had discovered they were related through his great-grandfather Raphel Westmoreland.

"Was your grandfather really married to all those women?" she asked after he told her the tale of how Raphel had become a black sheep in the family after running off in the early nineteen hundreds with the preacher's wife and all the other wives he supposedly collected along the way.

He took another sip of wine. "That's what everyone is trying to find out. We need to know if there are any more Westmorelands out there. Megan is hiring a private detective to help solve the puzzle about Raphel's wives. We've eliminated two and now we have two more to check out."

When they finished the main course Jason used his cell phone to call downstairs to say they were ready for dessert. Moments later banana pudding was delivered to them. Bella thought the dessert was simply delicious. She usually didn't eat a lot of sweets but once she'd taken a bite she couldn't help but finish the whole thing.

A short while later, after they'd devoured the dessert with coffee, Jason checked his watch. "We're right on schedule. I'll take you back in time to get your car so you can make your meeting with Marvin."

Jason stood, rounded the table and reached for her hand. The instant they touched it seemed a rush of heated sensations tore through the both of them at the same time. It was absorbed in their bones, tangled their flesh and he all but shuddered under the impact. The alluring scent of her filled his nostrils and his breath was freed on a ragged sigh.

Some part of his brain told him to take a step back and put distance between them. But then another part told him he was facing the inevitable. There had been this blazing attraction, this tantalizing degree of lust between them from the beginning. For him it had been since the moment he had seen her when she'd entered the ballroom with Kenneth Bostwick. He had known then he wanted her.

They stared at each other and for a second he thought she would avert her gaze from his but she didn't. She couldn't resist him any more than he could resist her and they both knew it, which was probably why, when he took a step closer and began lowering his head, she went on tiptoes and lifted her mouth to meet his.

The moment their lips connected, a low, guttural sound rumbled from deep in his throat and he deepened the kiss the moment she wrapped her arms around his neck. His tongue slid easily into her mouth, exploring one side and then another, as well as all the areas in

meeting this afternoon. He, Zane and Derringer
conference call with their partners in Montana in
than an hour. He hadn't forgotten about the meet-
out spending time with Bella had been something
adn't been willing to shorten. Now with the taste of
still lingering in his mouth, he was glad he hadn't.
He shook his head, still finding it hard to believe just
well they had connected with that kiss, which made
wonder how they would connect in other ways and
ces…like in the bedroom.

The thought of her naked, thighs opened while he en-
ed her, was something he couldn't get out of his mind.
was burning for her and although he'd like to think
was only a physical attraction he wasn't sure that was
case. But then if it wasn't the case, what was it?
He didn't get a chance to think any further because
that moment his cell phone rang. He pulled it off his
t and saw it was his cousin Derringer. The newlywed
ust a little over a month had been the last person he'd
ught would fall in love with any woman. But he had
Jason could see why. Lucia was as precious as they
e and everyone thought she was a great addition to
Westmoreland family.

"Yes, Derringer?"

"Hey, man, where are you? Did you forget about to-
's meeting?"

ason couldn't help but smile as he remembered how
called to ask Derringer the same question since he'd
en married. It seemed these days it was hard for
cousin to tear himself away from his wife at times.

No, I didn't forget and I'm less than thirty min-
away."

between before tangling with her own, mating deeply,
and when she reciprocated the move sent a jolt of desire all through his bones.

And then it was on.

Holy crap. Hunger the likes of he'd never felt before
infiltrated his mind. He felt a sexual connection with
her that he'd never felt with any woman before. As his
tongue continued to slide against hers, parts of him felt
primed and ready to explode at any moment. Never had
he encountered such overwhelming passion, such blatant desire and raw primal need.

His mouth was doing a good job tasting her, but the
rest of him wanted to feel her, draw her closer into his
arms. On instinct he felt her lean into him, plastering
their bodies from breast to knee, and as Jason deepened
the kiss even more, he groaned, wondering if he would
never get enough of her.

Bella was feeling the same way about Jason. No man
had ever held her this close, taken her mouth this passionately and made sensations she'd never felt before
rush through her quicker than the speed of light.

And she felt him, his erection, rigid and throbbing,
against her middle, pressing hard at the juncture of her
thighs, making her feel sensations there—right there—
she hadn't felt before. It was doing more than just tingling. She was left aching in that very spot. She felt
like a mass of kerosene and he was a torch set to ignite
her, making her explode into flames. He was all solid
muscle pressing against her and she wanted it all. She
wanted him. She wasn't sure what wanting him entailed
but she knew he was the only man who made her feel
this way. He was the only man she wanted to make her
feel this way.

When at last he drew his mouth away from her, his face remained close. Acting by instinct, she took her tongue and licked around his lips from corner to corner, not ready to relinquish the taste of him. When a guttural sound emitted from his throat, need rammed through her and when she tilted her lips toward his, he took her mouth once again. He eased his tongue into her mouth like it had every right to be there and at the moment she was of the conclusion that it did.

He slowly broke off the kiss and stared into her face for a long moment before caressing his thumb across her lips then running his fingers through the curls on her head.

"I guess we better leave now so you won't miss your meeting," he said in a deep, husky tone.

Unable to utter a single word she merely nodded.

And when he took her hand and entwined her fingers in his, the sensations she'd felt earlier were still strong, nearly overpowering, but she was determined to fight it this time. And every time after that. She could not become involved with anyone, especially someone like Jason. And especially not now.

She had enough on her plate in dealing with the ranch and her parents. She had to keep her head on straight and not get caught up in the desires of the flesh. She didn't need a lover; she needed a game plan.

And as Jason led her out of his office, she tried sorting out all the emotions she was feeling. She'd just been kissed senseless and now she was trying to convince herself that no matter what, it couldn't happen again.

Only problem with that was her mind was declaring one thing and her body was claiming another.

Chapter 3

He was in serious trouble.

Jason rubbed his hand across his face a[s] Bella rush off toward her car. He made sure [she'd got-]ten inside and driven off before pulling ou[t of the park-]ing lot behind her. The Westmoreland men [were known] to have high testosterone levels but his ha[d never made] him pause until today, and only with Bel[la.]

He wouldn't waste his time wonderin[g why he] kissed her since he knew the reason. She [was] femininity at its finest, temptation not t[oo many men] could resist and a lustful shot in any man'[s body. He'd] gotten a sampling of all three. And it hadn['t been a mere] taste but a whole whopping one. Now th[at he knew her] flavor he wanted to savor it again and ag[ain.]

When he brought his truck to a stop a[t the light,] he checked his watch. Bella wasn't the [only one with a min-]ute

"Okay. And I hear your lady is joining the family for dinner on Friday night."

He considered that for a moment. Had anyone else made that comment he probably would have gotten irritated by it, but Derringer was Derringer and the two people who knew more than anyone that he didn't have a "lady" were his cousins Derringer and Zane. Knowing that was the case he figured Derringer was fishing for information.

"I don't have a *lady* and you very well know it, Derringer."

"Do I? If that's the case when did you become a tea sipper?"

He laughed as his gaze held steady to the road. "Ah, I see our precious Bailey has been talking."

"Who else? Bella might have mentioned it to the ladies when they went visiting, but of course it's Bailey who's decided you have the hots for the Southern belle. And those were Bailey's words not mine."

"Thanks for clarifying that for me." The hots weren't all he had for Bella Bostwick. Blood was pumping fast and furious in his veins at the thought of the kiss they had shared.

"No problem. So level with me, Jason. What's going on with you and the Southern Bella?"

Jason smiled. The Southern Bella fit her. But then so did the Sensuous Bella. The Sexy Bella. The Sumptuous Bella. "And what makes you think something is going on?"

"I know you."

True. Derringer and Zane knew him better than any of the other Westmorelands because they'd always been close, thick as thieves while growing up. "I admit I'm attracted to her but what man wouldn't be? Otherwise, it's not that serious."

"You sure?"

Jason's hand tightened on his steering wheel—that was the crux of his problem. When it came to Bella the only thing he was sure about was that he wanted her in a way he'd never wanted any other woman. When they'd kissed she kissed him back in a way that had his body heating up just thinking how her tongue had mated with his. He had loved the way her silken curls had felt flowing through his fingers and how perfect their bodies fit together.

He was probably treading on dangerous ground but for reasons he didn't quite understand, he couldn't admit to being sure right now. So instead of outright lying he decided to plead the fifth by saying, "I'll get back to you on that."

Irritation spread all through his gut at the thought that he hadn't given Derringer an answer mainly because he couldn't. And for a man who'd always been decisive when it came to a woman's place in his heart, he could just imagine what Derringer was thinking.

He was trying not to think the same thing himself. Hell, he'd only set out to be a good neighbor and then realized how much he enjoyed her company. And then there had been the attraction he hadn't been able to overlook.

"I'll see you when you get here, Jason. Have a safe drive in," Derringer said without further comment about Bella.

"Will do."

* * *

Bella stood staring out her bedroom window at the mountains. Her meeting with Marvin had been informative as well as a little overwhelming. But she had been able to follow everything the man had said. Heading the list was Hercules. The horse was restless, agitated and it seemed when Hercules wasn't in a good mood everybody knew it.

According to Marvin, Hercules hadn't been ridden in a while mainly because very few men would go near him. The only man capable of handling Hercules was Jason. The same Jason she had decided to avoid from now on. She recognized danger when she saw it and in this case it was danger she could feel. Physically.

Even now she could remember Jason mesmerizing her with his smile, seducing her with his kiss and making her groan over and over again. And there was the way his gaze had scanned over her body while in the elevator as they left his office after lunch, or the hot, lusty look he gave her when she got out of the truck at the appliance store. That look had her rushing off as if a pack of pit bulls were nipping at her heels.

And last but not least were Jason's hands on her. Those big, strong hands had touched her in places that had made her pause for breath, had made sensations overtake her and had made her put her guard up in a way she didn't feel safe in letting down.

Of course she'd known they were attracted to each other from the first, but she hadn't expected that attraction to become so volatile and explosive. And she'd experienced all that from just one kiss. Heaven help them if they went beyond kissing.

If he continued to come around, if he continued to

spend time with her in any way, they would be tempted to go beyond that. Today proved she was virtually putty in his hands and she didn't want to think about what that could mean if it continued. She liked it but then she was threatened by it. She was just getting to feel free and the last thing she wanted to be was held in bondage by anything, especially by emotions she couldn't quite understand. She wasn't ready to become the other part of anyone. Jeez, she was just finding herself, enjoying her newfound independence. She didn't want to give it up before experiencing it fully.

At that moment her cell phone went off and she rolled her eyes when she saw the caller was her mother. She pulled in a deep breath before saying, "Yes, Mother?"

"I'm sure you've heard from your attorney about that little stipulation we found out about in your trust fund. My mother was definitely smart to think of it."

Bella frowned. "Yes, I heard all about it." Of course Melissa Bostwick would take the time to call and gloat. And of course she wanted to make it seem that they had discovered the stipulation by accident when the truth was that they'd probably hired a team of attorneys to look for anything in the trust fund they could use against her to keep her in line. If they had their way she would be dependent on them for life.

"Good. Your father and I expect you to stop this nonsense immediately and come home."

"Sorry, Mom, but I am home."

"No, you're not, and if you continue with this foolishness you will be sorry. With no money coming in, what on earth will you do?"

"Get a job I guess."

"Don't be ridiculous."

"I'm being serious. Sorry you can't tell the difference."

There was a pause and then her mother asked, "Why do you always want to have your way?"

"Because it's my way to have. I'm twenty-five for heaven's sake. You and Dad need to let me live my own life."

"We will but not there, and Hugh's been asking about you."

"That's nice. Is there anything else you wanted, Mom?"

"For you to stop being difficult."

"If wanting to live my life the way I want is being difficult then get prepared for more difficult days ahead. Goodbye, Mom."

Out of respect Bella didn't hang up the phone until she heard her mother's click. And when she did she clicked off and shook her head. Her parents were so sure they had her where they wanted her.

And that possibility bothered her more than anything.

Jason glanced around the room. All of his male cousins had Bella to the side conversing away with her. No doubt they were as fascinated by her intellect as well as her beauty. And things had been that way since she'd arrived. More than once he'd sent Zane dirty looks that basically told his cousin to back off. Why he'd done such a thing he wasn't sure. He and Bella weren't an item or anything of the sort.

In fact, to his way of thinking, she was acting rather coolly toward him. Although she was polite enough, no one would have thought he had devoured her mouth the

way he had three days ago in his office. And maybe
that was the reason she was acting this way. No one was
supposed to know. It was their secret. Right?

Wrong.

He knew his family well, a lot better than she did.
Their acting like cordial acquaintances only made them
suspect. His brother Riley had already voiced his suspicions. "Trouble in paradise with the Southern Bella?"

He'd frowned and had been tempted to tell Riley
there was no trouble in paradise because he and Bella
didn't have that kind of relationship. They had kissed
only once for heaven's sake. Twice, if you were to take
into consideration that he'd kissed her a second time
that day before leaving his office.

So, okay, they had kissed twice. No big deal. He drew
in a deep breath wondering if it wasn't a big deal, why
was he making it one? Why had he come early and anticipated her arrival like a kid waiting for Christmas
to get here?

Everyone who knew him, especially his family, was
well aware that he dated when it suited him and his reputation with women was nothing like Derringer's had
been or Zane's was. It didn't come close. The thought
of meeting someone and getting married and having a
family was something at the bottom of his list, but at
least he didn't mind claiming it was on his list. That
was something some of his other single brothers and
cousins refused to do.

"You're rather quiet tonight, Jason."

He glanced over and saw his cousin Bailey had come
to stand beside him and knew why she was there. She
wanted to not just pick his brain but to dissect his mind.
"I'm no quieter than usual, Bail."

She tilted her head and looked up at him. "Hmm, I think you are. Does Bella have anything to do with it?"

He took a sip of his wine. "And what makes you think that?"

She shrugged. "Because you keep glancing over there at her when you think no one is looking."

"That's not true."

She smiled. "Yes, it is. You probably don't realize you're doing it."

He frowned. Was that true? Had he been that obvious whenever he'd glanced over at Bella? Of course someone like Bailey—who made it her business to keep up with everything and everyone, or tried to—would notice such a thing.

"I thought we were just having dinner," he decided to say. "I didn't know it was an all-out dinner party."

Bailey grinned. "I remember the first time Ramsey brought Chloe to introduce her to the family. He'd thought the same thing."

Nodding, he remembered that time. "Only difference in that is that Ramsey *brought* Chloe. I didn't bring Bella nor did I invite her."

"Are you saying you wished she wasn't here?"

He hated when Bailey tried putting words into his mouth. And speaking of mouth…he glanced across the room to Bella and watched hers move and couldn't help remembering all he'd done to that mouth when he'd kissed her.

"Jason?"

He then recalled what Bailey had asked him and figured until he gave her an answer she wasn't going anywhere. "No, that's not what I'm saying and you darn well know it. I don't have a problem with Bella being here. I think it's important for her to get to know her neighbors."

But did his brothers and cousins have to stay in her face, hang on to her every word and check her out so thoroughly? He knew everyone who hadn't officially met her had been taken with her the moment Dillon had opened the door for her. She had walked in with a grace-fulness and pristine elegance that made every male in the house appreciate not only her beauty but her poise, refinement and charming personality.

Her outfit, an electric-blue wrap dress with a flatter-ing scoop neckline and a hem line that hit just above her knees greatly emphasized her small waist, firm breasts and shapely legs, and looked stylishly perfect on her. He would admit that his heart had slammed hard in his chest the moment she'd entered the room.

"Well, dinner is about to be served. You better hope you get a seat close to her. It won't take much for the others to boot you out of the way." She then walked off.

He glanced back over to where Bella was standing and thought that no one would boot him out of the way when it came to Bella. They better not even try.

Bella smiled at something Zane had said while trying not to glance across the room at Jason. He had spoken to her when she'd first arrived but since then had pretty much kept his distance, preferring to let his brothers and cousins keep her company.

You would never know they had been two people who'd almost demolished the mouths right off their faces a few days ago. But then maybe that was the point. Maybe he didn't want anyone to know. Come to think of it, she'd never asked if he even had a girlfriend.

For all she knew he might have one. Just because he'd dropped by for tea didn't mean anything other than he was neighborly. And she had to remember that he had never gotten out of the way with her.

Until that day in his office.

What had made him want to kiss her? There had been this intense chemistry between them from the first, but neither of them had acted on it until that day. Had stepping over those boundaries taken their relationship to a place where it couldn't recover? She truly hoped not. He was a nice person, a charmer if ever there was one. And although she'd decided that distance between them was probably for the best right now, she did want him to remain her friend.

"Pam's getting everyone's attention for dinner," Dillon said as he approached the group. "Let me escort you to the dining room," he offered and tucked Bella's arm beneath his.

She smiled at him. The one thing she noticed was that all the Westmoreland men resembled in some way. "Thank you."

She glanced over at Jason. Their gazes met and she felt it, the same sensations she felt whenever he was near her. That deep stirring in the pit of her stomach had her trying to catch her breath.

"You okay?" Dillon asked her.

She glanced up and saw concern in his deep dark eyes. He'd followed her gaze and noted it had lit on his brother. "Yes, I'm fine."

She just hoped what she'd said was true.

Jason wasn't surprised to discover he had been placed beside Bella at the dinner table. The women in the family tended to be matchmakers when they set their minds to it, which he could overlook considering three of them were all happily married themselves. The other two, Megan and Bailey, were in it for the ride.

He dipped his head, lower than he'd planned, to ask Bella if she was enjoying herself, and when she turned her head to look at him their lips nearly touched. He came close to ignoring everyone sitting at the table and giving in to the temptation to kiss her.

She must have read his mind and a light blush spread into her cheeks. He swallowed, pulled his lips back. "Are you having a good time?"

"Yes. And I appreciate your family for inviting me."

"And I'm sure they enjoy having you here," he said. Had she expected him to invite her? He shrugged off the thought as wrong. There had been no reason for him to invite her to meet his family. Come to think of it, he had never invited a woman home for dinner. Not even Emma Phillips and they'd dated close to a year before she tried giving him an ultimatum.

The meal went off without a hitch with various conversations swirling around the table. Megan informed everyone that the private investigator she had hired to dig deeper into their great-grandfather Raphel's past was Rico Claiborne, who just happened to be the brother of Jessica and Savannah, who were married to their cousins Chase and Durango. Rico, whom Megan hadn't yet met, was flying into Denver at some point in time to go over the information he'd collected on what was supposed to be Raphel's third wife.

By the time dinner was over and conversations wound down it was close to ten o'clock. Someone suggested given the lateness of the hour that Bella be escorted back home. Several of his cousins spoke up to do the honor and Jason figured he needed to end the nonsense once and for all and said in a voice that brooked no argument, "I'll make sure Bella gets home."

He noticed that all conversation automatically ceased and no one questioned his announcement. "Ready to go?" he asked Bella softly.

"Yes."

She thanked everyone and openly gave his cousins and brothers hugs. It wasn't hard to tell that they all liked her and had enjoyed her visit. After telling everyone good-night he followed her out the door.

Bella glanced out her rearview mirror and saw Jason was following her at a safe distance. She laughed, thinking when it came to Jason there wasn't a safe zone. Just knowing he was anywhere within her area was enough to rattle her. Even sitting beside him at dinner had been a challenge for her, but thanks to the rest of his family who kept lively conversation going on, she was able to endure his presence and the sexual tension she'd felt. Each time he talked to her and she looked into his face and focused on his mouth, she would remember that same mouth mating with hers.

A sigh of relief escaped her lips when they pulled into her yard. Figuring it would be dark when she returned she had left lights burning outside and her yard was practically glowing. She parked her car and was opening the door to get out when she saw Jason already standing there beside it. Her breathing quickened and panic set in. "You don't need to walk me to the door, Jason," she said quickly.

"I want to," he said simply.

Annoyance flashed in her eyes when she recalled how he'd gone out of his way most of the evening to avoid her. "Why would you?"

He gave her a look. "Why wouldn't I?" Instead of waiting for her to respond he took her hand in his and headed toward her front door.

Fine! she thought, fuming inside and dismissing the temptation to pull her hand away from his. Because her foreman lived on the ranch, she knew the last thing she needed to do was make a scene with Jason outside under the bright lights. He stood back while she unlocked the door and she had a feeling he intended to make sure she was safely inside before leaving. She was right when he followed her inside.

When he closed the door behind them she placed her hands on her hips and opened her mouth to say what was on her mind, but he beat her to the punch. "Was I out of line when I kissed you that day, Bella?"

The softly spoken question gave her pause and she dropped her hands to her sides. No, he hadn't been out of line mainly because she'd wanted the kiss. She had wanted to feel his mouth on hers, his tongue tangling with her own. And if she was downright truthful about it, she would admit to wanting his hands on her, all over her, touching her in ways no man had touched her before.

He was waiting for her response.

"No, you weren't out of line."

"Then why the coldness today?"

She tilted her chin. "I can be asking you the same thing, Jason. You weren't Mr. Congeniality yourself tonight."

He didn't say anything for a moment but she could

between before tangling with her own, mating deeply, and when she reciprocated the move sent a jolt of desire all through his bones.

And then it was on.

Holy crap. Hunger the likes of he'd never felt before infiltrated his mind. He felt a sexual connection with her that he'd never felt with any woman before. As his tongue continued to slide against hers, parts of him felt primed and ready to explode at any moment. Never had he encountered such overwhelming passion, such blatant desire and raw primal need.

His mouth was doing a good job tasting her, but the rest of him wanted to feel her, draw her closer into his arms. On instinct he felt her lean into him, plastering their bodies from breast to knee, and as Jason deepened the kiss even more, he groaned, wondering if he would never get enough of her.

Bella was feeling the same way about Jason. No man had ever held her this close, taken her mouth this passionately and made sensations she'd never felt before rush through her quicker than the speed of light.

And she felt him, his erection, rigid and throbbing, against her middle, pressing hard at the juncture of her thighs, making her feel sensations there—right there—she hadn't felt before. It was doing more than just tingling. She was left aching in that very spot. She felt like a mass of kerosene and he was a torch set to ignite her, making her explode into flames. He was all solid muscle pressing against her and she wanted it all. She wanted him. She wasn't sure what wanting him entailed but she knew he was the only man who made her feel this way. He was the only man she wanted to make her feel this way.

When at last he drew his mouth away from her, his face remained close. Acting by instinct, she took her tongue and licked around his lips from corner to corner, not ready to relinquish the taste of him. When a guttural sound emitted from his throat, need rammed through her and when she tilted her lips toward his, he took her mouth once again. He eased his tongue into her mouth like it had every right to be there and at the moment she was of the conclusion that it did.

He slowly broke off the kiss and stared into her face for a long moment before caressing his thumb across her lips then running his fingers through the curls on her head.

"I guess we better leave now so you won't miss your meeting," he said in a deep, husky tone.

Unable to utter a single word she merely nodded.

And when he took her hand and entwined her fingers in his, the sensations she'd felt earlier were still strong, nearly overpowering, but she was determined to fight it this time. And every time after that. She could not become involved with anyone, especially someone like Jason. And especially not now.

She had enough on her plate in dealing with the ranch and her parents. She had to keep her head on straight and not get caught up in the desires of the flesh. She didn't need a lover; she needed a game plan.

And as Jason led her out of his office, she tried sorting out all the emotions she was feeling. She'd just been kissed senseless and now she was trying to convince herself that no matter what, it couldn't happen again.

Only problem with that was her mind was declaring one thing and her body was claiming another.

Chapter 3

He was in serious trouble.

Jason rubbed his hand across his face as he watched Bella rush off toward her car. He made sure she had gotten inside and driven off before pulling out of the parking lot behind her. The Westmoreland men were known to have high testosterone levels but his had never given him pause until today, and only with Bella Bostwick.

He wouldn't waste his time wondering why he had kissed her since he knew the reason. She was walking femininity at its finest, temptation not too many men could resist and a lustful shot in any man's arms. He had gotten a sampling of all three. And it hadn't been a little taste but a whole whopping one. Now that he knew her flavor he wanted to savor it again and again and again.

When he brought his truck to a stop at a traffic light he checked his watch. Bella wasn't the only one who had a meeting this afternoon. He, Zane and Derringer had a conference call with their partners in Montana in less than an hour. He hadn't forgotten about the meeting but spending time with Bella had been something he hadn't been willing to shorten. Now with the taste of her still lingering in his mouth, he was glad he hadn't.

He shook his head, still finding it hard to believe just how well they had connected with that kiss, which made him wonder how they would connect in other ways and places…like in the bedroom.

The thought of her naked, thighs opened while he entered her, was something he couldn't get out of his mind. He was burning for her and although he'd like to think it was only a physical attraction he wasn't sure that was the case. But then if it wasn't the case, what was it?

He didn't get a chance to think any further because at that moment his cell phone rang. He pulled it off his belt and saw it was his cousin Derringer. The newlywed of just a little over a month had been the last person he'd thought would fall in love with any woman. But he had and Jason could see why. Lucia was as precious as they came and everyone thought she was a great addition to the Westmoreland family.

"Yes, Derringer?"

"Hey, man, where are you? Did you forget about today's meeting?"

Jason couldn't help but smile as he remembered how he'd called to ask Derringer the same question since he'd gotten married. It seemed these days it was hard for his cousin to tear himself away from his wife at times.

"No, I didn't forget and I'm less than thirty minutes away."

For all she knew he might have one. Just because he'd dropped by for tea didn't mean anything other than he was neighborly. And she had to remember that he had never gotten out of the way with her.

Until that day in his office.

What had made him want to kiss her? There had been this intense chemistry between them from the first, but neither of them had acted on it until that day. Had stepping over those boundaries taken their relationship to a place where it couldn't recover? She truly hoped not. He was a nice person, a charmer if ever there was one. And although she'd decided that distance between them was probably for the best right now, she did want him to remain her friend.

"Pam's getting everyone's attention for dinner," Dillon said as he approached the group. "Let me escort you to the dining room," he offered and tucked Bella's arm beneath his.

She smiled at him. The one thing she noticed was that all the Westmoreland men resembled in some way. "Thank you."

She glanced over at Jason. Their gazes met and she felt it, the same sensations she felt whenever he was near her. That deep stirring in the pit of her stomach had her trying to catch her breath.

"You okay?" Dillon asked her.

She glanced up and saw concern in his deep dark eyes. He'd followed her gaze and noted it had lit on his brother. "Yes, I'm fine."

She just hoped what she'd said was true.

Jason wasn't surprised to discover he had been placed beside Bella at the dinner table. The women in the family tended to be matchmakers when they set their minds to it, which he could overlook considering three of them were all happily married themselves. The other two, Megan and Bailey, were in it for the ride.

He dipped his head, lower than he'd planned, to ask Bella if she was enjoying herself, and when she turned her head to look at him their lips nearly touched. He came close to ignoring everyone sitting at the table and giving in to the temptation to kiss her.

She must have read his mind and a light blush spread into her cheeks. He swallowed, pulled his lips back. "Are you having a good time?"

"Yes. And I appreciate your family for inviting me."

"And I'm sure they enjoy having you here," he said. Had she expected him to invite her? He shrugged off the thought as wrong. There had been no reason for him to invite her to meet his family. Come to think of it, he had never invited a woman home for dinner. Not even Emma Phillips and they'd dated close to a year before she tried giving him an ultimatum.

The meal went off without a hitch with various conversations swirling around the table. Megan informed everyone that the private investigator she had hired to dig deeper into their great-grandfather Raphel's past was Rico Claiborne, who just happened to be the brother of Jessica and Savannah, who were married to their cousins Chase and Durango. Rico, whom Megan hadn't yet met, was flying into Denver at some point in time to go over the information he'd collected on what was supposed to be Raphel's third wife.

By the time dinner was over and conversations wound down it was close to ten o'clock. Someone suggested given the lateness of the hour that Bella be estell her comment had hit a mark with him. "No, I wasn't," he admitted.

Although she had made the accusation she was stunned by the admission. It had caught her off guard. "Why?" She knew the reason for her distance but was curious to know the reason for his.

"Ladies first."

"Fine," she said, placing her purse on the table. "We might as well get this little talk over with. Would you like something to drink?"

"Yes," he said, rubbing his hand down his face in frustration. "A cup of tea would be nice."

She glanced up at him, surprised by his choice. There was no need to mention since that first day when he'd shown up she had picked up a couple bottles of beer and wine at the store to give him more of a choice. Since tea was also her choice she said, "All right, I'll be back in a moment." She then swept from the room.

Jason watched her leave and felt more frustrated than ever. She was right, they needed to talk. He shook his head. When had things between them gotten so complicated? Had it all started with that kiss? A kiss that was destined to happen sooner or later given the intense attraction between them?

He sighed deeply, wondering how he would explain his coldness to her tonight. How could he tell her his behavior had been put in place as a safety mechanism stemming from the fact that he wanted her more than he'd ever wanted any other woman? And how could he explain that the thought of any woman getting under his skin to the extent she had scared the hell out of him?

Chances were if he hadn't run into her at the appliance store he would have sought out her company anyway. More than likely he would have dropped by later for tea, although he had tried limiting his visits for fear of wearing out his welcome.

Her phone rang and he wondered who would be calling her at this late hour but knew it was none of his business when she picked it up on the second rang. He'd never gotten around to asking if she had a boyfriend or not and assumed she didn't.

Moments later Jason glanced toward the kitchen door when he heard a loud noise, the sound of something crashing on her floor. He quickly moved toward the kitchen to see what had happened and to make sure she was all right.

He frowned when he entered the kitchen and saw Bella stooping to pick up the tray she'd dropped along with two broken cups.

He quickly moved forward. "Are you okay, Bella?" he asked.

She didn't look at him as she continued to pick up broken pieces of the teacups. "I'm fine. I accidentally dropped it."

He bent down toward her. "That's fine. At least you didn't have tea in the cups. You could have burned yourself. I can help you get that up."

She turned to look up at him. "I can do this, Jason. I don't need your help."

He met her gaze and would have taken her stinging words to heart if he hadn't seen the redness of her eyes. "What's wrong?"

Instead of answering she shook her head and averted her gaze, refusing to look at him any longer. Quickly recovering his composure at seeing her so upset, he was pushed into action and wrapped his arms around her waist and assisted her up off the floor.

He stood facing her and drew in a deep, calming breath before saying, "I want to know what's wrong, Bella."

She drew in her own deep breath. "That was my father. He called to gloat."

Jason frowned. "About what?"

He watched her when she swallowed deeply. "He and his attorney were able to get an injunction against my trust fund and wanted me to know my monthly funds are on hold."

He heard the tremor in her voice. "But I thought you had three months before your twenty-sixth birthday."

"I do, but some judge—probably a close friend of Dad's—felt my parents had grounds to place a hold on my money. They don't believe I'll marry before the trust fund's deadline date."

She frowned. "I need my money, Jason. I was counting on the income to pay my men as well as to pay for all the work I've ordered to be done around here. There were a number of things my grandfather hadn't taken care of around here that need to be done, like repairing the roof on the barn. My parents are deliberately placing me in a bind and they know it."

Jason nodded. He had started noticing a number of things Herman had begun overlooking that had needed to be done. He then shook his head. He'd heard of controlling parents but felt hers were ridiculous.

"Certainly there is something your attorney can do."

She drew in a deep breath. "He sent me a text moments ago and said there's nothing he can do now that a judge has gotten involved. And even if there were, it would take time and my parents know it. It is time they figure I don't have, which will work in their favor. True, I got this ranch free and clear but it takes money to keep it operational."

He shook his head. "And all because you won't get married?"

"Yes. They believe I was raised and groomed to be the wife of someone like Hugh who already has standing in Savannah's upper-class society."

Jason didn't say anything for a few moments. "Does your trust fund specifically state who you're to marry?"

"No, it just says I have to be a married woman. I guess my grandparents figured in their way of thinking that I would automatically marry someone they would consider my equal and not just anyone."

An idea suddenly slammed into Jason's head. It was a crazy one…but it would serve a purpose in the long run. In the end, she would get what she wanted and he would get what he wanted.

He reached out and took her hand in his, entwined their fingers and tried ignoring the sensations touching her caused. "Let's sit down for a moment. I might have an idea."

Bella allowed him to lead her over to the kitchen table and she sat down with her hands on top of the table and glanced up at him expectantly.

"Promise you'll keep an open mind when you hear my proposal."

"All right, I promise."

He paused a moment and then said, "I think you should do what your parents want and get married."

"What!"

"Think about it, Bella. You can marry anyone to keep your trust fund intact."

He could tell she was even more confused. "I don't understand, Jason. I'm not seriously involved with anyone, so who am I supposed to marry?"

"Me."

Chapter 4

Bella's jaw dropped open. "You?"

"Yes."

She stared at Jason for a long moment and then she adamantly shook her head.

"Why would you agree to marry me?" she asked, confused.

"Think about it, Bella. It will be a win-win situation for the both of us. Marriage to me will guarantee you'll keep your trust fund rolling in without your parents' interfering. And it will give me what I want, as well, which is your land and Hercules."

Her eyes widened. "A marriage of convenience between us?"

"Yes." He could see the light shining bright in her wide-eyed innocent gaze. But then caution eased into the hazel depths.

"And you want me to give you my land as well as Hercules?"

"Co-ownership of the land and total ownership of Hercules."

Bella nibbled on her bottom lip, giving his proposal consideration while trying not to feel the disappointment trying to crowd her in. She had come here to Denver to be independent and not dependent. But what he was proposing was not how she had planned things to go. She was just learning to live on her own without her parents looking over her shoulder. She wanted her own life and now Jason was proposing that he share it. Even if it was on a temporary basis, she was going to feel her independence snatched away. "And how long do we have to remain married?"

"For as long as we want but at least a year. Anytime after that either of us are free to file for a divorce to end things. But think about it, once we send your father's attorney proof we're officially married he'll have no choice but to release the hold on your trust fund."

Bella knew that her parents would always be her parents and although she loved them, she could not put up with their controlling ways any longer. She thought Jason's proposal might work but she still had a few reservations and concerns.

"Will we live in separate households?" she decided to ask.

"No, we will either live here or at my place. I have no problem moving in here but we can't live apart. We don't want to give your parents or anyone a reason to think our marriage isn't the real thing."

She nodded, thinking what he said made sense but she needed to ask another question. This one was of a

delicate nature but was one she definitely needed to
know the answer to. She cleared her throat. "If we lived
in the same house would you expect for us to sleep in
the same bed?"

He held her gaze intently. "I think by now it's apparent we're attracted to each other, which is the reason
I wasn't Mr. Congeniality tonight as you've indicated.
That kiss we shared only made me want more and I
think you know where wanting more would have led."

Yes, she knew. And because he was being honest
with her she might as well be honest with him. "And
the reason I acted 'cold,' as you put it, was that I felt
sensations kissing you that I'd never felt before and with
everything going on in my life, the last thing I needed
to take on was a lover. And now you want me to take
on a husband, Jason?"

"Yes, and only because you won't have all those issues you had before. And I would want us to share a
bed, but I'll leave the decision of what we do up to you.
I won't rush you into doing anything you're not comfortable with doing. But I think you can rightly say with
us living under the same roof such a thing is bound to
happen eventually."

She swallowed. Yes, she could rightly say that. Marrying him would definitely be a solution to her problem
and like he'd said, he would be getting what he wanted
out of the deal as well—co-ownership of her land and
Hercules. It would be a win-win situation.

But still.

"I need to think about it, Jason. Your proposal sounds
good but I need to make sure it's the right answer."

He nodded. "I have an attorney who can draw up the
papers so you won't have to worry about everything I'm

proposing being legit and binding. Your attorney can look at them as well if you'd like. He will be bound by attorney-client privilege not to disclose the details of our marriage to anyone."

"I still need time to think things through, Jason."

"And I'll give you that time but my proposal won't be out there forever."

"I understand."

And whether or not he believed her, she *did* understand, which was why she needed time to think about it. From his standpoint things probably looked simple and easy. But to her there were several "what ifs" she had to consider.

What if during that year she fell in love with him but he wanted out of the marriage? What if he was satisfied with a loveless marriage and like her parents wanted to be discreet in taking lovers? What if—

"How much time do you think you'll need to think about it?"

"No more than a week at the most. I should have my answer to you by then." And she hoped more than anything it would be the right one.

"All right, that will work for me."

"And you're not involved with anyone?" she asked, needing to know for certain.

He smiled. "No, I'm not. Trust me. I couldn't be involved with anyone and kiss you the way I did the other day."

Bringing up their kiss made her remember how it had been that day, and how easily her lips had molded to his. It had been so easy to feel his passion, and some of the things his tongue had done inside her mouth nearly short-circuited her brain. Even now her body was inwardly shuddering with the force of those memories. And she expected them to live under the same roof and not share a bed? That was definitely an unrealistic expectation on her part. It seemed since their kiss, being under the same roof for any period of time was a passionate time bomb waiting to happen for them and they both knew it.

She glanced across the table at him and her stomach clenched. He was looking at her the same way he'd done that day right before he'd kissed her. And she'd kissed him back. Mated with his mouth and loved every minute doing so.

Even now she recognized the look in his eyes. It was a dark, hungry look that did more than suggest he wanted her and if given the chance he would take her right here, on her kitchen table. And it would entail more than just kissing. He would probably want to sample her the same way she'd done the seafood bisque Pam had served at dinner. And heaven help her but she would just love to be sampled.

She knew what he wanted but was curious to know what he was thinking at this moment. He was staring at her with such intensity, such longing and such greed. Then she thought, maybe it was best that she didn't know. It would be safer to just imagine.

Swallowing hard, she broke eye contact with him and thought changing the subject was a good idea. The discussion of a possible marriage between them was not the way to go right now.

"At least I've paid for the appliances they are delivering next week," she said, glancing over at her stove that had seen better days. "I think that stove and refrigerator were here when my dad lived here," she added.

"Probably."

"So it was time for new ones, don't you think?"

"Yes. And I think we need to get those broken pieces of the teacups off the floor," he said.

"I'll do it later. It will give me something to do after you leave. I'm going to need to stay busy for a while. I'm not sleepy."

"You sure you won't need my help cleaning it up?"

"Yes, I'm sure" was her response.

"All right."

"I have beer in the refrigerator if you'd like one," she offered.

"No, I'm straight."

For the next ten minutes they continued to engage in idle chatter. Anything else was liable to set off sparks that could ignite into who knows what.

"Bella?"

"Yes."

"It's not working."

She knew just what he meant. They had moved the conversation from her appliances, to the broken teacups, to him not wanting a beer, to the furniture in her living room, to the movie that had made number one at the box office last weekend like either of them really gave a royal flip. "It's not?"

"No. It's okay to feel what we're feeling right now, no matter what decision you make a week from now. And on that note," he said, standing, "if you're sure you don't want me to help clean up the broken teacups, I think I'd better go before…"

"Before what?" she asked when he hesitated in completing the statement.

"Before I try eating you alive."

She sucked in a quick breath while a vision of him doing that very thing filtered through her mind. And then instead of leaving well enough alone, she asked something really stupid. "Why would you want to do something like that?"

He smiled. And the way he smiled had her pulse beating rapidly in several areas of her body. It wasn't a predatory smile but one of those "if you really want to know" smiles. Never before had she been aware of the many smiles a person's lips could convey.

In truth, with the little experience she had when it came to men, she was surprised she could read him at all. But for some strange reason she could read Jason and she could do so on a level that could set off passion fizzing to life inside of her.

Like it was doing now.

"The reason I'd try eating you alive is that the other day I only got a sample of your taste. But it was enough to give me plenty of sleepless nights since then. Now I find that I crave knowing how you taste all over. So if you're not ready for that to happen, come on and walk me to the door."

Honestly, at that moment she wasn't quite sure what she was ready for and figured that degree of uncertainty was reason to walk him to the door. She had a lot to think about and work out in her mind and only a week to do it.

She stood and moved around the table. When he extended his hand to her, she knew if they were to touch it would set off a chain of emotions and events she wasn't sure she was ready for. Her gaze moved away from his hand up to his face and she had a feeling that he knew it, as well. Was this supposed to be a challenge? Or was it merely a way to get her to face the facts of how living under the same roof with him would be?

She could ignore his outstretched hand but doing so would be rude and she wasn't a rude person. He was watching her. Waiting for her next move. So she made it and placed her hand in his. And the instant their hands touched she felt it. The heat of his warmth spread through her and instead of withstanding it she was drawn deeper and deeper into it.

Before she realized his intentions he let go of her hand to slide his fingertips up and down her arm in a caress so light and so mind-bogglingly sensual that she had to clamp down her mouth to keep from moaning.

The look in the dark eyes staring at her was intense and she knew at that moment his touch wasn't the only thing making her come apart. His manly scent was flowing through her nostrils and drawing him to her in a way that was actually making her panties wet.

My goodness.

"Maybe my thinking is wrong, Bella," he said in a deep, husky voice as his fingers continued to caress her arms, making her stomach clench with every heated stroke against her skin.

"Maybe you are ready for me to taste you all over, let my tongue glide across your skin, sample you in my mouth and feast on you with the deep hunger I need assuaged. And while your delicious taste sinks into my mouth, I will use my tongue to push you over the edge time and time again and drown you in a need that I intend to fulfill."

His words were pushing her over the edge just as much as his touch was doing. They were making her feel things. Want things. And increasing her desire to explore. To experience. To exert her freedom this way.

"Tell me you're ready," he urged softly in a heated voice. "Just looking at you makes me hot and hard," he said in a tone that heated her skin. "So please tell me you're ready for me."

Bella thought Jason's words had been spoken in the huskiest whisper she'd ever heard, and they did something to her both physically and mentally. They prodded her to want whatever it was he was offering. Whatever she was supposed to be ready for.

Like other women, sex was no great mystery to her. At least not since she had seen her parents' housekeeper Carlie have sex with the gardener when she was twelve. She hadn't understood at the time what all the moans and groans were about and why they had to be naked while making them. As she got older she'd been shielded from any encounters with the opposite sex and never had time to dwell on such matters.

But there had been a time when she'd become curious so she had begun reading a lot. Her parents would probably die of shame if they knew about all the romance novels Carlie would sneak in to her. It was there between the pages of those novels that she began to dream, fantasize and hope that one day she would fall in love and live happily ever after like the women she read about. Her most ardent desire was to one day find the one man who would make her sexually liberated. She wouldn't press her luck and hold out for love.

She swallowed deeply as she gazed up at Jason, knowing he was waiting for her response, and she knew at that moment what it would be. "Yes, Jason, I'm ready."

He didn't say anything for the longest time; he just stood there and stared at her. For a moment she wondered if he'd heard her. But his darkened eyes, the sound of his breathing alerted her that he had. And his eyes then traveled down the length of her throat and she knew he saw how erratically her pulse was throbbing there at the center.

And then before she could blink, he lowered his head to kiss her. His tongue drove between her lips at the same time his hand reached under her wrap dress. While his tongue relentlessly probed her mouth, his fingers began sliding up her thighs and the feel of his hands on that part of her, a part no other man had touched, made something inside of her uncoil and she released a breathless sigh. She knew at that moment the heat was on. Before she realized he'd done so, he had inched her backward and the cheeks of her behind aligned with the table.

He withdrew his mouth from hers long enough to whisper, "I can't wait to get my tongue inside of you."

His words sent all kinds of sensations swirling around in her stomach and a deep ache began throbbing between her legs. The heat was not just on, it was almost edging out of control. She felt it emitting even more when his fingers moved from her thighs to her panties.

And when he reclaimed her mouth again she moaned at how thoroughly he was kissing her and thinking her brain would overload from all the sensations ramming through her. She tried keeping up as his tongue did a methodical sweep of her mouth. And when she finally thought her senses were partially back under control, he proved her wrong when his fingers wiggled their way beneath the waistband of her panties to begin stroking her in a way that all but obliterated her senses.

"Jason…"

She felt her body being eased back onto the table at the same time her dress was pushed up to her waist. She was too full of emotions, wrapped up in way too many sensations, to take stock in what he was doing, but she got a pretty good idea when he eased her panties down her legs, leaving her open and bare to his sight. And when he eased her back farther on the table and placed her legs over his shoulders to nearly wrap around his neck she knew.

Her breath quickened at the smile that then touched his lips, a smile like before that was not predatory and this time wasn't even one of those "if you really want to know" smiles. This one was a "you're going to enjoy this" smile that curved the corners of his mouth and made a hidden dimple appear in his right cheek.

And before she could release her next breath he lifted her hips to bury his face between her legs. She bit her tongue to keep from screaming when his hot tongue slid between her womanly folds.

She squirmed frantically beneath his mouth as he drove her crazy with passion, using his tongue to coax her into the kind of climax she'd only read about. It was the kind that had preclimactic sensations rushing through her. He shoved his tongue deeper inside her, doing more than tasting her dewy wetness; he was using the hot tip of his tongue to greedily lick her from core to core.

She threw her head back and closed her eyes, as his

tongue began making all kinds of circles inside her, teasing her flesh, branding it. But he wouldn't let up and she saw he had no intentions of doing so. She felt the buildup right there at the center of her thighs where his mouth was. Pleasure and heat were taking their toll.

Then suddenly her body convulsed around his mouth and she released a moan from deep within her throat as sharp jolts of sexual pleasure set ripples off in her body. And she moaned while the aftershocks made her body shudder uncontrollably. What she was enduring was unbearably erotic, pleasure so great she thought she would pass out from it.

But she couldn't pass out, not when his tongue continued to thrust inside her, forcing her to give even more. And then she was shoved over the edge. Unable to take anymore, she tightened her legs around his neck and cried out in ecstasy as wave after turbulent wave overtook her.

It was only when the last spasm had eased from her body did he tear his mouth away from her, lower her legs, lean down and kiss her, letting her taste the essence of herself from his lips.

She sucked hard on his tongue, needing it like a lifeline and knowing at that moment he had to be the most sensual and passionate man to walk on the planet. He had made her feel things she'd never felt before, far greater than what she had imagined in any of those romance novels. And she knew this was just the beginning, an introduction to what was out there...and she had a feeling of what was to come.

She knew at that moment, while their tongues continued to mate furiously, that after tonight there was no way they could live under the same roof and not want

to discover what was beyond this. How far into pleasure could he take her?

She was definitely going to have to give the proposal
he'd placed out there some serious thought.

Jason eased Bella's dress back down her thighs before lifting her from the table to stand on her feet. He
studied her features and was pleased with what he saw.
Her eyes glowed, her lips were swollen and she looked
well rested when she hadn't slept.

But more than anything he thought she was the most
beautiful woman he'd ever seen. He hoped he'd given
her something to think about, something to anticipate,
because more than anything he wanted to marry her.

He intended to marry her.

"Come on, walk me to the door," he whispered
thickly. "And this time I promise to leave."

He took her hand in his and ignored the sensations
he felt whenever he touched her. "Have breakfast with
me tomorrow."

She glanced up at him. "You don't intend to make
my decision easy, do you?"

A soft chuckle escaped his lips. "Nothing's wrong
with me giving you something to think about. To remember. And to anticipate. It will only help you to make
the right decision about my proposal."

When they reached her door he leaned down and
kissed her again. She parted her lips easily for him and
he deepened the kiss, finding her tongue and then enjoying a game of hide-and-seek with it before finally
releasing her mouth on a deep, guttural moan. "What
about breakfast in the morning at my place?" he asked
huskily.

"That's all it's going to be, right? Breakfast and nothing more?" she asked, her voice lower than a whisper.

He smiled at her with a mischievous grin on his face. "We'll see."

"In that case I'll pass. I can't take too much of you, Jason Westmoreland."

He laughed as he pulled her closer into his arms. "Sweetheart, if I have my way, one of these days you're going to take *all* of me." He figured she knew just what he meant with his throbbing erection all but poking at her center. Maybe she was right and for them to share breakfast tomorrow wasn't a good idea. He would be pouncing on her before she got inside his house.

"A rain check, then?" he prompted.

"Um, maybe."

He lifted a brow. "You're not trying to play hard to get, are you?"

She smiled. "You can ask me that after what happened a short while ago in my kitchen? But I will warn you that I intend to build up some type of immunity to your charms by the time I see you again. You can be overwhelming, Jason."

He chuckled again, thinking she hadn't seen anything yet. Leaning over he brushed a kiss across her lips. "Think about me tonight, Bella."

He opened the door and walked out, thinking the next seven days were bound to be the longest he'd ever endured.

Later that night Bella couldn't get to sleep. Her body was tingling all over from the touch of a man. But it hadn't been any man, it had been Jason. When she tried closing her eyes all she could see was how it had been in her kitchen, the way Jason had draped her across the table and proceeded to enjoy her in such a scandalous way. The nuns at her school would have heart failure to know what had happened to her...and to know how much she had enjoyed it.

All her life she'd been taught—it had virtually been drilled into her head—all about the sins of the flesh. It was wrong for a woman to engage in any type of sexual encounter with a man before marriage. But how could something be so wrong if it felt so right?

Color tinted her cheeks. She needed to get to Confessions the first chance she got. She'd given in to temptation tonight and as much as she had enjoyed it, it would be something she couldn't repeat. Those kinds of activities belonged to people who were married and doing otherwise was improper.

She was just going to have to make sure she and Jason weren't under the same roof alone for a long period of time. Things could get out of hand. She was a weakling when it came to him. He would tempt her to do things she knew she shouldn't.

And now she was paying the price for her little indulgence by not being able to get to sleep. There was no doubt in her mind that Jason's mouth should be outlawed. She inwardly sighed. It was going to take a rather long time to clear those thoughts from her mind.

Chapter 5

"I like Bella, Jason."

He glanced over at his cousin Zane. It was early Monday morning and they were standing in the round pen with one of the mares while waiting for Derringer to bring the designated stallion from his stall for the scheduled breeding session. "I like her, too."

Zane chuckled. "Could have fooled me. Because you weren't giving her your attention at dinner Friday night. We all felt that it was up to us to make her feel welcome, because you were ignoring the poor girl."

Jason rolled his eyes. "And I bet it pained all of you to do so."

"Not really. Your Southern Bella is a real classy lady. If you weren't interested in her I'd make a play for her."

"But I *am* interested in her."

"I know," Zane said, smiling. "It was pretty obvious. I intercepted your dirty looks loud and clear. In any case, I hope things get straightened out between you two."

"I hope so, too. I'll find out in five more days."

Zane lifted a curious brow. "Five days? What's supposed to happen in five days?"

"Long story and one which I prefer not to share right now." He had intentionally not contacted Bella over the past two days to give her breathing space from him to think his proposal through. He'd thought it through and it made perfect sense to him. He was beginning to anticipate her answer. It would be yes; it just had to be.

But what if yes wasn't her answer? What if even after the other night and the sample lovemaking they'd shared that she thought his proposal wasn't worth taking the chance? He would be the first to admit that his proposal was a bit daring. But he felt the terms were fair. Hell, he was giving her a chance to be the first to file for a divorce after the first year. And he—

Zane snapped a finger in front of his face. "Hellooo. Are you with us? Derringer is here with Fireball. Are you up to this or are you thinking about mating of another kind?" Zane was grinning.

Jason frowned when he glanced over at Derringer and saw a smirk on his face, as well. "Yes, I'm up to this and it's none of your business what I'm thinking about."

"Fine, just keep Prancer straight while Fireball mounts her. It's been a while since he's had a mare and he might be overly eager," Zane said with a meaningful smile.

Just like me, Jason thought, remembering every vivid detail of Bella spread out on her kitchen table for him to enjoy. "All right, let's get this going. I have something to do later."

Both Zane and Derringer gave him speculative looks but said nothing.

Bella stepped out of the shower and began toweling herself dry. It was the middle of the day but after going for a walk around the ranch she had gotten hot and sticky. Now she intended to slip into something comfortable and have a cup of tea and relax…and think about Jason's proposal.

The walk had done her good and walking her land had made her even more determined to hold on to what was hers. But was Jason's proposal the answer? Or would she be jumping out of the pot and into the fire?

After Friday night and what had gone down in her kitchen, there was no doubt in her mind that Jason was the kind of lover women dreamed of having. And he had to be the most unselfish person she knew. He had given her pleasure without seeking his own. She had read enough articles on the subject to know most men weren't usually that generous. But he had been and her body hadn't been the same since. Every time she thought about him and that night in the kitchen, she had to pause and catch her breath.

She hadn't heard from him since that night but figured he was giving her time to think things through before she gave him her answer. She had talked to her attorney again and he hadn't said anything to make her think she had a chance of getting the hold on her trust fund lifted.

She had run into her uncle yesterday when she'd gone into town and he hadn't been at all pleasant. And neither had his son, daughter and two teenage grandsons. All of them practically cut her with their sharp looks. She just didn't get it. Jason had wanted her land as well but he hadn't been anything but supportive of her decision to keep it and had offered his help from the first.

She understood that she and her Denver relatives didn't have the same bond as the Westmorelands but she would think they wouldn't be dismissing her the way they were doing over some land.

She had dressed and was heading downstairs when something like a missile sailed through her living room window, breaking the glass in the process. "What on earth!" She nearly missed her step when she raced back up the stairs to her bedroom, closing the door and locking it behind her.

Catching her breath she grabbed her cell phone off the nightstand and called the police.

"Where is she, Marvin?" Jason asked, walking into Bella's house with Zane and Derringer on his heels.

"She's in the kitchen," the man answered, moving quickly out of Jason's way.

Jason had gotten a call from Pam to tell him what had happened. He had jumped in his truck and left Zane's ranch immediately with Derringer and Zane following close behind in their vehicles.

From what Pam had said, someone had thrown a large rock through Bella's window with a note tied to it saying, "Go back to where you came from." The thought of anyone doing that angered him. Who on earth would do such a thing?

He walked into the kitchen and glanced around, dismissing memories of the last time he'd been there, and his focus immediately went to Bella. She was sitting at the kitchen table talking to Pete Higgins, one of the sheriff's deputies and a good friend of Derringer's.

Everyone glanced up when he entered and the look on Bella's face was like a kick in his gut. He could tell she was shaken and there was a hurt expression in her eyes he'd never seen before. His anger flared at the thought that someone could hurt her in any way. The rock may not have hit her but she'd taken a hit just the same. Whoever had thrown that rock through the window had hit her spirit and left her shaken.

"Jason, Zane and Derringer," Pete said, acknowledging their arrival. "Why am I not surprised to see the three of you here?"

Jason didn't respond as he moved straight toward Bella and, disregarding the onlookers, he reached out to caress the soft skin beneath her ear. "Are you all right?" he whispered in a husky tone.

She held his gaze and nodded slowly. "Yes, I'm fine. I was on my way downstairs when that rock came flying through the window. It scared me more than anything."

He glanced at the rock that someone had placed on the table. It was a huge rock, big enough to hurt her had she been in her living room anywhere near the window. The thought of anyone harming one single hair on her head infuriated him.

He glanced over at Pete. "Do you have any idea who did it?"

Peter shook his head. "No, but both the rock and note have been dusted for fingerprints. Hopefully we'll know something soon."

Soon? He wanted to know something now. He glanced down at the note and read it.

"I was just asking Ms. Bostwick if she knew of anyone who wanted her off this property. The only people she could think of are her parents and possibly Kenneth Bostwick."

"I can't see my parents behind anything like this," Bella said in a soft voice. "And I don't want to think Uncle Kenneth is capable of doing anything like this, either. However, he does want me off the land because he knows of someone who wants to buy it."

Pete nodded. "What about Jason here? I think we all know he wants your land and Hercules, as well," the deputy said as if Jason wasn't standing right there listening to his every word. "Do you think he'd want you gone, too?"

Bella seemed surprised by the question and moved her gaze from Pete to Jason. Jason figured she saw remnants of passion behind the anger in his eyes.

"No, he'd want me to stay," she said with a soft sigh.

Pete closed his notepad, evidently deciding not to ask why she was so certain of that. "Well, hopefully we'll have something within a week if those fingerprints are identified," he said.

"And what is she supposed to do in the meantime, Pete?" Jason asked in a frustrated tone.

"Report anything suspicious," Pete responded drily. He turned to face Bella. "I'll request that the sheriff beef up security around here starting today."

"Thank you, Deputy Higgins," Bella said softly. "I'd appreciate that tremendously. Marvin is getting the window replaced and I'll be keeping the lights on in the yard all night now."

"Doesn't matter," Jason said. "You're staying at my place tonight."

Bella tilted her head to the side and met Jason's intense gaze. "I can't do that. You and I can't stay under the same roof."

Jason crossed his arms over his chest. "And why not?"

A flush stole into her cheeks when she noted Jason wasn't the only one waiting on her response. "You know why," she finally said.

Jason's forehead bunched up. Then when he remembered what could possibly happen if they stayed overnight under the same roof, he smiled. "Oh, yeah."

"Oh, yeah, what?" Zane wanted to know.

Jason frowned at his cousin. "None of your business."

Pete cleared his throat. "I'm out of here but like I said, Miss Bostwick, the department will have more police checking around the area." He slipped both the rock and note into a plastic evidence bag.

Zane and Derringer followed Pete out the door, which Jason appreciated since it gave him time alone with Bella. The first thing he did was lean down and kiss her. He needed the taste of her to know she was really okay.

She responded to his kiss and automatically he deepened it, drawing her up out of the chair to stand on her feet in the process. He needed the feel of all of her to know she was safe. He would protect her with his life if he had to. He'd aged a good twenty years when he'd gotten that call from Pam telling him what had happened. And speaking of Pam's phone call...

He broke off the kiss and with an irritated frown on his features he looked down at Bella. "Why didn't you call me? Why did I have to hear what happened from someone else?"

She gazed right back at him with an irritated frown of her own. "You've never given me your phone number."

Jason blinked in surprise and realized what she'd said was true. He hadn't given her his phone number.

"I apologize for that oversight," he said. "You will definitely have it from here on out. And we need to talk about you moving in with me for a while."

She shook her head. "I can't move in with you, Jason, and as I said earlier, we both know why."

"Do you honestly think if you gave me an order not to touch you that I wouldn't keep my hands off you?" he asked.

She shrugged delicate shoulders. "Yes, I believe you'd do as I ask, but I'm not sure given that same scenario, in light of what happened in this very kitchen Friday night, that I'd be able to keep my hands off you."

He blinked, stared down at her and blinked again. This time with a smile on his lips. "You don't say?"

"I do say and I know it's an awful thing to admit, but right now I can't make you any promises," she said, rubbing her hands together as if distressed by the very notion.

He wasn't distressed, not even a little bit. In fact, he was elated. For a minute he couldn't say a word and then said, "And you think I have a problem with you not being able to keep your hands off me?"

She nodded. "If you don't have a problem with it then you should. We aren't married. We aren't even engaged."

"I asked you to marry me Friday night."

She used her hand to wave off his reminder. "Yes, but it would be a marriage of convenience, which I haven't agreed to yet since the issue of the sleeping arrangements is still up in the air. Until I do decide I think it's best if you stay under your roof and I stay under mine. Yes, that's the proper thing to do."

He lifted a brow. "The proper thing to do?"

"Yes, proper, appropriate, suitable, fitting—which of those words do you prefer using?"

"What about none of them?"

"It doesn't matter, Jason. It's bad enough that we got carried away the other night in this kitchen. But we can't repeat something like that."

He didn't see why they couldn't and was about to say as much when he heard footsteps approaching and glanced over as Derringer and Zane entered the kitchen.

"Pete thinks he's found a footprint outside near the bushes and is checking it out now," Derringer informed them.

Jason nodded. He then turned back to Bella and his expression was one that would accept no argument on the matter. "Pack an overnight bag, Bella. You're staying at my place tonight even if I have to sleep in the barn."

Chapter 6

Bella glared at Jason. It was a ladylike glare but a glare nonetheless. She opened her mouth to say something then remembered they had an audience and immediately closed it. She cast a warm smile over at Zane and Derringer. "I'd like a few minutes alone with Jason to discuss a private matter, please."

They returned her smile, nodded and gave Jason "you've done it now" smiles before walking out of the kitchen.

It was then that she turned her attention back to Jason. "Now then, Jason, let's not be ridiculous. You are not sleeping in your barn just so I can sleep under your roof. I'm staying right here."

She could tell he did not appreciate his order not being obeyed when she saw his irritation with her increase. "Have you forgotten someone threw a rock through your window with a note demanding you leave town?"

She nibbled a minute on her bottom lip. "No, I didn't forget the rock or the note attached to it, but I can't let them think they've won by running away. I admit to being a little frightened at first but I'm fine now. Marvin is having the window replaced and I'll keep lights shining around here all night. And don't forget Marvin sleeps in the bunkhouse each night so technically, I won't be here by myself. I'll be fine, but I appreciate your concern."

Jason stared at her for a moment and didn't say anything. He hadn't lied about aging twenty years when he'd gotten that call from Pam. He had walked into her house not knowing what to expect. The thought that someone wanted her gone bothered him, because he knew she wasn't going anywhere and that meant he needed to protect her.

"Fine, you stay inside here and I'll sleep in your barn," he finally said.

She shook her head after crossing her arms over her chest. "You won't be sleeping in anyone's barn. You're going to sleep in your own bed tonight and I intend to sleep in mine."

"Fine," he snapped like he was giving in to her suggestion when he wouldn't do anything of the sort. But if she wanted to think it he would let her. "I need to take you to Pam's to show her and the others you're okay and in one piece."

A smile touched her lips. "They were worried about me?"

She seemed surprised by that. "Yes, everyone was worried."

"In that case let me grab my purse." ·

"I'll be waiting outside," he said to her fleeing back.

He shook his head and slowly left the kitchen and walked through the dining room to the living room where Marvin and a couple of the men were replacing the window. They had cleaned up all the broken glass but a scratch mark on the wooden floor clearly showed where the rock had landed once it entered the house.

He drew in a sharp breath at the thought of Bella getting hit by that rock. If anything would have happened to her he would have…

At that moment he wasn't sure just what he would do. The thought of anything happening to her sent sharp fear through him in a way he'd never known before. Why? Why were his feelings for her so intense? Why was he so possessive when it came to her?

He shrugged off the responses that flowed through his mind, not ready to deal with any of them. He walked out the front door to where Zane and Derringer were waiting.

"You aren't really going to let her stay here unprotected?" Derringer asked, studying his features.

Jason shook his head. "No."

"And why can't the two of you stay under the same roof?" Zane asked curiously.

"None of your business."

Zane chuckled. "If you don't give me an answer I'm going to think things."

That didn't move Jason. "Think whatever you want." He then checked his watch. "I hate to do this but I'm checking out for the rest of the day. I intend to keep an eye on Bella until Pete finds out who threw that rock through her window."

"You think Kenneth Bostwick had something to do with it?" Derringer asked.

"Not sure, but I hope for his sake he didn't," Jason said in a voice laced with tightly controlled anger.

He stopped talking when Bella walked onto the porch. Not only had she grabbed her purse but she'd also changed her dress. At his curious look, she said, "The dress I was wearing wasn't suitable for visiting."

He nodded and decided not to tell her she looked good now and had looked good then. Whatever she put on her body she wore with both grace and style. He met her in the middle of the porch and slipped her hand in his. "You look nice. And I thought we could grab dinner someplace before I bring you back here."

Her eyes glowed in a way that tightened his stomach and sent sensations rushing through his gut. "I'd like that, Jason."

It was close to ten at night when Bella returned home. Jason entered her house and checked around, turning on lights as he went from room to room. It made her feel extra safe when she saw a police patrol car parked near the turnoff to her property.

"Everything looks okay," Jason said, breaking into her thoughts.

"Thanks. I'll walk you to the door," she said quickly, heading back downstairs.

"Trying to rush me out of here, Bella?"

At the moment she didn't care what he thought. She just needed him gone so she could get her mind straightened out. Being with him for the past eight hours had taken its toll on her mind and body.

She hadn't known he was so touchy and each time

he'd touched her, even by doing something as simple as placing a hand in the center of her back when they'd been walking into the movies, it had done something to her in a way that had her hot and bothered for the rest of the evening.

But she had enjoyed the movies they'd gone to after dinner. She had enjoyed sitting beside him while he held her hand when he wasn't feeding her popcorn.

"No, I'm not trying to rush you, Jason, but it is late," she said. "If your goal this evening was to tire me out then you've done a good job of it. I plan to take a shower and then go to bed."

They were standing facing each other and he wrapped his arms around her and took a step closer, almost plastering his body to hers. She could feel all of him from chest to knee; but especially the erect body part in between.

"I'd love to take a shower with you, sweetheart," he whispered.

She didn't know what he was trying to do, but he'd been whispering such naughty come-ons to her all evening. And each and every one of them had only added to her torment. "Taking a shower together wouldn't be right, Jason, and you know it."

He chuckled. "Trying to send me home to an empty bed isn't right, either. Why don't you just accept my proposal? We can get married the same day. No waiting. And then," he said, leaning closer to begin nibbling around her mouth, "we can sleep under the same roof that night. Just think about that."

Bella moaned against the onslaught of his mouth on hers. She was thinking about it and could just imagine it. Oh, what a night that would be. But then she also had to think about what would happen if he got tired of her like her father had eventually gotten tired of her mother. The way her mother had gotten tired of her father. What if he approached her about wanting an open marriage? What if he told her after the first year that he wanted a divorce and she'd gotten attached to him? She could just imagine the heartbreak she would feel.

"Bella?"

She glanced up at him. "Yes?"

Jason Westmoreland was such a handsome man that it made her heart ache. And at the same time he made parts of her sizzle in desire so thick you could cut it with a knife. She thought his features were flawless and he had to have the most irresistible pair of lips born to any man. Staring at his mouth pushed her to recall the way their tongues would entangle in his mouth while they mated them like crazy. It didn't take much to wonder how things would be between them in the bedroom. But she knew as tempting as it was, there was more to a marriage than just great sex. But could she really ask for more from a marriage of convenience?

"Are you sure you don't want me to stay tonight? I could sleep on the sofa."

She shook her head. Even that would be too close for comfort for her. "No, Jason, I'll be fine. Go home."

"Not before I do this," he said, leaning down and capturing her mouth with his. She didn't have a problem offering him what he wanted and he proved he didn't have a problem taking it. He kissed her deeply, thoroughly and with no reservations about making her feel wanted, needed and desired. She could definitely feel heat radiating from his body to hers and wasn't put off by it. Instead it ignited passion within her so acute she had to fight to keep a level head or risk the kiss taking them places she wasn't ready to go.

Moments later she was the one who broke off the kiss. Desperately needing to breathe, she inhaled a deep breath. Jason just simply stood there staring and waiting, as if he was ready to go another round.

Bella knew she disappointed him when she took a step back. "Good night, Jason."

His lips curved into a too-sexy smile. "Tell me one thing that will be good about it once I walk out that door."

She really wasn't sure what she could say to that, and in those cases she'd always been told it was better not to say anything at all. Instead she repeated herself while turning the knob on the door to open it. "Good night, Jason."

He leaned in, brushed a kiss across her lips and whispered, "Good night, Bella."

Bella wasn't sure what brought her awake during the middle of the night. Glancing over at the clock on her nightstand she saw it was two in the morning. She was restless. She was hot. And she was definitely still bothered. She hadn't known just spending time with a man could put a woman in such an erotic state.

Sliding out of bed she slipped into her robe and house shoes. A full moon was in the sky and its light spread into the room. She was surprised by how easily sleep had come to her at first. But that had been a few hours ago and now she was wide-awake.

She moved over to the windows to look out. Under the moon-crested sky she could see the shape of the mountains in their majestic splendor. At night they were just as overpowering as they were in the daylight.

She was about to move away from the window when she happened to glance down below and saw a truck parked in her yard. She frowned and pressed her face closer to the window to make out just whose vehicle was parked in her yard and frowned when she recognized the vehicle was Jason's.

What was his truck doing in her yard at two in the morning? Was he in it?

She rushed downstairs. He couldn't be in a truck in front of her house at two in the morning. What would Marvin think? What would the police officers cruising the area think? His family?

When she made it to the living room she slowly opened the door and slipped out. She then released a disgusted sigh when she saw he was sitting in the truck. He had put his seat in a reclining position, but that had to be uncomfortable for him.

As if he'd been sleeping with one eye open and another one closed, he came awake when she rounded the truck and tapped on his window. He slowly tilted his Stetson back from covering his eyes. "Yes, Bella?"

She opened her mouth to speak and then closed it. If she thought he was a handsome man before, then he was even more now with the shadow covering his jaw. There was just something ultrasexy about a man who hadn't shaved.

She fought her attention away from his jaw back to his gaze. "What are you doing here? Why did you come back?"

"I never left."

She blinked. "You never left? You mean to tell me

you've been out here in the car since I walked you to the door?"

He smiled that sexy smile. "Yes, I've been here since you walked me to the door."

"But why?"

"To protect you."

That simple statement suddenly took the wind out of her sail for just a moment. Merely a moment. That was all the time she needed to be reminded that no one had tried truly protecting her before. She'd always considered her parents' antics more in the line of controlling than protecting.

She then recovered and remembered why he couldn't sit out here protecting her. "But you can't sit out here, Jason. It's not proper. What will your family think if any of them see your car parked in front of my house at this hour? What would those policemen think? What would—"

"Honestly, Bella, I really don't give a royal damn what anyone thinks. I refuse to let you stay here without being close by to make sure you're okay. You didn't want me to sleep in the barn so this is where I am and where I will stay."

She frowned. "You're being difficult."

"No, I'm being a man looking out for the woman I want. Now go back inside and lock the door behind you. You interrupted my sleep."

She stared at him for a long moment and then said, "Fine, you win. Come on inside."

He stared back at her. "That wasn't what this was about, Bella. I recognize the fact just as much as you do that we don't need to be under the same roof alone. I'm fine with being out here tonight."

"Well, I'm not fine with it."

"Sorry about that but there's nothing I can do about it."

She glared at him and seeing he was determined to be stubborn, she threw up her hands before going back into the house, closing the door behind her.

Jason heard the lock click in place and swore he could also hear her fuming all the way up the stairs. She could fume all she wanted but he wasn't leaving. He had been sitting out there for the past four hours thinking, and the more he thought the more he realized something vital to him. And it was something he could not deny or ignore. He had fallen in love with Bella. And accepting how he felt gave his proposal much more meaning than what he'd presented to her. Now he fully understood why Derringer had acted so strangely while courting Lucia.

He had dated women in the past but had never loved any of them. He'd known better than to do so after that fiasco with Mona Cardington in high school. He'd admitted he loved her and when a new guy moved to town weeks later she had dumped him like a hot potato. That had been years ago but the pain he'd felt that day had been real and at seventeen it had been what had kept him from loving another woman.

And now he had fallen head over heels in love with a Southern belle, and for the time being would keep how he felt to himself.

An hour later Bella lay in bed staring up at the ceiling, still inwardly fuming. How dare Jason put her in such a compromising position? No one would think he was sleeping in the truck. People were going to assume they were lovers and he was sleeping in her bed, lying with her between silken sheets with their limbs entwined and mouths fused while making hot, passionate and steamy love.

Her thighs began to quiver and the juncture between her legs began to ache just thinking of how it would probably be if they were to share a bed. He would stroke her senseless with his fingers in her most intimate spot first, taking his time to get her primed and ready for the next stage of what he would do to her.

She shifted to her side and held her legs tightly together, hoping the ache would go away. She'd never craved a man before and now she was craving Jason something fierce, more so than ever since he'd tasted her there. All she had to do was close her eyes and remember being stretched out on her kitchen table with his head between her legs and how he had lapped her into sweet oblivion. The memories sent jolts of electricity throughout her body, making the tips of her breasts feel sensitive against her nightgown.

And the man causing her so much torment and pleasure was downstairs sleeping in his truck just to keep her safe. She couldn't help but be touched that he would do such a thing. He had given up a nice comfortable bed and was sleeping in a position that couldn't be relaxing with his hat over his eyes to shield the brightness of the lights around her yard. Why? Was protecting her that important to him?

If it was, then why?

Deep down she knew the reason and it stemmed from him wanting her land and Hercules. He had been up-front about it from the beginning. She had respected him for it and for accepting the decision was hers to make. So, in other words, he wasn't really protecting her per se but merely protecting his interest, or what he hoped to be his interest. She figured such a thing made sense but...

Would accepting the proposal Jason placed on the table be in her best interest? Did she have a choice if she wanted the hold lifted on her trust fund? Was being legally bound to Jason as his wife for a minimum of a year something she wanted? What about sleeping under the same roof with him and sharing his bed—she'd accepted they would be synonymous—would they be in her best interest? Was it what she wanted to do, knowing in a year's time he could walk away without looking back? Knowing after that time he would be free to marry someone else? Free to make love to someone else the same way he'd make love to her?

And then there was the question of who was responsible for throwing the rock inside her house. Why was someone trying to scare her off? Although she doubted it, could it be her parents' doing to get her to run back home?

She yawned when she felt sleep coming down on her. Although she regretted Jason was sleeping in his truck, she knew she could sleep a lot more peacefully knowing he was the one protecting her.

Bella woke to the sound of someone knocking on her door and discovered it was morning. She quickly eased out of bed and slid into her bathrobe and bedroom shoes to head downstairs.

"I'm coming!" she called out, rushing to the door. She glanced out the peephole and saw it was Jason. Her heart began beating fast and furiously in her chest at the sight of him, handsome and unshaven with his Stetson low on his brow. Mercy!

Taking a deep breath she opened the door. "Good morning, Jason."

"Good morning, Bella. I wanted to let you know I'm leaving to go home and freshen up, but Riley is here."

"Your brother Riley?" she asked, looking over his shoulder to see the truck parked next to his and the man sitting inside. Riley threw up his hand in a wave, which she returned. She recalled meeting him that night at dinner. Jason was older than Riley by two and a half years.

"Yes, my brother Riley."

She was confused. "Why is he here?"

"Because I'm going home to freshen up." He tilted his head and smiled at her. "Are you awake yet?"

"Yes, I'm awake and I know you said you're going home to change but why does Riley have to be here? It's not like I need a bodyguard or something. A rock got thrown through my window, Jason. Not a scud missile."

He merely kept smiling at her while leaning in her doorway. And then he said, "Has anyone ever told you how beautiful you look in the morning?"

She stood there and stared at him. Not ready for him to change the subject and definitely not prepared for him to say something so nice about how she looked. She could definitely return the favor and ask, had anyone ever told him how handsome he looked in the morning? However, she was certain a number of women already had.

So she answered him honestly. "No one has ever told me that."

"Then let me go on record as being your first."

She drew in a deep breath. He didn't say "the" first

but had said "your" first. He had made it personal and exclusive. She wondered what he would think to know she had drifted off to sleep last night with images of him flittering through her mind. Memories of his mouth on her probably elicited pleasurable sighs from her even while she slept.

"Doesn't Riley have to go to work today?" she asked, remembering when he'd mentioned that Riley worked for Blue Ridge Management. She'd even seen his name on one of the doors when they'd exited from the elevator on the fortieth floor.

"Yes, but he'll leave whenever I get back."

She crossed her arms over her chest. "And what about you? Don't you have horses to breed or train?"

"Your safety is more important to me."

"Yeah, right."

He lifted a brow. "You don't believe me? Even after I spent the entire night in my truck?"

"You were protecting your interest."

"And that's definitely you, sweetheart."

Don't even go there. Bella figured it was definitely time to end this conversation. If she engaged in chatter with him too much longer he would be convincing her that everything he was saying was true.

"You will have an answer for me in four days, right, Bella?"

"That's my plan."

"Good. I'll be back by the time you're dressed and we can do breakfast with Dillon and Pam, and then I want to show you what I do for a living."

Before she could respond he leaned in and kissed her on the lips. "See you in an hour. And wear your riding attire."

She sucked in a deep breath and watched as he walked off the porch to his truck to drive away. The man was definitely something else. She cast a quick glance to where Riley sat in his own truck sipping a cup of coffee. There was no doubt in her mind Riley had seen his brother kiss her, and she could only imagine what he was thinking.

Deciding the least she could do was invite him in, she called out to him. "You're welcome to come inside, Riley," she said, smiling broadly at him.

The smile he returned was just as expansive as he leaned his head slightly out the truck's window and said, "Thanks, but Jason warned me not to. I'm fine."

Jason warned him not to? Of course he was just joking, although he looked dead serious.

Instead of questioning him about it, she nodded, closed the door and headed back upstairs. As she entered her bedroom she couldn't ignore the excitement she felt about riding with Jason and checking out his horse training business.

Jason had grabbed his Stetson off the rack and was about to head out the door when his cell phone rang. He pulled it off his belt and saw it was Dillon.

"Yes, Dil?"

"Pam wanted me to call and verify that you and Bella are coming for breakfast."

Jason smiled. "Yes, we'll be there. In fact, I'm about to saddle up one of the mares. I thought we'd ride over on horseback. We can enjoy the sights along the way."

"That's a good idea. Everything's okay at her place?"

"Yes, so far so good. The sheriff has increased the

patrols around Bella's house and I appreciate it. Thank him the next time the two of you shoot pool together."

Dillon chuckled. "I will. And just so you know, I like Bella. She has a lot of class."

Jason smiled. That meant a lot coming from his older brother. While growing up he'd always thought Dillon was smart with a good head on his shoulders. Jason's admiration increased when Dillon had worked hard to keep the family together.

"And thanks, Dillon."

"For what?"

"For being you. For being there when all of us needed you to be. For doing what you knew Mom and Dad, as well as Uncle Thomas and Aunt Susan, would have wanted you to do."

"You don't have to thank me, Jason."

"Yes, I do."

Dillon didn't say anything for a moment. "Then you're welcome. Now don't keep us waiting with Bella. We won't start breakfast until the two of you get here. At least all of us except Denver. He wakes up hungry. Pam has fed him already," Dillon said.

Jason couldn't help but smile, and not for the first time, as he thought of one day having a son of his own. Being around Denver had the tendency to put such thoughts into his head. He enjoyed his nephew immensely.

"We'll get there in good time, I promise," he said before clicking off the phone.

Bella glanced down at her riding attire and smiled. She wanted to be ready when Jason returned.

Grabbing her hat off the rack she placed it on her

head and opened the door to step outside on the porch. Riley had gotten out of the truck and was leaning against it. He glanced over at her and smiled.

"Ready to go riding I see," he said.

"Yes, Jason told me to be ready. We're having breakfast with Dillon and Pam."

"Yes, I had planned to have breakfast with them as well but I have a meeting at the office."

Bella nodded. "You enjoy working inside?"

Riley chuckled. "Yes, I'll leave the horses, dirt and grime to Jason. He's always liked being outdoors. When he worked at Blue Ridge I knew it was just a matter of time before wanderlust got ahold of him. He's good with horses, so are Zane and Derringer. Joining in with the Montana Westmorelands in that horse business was great for them."

Bella nodded again. "So exactly what do you do at Blue Ridge?"

"Mmm, a little bit of everything. I like to think of myself as Dillon's right-hand man. But my main job is PR. I have to make sure Blue Ridge keeps a stellar image."

Bella continued to engage in conversation with Riley while thinking he was another kind Westmoreland man. It seemed that all of them were. But she'd heard Bailey remark more than once that Riley was also a ladies' man, and she could definitely believe that. Like Jason, he was handsome to a fault.

"So, Riley, when will you settle down and get married?" she asked him, just to see what his response would be.

"Married? Me? Never. I like things just the way they are. I am definitely not the marrying kind."

Bella smiled, wondering if Jason wasn't the marrying kind, as well, although he'd given a marriage proposal to her. Did he want joint ownership of her land and Hercules that much? Evidently so.

Jason smiled as he headed back to Bella's ranch with a horse he knew she would love riding. Fancy Free was an even-tempered mare. In the distance, he could see Bella was standing on the porch waiting for him. He would discount the fact that she seemed to be having an enjoyable conversation with Riley, who seemed to be flirting with her.

He ignored the signs of jealousy seeping into his bones. Riley was his brother and if you couldn't trust your own brother who could you trust? A lightbulb suddenly went off in his head. Hell. Had Abel assumed the same thing about Cain?

He tightened his hands on his horse and increased his pace to a gallop. What was Riley saying to Bella to make her laugh so much anyway? Riley was becoming a regular ladies' man around town. It seemed he was trying to keep up with Zane in that aspect. Jason had always thought Riley's playboy ways were amusing. Until now.

Moments later he brought his horse to a stop by the edge of Bella's porch. He tilted his Stetson back on his head so it wouldn't shield his eyes. "Excuse me if I'm interrupting anything."

Riley had the nerve to grin up at him. "No problem but you're twenty minutes late. You better be glad I enjoy Bella's company."

Jason frowned at his brother. "I can tell."

His gaze then shifted to Bella. She looked beautiful

standing there in a pair of riding breeches that fitted her body to perfection, a white shirt and a pair of riding boots. She didn't just look beautiful, she looked hot as sin and a side glance at Riley told him that his brother was enjoying the view as much as he was.

"Don't you need to be on your way to work, Riley?"

His brother gave him another grin. "I guess so. Call if you need me as Bella's bodyguard again." He then got into his truck and drove off.

Jason watched him leave before turning his full attention back to Bella. "Ready to go riding, sweetheart?"

As Bella rode with Jason she tried concentrating on the sheer beauty of the rustic countryside instead of the sexiness of the man in the saddle beside her. He was riding Hercules and she could tell he was an expert horseman. And she could tell why he wanted to own the stallion. It was as if he and the horse had a personal relationship. It was evident Hercules had been glad to see him. Whereas the stallion had been like putty in Jason's hands, the horse had given the others grief in trying to handle him. Even now the two seemed in sync.

This was beautiful countryside and the first time she'd seen it. She was stunned by its beauty. The mare he'd chosen for her had come from his stable and was the one he'd rode over to her place. She liked how easily she and the horse were able to take the slopes that stretched out into valleys. The landscape looked majestic with the mountains in the distance.

First they rode over to Dillon and Pam's for breakfast. She had fallen in love with the Westmoreland Estate the first time she had seen it. The huge Victorian-style home with a wide circular driveway sat on three hundred acres of land. Jason had told her on the ride over that as the oldest cousin, Dillon had inherited the family home. It was where most of the family seemed to congregate the majority of the time.

She had met Pam's three younger sisters the other night at dinner and enjoyed their company again around the breakfast table. Everyone asked questions about the rock-throwing incident, and Dillon, who knew the sheriff personally, felt the person or persons responsible would eventually get caught.

After breakfast they were in the saddle again. Jason and Bella rode to Zane's place. She was given a front row seat and watched as Zane, Derringer and Jason exercised several of the horses. Jason had explained some of the horses needed both aerobic and anaerobic training, and that so many hours each day were spent on that task. She could tell that it took a lot of skill as well as experience for any trainer to be successful and achieve the goals they wanted for the horses they trained.

At noon Lucia arrived with box lunches for everyone and Bella couldn't help noticing how much the newlyweds were still into each other. She knew if she decided to marry Jason they would not share the type of marriage Derringer and Lucia did since their union would be more of a business arrangement than anything else. But it was so obvious to anyone around Derringer and Lucia they were madly in love with each other.

Later that day they had dinner with Ramsey and Chloe and enjoyed the time they spent with the couple immensely. Over dinner Ramsey provided tidbits about sheep ranching and how he'd made the decision to move from being a businessman to operating a sheep ranch.

The sun was going down when she and Jason

mounted their horses to return to her ranch. It had been a full day of activities and she had learned a lot about both the horse training business and sheep ranching.

She glanced over at Jason. He hadn't said a whole lot since they'd left his brother's ranch and she couldn't help wondering what he was thinking. She also couldn't help wondering if he intended to sleep in his truck again tonight.

"I feel like a freeloader today," she said to break the silence between them.

He glanced over at her. "Why?"

"Your family fed me breakfast, lunch and dinner today."

He smiled. "They like you."

"And I like them."

She truly did. One of the benefits of accepting Jason's proposal would be his family. But what would happen after the year was up and she'd gotten attached to them? Considered herself part of the family?

They had cleared his land and were riding on her property when up ahead in the distance they saw what appeared to be a huge fiery red ball filled with smoke. They both realized at the same time what it was.

Fire.

And it was coming from the direction of her ranch.

Chapter 7

Bella stood in what used to be the middle of her living room, glanced around and fought the tears stinging her eyes. More than half of her home was gone, destroyed by the fire. And according to the fire marshal it had been deliberately set. If it hadn't been for the quick thinking of her men who begun using water hoses to douse the flames, the entire ranch house would have gone up in smoke.

Her heart felt heavy. Oppressed. Broken. All she'd wanted when she had left Savannah was to start a new life here. But it seemed that was not going to happen. Someone wanted her gone. Who wanted her land that much?

She felt a touch to her arm and without looking up she knew it was Jason. Her body would recognize his touch anywhere. He had been by her side the entire time and watched as portions of her house went up in flames. And he had held her when she couldn't watch any longer and buried her face in his chest and clung to him. At that moment he had become the one thing that was unshakable in a world that was falling down all around her; intentionally being destroyed by someone who was determined to steal her happiness and joy. And he had held her and whispered over and over that everything was going to be all right. And she had tried to believe him and had managed to draw strength from him.

His family had arrived and had given their support as well and had let the authorities know they wanted answers and wanted the person or persons responsible brought to justice. Already they were talking about helping her rebuild and, like Jason had done, assured her that everything would be all right.

Sheriff Harper had questioned her, making inquiries similar to the ones Pete had yesterday when the rock had been thrown through her living room window. Did she know of anyone who wanted her out of Denver? Whoever was responsible was determined to get their message through to her loud and clear.

"Bella?"

She glanced up and met Jason's gaze. "Yes?"

"Come on, let's go. There's nothing more we can do here tonight."

She shuddered miserably and the lungs holding back her sob constricted. "Go? Go where, Jason? Look around you. I no longer have a home."

She couldn't stop the single tear that fell from her eyes. Instead of responding to what she'd said Jason brushed the tear away with the pad of his thumb before entwining his fingers in hers. He then led her away toward the barn for a moment of privacy. It was then that he turned her to face him, sweeping the curls back from her face. He fixed her with a gaze that stirred everything inside of her.

"As long as I have a home, Bella, you do, too."

He then drew in a deep breath. "Don't let whoever did this win. This is land that your grandfather gave you and you have every right to be here if that's what you want. Don't let anyone run you off your land," Jason said in a husky whisper.

She heard his words, she felt his plea, but like she'd told him, she no longer had a home now. She didn't want to depend on others, become their charity case. "But what can I do, Jason? It takes money to rebuild and thanks to my parents, my trust fund is on hold." She paused and then with sagging shoulders added, "I don't have anything now. The ranch was insured, but it will take time to rebuild."

"You have me, Bella. My proposal still stands and now more than ever you should consider taking it. A marriage between us means that we'll both get what we want and will show the person who did this that you aren't going anywhere. It will show them they didn't win after all and sooner or later they will get caught. And even if it happens to be a member of your family, I'm going to make sure they pay for doing this."

Jason lowered his gaze to the ground for a moment and then returned it to her. "I am worse than mad right now, Bella. I'm so full of rage I could actually hurt someone for doing this to you. Whoever is behind this probably thought you were inside the house. What if you had been? What if you hadn't spent the day with me?"

Bella took a deep breath. Those were more "what ifs" she didn't want to think about or consider. The only thing she wanted to think about right now was the proposal; the one Jason had offered and still wanted her to take. And she decided at that very moment that she would.

She would take her chances on what might or might not happen within that year. She would be the best wife possible and hopefully in a year's time even if he wanted a divorce they could still be friends.

"So what about it, Bella? Will you show whoever did this today that you are a fighter and not a quitter and that you will keep what's yours? Will you marry me so we can do that together?"

She held his gaze, exhaled deeply. "Yes, I'll marry you, Jason."

She thought the smile that touched his lips was priceless and she had to inwardly remind herself he wasn't happy because he was marrying her but because marrying her meant he would co-own her land and get full possession of Hercules. And in marrying him she would get her trust fund back and send a message to whomever was behind the threats to her that they were wasting their time and she wasn't going anywhere.

He leaned down, brushed a kiss across her lips and tightened his hold on her hand. "Come on. Let's go tell the family our good news."

If Jason's brothers and cousins were surprised by their announcement they didn't let on. Probably because they were too busy congratulating them and then making wedding plans.

She and Jason had decided the true nature of their

marriage was between them. They planned to keep it that way. The Westmorelands didn't so much as bat an eye when Jason further announced they would be getting married as soon as possible. Tomorrow in fact. He assured everyone they could plan a huge reception for later.

Bella decided to contact her parents *after* the wedding tomorrow. A judge who was a friend of the Westmorelands was given a call and he immediately agreed to perform the civil ceremony in his chambers around three in the afternoon. Dillon and Ramsey suggested the family celebrate the nuptials by joining them for dinner after the ceremony at a restaurant downtown.

The honeymoon would come later. For now they would spend the night at a hotel downtown. With so many things to do to prepare for tomorrow, Bella was able to put the fire behind her and she actually looked forward to her wedding day. She was also able to put out of her mind the reason they were marrying in the first place. Dillon and Pam invited her to spend the night in their home, and she accepted their invitation.

"Come walk me out to my truck," Jason whispered, taking her hand in his.

"All right."

When they got to where his truck was parked, he placed her against it and leaned over and kissed her in a deep, drugging kiss. When he released her lips he whispered, "You can come home with me tonight, you know."

Yes, she knew but then she also knew if she did so, they would consummate a wedding that was yet to take place. She wanted to do things in the right order. The way she'd always dreamed of doing them when she read all those romance novels.

"Yes, I know but I'll be fine staying with Dillon and Pam tonight. Tomorrow will be here before you know it." She then paused and looked up at him, searched his gaze. "And you think we're doing the right thing, Jason?"

He smiled, nodding. "Yes, I'm positive. After the ceremony we'll contact your parents and provide their attorney with whatever documentation needed to kick your trust fund back in gear. And I'm sure word will get around soon enough for whoever has been making those threats to hear Bella Bostwick Westmoreland is here to stay."

Bella Bostwick Westmoreland. She liked the sound of it already but deep down she knew she couldn't get attached to it. She stared into his eyes and hoped he wouldn't wake up one morning and think he'd made a mistake and the proposal hadn't been worth it.

"Everything will work out for the best, Bella. You'll see." He then pulled her into his arms and kissed her again.

"I now pronounce you man and wife. Jason, you may kiss your bride."

Jason didn't waste any time pulling Bella into his arms and devouring her mouth the way he'd gotten accustomed to doing.

He had expected a small audience but every Westmoreland living in Denver was there, except Micah, his brother who was a year older and an epidemiologist with the federal government, as well as his brothers Canyon and Stern who were away attending law school. And

of course he missed his cousin Gemma who was living
with her husband in Australia, and his younger brother
Bane who was in the navy. Jason also missed the twins,
Aidan and Adrian. They were away at college.

When he finally released Bella's mouth, cheers went
up and he glanced at Bella and knew at that moment
just how much he loved her. He would prove the depth
of his love over the rest of their lives. He knew she assumed after the first year either of them could file for
divorce, but he didn't intend for that to happen. Ever.
There would be no divorce.

He glanced down at the ring he'd placed on her finger. He had picked her up at eight that morning, taken
her into town for breakfast and from there a whirlwind
of activities had begun with a visit to the jeweler. Then
to the courthouse to file the necessary papers so they
could marry on time. Luckily there was no waiting period in Colorado and he was grateful for that.

"Hey, Jason and Bella. Are the two of you ready for
dinner?" Dillon asked, smiling.

Jason smiled back. "Yes, we are." He took Bella's
hand in his, felt the sensations touching her elicited
and knew that, personally, he was ready for something
else, as well.

Bella cast a quick glance over at Jason as they
stepped on the elevator that would take them up to their
hotel room in the tower—the honeymoon suite—compliments of the entire Westmoreland family. She realized she hadn't just married the man but had also
inherited his entire family. For someone who'd never
had an extended family before, she could only be elated.

Dinner with everyone had been wonderful and Jason's brothers and cousins had stood to offer toasts to what everyone saw as a long marriage. There hadn't been anything in Jason's expression indicating they were way off base in that assumption or that it was wishful thinking on their parts.

All of the Westmoreland ladies had given her hugs and welcomed her to the family. The men had hugged her, as well, and she could tell they were genuinely happy for her and Jason.

And now they were on the elevator that would carry them to the floor where their room was located. They would be spending the night, sleeping under the same roof and sharing the same bed. They hadn't discussed such a thing happening, but she knew it was an unspoken understanding between them.

Jason had become quiet and she wondered if he'd already regretted making the proposal. The thought that he had sent her into a panic mode made her heart begin to break a piece at a time. Then without warning, she felt his hand touch her arm and when she glanced over at him he smiled and reached for her and pulled her closer to his side, as if refusing to let her stand anywhere by herself…without him. It was as if he was letting her know she would never ever be alone again.

She knew a part of her was probably rationalizing things the way she wished they were, the way she wanted them to be but not necessarily how they really were. But if she had to fantasize then she would do that. If she had to pretend they had a real marriage for the next year then she would do that, too. However, a part of her would never lose sight of the real reason she was here. A part of her would always be prepared for the inevitable.

"You were a beautiful bride, Bella."

"Thank you." Warmth spread through her in knowing that he'd thought so because she had tried so hard to be. She had been determined to make some part of today resemble a real wedding—even if it was a civil one in the judge's chambers. The ladies in the family had insisted that she be turned over to them after securing a license at the Denver County Court House and had promised Jason she would be on time for her wedding.

It had taken less than an hour to obtain the marriage license and Lucia had been there to pick her up afterward. Bella had been whisked away for a day of beauty and to visit a very exclusive bridal shop to pick up the perfect dress for her wedding. Since time was of the essence, everything had been arranged beforehand. When they had delivered her back to Jason five hours later, the moment she'd joined him in the judge's chambers his smile had let her know he thought her time away from him had been well worth it. She would forever be grateful to her new in-laws and a part of her knew that Pam, Chloe, Megan, Lucia and Bailey would also be friends she could count on for life.

"You look good yourself," she said softly.

She thought that was an understatement. She had seen him in a suit the night at the charity ball. He had taken her breath away then and was taking it away now. Tall, dark and handsome, he was the epitome of every woman's fantasy and dream. And for at least one full year, he would be hers.

The elevator stopped on their floor and, tightening hand on hers, they stepped out. Her breath caught the elevator doors whooshed closed behind them began walking toward room 4501. She knew

once they reached those doors and she stepped inside
there would be no turning back.

They silently strolled side by side holding hands.
Everything about the Four Seasons Hotel spoke of its
elegance and the decorative colors all around were vi-
brant and vivid.

Jason released her hand when they reached their
room to pull the passkey from the pocket of his suit
jacket. Once he opened the door he extended his hand to
her and she took it, felt the sensations flowing between
them. She gasped when she was suddenly swept off her
feet and into his arms and carried over the threshold
into the honeymoon suite.

Jason kicked the door closed with his foot before
placing Bella on her feet. And then he just stood there
and looked at her, allowing his gaze to roam all over
her. What he'd told her earlier was true. She was a beautiful bride.

And she was his.

Absolutely and positively his.

Her tea-length dress was ivory in color and made
of silk chiffon and fitted at her small waist with a rose
in the center. It was a perfect match for the ivory satin
rose-heeled shoes on her feet. White roses were her favorite flower and she'd used them as the theme in their
wedding. Even her wedding bouquet had consisted of
white roses.

His chest expanded with so much love for her, love
she didn't know about yet. He had a year to win her ove
and intended to spend the next twelve months doi
just that. But now, he needed for her to know just
much she was desired.

He lowered his head and kissed her, letting his tongue tangle with hers, reacquainting himself with the taste of her, a taste he had not forgotten and had so desperately craved since the last time. He kissed her deeply, not allowing any part of her mouth to go untouched. And she returned the kiss with a hunger that matched his own and he was mesmerized by how she was making him feel.

He tightened his hold on her, molding his body to hers, and was certain she could feel the hot ridge of his erection pressing against her. It was throbbing something awful with a need for her that was monumental. He had wanted her for a long time…ever since he'd seen her that night at the ball, and his desire for her hadn't diminished any since. If anything, it had only increased to a level that even now he could feel his gut tighten in desire. Taking her hands he deliberately began slowly lifting her dress up toward her waist.

"Wrap your legs around me, Bella," he whispered and assisted by lifting her hips when she wrapped her legs around him to walk her toward the bedroom. It was a huge suite and he was determined that later, after they took care of business in the bedroom, they would check out all the amenities the suite had to offer; especially the large Jacuzzi bathtub. Already he saw the beauty of downtown Denver from their hotel room window. But downtown Denver was the last thing on his mind right now. Making love to his wife was.

His wife.

He began kissing her again, deeper and longer, loving the way her tongue mated with his over and over again. He placed her on the bed while reaching behind her to unfasten her dress and slide it from her body. It was then that he took a step back and thought he was dreaming. No fantasy could top what he was seeing now.

She was wearing a white lace bra and matching panties. On any other woman such a color would come across as ultrainnocence, but on Bella it became the epitome of sexual desire.

He needed to completely undress her and did so while thinking of everything he wanted to do to her. When she was on her knees in the middle of the bed naked, he could tell from her expression that this was the first time a man had seen her body and the thought sent shivers through him as his gaze roamed over her in male appreciation. A shudder of primal pride flowed through him and he could only stand there and take her all in.

An erection that was already hard got even harder when he looked at her chest, an area he had yet to taste. Her twin globes were firm. His tongue tingled at the thought of being wrapped around those nipples.

No longer able to resist temptation, he moved toward the bed and placed a knee on it and immediately leaned in to capture a nipple in his mouth. His tongue latched on the hard nub and began playing all kinds of games with it. Games she seemed to enjoy if the way she was pushing her breasts deeper into his mouth was anything to go by.

He heard her moan as he continued to torture her nipples, with quick nips followed by sucking motions, and when he reached down to let his hands test her to see how ready she was, he found she was definitely ready for him. Pulling back he eased from the bed to remove his clothes as she watched.

"I'm not on the Pill, Jason."

He glanced over at her. "You're not?"

"No."

And evidently thinking she needed to explain further she said, "I haven't been sexually active with anyone."

"Since?"

"Never."

A part of him wasn't surprised. In fact, he had suspected as much. He'd known no other man had performed oral sex on her but hadn't been sure of the depth of any other sexual experience. "Any reason you hadn't?"

She met his gaze and held it. "I've been waiting for you."

He drew in a sharp breath and wondered if she knew what she'd just insinuated and figured she hadn't. Maybe she hadn't insinuated anything and it was just wishful thinking on his part. He loved her and would give just about anything for her to love him in return. And until she said the words, he wouldn't assume anything.

"Then your wait is over, sweetheart," he said, sliding on a condom over the thickness of his erection while she looked on. And from the fascinated expression on her face he could tell what she was seeing was another first for her.

When he completed that task he moved to the bed and toward her. "You are so beautifully built, Jason," she said softly, and as if she needed to test her ability to arouse him, she leaned up and flicked out her tongue, licking one of the hardened nubs on his breast like he'd done earlier to her.

He drew in a sharp intake of breath. "You're a quick learner," he said huskily.

"Is that good or bad?"

He smiled at her. "For us it will always be good."

Since this would be her first time he wanted her more than ready and knew of one way to do it. He eased her down on the bed and decided to lick her into an orgasm. Starting at her mouth, he slowly moved downward to her chin, trekked down her neck to her breasts. By the time he'd made it past her midriff to her flat tummy she was writhing under his mouth but he didn't mind. That was a telltale sign of how she was feeling.

"Open your legs, baby," he whispered. The moment she did so he dipped his head to ease his tongue between the folds of her femininity. He recalled doing this to her the last time and knew just what spots would make her moan deep in her throat. Tonight he wanted to do better than that. He wanted to make her scream.

Over and over again he licked her to the edge of an orgasm then withdrew his tongue and began torturing her all over again. She sobbed his name, moaned and groaned. And then, when she was on the verge of an explosion he shifted upward and placed his body over hers.

When he guided his erection in place, he held her gaze and lowered his body to join with hers, uniting them as one. She was tight and he kept a level of control as he eased inside her, feeling how firm a hold her clenched muscles had on him. He didn't want to hurt her and moved inch by slow inch inside her. When he had finally reached the hilt, he closed his eyes but didn't move. He needed to be still for a moment and grasp the significance of what was taking place. He was making love to his wife and she was a wife he loved more than life.

He slowly opened his eyes and met hers and saw she had been watching…waiting and needing him to finish what he'd started. So he did. He began moving slowly, with an extremely low amount of pressure as he began moving in and out of her. When she arched her back, he increased the pressure and the rhythm.

The sounds she began making sent him spiraling and let him know she was loving it. The more she moaned, the more she got. Several times he'd gone so deep inside her he knew he had touched her womb and the thought that he had done so made him crave her that much more.

She released a number of shuddering breaths as he continued to thrust, claiming her as his while she claimed him as hers. And then she threw her head back and screamed out his name.

That's when he came, filling her while groaning thickly as an orgasm overtook them both. The spasms that rammed through his body were so powerful he had to force himself to breathe. He bucked against her several times as he continued to ride her through the force of his release.

He inhaled the scent of their lovemaking before leaning down to capture her mouth, and knew at that moment the night for them was just beginning.

Sometime during the night Jason woke up from the feel of Bella's mouth on him. Immediately his erection began to swell.

"Oh." She pulled her mouth away and looked up

at him with a blush on her face. "I thought you were asleep."

His lips curved into a smile. "I was, but there are some things a man can't sleep through. What are you doing down there?"

She raised her head to meet his gaze. "Tasting you the way you tasted me," she said softly.

"You didn't have to wait until I was asleep, you know," he said, feeling himself get even harder. Although he was no longer inside her mouth, it was still close. Right there. And the heat of her breath was way too close.

"I know, but you were asleep and I thought I would practice first. I didn't want to embarrass myself while you were awake and get it wrong," she said, blushing even more.

He chuckled, thinking her blush was priceless. "Baby, this is one of those things a woman can never get wrong."

"Do you want me to stop?"

"What do you think?"

She smiled up at him shyly. Wickedly. Wantonly. "I think you don't. Just remember this is a practice session."

She then leaned closer and slid him back into her mouth. He groaned deep in his throat when she began making love to him this way. Earlier that night he had licked her into an orgasm and now she was licking him to insanity. He made a low sound in the back of his throat when she began pulling everything out of him with her mouth. If this was a practice session she would kill him when it came to the real thing.

"Bella!"

He quickly reached down and pulled her up to him and flipped her onto her back. He moved on top of her and pushed inside of her, realizing too late when he felt himself explode that he wasn't wearing a condom. The thought that he could be making her pregnant jutted an even bigger release from his body into hers.

His entire body quivered from the magnitude of the powerful thrusts that kept coming, thrusts he wasn't able to stop. The more she gave, the more he wanted and when her hips arched off the bed, he drove in deeper and came again.

"Jason!"

She was following him to sweet oblivion and his heart began hammering at the realization that this was lovemaking as naked as it could get, and he clung to it, clung to her. A low, shivering moan escaped his lips and when her thighs began to tremor, he felt the vibration to the core.

Moments later he collapsed on top of her, moaned her name as his manhood buried inside of her continued to throb, cling to her flesh as her inner muscles wouldn't release their hold.

What they'd just shared as well as all the other times they'd made love tonight was so unbearably pleasurable he couldn't think straight. The thought of what she'd been doing when he had awakened sent sensuous chills down his body.

He opened his mouth to speak but immediately closed it when he saw she had drifted off to sleep. She made such an erotic picture lying there with her eyes closed, soft dark curls framing her face and the sexiest lips he'd ever had the pleasure of kissing slightly parted.

He continued to look at her, thinking he would let her get some rest now. Later he intended to wake her up the same way she'd woken him.

Chapter 8

The following morning after they'd enjoyed breakfast in bed, Bella figured now was just as good a time as any to let her parents know she was a married woman.

She picked up her cell phone and then glanced over at Jason and smiled. That smile gave her the inner strength for the confrontation she knew was coming. The thought of her outwitting them by marrying—and someone from Denver—would definitely throw her parents into a tizzy. She could just imagine what they would try to do. But just as Jason had said, they could try but wouldn't succeed. She and Jason were as married as married could get and there was nothing her parents could do about it.

Taking a deep breath she punched in their number and when the housekeeper answered she was put on hold, waiting for her father to pick up the line.

"Elizabeth. I hope you're calling to say you've come to your senses and have purchased a one-way plane ticket back home."

She frowned. He didn't even take the time to ask how she was doing. Although she figured her parents had nothing to do with those two incidents this week, she decided to ask anyway. "Tell me something, Dad. Did you and Mom think using scare tactics to get me to return to Savannah would work?"

"What are you talking about?"

"Three days ago someone threw a rock through my living room window with a threatening note for me to leave town, and two days ago someone torched my house. Luckily I wasn't there at the time."

"Someone set Dad's house on fire?"

She'd heard the shock in his voice and she heard something else, too. Empathy. This was the first time she'd heard him refer to Herman as "Dad."

"Yes."

"I didn't have anything to do with that, Elizabeth. Your mother and I would never put you in danger like that. What kind of parents do you think we are?"

"Controlling. But I didn't call to exchange words, Dad. I'm just calling for you and Mother to share my good news. I got married yesterday."

"What!"

"That's right. I got married to a wonderful man by the name of Jason Westmoreland."

"Westmoreland?"

"Yes."

"I went to schools with some Westmorelands. Their land was connected to ours."

"Probably his parents. They're deceased now."

"Sorry to hear that, but I hope you know why he married you. He wants that land. But don't worry about it, dear. It can easily be remedied once you file for an annulment."

She shook her head. Her parents just didn't get it. "Jason didn't force me to marry him, Dad. I married him of my own free will."

"Listen, Elizabeth, you haven't been living out there even a full month. You don't know this guy. I will not allow you to marry him."

"Dad, I am already married to him and I plan to send your attorney a copy of our marriage license so the hold on my trust fund will be lifted."

"You think you're smart, Elizabeth. I know what you're doing and I won't allow it. You don't love him and he can't love you."

"Sounds pretty much like the same setup you and Mom have got going. The same kind of marriage you wanted me to enter with Hugh. So what's the problem? I don't see where there is one and I refuse to discuss the matter with you any longer. Goodbye, Dad. Give Mom my best." She then clicked off the phone.

"I take it the news of our marriage didn't go over well with your father."

She glanced over at Jason who was lying beside her and smiled faintly. "Did you really expect that it would?"

"No and it really doesn't matter. They'll just have to get over it."

She snuggled closer to him. That was one of the things she liked about Jason. He was his own man. "What time do we have to check out of here?"

"By noon. And then we'll be on our way to Jason's Place."

She had to restrain the happiness she felt upon knowing they would be going to his home where she would live for at least the next twelve months. "Are there any do's and don'ts that I need to know about?"

He lifted a brow. "Do's and don'ts?"

"Yes. My time at your home is limited. I don't want to jeopardize my welcome." She could have sworn she'd seen something flash in his eyes but couldn't be certain.

"You'd never jeopardize your welcome and no, there are no do's and don'ts that will apply to you, unless…"

Now it was her turn to raise a brow. "Unless what?"

"You take a notion to paint my bedroom pink or something."

She couldn't help bursting out in laughter. She calmed down enough to ask, "What about yellow? Will that do?"

"Not one of my favorite colors but I guess it will work."

She smiled as she snuggled even closer to him. She was looking forward to living under the same roof with Jason.

"Bella?"

She glanced up. "Yes?"

"The last time we made love, I didn't use a condom."

She'd been aware of it but hadn't expected him to talk about it. "Yes, I know."

"It wasn't intentional."

"I know that, too," she said softly. There was no reason he would want to get her pregnant. That would only throw a monkey wrench in their agreement.

They didn't say anything for a long moment and then he asked, "Do you like children?"

She wondered why he was asking such a thing. Surely he had seen her interactions with Susan and Denver enough to know that she did. "Yes, I like children."

"Do you think you'd want any of your own one day?"

Was he asking because he was worried that she would use that as a trap to stay with him beyond the one year? But he'd asked and she needed to be honest. "Yes, I'd love children, although I haven't had the best of childhoods. Don't get me wrong, my parents weren't monsters or anything like that but they just weren't affectionate…at least not like your family."

She paused for a moment. "I love my parents, Jason, although I doubt my relationship with them will ever be what I've always wished for. They aren't those kind of people. Displaying affection isn't one of their strong points. If I become a mother I want to do just the opposite. There will never be a day my child will not know he or she is loved." She hadn't meant to say all of that and now she couldn't help wondering if doing so would ruin things between them.

"I think you would make a wonderful mother."

His words touched her. "Thank you for saying that."

"You're welcome, and I meant it."

She drew in a deep breath, wondering how he could be certain of such a thing. She continued to stare at him for a long moment. He would be a gift to any woman and he had sacrificed himself to marry her—just because he'd wanted her land and Hercules. When she thought about it she found it pitiful that it had taken that to make him want to join his life to hers.

He lifted her hand and looked at the ring he'd placed

there. She looked at it, too. It was beautiful. More than she'd expected and everyone had oohed and ahhed over it.

"You're wearing my ring," he said softly.

The sound of his deep, husky voice made her tummy tingle and a heated sensation spread all through her. "Yes, I'm wearing your ring. It's beautiful. Thank you."

Then she lifted his hand. Saw the gold band brilliantly shining in the sunlight. "And you're wearing mine."

And then she found herself being kissed by him and she knew that no matter how their marriage might end up, right now it was off to a great beginning.

For the second time in two days Jason carried the woman he loved over the threshold. This time he walked into his house. "Welcome to Jason's Place, sweetheart," he said, placing her on her feet.

Bella glanced around. This was the first time she'd been inside Jason's home. She'd seen it a few times from a distance and thought the two-story dwelling flanked by a number of flowering trees was simply beautiful. On the drive from town he'd given her a little history of his home. It had taken an entire year to build and he had built it himself, with help from all the other Westmorelands. And with all the pride she'd heard when he spoke of it, she knew he loved his home. She could see why. The design was magnificent. The decorating—which had been done by his cousin Gemma—was breathtaking and perfect for the single man he'd been.

Jason's eyes never left Bella's as he studied her reaction to being in his home. As far as he was concerned, she would be a permanent fixture. His heart would beat when hers did. His breath was released the same time hers was. He had shared something with her he had never done with any woman—the essence of himself. For the first time in his life he had made love to a woman without wearing a condom. It had felt wonderful being skin to skin, flesh to flesh with her—but only with her. The wife he adored and intended to keep forever.

He knew he had a job to do where she was concerned and it would be one that would give him the greatest of pleasure and satisfaction. Her pain was his pain, her happiness was his. Their lives were now entwined and all because of the proposal he'd offered and she'd taken.

Without thought he turned her in his arms and lowered his head to kiss her, needing the feel of his mouth on hers, her body pressed against his. The kiss was long, deep and the most satisfying experience he could imagine. But then, he'd had nothing but satisfying experiences with her. And he planned on having plenty more.

"Aren't you going to work today?" Bella asked Jason the following day over breakfast. She was learning her way around his spacious kitchen and loved doing it. They had stayed inside yesterday after he'd brought her here. He had kept her mostly in the bedroom, saying their honeymoon was still ongoing. And she had been not one to argue considering the glow she figured had to be on her face. Jason was the most ardent and generous of lovers.

Her mother had called last night trying to convince her she'd made a mistake and that she and her father would be flying into Denver in a few days to talk some sense into her. Bella had told her mother she didn't think coming to Denver was a good idea, but of course Melissa Bostwick wouldn't listen.

When Bella had told Jason about the latest developments—namely her parents' planned trip to Denver—he'd merely shrugged and told her not to worry about it. That was easy for him to say. He'd never met her parents.

"No, I'm not going to work today. I'm still on my honeymoon," Jason said, breaking into her thoughts. "You tell me what you want to do today and we'll do it."

She turned away from the stove where she'd prepared something simple like French toast. "You want to spend more time with me?"

He chuckled. "Of course I do. You sound surprised."

She was. She figured as much time as they'd spent in the bedroom he would have tired of her by now. She was about to open her mouth when his house phone rang. He smiled over at her. "Excuse me for a minute while I get that."

Bella figured the caller was one of his relatives. She turned back to the stove to turn it off. She couldn't help but smile at the thought that he wanted to spend more time with her.

A few moments later Jason hung up the phone. "That was Sheriff Harper."

She turned back around to him. "Has he found out anything?"

"Yes, they've made some arrests."

A lump formed in her throat. She crossed the floor to sit down at the table, thinking she didn't want to be standing for this. "Who did it?"

He came to sit across from her. "Your uncle Kenneth's twin grandsons."

Bella's hand flew to her chest. "But they're only four-teen years old."

"Yes, but the footprints outside your window and the fingerprints on the rock matched theirs. Not to mention that the kerosene can they used to start the fire at your ranch belonged to their parents."

Bella didn't say anything. She just continued to stare at him.

"Evidently they heard their grandfather's grumblings about you and figured they were doing him a favor by scaring you away," Jason said.

"What will happen to them?" she asked quietly.

"Right now they're in police custody. A judge will decide tomorrow if they will be released into the custody of their parents until a court date is set. If they are found guilty, and chances are they will be since the evidence against them is so strong, they will serve time in a detention center for youth for about one or two years, maybe longer depending on any prior arrests."

Jason's face hardened. "Personally, it wouldn't bother me in the least if they locked them up and threw away the key. I'm sure Kenneth is fit to be tied, though. He thinks the world of those two."

Bella shook her head sadly. "I feel so bad about this."

A deep scowl covered Jason's face. "Why do you feel bad? You're the victim and they broke the law."

She could tell by the sound of his voice that he was still upset. "But they're just kids. I need to call Uncle Kenneth."

"Why? As far as I'm concerned this is all his fault for spouting off at the mouth around them about you."

A part of Bella knew what Jason said was true and could even accept he had a right to be angry, but still, the thought that she was responsible for the disruption of so many lives was getting to her. Had she made a mistake in moving to Denver after all?

"Don't even think it, Bella."

She glanced across the table at Jason. "What?"

"I know what's going through your mind, sweetheart. I can see it all over your face and you want to blame yourself for what happened but it's not your fault."

"Isn't it?"

"No. You can't hold yourself responsible for the actions of others. What if you had been standing near the window the day that rock came flying through, or worse yet, what if you'd been home the day they set fire to the house? If I sound mad it's because I still am. And I'm going to stay mad until justice is served."

He paused a moment and then said, "I don't want to talk about Kenneth or his grandsons any longer. Come on, let's get dressed and go riding."

When they returned from riding and Bella checked her cell phone, she had received a call from her parents saying that they had changed their minds and would not be coming to Denver after all. She couldn't help wondering why, but she figured the best thing to do was count her blessings and be happy about their change in plans.

Jason was outside putting the horses away and she decided to take a shower and change into something relaxing. So far, other than the sheriff, no one else had called. She figured Jason's family was treating them as honeymooners and giving them their privacy.

When her cell phone rang, she didn't recognize the

caller but figured it might be one of her parents calling from another number. "Yes?"

"This is all your fault, Bella."

She froze upon hearing her uncle's voice. He was angry. "My grandsons might be going to some youth detention center for a couple of years because of you."

Bella drew in a deep breath and remembered the conversation she and Jason had had earlier that day. "You should not have talked badly about me in front of them."

"Are you saying it's my fault?"

"Yes, Uncle Kenneth, that's exactly what I'm saying. You have no one else to blame but yourself."

"Why you… How dare you speak to me that way. You think you're something now that you're married to a Westmoreland. Well, you'll see what a mistake you made. All Jason Westmoreland wanted was your land and that horse. He doesn't care anything about you. I told you I knew someone who wanted to buy your land."

"And I've always told you my land isn't for sale."

"If you don't think Westmoreland plans to weasel it from you then you're crazy. Just mark my word. You mean nothing to him. All he wants is that land. He is nothing but a controller and a manipulator."

Her uncle then hung up the phone on her.

Bella tried not to let her uncle's words get to her. No one knew the details of their marriage so her uncle had no idea that she was well aware that Jason wanted her land and horse. For what other reason would he have presented her with that proposal? She wasn't the crazy person her uncle evidently assumed she was. She was operating with more than a full deck and was also well aware Jason didn't love her.

She glanced up when Jason walked through the back

door. He smiled when he saw her. "I thought you were going to take a shower."

"I was, but I got a phone call."

"Oh, from who?"

She knew now was not the time to tell him about her uncle's call—especially after all he'd said earlier. So she decided to take that time to tell him about her parents' decision.

"Dad and Mom called. They aren't coming after all."

"What changed their minds?" he asked, taking a seat on the sofa.

"Not sure. They didn't say."

He caught her wrist and pulled her down on the sofa beside him. "Well, I have a lot to say, none of it nice. But the main thing is they've decided not to come and I think it's a good move on their part because I don't want anyone to upset you."

"No one will," she said softly. "I'm fine."

"And I want to make sure you stay that way," he said and pulled her closer into his arms.

She was quiet as her head lay rested against his chest and could actually hear his heart pounding. She wondered if he could hear the pounding of her heart. She still found it strange how attracted they were to each other. Getting married hadn't lessened that any.

She lifted her head to look up at him and saw the intense look that was there in his eyes. It was a look that was so intimate it sent a rush of heat sprinting all through her.

And when he began easing his mouth toward hers, all thoughts left her mind except for one, and that was how much he could make her feel loved even when he was pretending. The moment their lips touched she refused to believe her uncle Kenneth's claim that he was controlling.

Instead she concentrated on how he was making her feel with the way his mouth was mating with hers. And she knew this kiss was just the beginning.

Chapter 9

During the next few weeks Bella settled into what she considered a comfortable routine. She'd never thought being married would be such a wonderful experience and could only thank Jason for making the transition easy for her.

They shared a bed and made passionate love each night. Then in the morning they would get up early and while he sat at the table drinking coffee she would enjoy a cup of tea while he told her about what horses he would be training that day.

While he was away she usually kept busy by reading her grandfather's journals, which had been upstairs in her bedroom and so were spared by the fire. Because she'd been heavily involved with a lot of charity work while living in Savannah, she'd already volunteered a lot of her time at the children's hospital and the West-moreland Foundation.

Hercules was now in Jason's stalls and Jason was working with the insurance company on the repairs of her ranch. He had arranged for all the men who'd worked with her before the fire to be hired on with his horse training business.

Although she appreciated him stepping in and taking charge of her affairs the way he'd done, she hadn't been able to put her uncle Kenneth's warning out of her mind. She knew it was ludicrous to worry about Jason's motivation because he had been honest with her from the beginning and she knew why he'd made the proposal for their marriage. She was well aware that he didn't love her and that he was only married to her for the land and Hercules. But now that he had both was it just a matter of time for him before he tried to get rid of her?

She would be the first to admit he never acted as if he was getting tired of her and still treated her as if he enjoyed having her around. In the afternoons when he returned home from work, the first thing he did after placing his Stetson on the hat rack was to seek her out. Usually he didn't have far to look because she would be right there, close by. Anticipating his return home always put her near the door when he entered the house.

Bella couldn't help noticing that over the past couple of days she had begun getting a little antsy where Jason was concerned because she was uncertain as to her future with him. And to make matters even worse, she was late, which was a good sign she might be pregnant. She hadn't told him of her suspicions because she wasn't sure how he would take the news.

If she were pregnant, the baby would be born within

the first year of their marriage. Would he still want
a divorce even if she was the mother of his child, or
would he want to keep her around for that same reason;
because he felt obligated to do so? But an even more
important question was, did he even want to become
a father? He had questioned her feelings on mother-
hood but she'd never questioned his. She could tell from
his interactions with Susan and Denver that he liked
kids, but that didn't necessarily mean he wanted any of
his own.

Bella knew she should tell him about the possibility
she could be pregnant and discuss her concerns with
him now, but each time she was presented with the opportunity to do so, she would get cold feet.

She walked into an empty room he'd converted into
an office and sat down at the desk to glance out the
window. She would finally admit that another reason
she was antsy was that she knew without a shadow of
doubt that she had fallen in love with Jason and could
certainly understand how such a thing had happened.
She could understand it, but would he? He'd never asked
for her love, just her land and horse.

She heard the sound of a vehicle door closing and
stood from the desk, went to the window and looked
down. It was Jason. He glanced up and saw her and a
smile touched the corners of his mouth. Instantly she
felt the buds of her nipples harden against her blouse.
A flush of desire rushed through her and she knew at
that moment her panties had gotten wet. The man could
turn her on with a single look. He was home earlier than
usual. Three hours earlier.

Now that he was here a lot of ideas flowed in her
mind on how they could use those extra hours. What

she wanted to do first was to take him into her mouth, something she discovered she enjoyed doing. And then he could return the favor by putting that tongue of his to work between her legs. She shuddered at the thought and figured her hormones were on the attack; otherwise, she wouldn't be thinking such scandalous things. They were definitely not things a Miss Prim and Proper lady would think.

He broke eye contact with her to walk up the steps to come into the house and she rushed out of the office to stand at the top of the stairs. She glanced down the moment he opened the door. Jason's dark gaze latched on her and immediately her breath was snatched from her lungs. As she watched, he locked the door behind him and slowly began removing the clothes from his body, first tossing his hat on the rack and then unbuttoning his shirt.

She felt hot as she watched him and he didn't stop. He had completely removed his shirt and she couldn't help admiring the broad shoulders and sinewy muscular thighs in jeans. The masculine sight had blood rushing fast and furious through her veins.

"I'm coming up," he said in a deep, husky voice.

She slowly began backing up when he started moving up the stairs with a look in his eyes that was as predatory as anything she'd ever seen. And there was a deep, intense hunger in his gaze that had her heart hammering like crazy in her chest.

When he cleared the top stair and stepped onto the landing, she breathed in deeply, taking in his scent, while thinking that no man had a right to smell so good, look so utterly male and be so damn hot in a way that would overwhelm any woman's senses.

At least no man but Jason Westmoreland.

"Take off your clothes, Bella," he said in a deep, throaty voice.

She then asked what some would probably think was a dumb question. "Why?"

He moved slowly toward her and it was as if her feet were glued to the spot and she couldn't move. And when he came to a stop in front of her, she tilted back her head to look up at him, saw the hunger in his dark brown gaze. The intensity of that look sent a shudder through her.

He reached out and cupped her face in the palms of his hands and lowered his head slightly to whisper, "I came home early because I need to make love to you. And I need to do it now."

And then he captured her mouth with his, kissing her with the same intensity and hunger she'd seen in his eyes. She returned his kiss, not understanding why he needed to make love to her and why now. But she knew she would give him whatever he wanted and whatever way he wanted it.

He was ravishing her mouth, making her moan deep in her throat. His kiss seemed to be making a statement and staking a claim all at the same time. She couldn't do anything but take whatever he was giving, and she did so gladly and without shame. He had no idea she loved him. How much sharing these past few weeks had meant to her.

And then he jerked his mouth away and quickly removed his boots. Afterward, he carried her into the office and stood her by the desk as he began taking off her clothes with a frenzy that had her head spinning. One part of her wanted to tell him to slow down and to assure him she wasn't going anywhere. But another part was just as eager and excited as he was to get naked, and kept insisting that he hurry up.

Within minutes, more like seconds, spooned between his body and the desk, she was totally naked. The cool air from the air conditioner that swept across her heated skin made her want to cover herself with her hands, but he wouldn't let her. He gently grabbed her wrists in his and held them up over her head, which made her breasts tilt up in perfect alignment to his lips when he leaned down.

On a breathless sigh he eased a nipple into his mouth, sucking it in between his lips and then licking the throbbing tip. She arched her back, felt him gently ease her onto the desk and realized he was practically on the desk with her. The metal surface felt cool to her back, but the warmth of his body felt hot to her front.

He lowered his hand to her sex and the stroke of his fingers on the folds of her labia made her groan out sounds she'd never made before. She'd thought from the first that he had skillful fingers and they were thrumming through her, stirring all kinds of sensations within her. Their lovemaking would often range from gentle to hard and she knew today would be one of those hard times. For whatever reason, he was driven to take her now, without any gentleness of any kind. He was stroking a need within her that wanted it just as fast and hard as he could deliver.

He took a step back and quickly removed his jeans and boxers. When she saw him—in his engorged splendor—a sound of dire need erupted from deep within her throat. He was bringing her to this, this intense state of want and need that was fueled by passion and desire.

"I want to know your taste, baby."

It was on the tip of her tongue to say that as many times as he'd made a meal out of her that he should know it pretty well by now. Instead when he crouched down in front of her body, which was all but spread out on the desk, and proceeded to wrap her legs over his shoulders, she automatically arched her back.

And when she felt his hot mouth close in on her sex, slide his tongue through her womanly folds, she lifted her hips off the table with the intimate contact. And when he began suckling hard, using his tongue to both torture and pleasure, she let out an intense moan as an orgasm tore through her body; sensations started at the soles of her feet and traveled like wildfire all the way to the crown of her head. And then she screamed at the top of her lungs.

Shudders continued to rip through her, made her muscles both ache and rejuvenate. And she couldn't help but lie there while Jason continued to get the taste he wanted.

When her shudders finally subsided, he gave her body one complete and thorough lick before lifting his head and looking up at her with a satisfied smile on his face, and the way he began licking his lips made her feel hot all over again.

He reached out and spread her legs wide and began stroking her again and she began moaning at the contact. "My fingers are all wet, which means you're ready," he said. "Now for me to get ready."

And she knew without looking that he was tearing into a condom packet and soon would be sliding the latex over his erection. After that first time in the hotel he'd never made love to her unprotected again, which gave her even more reason to think he wasn't ready for children. At least not with her, anyway.

From the feel of his erection pressing against her thigh she would definitely agree that at least he was ready for this, probably more ready than any man had a right to be, but she had no complaints.

She came to full attention when she felt his swollen, engorged member easing between her legs, and when he centered it to begin sliding between the folds of her labia and then suddenly thrust forward without any preamble, she began shuddering all over again.

"Look at me, baby. I want to be looking in your eyes when you come. I need to see it happen, Bella."

She looked up and met his gaze. He was buried deep inside of her and then holding tight to her gaze, he began moving, holding tight to the hips whose legs were wrapped firmly around him. They began moving together seemingly in perfect rhythm, faultless harmony and seamless precision. With each deep and thorough stroke, she felt all of him…every glorious inch.

"You tasted good and now you feel good," he said in a guttural voice while holding steadfast to her gaze. "Do you have any idea how wonderful you are making me feel?"

She had an idea. If it was anything close to how he was making her feel then the feelings were definitely mutual. And to show him just how mutual, her inner muscles began clamping down on him, milking him. She could tell from the look in his eyes the exact moment he realized what she was doing and the effect it was having on him. The more she milked him the bigger he seemed to get inside of her, as if he intended for her to have it all.

Today she felt greedy and was glad he intended to supply her needs. She dug her nails into his shoulders, at the moment not caring if she was branding him for life. And then he picked up the tempo and pleasure, the likes of nothing she'd experienced before dimming her vision. But through it all, she kept her gaze locked on his and saw how every sound, every move she made, got to him and triggered him to keep it coming.

And then when she felt her body break into fragments, she screamed out his name and he began pumping into her as if his very life depended on it. The orgasm that ripped through her snatched the breath from her lungs as his intense, relentless strokes almost drove her over the edge. And when she heard the hoarse cry from his own lips, saw the flash of something dark and turbulent in the depths of his eyes, she lost it and screamed again at the top of her lungs as another orgasm shook the core of everything inside her body.

And he followed her, pushed over the edge, while he continued to thrust even deeper. He buried his fingers into her hair and leaned down and captured her mouth to kiss the trembles right off her lips. At that moment she wished she could say all the words that had formed in her heart, words of love she wanted him to know. But she couldn't. This was all there was between them. She had accepted that long ago. And for the moment she was satisfied and content.

And when the day came that he wanted her gone, memories like these would sustain her, get her through each day without him.

And she prayed to God the memories would be enough.

* * *

"So when can we plan your wedding reception?" Megan asked when the Westmorelands had assembled around the dinner table at Dillon's place a few weeks later.

When Bella didn't say anything but looked over at Jason, he shrugged and said, "Throw some dates out to see if they will work for us."

Megan began rambling off dates, saying the first weekend in August would be perfect since all the Westmorelands away at college would be home and Micah, who was presently in Beijing, had sent word he would be back in the States during that time, as well. Gemma, who was expecting, had gotten the doctor's okay to travel from Australia then.

"And," Megan continued, "I spoke with Casey yesterday and she's checked with the other Westmorelands and that will give them plenty of time to make plans to be here, as well. I'm so excited."

Jason glanced over at Bella again thinking he was glad someone was. There was something going on with his wife that he just couldn't put a finger on and whatever it was had put him at a disadvantage. He knew she was upset with the outcome of the Bostwick twins. With all the evidence mounted against the twins, their attorney had convinced their parents to enter a guilty plea in hopes they would get a lesser sentence.

However, given prior mischievous pranks that had gotten the pair into trouble with the law before, the judge was not all that lenient and gave them two years. Bella had insisted on going to the sentencing hearing and he'd warned her against it but she'd been adamant. Things hadn't gone well when Kenneth, who still refused to accept blame for his part in any of it, made a scene, accusing Bella as the one responsible for what had happened to his grandsons. Since that day Jason had noted a change in her and she'd begun withdrawing from him. He'd tried getting her to talk, but she refused to do so.

"So what do the two of you think?" Megan asked, drawing his attention again.

He glanced at Bella. "What do you think, sweetheart?"

She placed a smile on her lips that he knew was forced. "That time is fine with me, but I doubt Mom and Dad will come either way."

"Then they will miss a good party," Jason replied. He then turned to Megan. "The first weekend in August is fine."

Later, on the ride back to their place, Jason finally found out what was troubling Bella. "I rode over to my ranch today, Jason. Why didn't you tell me work hadn't begun on the house yet?"

"There was no reason to tell you. You knew I was taking care of things, didn't you?"

"Yes. But I assumed work had gotten started already."

"I saw no reason to begin work on the place yet, given we're having a lot of rainy days around here now. It's not a good time to start any type of construction. Besides, it's not like you're going to move into the house or anything."

"You don't know that."

He had pulled into the yard and brought the truck to a stop and turned the ignition off. He glanced over at her. "I don't? I thought I did."

He tilted his hat back from his eyes and stared over at her. "Why would you need to move back into the house?"

Instead of holding his gaze she glanced out the window and looked ahead at his house, which he now considered as their house. "Our marriage is only supposed to last a year and I'm going to need somewhere to live when it ends."

Her words were like a kick in the gut. She was already planning for the time when she would be leaving him? Why? He thought things were going great between them. "What's going on, Bella?"

"Nothing is going on. I just need to be realistic and remember that although we enjoy being bed partners, the reason we married stemmed from your proposal, which I accepted knowing full well the terms. And they are terms we must not forget."

Jason simply looked at her as he swore under his breath. She thought the only thing between them was the fact they were bed partners? "Thanks for reminding me, Bella." He then got out of the truck.

That was the first night they slept in the same bed but didn't make love and Bella lay there hurting inside and wasn't sure what she could do about it. She was trying to protect her heart, especially after the results of the pregnancy test she'd taken a few days ago.

Jason was an honorable man. Just the kind of man who'd keep her around just because she was the mother of his child. She wasn't particularly thinking of herself per se but of her child. She had grown up in a loveless household and simply refused to subject her child to one. Jason would never understand how that could be because he'd grown up with parents who'd loved each other and had set a good example for their children to follow. That was evident in the way his cousins and brother treated the wives they loved. It was easy to see their relationships were loving ones, the kinds that last until death. She didn't expect that kind of long-term commitment from Jason. That was not in the plan and had not been in his proposal.

She knew he was awake by the sound of his breathing but his back was to her as hers was to him. When he had come up to bed he hadn't said anything. In fact, he had barely cast a glance her way before sliding under the covers.

His family was excited about hosting a wedding reception for them but she had been tempted to tell them not to bother. Their year would be up before she knew it anyway. However, she had sat there and listened while plans were being made and fighting the urge to get pulled into the excitement.

The bed shifted and she held her breath hoping that, although she'd given him that reminder, he would still want her. He dashed that hope when instead of sliding toward her he got out of the bed and left the room. Was he coming back to bed or did he plan on sleeping somewhere else tonight? On the sofa? In his truck?

She couldn't help the tears that began falling from her eyes. She only had herself to blame. No one told her to fall in love. She should have known better. She should not have put her heart out there. But she had and now she was paying the price for doing so.

"Okay, what the hell is wrong with you, Jason? It's not like you to make such a stupid mistake and the one you just made was a doozy," Zane stormed. "That's the sheikh's prized horse and what you did could have cost him a leg."

Anger flared up inside of Jason. "Dammit, Zane, I know what I did. You don't have to remind me."

He then glanced over at Derringer and waited to see what he had to say and when he didn't say anything, Jason was grateful.

"Look, guys, I'm sorry about the mistake. I've got a lot on my mind. I think I'll call it a day before I cause another major screwup." He then walked off toward Zane's barn.

He was in the middle of saddling his horse to leave when Derringer walked up. "Hey, man, you want to talk about it?"

Jason drew in a deep breath. "No."

"Come on, Jas, there's evidently trouble in paradise at Jason's Place. I don't profess to be an expert when it comes to such matters, but even you will admit that me and Lucia had a number of clashes before we married."

Jason glanced over at him. "What about *after* you married?"

Derringer threw his head back and laughed. "Want a list? The main thing to remember is the two of you are people with different personalities and that in itself is bound to cause problems. The most effective solution is good, open communication. We talk it out and then we make love. Works every time. Oh, and you need to remind her every so often how much you love her."

Jason chuckled drily. "The first two things you said I should do are things I can handle but not the latter."

Derringer raised a brow. "What? You can't tell your wife you love her?"

Jason sighed. "No, I can't tell her."

Derringer looked confused. "Why? You do love her, don't you?"

"Yes, more than life."

"Then what's the problem?"

Jason stopped what he was doing and met Derringer's gaze. "She doesn't love me back."

Derringer blinked and then drew back slightly and said, "Of course she loves you."

Jason shook his head. "No, she doesn't." He paused for a moment and then said, "Our marriage was based on a business proposition, Derringer. She needed a husband to retain her trust fund and I wanted her land—at least co-ownership of her land—and Hercules."

Derringer stared at him for a long moment and then said, "I think you'd better start from the beginning."

It took Jason less than ten minutes to tell Derringer everything, basically because his cousin stood there and listened without asking any questions. But once he'd finished the questions had begun…as well as the observations.

Derringer was certain Bella loved him because he claimed she looked at Jason the way Lucia looked at him, the way Chloe looked at Ramsey and the way Pam looked at Dillon—when they thought no one was supposed to be watching.

Then Derringer claimed that given the fact Jason and Bella were still sharing the same bed—although no hanky-panky had been going on for almost a week now—had significant meaning.

Jason shook his head. "If Bella loves me the way you think she does then why hasn't she told me?"

Derringer crossed his arms over his chest. "And why haven't you told her?" When Jason couldn't answer, Derringer smiled and said, "I think the two of you have a big communication problem. It happens and is something that can easily be corrected."

Jason couldn't help but smile. "Sounds like you've gotten to be a real expert on the subject of marriage."

Derringer chuckled. "I have to be. I plan on being a married man for life so I need to know what it takes to keep my woman happy and to understand that when wifey isn't happy, hubby's life can be a living hell."

Derringer then tapped his foot on the barn's wooden floor as if he was trying to make up his mind about something. "I really shouldn't be telling you this because it's something I overheard Chloe and Lucia discussing yesterday and if Lucia found out I was eavesdropping she—"

"What?"

"Maybe you already know but just hadn't mentioned anything."

"Dammit, Derringer, what the hell are you talking about?"

A sly smile eased across Derringer's lips. "The ladies in the family suspect Bella might be pregnant."

Bella walked out of the children's hospital with a smile on her face. She loved kids and being around them always made her forget her troubles, which was why she would come here a couple of days a week to spend time with them. She glanced at her watch. It was still early yet and she wasn't ready to go home.

Home.

She couldn't help but think of Jason's Place as her

home. Although she'd made a stink with Jason about construction on her ranch, she didn't relish the thought of going back there to live. She had gotten accustomed to her home with Jason.

She was more confused than ever and the phone call from her mother hadn't helped. Now her parents were trying to work out a bargain with her—another proposal of a sort. They would have their attorney draw up a legal document that stated if she returned home they would give her the space she needed. Of course they wanted her to move back onto their estate, although she would be given the entire east wing as her own. They claimed they no longer wanted to control her life, but just wanted to make sure she was living the kind of life she was entitled to live.

Their proposal sounded good but she had gotten into enough trouble accepting proposals already. Besides, even if things didn't work out between her and Jason, he deserved to be around his child. When they divorced, at least his son or daughter would be a stone's throw away.

She was crossing the parking lot to her car when she heard someone call her name. She turned and cringed when she saw it was her uncle Kenneth's daughter, who was the mother of the twins. Although Uncle Kenneth had had an outburst at the trial, Elyse Bostwick Thomas had not. She'd been too busy crying.

Drawing in a deep breath Bella waited for the woman to catch up with her. "Elyse."

"Bella. I just wanted to say how sorry I was for what Mark and Michael did. I know Dad is bitter and I've tried talking to him about it but he refuses to discuss it. He's always spoiled the boys and there was nothing I could do about it, mainly because my husband and I are divorced. My ex moved away, but I wanted a father figure in their lives."

Elyse didn't say anything for a moment. "I hope Dad will eventually realize his part in all this, and although I miss my sons, they were getting too out of hand. I've been assured the place they are going will teach them discipline. I just wanted you to know I was wrong for listening to everything Dad said about you and when I found out you even offered to help pay for my sons' attorney I thought that was generous of you."

Bella nodded. "Uncle Kenneth turned down my offer."

"Yes, but just the thought touched me deeply, considering everything. You and I are family and I hope that one day we can be friends."

A smile touched Bella's lips. "I'd like that, Elyse. I really would."

"Bella, are you sure you're okay? You might want to go see the doctor about that stomach virus."

Bella glanced over at Chloe. On her way home she had dropped by to visit with her cousin-in-law and little Susan. Bella had grown fond of the baby who was a replica of both of her parents. The little girl had Ramsey's eyes and skin tone and Chloe's mouth and nose. "Yes, Chloe, I'm fine."

She decided not to say anything about her pregnancy just yet until after she figured out how and when she would tell Jason. Evidently Chloe had gotten suspicious because Bella had thrown up the other day when Chloe had come to deliver a package to Jason from Ramsey.

Bella knew from the bits and pieces of the stories she'd heard from the ladies that Chloe was pregnant when she and Ramsey had married. However, Bella doubted that was the reason Ramsey had married her. Anyone around the pair for any period of time could tell how in love they were.

Bella never had a best friend, no other woman to share her innermost feminine secrets with. That was one of the reasons she appreciated the bond she felt toward all the Westmoreland women. They were all friendly, understanding and supportive. But she was hoping that because Chloe had been pregnant when she'd married Ramsey, her in-law could help her understand a few things. She had decisions to make that would impact her baby's future.

"Chloe, can I ask you something?"

Chloe smiled over at her. "Sure."

"When you found out you were pregnant were you afraid to tell Ramsey for fear of how he would react?"

Chloe placed her teacup down on the table and her smile brightened as if she was recalling that time. "I didn't discover I was pregnant until Ramsey and I broke up. But the one thing I knew was that I was going to tell him because he had every right to know. The one thing that I wasn't sure about was when I was going to tell him. One time I thought of taking the coward's way out and waiting until I returned to Florida and calling him from there."

Chloe paused for a moment and then said, "Ramsey made things easy for me when he came to me. We patched up things between us, found it had been nothing more than a huge misunderstanding and got back together. It was then that I told him about my pregnancy and he was happy about it."

Bella took a sip of her tea and then asked, "When the two of you broke up did you stay apart for long?"

"For over three weeks and they were the unhappiest three weeks of my life." Chloe smiled again when she added, "A Westmoreland man has a tendency to grow on you, Bella. They become habit-forming. And when it comes to babies, they love them."

There was no doubt in Bella's mind that Jason loved children; that wasn't what worried her. The big question was if he'd want to father any with her considering the nature of their marriage. Would he see that as a noose around his neck? For all she knew he might be counting the days until their year would be up so he could go his way and she go hers. A baby would definitely change things.

She glanced back over at Chloe. "Ramsey is a wonderful father."

Chloe smiled. "Yes, and Jason would be a wonderful father, as well. When their parents died all the Westmorelands had to pitch in and raise the younger ones. It was a team effort and it wasn't easy. Jason is wonderful with children and would make any child a fantastic father."

Chloe chuckled. "I can see him with a son while teaching him to ride his first pony, or a daughter who will wrap him around her finger the way Susan does Ramsey. I can see you and Jason having a houseful of kids."

Bella nodded. Chloe could only see that because she thought she and Jason had a normal marriage.

"Don't ever underestimate a Westmoreland man, Bella."

Chloe's words interrupted her thoughts. "What do you mean?"

"I mean that from what I've discovered in talking with all the other wives, even those spread out in Montana, Texas, Atlanta and Charlotte, a Westmoreland man is loyal and dedicated to a fault to the woman he's chosen as a mate. The woman he loves. And although they can be overly protective at times, you can't find a man more loving and supportive. But the one thing they don't care too much for is when we hold secrets from them. Secrets that need to be shared with them. Jason is special, and I believe the longer you and he are married, the more you will see just how special he is."

Chloe reached out and gently touched Bella's hand. "I hope what I've said has helped in some way."

Bella returned her smile. "It has." Bella knew that she needed to tell Jason about the baby. And whatever decision he made regarding their future, she would have to live with it.

Chapter 10

Jason didn't bother riding his horse back home after his discussion with Derringer. Instead he borrowed Zane's truck and drove home like a madman only to discover Bella wasn't there. She hadn't mentioned anything at breakfast about going out, so where was she? But then they hadn't been real chatty lately, so he wasn't really surprised she hadn't told him anything.

He glanced around his home—their home—and took in the changes she'd made. Subtle changes but changes he liked. If she were to leave his house—their house—it wouldn't be the same. He wouldn't be the same.

He drew in a deep breath. What if the ladies' suspicions were true and she was pregnant? What if Derringer's suspicions were true and she loved him? Hell, if both suspicions were true then they had one hell of a major communication problem between them, and it was one he intended to remedy today as soon as she returned.

He walked into the kitchen and began making, of all things, a cup of tea. Jeez, Bella had definitely rubbed off on him but he wouldn't have it any other way. And what if she was really pregnant? The thought of her stomach growing big while she carried his child almost left him breathless. And he could recall when it happened.

It had to have been their wedding night spent in the honeymoon suite of the Four Seasons. He had awakened to find her mouth on him and she had driven him to more passion than he'd ever felt in his entire life. He'd ended up flipping her on her back and taking her without wearing a condom. He had exploded the moment he'd gotten inside her body. Evidently she had been good and fertile that night.

He certainly hoped so. The thought of her having his baby was his most fervent desire. And no matter what she thought, he would provide both her and his child with a loving home.

He heard the sound of the front door opening and paused a moment not to rush out and greet her. They needed to talk and he needed to create a comfortable environment for them to do so. He was determined that before they went to bed tonight there would be a greater degree of understanding between them. With that resolution, he placed the teacup on the counter to go greet his wife.

Bella's grooming and social training skills had prepared her to handle just about anything, but now that she was back at Jason's Place she was no longer sure of her capabilities. So much for all the money her parents had poured into those private schools.

She placed her purse on the table thinking at least she'd had one bright spot in her day other than the time spent with the kids. And that was her discussion with Elyse. They had made plans to get together for tea later in the week. She could just imagine how her uncle would handle it when he found out she and Elyse had decided to be friends.

And then there had been her conversation with Chloe. It had definitely been an eye-opener and made her realize she couldn't keep her secret from Jason any longer. He deserved to know about the baby and she would tell him tonight.

"Bella. You're home."

She was pulled from her reverie by the pure masculine tone of Jason's voice when he walked out of the kitchen. Her pulse hammered in the center of her throat and she wondered if he would always have this kind of effect on her. She took a second or two to compose herself, before she responded to him. "Yes, I'm home. I see you have company."

He lifted a brow. "Company?"

"Yes. Zane's truck is parked outside," she replied, allowing her gaze to roam over her husband, unable to stop herself from doing so. He was such a hunk and no matter what he wore it only enhanced his masculinity. Even the jeans and chambray shirt he was wearing now made him look sexy as hell.

"I borrowed it. He's not here."

"Oh." That meant they were alone. Un roof. And hadn't made love in almost a wee to reason that the deep vibrations of his v stir across her skin and that turn-you-on mouth of his would make her panties start to feel damp.

She met his gaze and something akin to potent sexual awareness passed between them, charging the air, electrifying the moment. She felt it and was sure he felt it, as well. She studied his features and knew she wanted a son or daughter who looked just like him.

She knew she needed to break into the sensual vibe surrounding them and go up the stairs, or else she would be tempted to do something crazy like cross the room and throw herself in his arms and beg him to want her, to love her, to want the child they had conceived together.

"Well, I guess I'll go upstairs a moment and—"

"Do you have a moment so we can talk, Bella?"

She swallowed deeply. "Talk?"

"Yes."

That meant she was going to have to sit across from him and watch that sensual mouth of his move, see his tongue work and remember what it felt like dueling nonstop with hers and—

"Bella, could we talk?"

She swallowed again. "Now?"

"Yes."

"Sure," she murmured and then she followed him toward the kitchen. Studying his backside she could only think that the man she had married was such a hottie.

Jason wasn't sure where they needed to begin but he did know they needed to begin somewhere.

"I was about to have a cup of tea. Would you like a cup, as well?"

He wondered if she recalled those were the exact

words she had spoken to him that first time she had invited him inside her house. They were words he still remembered to this day. And from the trace of amusement that touched her lips, he knew that she had recalled them.

"Yes, I'd love a cup. Thank you," she said, sitting down at the table, unintentionally flashing a bit of thigh.

He stepped back and quickly moved to the counter, trying to fight for control and to not remember this was the woman whom he'd given her first orgasm, the woman who'd awakened him one morning with her mouth on him, the first woman he'd had unprotected sex with, the only woman he'd wanted to shoot his release inside of, but more than anything, this was the woman he loved so very much.

Moments later when he turned back to her with cups of tea in his hands, he could tell she was nervous, was probably wondering what he wanted to talk about and was hoping he would hurry and get it over with.

"So, how was your day today?" he asked, sitting across from her at the table.

She shrugged those delicate shoulders he liked running his tongue over. She looked so sinfully sexy in the sundress she was wearing. "It was nice. I spent a lot of it at the children's hospital. Today was 'read-a-story' day and I entertained a bunch of them. I had so much fun."

"I'm glad."

"I also ran into Uncle Kenneth's daughter, Elyse."

"The mother of the twins, right?"

"Yes."

"And how did that go?" Jason asked.

"Better than I expected. Unlike Uncle Kenneth, she's not holding me responsible for what happened to her sons. She says they were getting out of hand anyway and is hoping the two years will teach them discipline," Bella said.

"We can all hope for that" was Jason's response.

"Yes, but in a way I feel sorry for her. I can only imagine how things were for her having Kenneth for a father. My dad wouldn't get a 'Father of the Year' trophy, either, but at least I had friends I met at all those schools they shipped me off to. It never bothered me when I didn't go home for the holidays. It helped when I went home with friends and saw how parents were supposed to act. Not as business partners but as human beings."

Bella realized after she'd said it that in a way Jason was her business partner, but she'd never thought of him that way. From the time he'd slipped a ring on her finger she had thought of him as her husband—for better or worse.

The kitchen got silent as they sipped tea.

"So what do you want to talk about, Jason?"

Good question, Jason thought. "I want to talk about us."

He saw her swallow. "Us?"

"Yes, us. Lately, I haven't been feeling an 'us' and I want to ask you a question."

She glanced over at him. "What?"

"Do you not want to be married to me anymore?"

She broke eye contact with him to study the pattern design on her teacup. "What gave you that idea?"

"Want a list?"

She shot her gaze back to him. "I didn't think you'd notice."

"Is that what this is about, Bella, me not noticing you, giving you attention?"

She quickly shook her head. Heaven help her or him if he were to notice her any more or give her more attention than she was already getting. To say Jason Westmoreland was all into her was an understatement. Unfortunately he was all into her, literally. And all for the wrong reasons. Sex was great but it couldn't hold a marriage together. It couldn't replace love no matter how many orgasms you had a night.

"Bella?"

"No, that's not it," she said, nervously biting her bottom lip.

"Then what is it, sweetheart? What do you need that I'm not giving you? What can I do to make you happy? I need to know because your leaving me is not an option. I love you too much to let you go."

The teacup froze midway to her lips. She stared over at him in shock. "What did you just say?"

"A number of things. Do I need to repeat it all?"

She shook her head, putting her cup down. "No, just the last part."

"About me loving you?"

"Yes."

"I said I loved you too much to let you go. Lately you've been reminding me about the year I mentioned in my proposal, but there isn't a year time frame, Bella. I threw that in as an adjustment period to not scare you off. I never intended to end things between us."

He saw the single tear flow from her eyes. "You didn't?"

"No. I love you too much to let you go. There, I've

said it again and I will keep saying it until you finally hear it. Believe it. Accept it."

"I didn't know you loved me, Jason. I love you, too. I think I fell in love with you the first time I saw you at your family's charity ball."

"And that's when I believe I fell in love with you, as well," he said, pushing the chair back to get up from the table. "I knew there was a reason every time we touched a part of my soul would stir, my heart would melt and my desire for you would increase."

"I thought it was all about sex."

"No. I believe the reason the sex between us was so good, so damn hot, was that it was fueled by love of the most intense kind. More than once I wanted to tell you I loved you but I wasn't sure you were ready to hear it. I didn't want to run you off."

"And knowing you loved me is what I needed to hear," she said, standing. "I've never thought I could be loved and I wanted so much for you to love me."

"Sweetheart, I do. I love every single thing about you."

"Oh, Jason."

She went to him and was immediately swept up into his arms, held tight. And when he lowered his head to kiss her, her mouth was ready, willing and hungry. That was evident in the way her tongue mated with his with such intensity.

Moments later he pulled back and swept her off her feet and into his arms then walked out of the kitchen.

Somehow they made it upstairs to the bedroom. And there in the middle of the room, he kissed Bella again with a hunger that she greedily returned. He finally released her mouth to draw in a deep breath, but before she could draw in one of her own, he flipped her dress up to her waist and was pulling a pair of wet panties down her thighs. She barely had time to react before he moved to her hips to bury his head between her legs.

"Jason!"

She came the moment his tongue whipped inside of her and began stroking her labia, but she quickly saw that wouldn't be enough for him. He sharpened the tip of his tongue and literally stabbed deep inside of her and proceeded to lick circles around her clitoris before drawing it in between his lips.

Her eyes fluttered closed as he then began suckling her senseless as desire, more potent than any she'd ever felt, started consuming her, racing through every part of her body and pushing her toward another orgasm.

"Jason!"

And he still didn't let up. She reached for him but couldn't get a firm hold as his tongue began thrusting inside her again. His tongue, she thought, should be patented with a warning sign. Whenever he parted this life it should be donated to the Smithsonian.

And when she came yet again, he spread her thighs wide to lap her up. She moaned deep in her throat as his tongue and lips made a plaything of her clitoris, driving her demented, crazy with lust, when sensation after earth-shattering sensation rammed through her.

And then suddenly he pulled back and through glazed eyes she watched as he stood and quickly undressed himself and then proceeded to undress her, as well. Her gaze went to his erection.

Without further ado, he carried her over to the bed, placed her on her back, slid over her and settled between her legs and aimed his shaft straight toward the damp folds of her labia.

"Yes!" she almost screamed out, and then she felt him, pushing inside her, desperate to be joined with her.

He stopped moving. Dropped his head down near hers and said in a sensual growl, "No condom tonight."

Bella gazed up at him. "No condom tonight or any other night for a while," she whispered. "I'll tell you why later. It's something I planned to tell you tonight anyway." And before she could dwell too much on just what she had to tell him, he began thrusting inside of her.

And when he pushed all the way to the hilt she gasped for breath at the fullness of having him buried so deep inside her. Her muscles clung to him, she was holding him tight and she began massaging him, milking his shaft for everything she had and thought she could get, while thinking a week had been too long.

He widened her legs farther with his hands and lifted her hips to drive deeper still and she almost cried when he began a steady thrusting inside of her, with relentless precision. This was the kind of ecstasy she'd missed. She hadn't known such degrees of pleasure existed until him and when he lifted her legs onto his shoulders while thrusting back and forth inside her, their gazes met through dazed lashes.

"Come for me, baby," he whispered. "Come for me now."

Her body complied and began to shudder in a climax so gigantic she felt the house shaking. She screamed. There was no way she could not, and when he began coming inside her, his hot release thickened by the intensity of their lovemaking, she could only cry out as she was swept away yet again.

And then he leaned up and kissed her, but not before whispering that he loved her and that he planned to spend the rest of his life making her happy, making her feel loved. And she believed him.

With all the strength she could muster, she leaned up to meet him.

"And I love you so very much, too."

And she meant it.

"Why don't I have to wear a condom for a while?" Jason asked moments later with her entwined in his arms, their limbs tangled as they enjoyed the aftermath of their lovemaking together. He knew the reason, but he wanted her to confirm it.

She lifted her head slightly, met his gaze and whispered, "I'm having your baby."

Her announcement did something to him. Being given confirmation that a life they had created together was growing inside her made him shudder. He knew she was waiting for him to say something.

He planned to show her he had taken it well. She needed to know just how happy her announcement had made him. "Knowing that you are pregnant with my child, Bella, is the greatest gift I could ever hope to receive."

"Oh, Jason."

And then she was there, closer into his arms with her arms wrapped around his neck. "I was afraid you wouldn't be happy."

"You were afraid for nothing. I am ecstatic, overjoyed at the prospect of being a father. Thank you for everything you've done, all the happiness you've brought me."

She shook her head. "No, it's I who needs to thank

you for sharing your family with me, for giving me your support when my own family tried to break me down. And for loving me."

And then she leaned toward his lips and he gave her what she wanted, what he wanted. He knew at that moment the proposal had worked. It had brought them together in a way they thought wasn't possible. And he would always appreciate and be forever thankful that Bella had come into his life.

Two days later the Westmorelands met at Dillon's for breakfast to celebrate. It seemed everyone had announcements to make and Dillon felt it was best that they were all made at the same time so they could all rejoice and celebrate.

First Dillon announced he'd received word from Bane that he would be graduating from the naval academy in a few months with honors. Dillon almost choked up when he'd said it, which let everyone know the magnitude of Bane's accomplishments in the eyes of his family. They knew Bane's first year in the navy had been hard since he hadn't known the meaning of discipline. But he'd finally straightened up and had dreams of becoming a SEAL. He'd worked hard and found favor with one of the high-ranking chief petty officers who'd recognized his potential and recommended him for the academy.

Zane then announced that Hercules had done his duty and had impregnated Silver Fly and everyone could only anticipate the beauty of the foal she would one day deliver.

Ramsey followed and said he'd received word from Storm Westmoreland that his wife, Jayla, was expecting and so were Durango and his wife, Savannah. Reggie and Libby's twins were now crawling all over the place. And then with a huge smile on his face Ramsey announced that he and Chloe were having another baby. That sent out loud cheers and it seemed the loudest had come from Chloe's father, Senator Jamison Burton of Florida, who along with Chloe's stepmother, had arrived the day before to visit with his daughter, son-in-law and granddaughter.

Everyone got quiet when Jason stood to announce that he and Bella would be having a baby in the spring, as well. Bella's eyes were glued to Jason as he spoke and she could feel the love radiating from his every word.

"Bella and I are converting her grandfather's ranch into a guest house and combining our lands for our future children to enjoy one day," he ended by saying.

"Does that mean the two of you want more than one child?" Zane asked with a sly chuckle.

Jason glanced over at Bella. "Yes, I want as many children as my wife wants to give me. We can handle it, can't we, sweetheart?"

Bella smiled. "Yes, we can handle it." And they would because what had started out as a proposal had ended up being a whole lot more and she was filled with overflowing joy at how Jason and his family had enriched her life.

He reached out his hand to her and she took it. Hers felt comforting in his and she could only be thankful for her Westmoreland man.

Epilogue

"When I first heard you'd gotten married I wondered about the quickness of it, Jason, but after meeting Bella I understand why," Micah said to his brother. "She's beautiful."

"Thanks." Jason smiled as he glanced around the huge guest house on his and Bella's property. The weather had cooperated and the construction workers had been able to transform what had once been a ranch house into a huge fifteen-room guest house for family, friends and business associates of the Westmorelands. Combining the old with the new, the builder and his crew had done a fantastic job and Jason and Bella couldn't be more pleased.

He glanced across the way and saw Dillon was talking to Bane who'd surprised everyone by showing up. It was the first time he'd returned home since he had left nearly three years ago. Jason had gotten the chance to have a long conversation with his youngest brother. He was not the bad-assed kid of yesteryears but standing beside Dillon in his naval officer's uniform, the family couldn't be more proud of the man he had become. But there still was that pain behind the sharpness of Bane's eyes. Although he hadn't mentioned Crystal's name, everyone in the family knew the young woman who'd been Bane's first love, his fixation probably since puberty, was still in his thoughts and probably had a permanent place in his heart. He could only imagine the conversation Dillon was having with Bane since they both had intense expressions on their faces.

"So you've not given up on Crystal?" Dillon asked his youngest brother.

Bane shook his head. "No. A man can never give up on the woman he loves. She's in my blood and I believe that no matter where she is, I'm in hers." Bane paused a moment. "But that's the crux of my problem. I have no idea where she is."

Bane then studied Dillon's features. "And you're sure that you don't?"

Dillon inhaled deeply. "Yes, I'm being honest with you, Bane. When the Newsomes moved away they didn't leave anyone a forwarding address. I just think they wanted to put as much distance between you and them as possible. But I'll still go on record and say that I think the time apart for you and Crystal was a good thing. She was young and so were you. The two of you were headed for trouble and both of you needed to grow up. I am proud of the man you've become."

"Thanks, but one day when I have a lot of time I'm

going to find her, Dillon, and nobody, her parents or anyone, will keep me from claiming what's mine."

Dillon saw the intense look in Bane's face and only hoped that wherever Crystal Newsome was that she loved Bane just as much as Bane still loved her.

Jason glanced over at Bella who was talking to her parents. The Bostwicks had surprised everyone by flying in for the reception. So far they'd been on their best behavior, probably because they were still in awe by the fact that Jason was related to Thorn Westmoreland—racing legend; Stone Westmoreland—aka Rock Mason, *New York Times* bestselling author; Jared Westmoreland, whose reputation as a divorce attorney was renowned; Senator Reggie Westmoreland, and that Dillon was the CEO of Blue Ridge. Hell, they were even speechless when they learned there was even a sheikh in the family.

He saw that Bella was pretending to hang on to her parents' every word. He had discovered she knew how to handle them and refused to let them treat her like a child. He hadn't had to step in once to put them in their place. Bella had managed to do that rather nicely on her own. They had opted to stay at a hotel in town, which had been fine with both him and Bella. There was only so much of her parents that either of them could take.

He inwardly smiled as he studied Bella's features and could tell she was ready to be rescued. "Excuse me a minute, Micah, I need to go claim my wife for a second." Jason moved across the yard to her and as if she felt his impending presence, she glanced his way and smiled. She then excused herself from her parents and headed to meet him.

The dress she was wearing was beautiful and the style hid the little pooch of her stomach. The doctor had warned them that because of the way her stomach was growing they shouldn't be surprised if she was having twins. It would be a couple of months before they knew for sure.

"Do you want to go somewhere for tea…and me," Jason leaned over to whisper close to her ear.

Bella smiled up at him. "Think we'll be missed?"

Jason chuckled. "With all these Westmorelands around, I doubt it. I don't even think your parents will miss us. Now they're standing over there hanging on to Sheikh Jamal Yasir's every word."

"I noticed."

Jason then took his wife's hand in his. "Come on. Let's take a stroll around our land."

And their land was beautiful, with the valley, the mountains, the blooming flowers and the lakes. Already he could envision a younger slew of Westmorelands that he and Bella would produce who would help take care of their land. They would love it as much as their parents did. Not for the first time he felt as if he was a blessed man, his riches abundant not in money or jewelry but in the woman walking by his side. His Southern Bella, his Southern beauty, the woman that was everything to him and then some.

"I was thinking," he said.

She glanced over at him. "About what?"

He stopped walking and reached out and placed a hand on her stomach. "You, me and our baby."

She chuckled. "Our babies. Don't forget there is that possibility."

He smiled at the thought of that. "Yes, our babies. But mainly about the proposal."

She nodded. "What about it?"

"I suggest we do another."

She threw her head back and laughed. "I don't have any more land or another horse to bargain with."

"A moot point, Mrs. Westmoreland. This time the stakes will be higher."

"Mmm, what do you want?"

"Another baby pretty soon after this one."

She chuckled again. "Don't you know you never mention having more babies to a pregnant woman? But I'm glad to hear that you want a house filled with children because I do, too. You'll make a wonderful father."

"And you a beautiful mother."

And then he kissed her with all the love in his heart, sealing yet another proposal and knowing the woman he held in his arms would be the love of his life for always.

* * * * *

FEELING THE HEAT

Chapter 1

Micah Westmoreland glanced across the ballroom at the woman just arriving and immediately felt a tightening in his gut. Kalina Daniels was undeniably beautiful, sensuous in every sense of the word.

He desperately wanted her.

A shadow of a smile touched his lips as he took a sip of his champagne.

But if he knew Kalina, and he *did* know Kalina, she despised him and still hadn't forgiven him for what had torn them apart two years ago. It would be a freezing-cold day in hell before she let him get near her, which meant sharing her bed again was out of the question.

He inhaled deeply and could swear that even with the distance separating them he could pick up her scent, a memory he couldn't seem to let go of. Nor could he let go of the memories of the time they'd shared together while in Australia. And there had been many. Even now, it didn't take much to recall the whisper of her breath on him just seconds before her mouth—

"Haven't you learned your lesson yet, Micah?"

He frowned and shot the man standing across from him a narrowed look. Evidently his best friend, Beau Smallwood, was also aware of Kalina's entry, and Beau, more than anyone, knew their history.

Micah took a sip of his drink and sat back on his heels. "Should I have?"

Beau merely smiled. "Yes, if you haven't, then you should. Need I remind you that I was there that night when Kalina ended up telling you to go to hell and not to talk to her ever again?"

Micah flinched, remembering that night, as well. Beau was right. After Kalina had overheard what she'd assumed to be the truth, she'd told him to kiss off in several languages. She was fluent in so damn many. The words might have sounded foreign, but the meaning had been crystal clear. She didn't want to see him again. Ever. With the way she'd reacted, she could have made that point to a deaf person.

"No, you don't need to remind me of anything." He wondered what she would say when she saw him tonight. Had she actually thought he wouldn't come? After all, this ceremony was to honor all medical personnel who worked for the federal government. As epidemiologists working for the Centers for Disease Control, they both fell within that category.

Knowing how her mind worked, he suspected she probably figured he wouldn't come. That he would be reluctant to face her. She thought the worst about him and had believed what her father had told her. Initially, her believing such a thing had pissed him off—until he'd accepted that given the set of circumstances, not to mention how well her father had played them both for fools, there was no way she could not believe it.

A part of him wished he could claim that she should have known him better, but even now he couldn't make that assertion. From the beginning, he'd made it perfectly clear to her, as he'd done with all women, that he wasn't interested in a serious relationship. Since Kalina was as into her career as he'd been into his, his suggestion of a no-strings affair hadn't bothered her at all and she'd agreed to the affair knowing it wasn't long-term.

At the time, he'd had no way of knowing that she would eventually get under his skin in a way that, even now, he found hard to accept. He hadn't been prepared for the serious turn their affair had taken until it had been too late. By then her father had already deliberately lied to save his own skin.

"Well, she hasn't seen you yet, and I prefer not being around when she does. I do remember Kalina's hostility toward you even if you don't," Beau said, snagging a glass of champagne from the tray of a passing waiter. "And with that said, I'm out of here." He then quickly walked to the other side of the room.

Micah watched Beau's retreating back before turning his attention to his glass, staring down at the bubbly liquid. Moments later, he sighed in frustration and glanced up in time to see Kalina cross the room. He couldn't help noticing he wasn't the only man watching her. That didn't surprise him.

One thing he could say, no matter what function she attended, whether it was in the finest restaurant in England or in a little hole in the wall in South Africa, she carried herself with grace, dignity and style. That kind of presence wasn't a necessity for her profession. But she made it one.

It had been clear to him the first time he'd met her—that night three years ago when her father, General Neil Daniels, had introduced them at a military function here in D.C.—that he and Kalina shared an intense attraction that had foretold a heated connection. What had surprised him was that she had captivated him without even trying.

She hadn't made things easy for him. In fact, to his way of thinking, she'd deliberately made things downright difficult. He'd figured he could handle just about anything. But when he'd later run into her in Sydney, she'd almost proven him wrong.

They'd been miles away from home, working together while trying to keep a deadly virus from spreading. He hadn't been ready to settle down. While he didn't consider himself a player in the same vein as some of his brothers and cousins, women had shifted in and out of his life with frequency once they saw he had no intention of putting a ring on anyone's finger. And he enjoyed traveling and seeing the world. He had a huge spread back in Denver just waiting for the day he was ready to retire, but he didn't see that happening for many years to come. His career as an epidemiologist was important to him.

But those two months he'd been involved with Kalina he had actually thought about settling down on his one hundred acres and doing nothing but enjoying a life with her. At one point, such thoughts would have scared the hell out of him, but with Kalina, he'd accepted that they couldn't be helped. Spending time with a woman like her would make any man think about tying his life with one woman and not sowing any more wild oats.

When he'd met the Daniels family, he'd known immediately that the father was controlling and the daughter was determined not to be controlled. Kalina was a woman who liked her independence. Wanted it. And she was determined to demand it—whether her father went along with it or not.

In a way, Micah understood. After all, he had come from a big family and although he didn't have any sisters, he did have three younger female cousins. Megan and Gemma hadn't been so bad. They'd made good decisions and stayed out of trouble while growing up. But the youngest female Westmoreland, Bailey, had been out of control while following around her younger hellion brothers, the twins Aidan and Adrian, as well as Micah's baby brother, Bane. The four of them had done a number of dumb things while in their teens, earning a not-so-nice reputation in Denver. That had been years ago. Now, thank God, the twins and Bailey were in college and Bane had graduated from the naval academy and was pursuing his dream of becoming a SEAL.

His thoughts shifted back to Kalina. She was a woman who refused to be pampered, although her father was determined to pamper her anyway. Micah could understand a man wanting to look out for his daughter, wanting to protect her. But sometimes a parent could go too far.

When General Daniels had approached Micah about doing something to keep Kalina out of China, he hadn't gone along with the man. What had happened between him and Kalina had happened on its own and hadn't been motivated by any request of her father's, although she now thought otherwise. Their affair had been one of those things that just happened. They had been attracted to each other from the first. So why she would assume he'd had ulterior motives to seek an affair was beyond him.

Kalina was smart, intelligent and beautiful. She possessed the most exquisite pair of whiskey-colored eyes, which made her honey-brown skin appear radiant. And the lights in the room seemed to highlight her shoulder-length brown hair and show its luxuriance. The overall picture she presented would make any male unashamedly aware of his sexuality. As he took another sip of his drink and glanced across the room, he thought she looked just as gorgeous as she had on their last date together, when they had returned to the States. It had been here in this very city, where they'd met, when their life together had ended after she discovered what she thought was the truth. To this day, he doubted he would ever forgive her father for distorting the facts and setting him up the way he had.

Micah sighed deeply and took the last sip of his drink, emptying his glass completely. It was time to step out of the shadows and right into the line of fire. And he hoped like hell that he survived it.

Micah was here.

The smile on Kalina's face froze as a shiver of awareness coursed through her and a piercing throb hit her right between the legs. She wasn't surprised at her body's familiar reaction where he was concerned, just annoyed. The man had that sort of effect on her and even after all this time the wow factor hadn't diminished.

It was hard to believe it had been two years since she had found out the truth, that their affair in Australia had been orchestrated by her father to keep her out of Beijing. Finding out had hurt—it still did—but what Micah had done had only reinforced her belief that men couldn't be trusted. Not her father, not Micah, not any of them.

And especially not the man standing in front of her with the glib tongue, weaving tales of his adventures in the Middle East and beyond. If Major Brian Rose thought he was impressing her, he was wrong. As a military brat, no one had traveled the globe as much as she had. But he was handsome enough, and looked so darn dashing in his formal military attire, he was keeping her a little bit interested.

Of course, she knew that wherever Micah was standing he would look even more breathtaking than Major Rose. The women in attendance had probably all held their breath when he'd walked into the room. As far as she was concerned, there wasn't any man alive who could hold a candle to him, in or out of clothes. That conclusion reminded her of when they'd met, almost three years ago, at a D.C. event similar to this one.

Her father had been honored that night as a commissioned officer. She'd had her own reason to celebrate in the nation's capital. She had finally finished medical school and accepted an assignment to work as a civilian for the federal government's infectious-disease research team.

It hadn't taken her long to hear the whispers about the drop-dead-gorgeous and handsome-as-sin Dr. Micah Westmoreland, who had graduated from Harvard Medical School before coming to work for the government as an infectious-disease specialist. But nothing could have prepared her for coming face-to-face with him.

She had been rendered speechless. Gathering the absolute last of her feminine dignity, she had picked up her jaw, which had fallen to the floor, and regained her common sense by the time her father had finished the introductions.

When Micah had acknowledged her presence, in a voice that had been too sexy to belong to a real man, she'd known she was a goner. And when he had taken her smaller hand in his in a handshake, it had been the most sensuous gesture she'd ever experienced. His touch alone had sent shivers up and down her spine and put her entire body in a tailspin. She had found it simply embarrassing to know any man could get her so aroused, and without even putting forth much effort.

"So, Dr. Daniels, where is your next assignment taking you?"

She was jerked out of her thoughts by the major's question. Was that mockery she'd heard in his voice? She was well aware of the rumor floating around that her father pretty much used his position to control her destinations and would do anything within his power to keep her out of harm's way. That meant she would never be able to go anyplace where there was some real action.

She'd been trying to get to Afghanistan for two years and her request was always denied, saying she was needed elsewhere. Although her father swore up and down he had nothing to do with it, she knew better. Losing her mother had been hard on him, and he was determined not to lose his only child, as well. Hadn't he proven just how far he would go when he'd gotten

Micah to have that affair with her just to keep her out of Beijing during the bird-flu epidemic?

"I haven't been given an assignment yet. In fact, I've decided to take some time off, an entire month, starting tomorrow."

The man's smile widened. "Really, now, isn't that a coincidence. I've decided to take some time off, too, but I have only fourteen days. Anywhere in particular that you're going? Maybe we can go there together."

The man definitely didn't believe in wasting time, Kalina thought. She was just about to tell the major, in no uncertain terms, that they wouldn't be spending any time together, not even if her life depended on it, when Brian glanced beyond her shoulder and frowned. Suddenly, her heart kicked up several beats. She didn't have to imagine why. Other men saw Micah as a threat to their playerhood since women usually drooled when he was around. She had drooled the first time *she'd* seen him.

Kalina refused to turn around, but couldn't stop her body's response when Micah stepped into her line of vision, all but capsizing it like a turbulent wave on a blast of sensual air.

"Good evening, Major Rose," he said with a hard edge to his voice, one that Kalina immediately picked up on. The two men exchanged strained greetings, and she watched how Micah eyed Major Rose with cool appraisal before turning his full attention to her. The hard lines on his face softened when he asked, "And how have you been, Kalina?"

She doubted that he really cared. She wasn't surprised he was at this function, but she *was* surprised he had deliberately sought her out, and there was no doubt in her mind he'd done so. Any other man who'd done what he had done would be avoiding her like the plague. But not Dr. Micah Westmoreland. The man had courage of steel, but in this case he had just used it foolishly. He was depending on her cultured upbringing to stop her from making a scene, and he was right about her. She had too much pride and dignity to cause a commotion tonight, although she'd gone off on him the last time they had seen each other. She still intended to let him know exactly how she felt by cutting him to the core, letting it be obvious that he was the last person she wanted to be around.

"I'm fine, and now if you gentlemen will excuse me, I'll continue to make my rounds. I just arrived, and there are a number of others I want to say hello to."

She needed to get away from Micah, and quick. He looked stunning in his tux, which was probably why so many women in the room were straining their necks to get a glimpse of him. Even her legs were shaky from being this close to him. She suddenly felt hot, and the cold champagne she'd taken a sip of wasn't relieving the slow burn gathering in her throat.

"I plan to mingle, myself," Micah said, reaching out and taking her arm. "I might as well join you since there's a matter we need to discuss."

She fought the urge to glare up at him and tell him they had nothing to discuss. She didn't want to snatch her arm away from him because they were already getting attention, probably from those who'd heard what happened between them two years ago. Unfortunately, the gossip mill was alive and well, especially when it came to Micah Westmoreland. She had heard about him long before she'd met him. It wasn't that he'd been the type of man who'd gone around hitting on women. The problem was that women just tended to place him on their wish list.

"Fine, let's talk," she said, deciding that if Micah thought he was up to such a thing with her, then she was ready.

Fighting her intense desire to smack that grin right off his face, she glanced over at Major Rose and smiled apologetically. "If you will excuse me, it seems Dr. Westmoreland and I have a few things to discuss. And I haven't decided just where I'll be going on vacation, but I'll let you know. I think it would be fun if you were to join me." She ignored the feel of Micah's hand tightening on her arm.

Major Rose nodded and gave her a rakish look. "Wonderful. I will await word on your plans, Kalina."

Before she could respond, Micah's hand tightened on her arm even more as he led her away.

"Don't count on Major Rose joining you anywhere," Micah all but growled, leaning close to Kalina's ear while leading her across the ballroom floor toward an exit. He had checked earlier and the French doors opened onto the outside garden. It was massive and far away from the ball, so no one could hear the dressing-down he was certain Kalina was about to give him.

She glared at him. "And don't count on him doing otherwise. You don't own me, Micah. Last I looked, there's nothing of yours on my body."

"Then look again, sweetheart. Everything of mine is written all over that body of yours. I branded you. Nothing has changed."

They came to a stop in front of what was the hotel's

replica of the White House's prized rose garden. He was glad no one was around. No prying eyes or over-eager ears. The last time she'd had her say he hadn't managed to get in a single word for dodging all the insults and accusations she'd been throwing at him. That wouldn't be the case this time. He had a lot to say and he intended for her to hear all of it.

"Nothing's changed? How dare you impose your presence on me after what you did," she snarled, transforming from a sophisticated lady to a roaring lioness. He liked seeing her shed all that formality and cultural adeptness and get downright nasty. He especially liked that alteration in the bedroom.

He crossed his arms over his chest. "And what exactly did I do, other than to spend two months of what I consider the best time of my life with you, Kalina?"

He watched her stiffen her spine when she said, "And I'm supposed to believe that? Are you going to stand here and lie to my face, Micah? Deny that you weren't in cahoots with my father to keep me away from Beijing, using any means necessary? I wasn't needed in Sydney."

"I don't deny that I fully agreed with your father that Beijing was the last place you needed to be, but I never agreed to keep you out of China."

He could tell she didn't want to hear the truth. She'd heard it all before but still refused to listen. Or to believe it. "And it wasn't that you weren't needed in Sydney," he added, remembering how they'd been sent there to combat the possible outbreak of a deadly virus. "You and I worked hard to keep the bird-flu epidemic from spreading to Australia, so it wasn't just sex, sex and more sex for us, Kalina. We worked our asses off, or have you forgotten?"

He knew his statement threw her for a second, made her remember. Yes, they might have shared a bed every night for those two months, but their daytime hours weren't all fun and games. No one except certain members of the Australian government had been aware that their presence in the country had been for anything other than pleasure.

And regardless of what she'd thought, she had been needed there. He had needed her. They had worked well together and had combated a contagious disease. He had already spent a year in Beijing and had needed to leave when his time was up. Depression had started to set in with the sight of people dying right before his eyes, mostly children. It had been so frustrating to work nonstop trying unsuccessfully to find a cure before things could get worse.

Kalina had wanted to go to Beijing and get right in the thick of things. He could just imagine how she would have operated. She was not only a great epidemiologist, she was also a compassionate one, especially when there was any type of outbreak. He could see her getting attached to the people—especially the children—to the point where she would have put their well-being before her own.

That, and that alone, was the reason he had agreed with her father, but at no time had he plotted to have an affair with her to keep her in Sydney. He was well aware that all her hostility was because she believed otherwise. And for two years he had let her think the worst, mainly because she had refused to listen to anything he had to say. It was apparent now that she was still refusing to listen.

"Have you finished talking, Micah?"

Her question brought his attention back to the present. "No, not by a long shot. But I can't say it all tonight. I need to see you tomorrow. I know you'll be in town for the next couple of days and so will I. Let's do lunch. Even better, let's spend that time together to clear things up between us."

"Clear things up between us?" Kalina sneered in an angry whisper as red-hot fury tore through her. She was convinced that Micah had lost his ever-loving mind. Did he honestly think she would want to spend a single minute in his presence? Even being here now with him was stretching her to the limit. Where was a good glass of champagne when she wanted it? Nothing would make her happier right now than to toss a whole freakin' glass full in his face.

"I think I need to explain a few things to you, Micah. There's really nothing to clear up. Evidently you think I'm a woman that a man can treat any kind of way. Well, I have news for you. I won't take it. I don't need you any more than you need me. I don't appreciate the way you and Dad manipulated things to satisfy your need to exert some kind of power over me. And I—"

"Power? Do you think that's what I was trying to do, Kalina? Exert some kind of *power* over you? Just what kind of person do you honestly think I am?"

She ignored the tinge of disappointment she heard in his voice. It was probably just an act anyway. At the end of those two months, she'd discovered just what a great actor Micah could be. When she'd found out the truth, she had dubbed him the great pretender.

Kalina lifted her chin and straightened her spine. "I think you are just like all the other men my father tried throwing at me. He says jump and you all say how high.

I thought you were different and was proven wrong. You see Dad as some sort of military hero, a legend, and whatever he says is gospel. And although Micah is a book in the Bible, last time I checked, my father's name was not. I am twenty-seven and old enough to make my own decisions about what I want to do and where I want to go. And neither you nor my father have anything to say about it. Furthermore—"

The next thing she knew, she was swept off her feet and into Micah's arms. His mouth came down hard, snatching air from her lungs and whatever words she was about to say from her lips.

She struggled against him, but only for a minute. That was all the time it took for those blasted memories of how good he tasted and just how well he kissed to come crashing over her, destroying her last shred of resistance. And then she settled down and gave in to what she knew had to be pleasure of the most intense kind.

God, he had missed this, Micah thought, pulling Kalina closer into his embrace while plundering her mouth with an intensity he felt in every part of his body. She had started shooting off her mouth, accusing him of things he hadn't done. Suddenly, he'd been filled with an overwhelming urge to kiss her mouth shut. So he had.

And with the kiss came memories of how things had been between them their last time together, before anger had set in and destroyed their happiness. Had it really been two years since he'd tasted this, the most delectable tongue any woman could possess? And the body pressed against his was like none other. A perfect fit.

The way she was returning the kiss was telling him she had missed this intimate connection as much as he had.

Her accusations bothered him immensely because there was no truth to what she'd said. He, of all people, was not—and never would be—a yes-man to her father, or to anyone. Her allegations showed just how little she knew him, and he intended to remedy that. But for now, he just wanted to enjoy this.

He deepened the kiss and felt the simmer sear his flesh, heat his skin and sizzle through to his bones. Then there was that surge of desire that flashed through his veins and set off a rumble of need in his chest. He'd found this kind of effect from mouth-to-mouth contact with a woman only happened with Kalina. She was building an ache within him, one only she had the ability to soothe.

Over the past two years he'd thought he was immune to this and to her, but the moment she had walked into the ballroom tonight, he'd known that Kalina was in his blood in a way no other woman could or would ever be. Even now, his heart was knocking against his ribs and he was inwardly chanting her name.

Lulled by the gentle breeze as well as the sweetness of her mouth, he wrapped his arms around her waist as something akin to molten liquid flowed over his senses. Damn, he was feeling the heat, and it was causing his pulse to quicken and his body to become aroused in a way it hadn't in years. Two years, to be exact.

And now he wanted to make up for lost time. How could she think he had pretended the passion that always flowed through his veins whenever he held her, kissed her or made love to her? He couldn't help tunneling his fingers through her hair. He'd noticed she was wearing it differently and liked the style on her. But there was very little about Kalina Daniels that he didn't like. All of which he found hard to resist.

He deepened the kiss even more when it was obvious she was just as taken, just as aroused and just as needy as he was. She could deny some things, but she couldn't deny this. Oh, she was mad at him and that was apparent. But it was also evident that all her anger had transformed to passion so thick that the need to make love to her was clawing at him, deep.

Conversation between an approaching couple had Kalina quickly pulling out of his arms. All it took was one look in her eyes beneath the softly lit lanterns to see the kiss had fired her up.

He leaned in, bringing his lips close to hers. "You are wrong about me, Kal. I never sold out to your father. I'm my own man. No one tells me what to do. If you believe otherwise, then you don't really know me."

He saw something flicker in her eyes. He also felt the tension surrounding them, the charged atmosphere, the electrified tingle making its way up his spine. Now more than ever, he was fully aware of her. Her scent. Her looks.

She was breathtaking in the sexy, one-shoulder, black cocktail dress that hugged her curves better than any race car could hug the curves at Indy. There was a sensuality about her that would make any man's pulse rise. Other men had been leery of approaching her that night in D.C. when he'd first flirted with her. After all, she was General Daniels's daughter and it was a known fact the man had placed her on a pedestal. But unlike the other men, Micah wasn't military under her father's command. He was civilian personnel who didn't have to take orders from the general.

She surprised him out of his thoughts when she leaned forward. He reached out for her only to have his hands knocked out of the way. The eyes staring at him were again flaring in anger. "I'm only going to say this once more, Micah. Stay away from me. I don't want to have anything else to do with you," she hissed, her breath fanning across his lips.

He sighed heavily. "Obviously you weren't listening, Kalina. I didn't have an affair with you because your father ordered me to. I was with you because I wanted to be. And you're going to have a hard time convincing me that you can still be upset with me after having shared a kiss like that."

"Think what you want. It doesn't matter anymore, Micah."

He intended to make it matter. "Spend tomorrow with me. Give it some thought."

"There's nothing to think about. Go use someone else."

Anger flashed through him. "I didn't use you." And then in a low husky tone, he added, "You meant a lot to me, Kalina."

Kalina swallowed. There was a time when she would have given anything to hear him say that. Even now, she wished that she could believe him, but she could not forget the look of guilt on his face when she'd stumbled across him discussing her with her father. She had stood in the shadows and listened. It hadn't been hard to put two and two together. She had fled from the party, caught a cab and returned to the hotel where she quickly packed her stuff and checked out.

Her father had been the first one she'd confronted, and he'd told her everything. How he had talked Micah into doing whatever it took to keep her in Sydney and away from Beijing. Her father claimed he'd done it for her own good, but he hadn't thought Micah would go so far as to seduce her. An affair hadn't been in their plan.

"You don't believe you meant something to me," he said again when she stood there and said nothing.

She lifted her chin. "No, I don't believe you. How can I think I meant anything to you other than a good time in bed when you explicitly told me in the very beginning that what we were sharing was a no-strings affair? And other than in the bedroom, you'd never let me get close to you. There's so much about you I don't know. Like your family, for instance. So how can you expect me to believe that I meant anything to you, Micah?"

Then, without saying another word, she turned and walked back toward the ballroom. She hoped that would be the end of it. Micah had hurt her once, and she would not let him do so again.

Chapter 2

By the time Micah got to his hotel room he was madder than hell. He slammed the door behind him. When he had returned to the ballroom, Kalina was nowhere to be found. Considering his present mood, that had been a good thing.

Now he moved across the room to toss his car keys on a table while grinding his teeth together. If she thought she'd seen the last of him then he had news for her. She was sadly mistaken. There was no way he would let her wash him off. No way and no how.

That kiss they'd shared had pretty much sealed things, whether she admitted it or not. He had not only felt her passion, he'd tasted it. She was still upset with him, but that hadn't stopped them from arousing each other. After the kiss, there had been fire in her eyes. However, the fire hadn't just come from her anger.

He stopped at a window and looked out, breathing heavily from the anger consuming him. Even at this hour the nation's capital was busy, if the number of cars on the road was anything to go by. But he didn't want to think about what anyone else was doing at the moment.

Micah rubbed his hand down his face. Okay, so Kalina had told the truth about him not letting her get too close. Thanks to an affair he'd had while in college, he'd been cautious. As a student, he'd fallen in love with a woman only to find out she'd been sleeping with one of her professors to get a better grade. The crazy thing about the situation was that she'd honestly thought he should understand and forgive her for what she'd done. He hadn't and had made up in his mind not to let another woman get close again. He hadn't shared himself emotionally with another woman since then.

But during his affair with Kalina, he had begun to let his guard down. How could she not know when their relationship had begun to change from a strictly no-strings affair to something more? Granted, there hadn't been any time for candlelight dinners, strolls in the park, flowers and such, but he had shared more with her than he had with any other woman…in the bedroom.

He drew in a deep breath and had to ask himself, "But what about outside the bedroom, man? Did you give her reason to think of anything beyond that?" He knew the answer immediately.

No, he hadn't. And she was right, he hadn't told her anything about his family and he knew why. He'd taken his college lover, Patrice, home and introduced her to the family as the woman he would one day marry. The woman who would one day have his children. She had gotten close to them. They had liked her and in the end she had betrayed them as much as she had betrayed him.

He lifted his head to stare up at the ceiling. Now he could see all his mistakes, and the first of many was letting two years go by without seeking out Kalina. He'd been well aware of what her father had told her. But he'd assumed she would eventually think things through and realize her dad hadn't been completely truthful with her. Instead, she had believed the worst. Mainly because she truly hadn't known Micah.

His BlackBerry suddenly went off. He pulled it out of his pocket and saw it was a call from home. His oldest brother, Dillon. There was only a two-year difference in their ages, and they'd always been close. Any other time he would have been excited about receiving a call from home, but not now and not tonight. However, Dillon was family, so Micah answered the call.

"Hello?"

"We haven't heard from you in a while, and I thought I would check in," Dillon said.

Micah leaned back against the wall. Because Dillon was the oldest, he had pretty much taken over things when their parents, aunt and uncle had died in a plane crash. There had been fifteen Westmorelands—nine of them under the age of sixteen—and Dillon had vowed to keep everyone together. And he had.

Micah had been in his second year of college and hadn't been around to give Dillon a hand. But Ramsey, their cousin, who was just months younger than Dillon, had pitched in to help manage things.

"I'm fine," Micah heard himself saying when in all honesty he was anything but. He drew in a deep breath and said, "I saw Kalina tonight."

Although Dillon had never met Kalina he knew who she was. One night while home, Micah had told Dillon all about her and what had happened to tear them apart. Dillon had suggested that he contact Kalina and straighten things out, as well as admit how he felt about her. But a stubborn streak wouldn't let Micah do so. Now he wished he would have acted on his brother's advice.

"And how is she?"

Micah rubbed another hand down his face. "She still hates my guts, if that's what you want to know. Go ahead and say I told you so."

"I wouldn't do that."

No, he wouldn't. That wasn't Dillon's style, although saying so would have been justified.

"So what are you going to do, Micah?"

Micah figured the only reason Dillon was asking was because his brother knew how much Kalina meant to him…even if *she* didn't know it. And her not knowing was no one's fault but his.

"Not sure what I'm going to do because no matter what I say, she won't believe me. A part of me just wants to say forget it, I don't need the hassle, but I can't, Dil. I just can't walk away from her."

"Then don't. You've never been a quitter. The Micah Westmoreland I know goes after what he wants and has never let anyone or anything stand in his way. But if you don't want her enough to fight for her and make her see the truth, then I don't know what to tell you."

Then, as if the subject of Kalina was a closed one, Dillon promptly began talking about something else. He told Micah how their sister-in-law, Bella, was coming along in her pregnancy, and that the doctors had verified twins, both girls.

"They're the first on our side," he said. Their parents had had all boys. Seven of them.

"I know, and everyone is excited and ready for them to be born," Dillon replied. "But I don't think anyone is as ready as Jason," he said of their brother and the expectant father.

The rest of the conversation was spent with Dillon bringing Micah up to date on what was going down on the home front. His brother Jason had settled into wedded bliss and so had his cousin Derringer. Micah shook his head. He could see Jason with a wife, but for the life of him, considering how Derringer used to play the field and enjoy it immensely, the thought of him settled down with one woman was still taking some getting used to. Dillon also mentioned that Ramsey and Chloe's son would be born in a few months.

"Do you think you'll be able to be here for li'l Callum's christening?"

Micah shook his head. Now, that was another one it was hard to believe had settled down. His cousin Gemma had a husband. She used to be a real pistol where men were concerned, but it seemed that Callum Austell had changed all that. She was now living in Australia with him and their two-month-old son.

"I plan to be there," Micah heard himself saying. "In a few weeks, I'll have thirty days to kill. I leave for Bajadad the day after tomorrow and I will be there for two weeks. I'll fly home from there." Bajadad was a small and beautiful city in northern India near the Himalayan foothills.

"It will be good seeing you again."

Micah couldn't help chuckling. "You make it sound like I haven't been home in years, Dil. I was just there seven months ago for Jason's wedding reception."

"I know, but anytime you come home and we can get everyone together is good."

Micah nodded. He would agree to that, and for Gemma's baby's christening, all the Westmorelands would be there, including their cousins from Atlanta, Texas and Montana.

Moments later, Micah ended his phone conversation with Dillon. He headed for the bedroom to undress and take a shower. The question Dillon asked him rang through his head. What was he going to do about Kalina?

Just like that, he remembered the proposition she'd made to Major Rose. And as he'd told her, he had no intention of letting the man go anywhere with her.

And just how are you going to stop her? his mind taunted. *She doesn't want to have anything to do with you. Thanks to her daddy's lie, you lost her. Get over it.*

He drew in a deep breath, knowing that was the kicker. He couldn't get over it. Dillon was right. Micah was not a quitter, and it was about time he made Kalina aware of that very fact.

Micah was pulled from his thoughts when his cell phone rang again. Pulling it from his pants pocket, he saw it was an official call from the Department of Health and Human Services. "Yes, Major Harris?"

"Dr. Westmoreland, first I want to apologize for calling you so late. And secondly, I'm calling to report changes in the assignment to India."

"And what are the changes, Major?"

"You will leave tomorrow instead of Monday. And

Dr. Moore's wife went into labor earlier today so he has to be pulled off the team. We're going to have to send in a replacement."

Micah headed the U.S. epidemic response team consisting of over thirty epidemiologists, so calling to let him know of any changes was the norm. "That's fine."

He was about to thank her for calling and hang up when she said, "Now I need to call Dr. Daniels. Unfortunately, her vacation has to be canceled so she can take Dr. Moore's place."

Micah's pulse rate shot up and there was a deep thumping in his chest, close to his heart. "What did you say?" he asked, to make sure he'd heard her correctly.

"I said Dr. Daniels will be Dr. Moore's replacement since she's next in line on the on-call list. Unfortunately, her vacation was supposed to start tomorrow."

"What a pity," he said, not really feeling such sympathy. What others would see as Kalina's misfortune, he saw as his blessing. This change couldn't be any better if he'd planned it himself, and he intended to make sure Kalina's canceled vacation worked to his advantage.

Of course, when she found out she would automatically think the worst. She would assume the schedule change was his idea and that he was responsible for ruining her vacation. But it wouldn't be the first time she'd falsely accused him of something.

"Good night, Dr. Westmoreland."

He couldn't help smiling, feeling as if he had a new lease on life. "Good night, Major Harris."

He clicked off the phone thinking someone upstairs had to like him, and he definitely appreciated it. Now he would have to come up with a plan to make sure he didn't screw things up with Kalina this time.

* * *

Kalina paced her hotel room. *What was she going to do about Micah?*

She came to a stop long enough to touch her lips. She'd known letting him kiss her had been a bad move, but she hadn't been able to resist the feel of his mouth on hers. She should have been prepared for it. She'd seen the telltale signs in his eyes. He hadn't taken her off to a secluded place to talk about the weather. She'd been prepared for them to face off, have it out. And they'd done that. Then they'd ended up kissing each other senseless.

As much as she would like to do so, she couldn't place the blame solely at his feet. She had gone after his mouth just as greedily as he'd gone after hers. A rush of heat had consumed her the moment he'd stuck his tongue inside her mouth. So, okay, they were still attracted to each other. No big deal.

Kalina frowned. It *was* a big deal, especially when, even now, whirling sensations had taken over her stomach. She knew with absolute certainty that she didn't want to be attracted to Micah Westmoreland. She didn't want to have anything to do with him, period.

She glanced over at the clock and saw it was just past midnight. She was still wearing her cocktail dress, since she hadn't changed out of her clothes. She had begun pacing the moment she'd returned to her hotel room. Why was she letting him do this to her? And why was he lying, claiming he had not been in cahoots with her father when she knew differently?

Moving to the sofa, she sat down, still not ready to get undressed, because once she got in bed all she would do was dream about Micah. She leaned back in her seat, remembering the first time they'd worked together. She had arrived in Sydney, and he had been the one to pick her up from the airport. They had met a year earlier and their attraction to each other had been hot and instantaneous. It had taken less than five minutes in his presence that day to see that the heat hadn't waned any.

She would give them both credit for trying to ignore it. After all, they'd had an important job to do. And they'd made it through the first week, managing to keep their hands off each other. But the beginning of the next week had been the end of that. It had happened when they'd worked late one night, sorting out samples, dissecting birds, trying to make sure the bird flu didn't spread to the continent of Australia.

Technically, he had been her boss, since he headed the government's epidemic response team. But he'd never exerted the power of that position over her or anyone. He had treated everyone as a vital and important part of the team. Micah was a born leader and everyone easily gave him the respect he deserved.

And on that particular night, she'd given him something else. He had walked her to her hotel room, and she had invited him in. It hadn't been a smart move, but she had gotten tired of playing games. Tired of lusting after him and trying to keep her distance. They were adults and that night she'd figured they deserved to finally let go and do what adults did when they had the hots for each other.

Until that night, she'd thought the whole sex act was overrated. Micah had proven her wrong so many times that first night that she still got a tingling sensation just remembering it. She'd assumed it was a one-night stand, but that hadn't been the case. He had invited her out to dinner the following night and provided her with the terms of a no-strings affair, if she was interested. She had been more than interested. She was dedicated to her career and hadn't wanted to get involved in a serious relationship any more than he did.

That night they had reached a mutual agreement, and from then on they'd been exclusively involved during the two months they'd remained in Sydney. She was so content with their affair that when her earlier request for an assignment to Beijing had been denied, it really hadn't bothered her.

That contentment had lasted until she'd returned to the States and discovered the truth. Not only had her father manipulated her orders, but he'd solicited Micah's help in doing whatever he had to do to make sure she was kept happy in Sydney. She had been the one left looking like a complete fool, and she doubted she would forgive either of them for what they'd done.

Thinking she'd had enough of strolling down memory lane where the hurt was too much to bear, Kalina got up from the sofa and was headed toward the bedroom to change and finally attempt to sleep, when her cell phone rang. She picked it up off the table and saw it was Major Sally Harris, the administrative coordinator responsible for Kalina's assignments. She wondered why the woman would be calling her so late at night.

Kalina flipped on the phone. "Yes, Major Harris?"

"Dr. Daniels, I regret calling you so late and I want to apologize, because I have to deliver bad news."

Kalina frowned. "And what bad news is that?"

"Dr. Moore's wife went into labor earlier today so he has to be pulled off the epidemic response team headed out for Bajadad. I know your vacation was to start tomorrow, but we need your assistance in India."

Kalina drew in a deep breath. Although she hadn't made any definite vacation plans, she had looked forward to taking time off. "How long will I be needed in Bajadad?"

"For two weeks, beginning tomorrow, and then you can resume your vacation."

She nodded. There was no need to ask if there was someone else they could call since she knew the answer to that already. The epidemic response team had thinned out over the past few years with a war going on. And since the enemy liked to engage in chemical warfare, a number of epidemiologists had been sent to work in Afghanistan and Iraq.

"Dr. Daniels?"

Resigned, she said, "Yes, of course." Not that she had a choice in the matter. She was civilian, but orders from her boss were still meant to be followed, and she couldn't rightly get mad at Jess Moore because his wife was having a baby. "I'll be ready to head out tomorrow."

"Thanks. I'll send your information to your email address," Major Harris said.

"That will be fine."

"And Dr. Westmoreland has been notified of the change in personnel."

Kalina almost dropped the phone. "Dr. Westmoreland?"

"Yes?"

She frowned. "Why was he notified?"

"Because he's the one heading up the team."

Kalina's head began spinning. No one would be so cruel as to make her work with Micah again. She drew in a deep breath when a suspicion flowed through her mind. "Was Dr. Westmoreland the one to suggest that I replace Dr. Moore?"

"No, the reason you were called is that you're the next doctor on the on-call list."

Lucky me. Kalina shook her head, feeling anything but lucky. The thought of spending two weeks around Micah had her fuming inside. And regardless of what Major Harris said, it was hard to believe it was merely a coincidence that she was next on the call list. Micah was well liked and she knew all about his numerous connections and contacts. If she found out he had something to do with this change then…

"Dr. Daniels?"

"Yes?"

"Is there anything else you'd like to know?"

"No, there's nothing else."

"Thank you, Dr. Daniels, and good night."

"Good night, Major Harris."

Kalina hung up the phone knowing she couldn't let her feelings for Micah interfere with her work. She had a job to do, and she intended to do it. She would just keep her distance from him. She went into the bedroom and began tugging off her clothes as she became lost in a mix of disturbing thoughts.

The first thing she would do would be to set ground rules between her and Micah. If he saw this as a golden opportunity to get back in her bed then he was sadly mistaken. She was not the type of woman to forgive easily. Just as she'd told him earlier tonight, there was nothing else they had to say to each other regarding what happened between them two years ago. It was over and done with.

But if that kiss was anything to go by, she would need to be on guard around him at all times. Because their relationship might be over and done with, but the attraction between them was still alive and well.

Chapter 3

Micah saw the fire in Kalina's eyes from ten feet away. She glared as she moved toward him, chin up and spine stiff. She meant business. He slid a hand into the pocket of his jeans, thinking that he was glad it was Sunday and there were few people around. It seemed they were about to have it out once again.

This morning, upon awakening, he had decided the best way to handle her was to let her assume he wasn't handling her at all, to make her think that he had accepted her decision about how things would be between them. And when he felt the time was right, he would seize every opportunity he could get and let her know in no uncertain terms that her decision hadn't been his.

His gaze swept over her now. She was dressed for travel, with her hair pulled back in a ponytail and a pair of comfortable shoes on her feet. She looked good in her jeans and tank top and lightweight jacket. But then, she looked better than any woman he knew, in clothes or out of them.

He continued to stare at her while remembering her body stretched out beneath his when he'd made love to her. Even now, he could recall how it felt to skim his hands down the front of her body, tangle his fingers in her womanly essence while kissing her with a degree of passion he hadn't been aware of until her.

His heart began racing, and he could feel the zipper of his pants getting tight. He withdrew his hand from his pocket. The last thing he needed was for her to take note of his aroused state, so he turned and entered the private office he used whenever he was in D.C. on business. Besides, he figured the best place to have the encounter he knew was coming was behind closed doors.

By the time she had entered the office, all but slamming the door behind her, he was standing behind the desk.

He met her gaze, and felt the anger she wasn't trying to hide. As much as he wanted to cross the room and pull her into his arms and kiss her, convince her how wrong she was about him, common sense dictated he stay put. He intended to do what he hadn't done two years ago. Give her the chance to get to know him. He was convinced if she'd truly known him, she would not have been so quick to believe the worst about him.

"Dr. Daniels, I take it you're ready to fly out to Bajadad."

Her gaze narrowed. "And you want me to believe you had nothing to do with those orders, Micah?"

He crossed his arms over his chest and met her stare head-on. "At this point, Kalina, you can believe whatever you like. For me to deny it wouldn't matter since you wouldn't believe me anyway."

"And why should I?" she snapped.

"Because I have no reason to lie," he said simply. "Have you ever considered the possibility that I could be telling the truth? Just in case you need to hear it from me—just like I had nothing to do with your father's plan to keep you out of Beijing, your orders to go to Bajadad were not my idea. Although I embrace the schedule change wholeheartedly. You're a good doctor, and I can't think of anyone I want more on my team. We're dealing with a suspicious virus. Five people have died already and the government suspects it might be part of something we need to nip in the bud as soon as possible. However, we won't know what we're dealing with until we get there."

He watched as her whole demeanor changed in the wake of the information he had just provided. Her stiffened spine relaxed and her features became alert. No matter what, she was a professional, and as he'd said, she was good at what she did.

"What's the point of entry?" she asked, moving to stand in front of the desk.

"So far, only by ingestion. It's been suspected that something was put in the water supply. If that's true, it will be up to us to find out what it is."

She nodded, and he knew she completely understood. The government's position was that if the enemy had developed some kind of deadly chemical then the United States needed to know about it. It was important to determine early on what they were up against and how they could protect U.S. military personnel.

"And how was it detected, Micah?" She was calm

and relaxed as she questioned him. He moved to sit on the edge of his desk. Not far from where she stood. He wondered if she'd taken note of their proximity.

He wished she wasn't wearing his favorite perfume and that he didn't remember just how dark her eyes would become in the heat of passion. Kalina Daniels was an innately sensuous woman. There was no doubt about it.

"Five otherwise healthy adults over the age of fifty were found dead within the same week with no obvious signs of trauma," he heard himself saying. "However, their tongues had enlarged to twice the normal size. Other than that, there was nothing else, not even evidence of a foreign substance in their bloodstream."

He saw the look in her eyes while she was digesting what he'd said. Most terrorist groups experimented on a small number of people before unleashing anything in full force, just to make sure their chemical warfare weapon was effective. It was too early to make an assumption about what they would be facing, but the researcher who was already there waiting on them had stated his suspicions. Before 9/11 chemical weapons were considered a poor-man's atomic bomb. However, because of their ability to reach millions of people in so many different ways, these weapons were now considered the worst and most highly effective of all forms of warfare.

"Have you ever been to Bajadad?" she asked him.

He met her gaze. "Yes, several years ago, right after the first democratic elections were held. It was my first assignment after leaving college and coming to work for the federal government. We were sent there on a peace-finding mission when members of the king's household had become ill. Some suspected foul play. However, it didn't take us long to determine it hadn't been all that serious, just a contaminated sack of wheat that should never have been used."

He could tell by the look in her eyes that she'd become intrigued. That's how it had always been with her. She would ask a lot of questions to quench that curiosity of hers. She thought he'd lived an adventurous life as an epidemiologist, while, thanks to her father, she'd been deliberately kept on the sidelines.

In a way, he was surprised she was going to Bajadad. Either the old man had finally learned his lesson or he was getting lax in keeping up with his daughter's whereabouts. He knew her father had worked behind the scenes, wielding power, influencing his contacts, to make sure Kalina had assignments only in the States or in first-world countries. He'd discovered, after the fact, that her time in Sydney had been orchestrated to keep her out of Beijing without giving her a reason to get suspicious.

Micah stood and decided to shift topics. He met Kalina's gaze when he said, "I think we need to talk about last night."

He watched her spine stiffen as she once again shifted into a defensive mode. "No, we don't."

"Yes, we do, Kalina. We're going out on a mission together, and I think it's going to be important that we're comfortable around each other and put our personal differences aside. I'd be the first to admit I've made a lot of mistakes where you're concerned, and I regret making them. Now you believe the worst of me and nothing I can say or do will change that."

He paused a moment, knowing he had to choose his

words carefully. "You don't have to worry about me mixing business with pleasure, because I refuse to become involved with a woman who doesn't trust me. So there can never be anything between us again."

There, he'd said it. He tasted the lie on his tongue, but knew his reasons for his concocted statement were justified. He had no intention of giving her up. Ever. But she had to learn to trust him. And he would do whatever he had to do to make that happen.

Although she tried to shelter her reaction, he'd seen how his words had jolted her body. There was no doubt in his mind she had felt the depth of what he'd said. A part of him wanted to believe that deep down she still cared for him.

She lifted her chin in a stubborn frown. "Good. I'm glad we got that out of the way and that we understand each other."

He glanced down at his watch. "Our flight leaves in a few hours. I would offer you a ride to the airport, but I'm catching a ride with someone myself."

She tilted her head back and looked at him. "No problem. I reserved a rental car."

Kalina looked at her own watch and slipped the straps of her purse onto her shoulders. "I need to be going."

"I'll walk out with you," he said, falling into step beside her. He had no problem offering her a ride if she needed one, but he hadn't wanted to appear too anxious to be in her company. "We're looking at a twelve-hour flight. I'd advise you to eat well before we fly out. The food we're going to be served on the plane won't be the best."

She chuckled and the sound did something to him.

It felt good to be walking beside her. "Don't think I don't know about military-airplane food. I'm going to stop and grab me a sandwich from Po'Boys," she said.

He knew she regretted mentioning the restaurant when he glanced over and saw the blush on her face. Chances were, like him, she was remembering the last time they'd gone there together. It had been their first night back in the States after Australia. He might not recall what all they'd eaten that night, but he did remember everything they'd done in the hotel room afterward.

"Whatever you get, eat enough for the both of us," he said, breaking the silence between them.

She glanced over at him. "I will."

They were now outside, standing on the top steps of the Centers for Disease Control. "Well, I guess I'll be seeing you on the flight. Take care until then, Kal."

Then, without looking back, he moved to the car that pulled up to the curb at that very moment. He smiled, thinking the timing was perfect when he saw who was driving the car.

He glanced up at the sky. He had a feeling someone up there was definitely on his side. His cousin, Senator Reggie Westmoreland, had called him that morning, inviting him to lunch. Reggie, his wife, Olivia, and their one-year-old twin sons made Washington their home for part of the year. It was Olivia and not Reggie who'd come to pick him up to take him to their house in Georgetown. She was a beautiful woman, and he could just imagine the thoughts going through Kalina's mind right now.

Kalina stood and watched Micah stroll down the steps toward the waiting car. He looked good in a cham-

bray shirt that showed the width of his broad shoulders
and jeans that hugged his masculine thighs, making
her appreciate what a fine specimen of a man he was.

He worked out regularly and it showed. No matter
from what angle you saw him—front, back or side—
one looked just as good as the other. And from the
side-glances of several women who were climbing the
steps and passing by him as he moved down, she was
reminded again that she wasn't the only one who appreciated that fact.

Oh, why did he have to call her Kal? It was the nick-
name he'd given her during their affair. No one else
called her that. Her father detested nicknames and always referred to her by her first and middle name. To
her dad she was Kalina Marie.

She tried not to show any emotion as she watched a
woman get out of the car, smiling brightly while moving
toward Micah. She was almost in his face by the time
his foot touched the last step, and he gave the woman
a huge hug and a warm smile as if he was happy to see
her, as well.

No wonder he's so quick to write you off, she thought
in exasperated disgust, hating that seeing Micah with
another woman bothered her. *He's already involved
with someone else. Well, what did you expect? It's been
two years. Just because you haven't been in a serious
relationship since then doesn't mean he hasn't. And
besides, you're the one who called things off. Accused
him of being in league with your father...*

Kalina shook her head as the car, with Micah in it,
pulled off. Why was she trying to rehash anything? She
knew the truth, and no matter how strenuously Micah
claimed otherwise, she believed her father. Yes, he was

controlling, but he loved her. He had no reason to lie. He had confessed his part and had admitted to his involvement in Micah's part, as well. So why couldn't Micah just come clean and fess up? And why had she felt a bout of jealousy when he'd hugged that woman? Why did she care that the woman was jaw-droppingly beautiful, simply gorgeous with not a hair on her head out of place?

Tightening her hand on her purse, Kalina walked down the steps toward the parking lot. She had to get a grip on more than her purse. She needed to be in complete control of her senses while dealing with Micah.

"Sorry to impose, but I think this is the only seat left on the plane," Micah said as he slid into the empty seat next to Kalina.

Her eyes had been closed as she waited for take-off, but she immediately opened them, looking at him strangely before lifting up slightly to glance around, as if to make sure he was telling the truth.

He smiled as he buckled his seat belt. "You need to stop doing that, you know."

She arched an eyebrow. "Doing what?"

"Acting like everything coming out of my mouth is a lie."

She shrugged what he knew were beautiful shoulders. "Well, once you tell one lie, people have a tendency not to believe you in the future. Sort of like the boy who cried wolf." She then closed her eyes again as if to dismiss him.

He didn't plan to let her response be the end of it. "What's going to happen when you find out you've been wrong about me?"

She opened her eyes and glanced over at him, looking as if the thought of her being wrong was not even a possibility. "Not that I think that will happen, but if it does then I'll owe you an apology."

"And when it does happen I might just be reluctant to accept your apology." He then leaned back in his seat and closed his eyes, this time dismissing her and leaving her with something to chew on.

The flight attendant prevented further conversation between them when she came on the intercom to provide flight rules and regulations. He kept his eyes closed. Kalina's insistence that he would conspire with her father grated on a raw nerve each and every time she said it.

Moments later, he felt the movement of the plane glide down the runway before tilting as it eased into the clouds. Over the years, he'd gotten used to air travel, but that didn't mean he particularly liked it. All he had to do was recall that he had lost four vital members of his family in a plane crash. And he couldn't help remembering that tragic and deep-felt loss each and every time he boarded a plane, even after all these years.

"She's pretty."

He opened his eyes and glanced over at Kalina. "Who is?"

"That woman who picked you up from the CDC today."

He nodded. "Thanks. I happen to think she's pretty, too," he said honestly. In fact, he thought all his cousins and brothers had married beautiful women. Not only were they beautiful, they were smart, intelligent and strong.

"Have the two of you been seeing each other long?"

It would be real simple to tell her that Olivia was a relative, but he decided to let her think whatever she wanted. "No, and we really aren't seeing each other now. We're just friends," he said.

"Close friends?"

He closed his eyes again. "Yes." He had been tempted to keep his eyes open just to see her expression, but knew closing them would make his nonchalance more effective.

"How long have the two of you known each other?"

He knew she was trying to figure out if Olivia had come before or after her. "Close to five years now."

"Oh."

So far everything he'd said had been the truth. He just wasn't elaborating. It was his choice and his right. Besides, he was giving her something to think about.

Deciding she'd asked enough questions about Olivia, he said, "You might want to rest awhile. We have a long flight ahead of us."

And he intended on sharing every single hour of it with her. It wasn't a coincidence that the last seat on the military jet had been next to her and that he'd taken it. There hadn't been any assigned seats on this flight. Passengers could sit anywhere, and, with the help of the flight attendant, he'd made sure they had sat everywhere but next to Kalina. The woman just happened to know that *New York Times* bestselling author Rock Mason, aka Stone Westmoreland, was Micah's cousin. The woman was a huge fan and the promise of an autographed copy of Stone's next action thriller had gone a long way.

Micah kept his eyes closed but could still inhale Kalina's scent. He could envision her that morning, dabbing cologne all over her body, a body he'd had intimate knowledge of for two wonderful months. He was convinced he knew where every mole was located, and he was well acquainted with that star-shaped scar near her hip bone that had come as a result of her taking a tumble off a skateboard at the age of twelve.

He drew in a deep breath, taking in her scent one more time for good measure. For now, he needed to pretend he was ignoring her. Sitting here lusting after Kalina wasn't doing him any good and was just weakening his resolve to keep her at a distance while he let her get to know him. He couldn't let that happen. But he couldn't help it when he opened his eyes, turned to her and said, "Oh, by the way, Kalina. You still have the cutest dimples." He then turned to face straight ahead before closing his eyes once again.

Satisfied he might have soothed her somewhat, he stretched his long legs out in front of him, at least as far as they could go, and tilted his seat back. He might as well get as comfortable as he could for the long flight.

He'd been given a good hand to play and he planned on making the kind of win that the gambler in the family, his cousin Ian, would be proud of. The stakes were high, but Micah intended to be victorious.

So Micah had known the woman during their affair. Did that mean he'd taken back up with her after their time together had ended? Kalina wondered. He said he and the woman were only friends, but she'd known men to claim only friendship even while sleeping with a woman every night. Men tended not to place the same importance on an affair as women did. She, of all people, should know that.

And how dare he compliment her on her dimples at a time like this and in the mood she was in. She had to work with him, but she was convinced she didn't even like him anymore. Yet in all fairness, she shouldn't be surprised by the comment about her dimples. He'd told her numerous times that her dimples were the first thing he'd noticed about her. They were permanent fixtures on her face, whether she smiled or not.

And then there was the way he'd looked at her when he'd said it. Out of the clear blue sky, he had turned those gorgeous bedroom-brown eyes on her and re-marked on her dimples. Her stomach had clenched. It had been so unexpected it had sent her world tilting for a minute. And before she'd recovered, he'd turned back around and closed his eyes.

Now he was reclining comfortably beside her. All man. All sexy. All Westmoreland. And seemingly all bored...at least with her. She had a good mind to wake him up and engage in some conversation just for the hell of it, but then she thought better of it. Micah West-moreland was a complex man and just thinking about how complex he could be had tension building at her temples.

She couldn't help thinking about all the things she didn't know about him. For some reason, he'd never shared much about himself or his family. She knew he had several brothers, but that fact was something she'd discovered by accident and not because he'd told her about them. She'd just so happened to overhear a con-versation between him and his good friend Dr. Beau Smallwood. And she did know his parents had died in a plane crash when he was in college. He'd only told her that because she'd asked.

Her life with her military father was basically an open book. After her mother had died of cervical cancer when Kalina was ten, her father had pretty much clung to her like a vine. The only time they were separated was when he'd been called for active duty or another assignment where she wasn't allowed. Those were the days she spent on her grandparents' farm in Alabama. Joe and Claudia Daniels had passed away years ago, but Kalina still had fond memories of the time she'd spent with them.

Kalina glanced over at Micah again. It felt strange casually sitting next to a man who'd been inside her body…numerous times. A man whose tongue had licked her in places that made her blush to think about. Someone who had taken her probably in every position known to the average man and in some he'd probably created himself. He was the type of man a woman fantasized about. A shiver raced through her body just thinking about being naked with him.

Up to now, she had come to terms with the fact that she'd be working with Micah again, especially after what he'd said in his office earlier that morning. He didn't want to become involved with her, just as she didn't want to become involved with him. So why was she tempted to reach out and trace the line of his chin with her fingers or use the tip of her tongue to glisten his lips?

Oh, by the way, you still have the cutest dimples. If those words had been meant to get next to her, they had. And she wished they hadn't. She didn't want to remember anything about the last time they were together or what sharing those two months with him had meant to her.

And she especially did not want to remember what the man had meant to her.

Having no interest in the movie currently being shown and wanting to get her mind off the man next to her, she decided to follow Micah's lead. She tilted her seat back, closed her eyes and went to sleep.

Chapter 4

Micah awakened the next morning and stretched as he glanced around his bedroom. He'd been too tired when he'd arrived at the private villa last night to take note of his surroundings, but now he couldn't help smiling. He would definitely like it here. Kalina's room was right next door to his.

He slid out of bed and headed for the bathroom, thinking the sooner he got downstairs the better. The government had set up a lab for them in the basement of the villa and, according to the report he'd read, it would be fully equipped for their needs.

Twelve hours on a plane hadn't been an ideal way to spend time with Kalina, but he had managed to retain his cool. He'd even gone so far as to engage in friendly conversation about work. Otherwise, like him, she'd slept most of the time. Once he'd found her watching some romantic movie. Another time she'd been reading a book on one of those eReaders.

A short while after waking, Micah had dressed and was headed downstairs for breakfast. The other doctor on the team had arrived last week and Micah was looking forward to seeing him again. Theodus Mitchell was a doctor he'd teamed with before, who did excellent work in the field of contagious diseases.

Micah opened his bedroom door and walked out into the hallway the same time Kalina did. He smiled when he saw her, although he could tell by her expression that she wasn't happy to see him. "Kalina. Good morning."

"Good morning, Micah. You're going down for breakfast?"

"Yes, what about you?" he asked, falling into step beside her.

"Yes, although I'm not all that hungry," she said.

He definitely was, and it wasn't all food that had him feeling hungry. She looked good. Well rested. Sexy as hell in a pair of brown slacks and a green blouse. And she'd gotten rid of the ponytail. She was wearing her hair down to her shoulders. The style made her features appear even more beautiful.

"Well, I'm starving," he said as they stepped onto the elevator. "And I'm also anxious to get to the lab to see what we're up against. Did you get a chance to read the report?"

She nodded as the elevator door shut behind them. "Yes, I read it before going to bed. I wasn't all that sleepy."

They were the only ones in the elevator and suddenly memories flooded his brain. The last time they had been in an elevator alone she had tempted him so much that he had ended up taking her against a wall in one hell of a quickie. Thoughts of that time fired his blood.

Now, she had moved to stand at the far side of the elevator. She was staring into space, looking as if she didn't have a care in the world. He wanted to fire her blood the way she was firing his.

The elevator stopped on the first floor and as soon as the doors swooshed open, she was out. He couldn't help chuckling to himself as he followed her, thinking she was trying to put distance between them. Evidently, although she'd pretended otherwise, she had remembered their last time in an elevator together, as well.

A buffet breakfast was set up on the patio, and the moment he walked out onto the terrace, his glance was caught by the panoramic view of the Himalayas, looming high toward a beautiful April sky.

"Theo!"

"Kalina, good seeing you again."

He turned and watched Theo and Kalina embrace, not feeling the least threatened since everyone knew just how devoted Theo was to his beautiful wife, Renee, who was an international model. Inhaling the richness of the mountain air, Micah strolled toward the pair. The last time the three of them had teamed up together on an assignment had been in Sydney. Beau had also been part of their team.

Theo released Kalina and turned to Micah and smiled. "Micah, it's good seeing you, as well. It's like old times," Theo said with a hearty handshake.

Micah wondered if Theo assumed the affair with Kalina was still ongoing since he'd been there with them in Australia when it had started. "Yes, and from what I understand we're going to be busy for the next two weeks."

Theo nodded and a serious expression appeared on his face. "So far there haven't been any more deaths and that's a good thing."

Micah agreed. "The three of us can discuss it over breakfast."

Kalina sat beside Micah and tried to unravel her tangled thoughts. But there was nothing she could do with the heat that was rushing through her at that moment. There was no way she could put a lid on it. The desire flowing within her was too thick to confine. For some reason, even amidst the conversations going on—mostly between Micah and Theo—she couldn't stop her mind from drifting and grabbing hold of memories of what she and Micah had once shared.

"So what do you think, Kalina?"

She glanced over at Micah. Had he suspected her of daydreaming when she should have been paying attention? Both men had worked as epidemiologists for a lot longer than she had and had seen and done a lot more. She had enjoyed just sitting and listening to how they analyzed things, figuring she could learn a lot from them.

Micah, Theo and another epidemiologist by the name of Beau Smallwood had begun work for the federal government right out of medical school and were good friends; especially Beau and Micah who were the best of friends.

"I think, although we can't make assumptions until we have the data to support it, I agree that the deaths are suspicious."

Micah smiled, and she tried downplaying the effect that smile had on her. She had to remind herself that smile or no smile, he was someone who couldn't be trusted. Someone who had betrayed her.

"Well, then, I think we'd better head over to the lab to find out what we're up against," Micah said, standing.

He reached for her tray and she pulled it back. "Thanks, but I can dispense with my own trash."

He nodded. "Suit yourself."

She stood and turned to walk off, but not before hearing Theo whisper to Micah, "Um, my friend, it sounds like there's trouble in paradise."

She was tempted to turn and alert Theo to the fact that "paradise" for them ended two years ago. Shaking off the anger she felt when she thought about that time in her life and the hurt she'd felt, she continued walking toward the trash can. She'd known at the start of her affair with Micah that it would be a short-term affair. He'd made certain she understood there were no strings, and she had.

But what she couldn't accept was knowing the entire thing had been orchestrated by her controlling father. The only reason she was here in India now was because the general was probably too busy with the war in Afghanistan to check up on her whereabouts. He probably felt pretty confident she was on vacation or assigned to some cushy job in the States. Although he claimed otherwise, she knew he was the reason she hadn't been given any hard-hitting assignments. If it hadn't been for Dr. Moore's baby, chances are she wouldn't be here now.

She was about to turn, when Micah came up beside her to toss out his own trash. "Stop being so uptight with me, Kalina."

She glanced over at him and drew in a deep breath to keep from saying something that was totally rude. Instead, she met his gaze and said, "My being uptight, Micah, should be the least of your worries." She then walked off.

Micah watched her go, admiring the sway of her hips with every step she took. His feelings for Kalina were a lot more than sexual, but he was a man, and the woman had a body that any man would appreciate.

"I see she still doesn't know how you feel about her, Micah."

Micah glanced over and saw the humor in Theo's blue gaze. There was no reason to pretend he didn't know what the man was talking about. "No, she doesn't know."

"Then don't you think you ought to tell her?"

Micah chuckled. "With Kalina it won't be that easy. I need to show her rather than tell her because she doesn't believe anything I say."

"Ouch. Sounds like you have your work cut out for you then."

Micah nodded. "I do, but in the end it will be worth it."

Kalina was fully aware of the moment Micah entered the lab. With her eyes glued to the microscope, she hadn't looked up, but she knew without a doubt he was there and that he had looked her way. It was their first full day in Bajadad, and it had taken all her control to fight the attraction, the pull, the heat between them. She had played the part of the professional and had, hopefully, pulled it off. At least she believed Theo hadn't picked up on anything. He was too absorbed in the findings of today's lab reports to notice the air around them was charged.

But *she* had noticed. Not only had she picked up on the strong chemistry flowing between her and Micah, she had also picked up on his tough resistance. He would try to resist her as much as she would try to resist him, and she saw that as a good thing.

Even if they hadn't been involved two years ago, there was no way they would not be attracted to each other. He was a man and she was a woman, so quite naturally there would be a moment of awareness between them. Some things just couldn't be helped. But hopefully, by tomorrow, that awareness would have passed and they would be able to get down to the business they were sent here to carry out.

What if it didn't pass?

A funny feeling settled in her stomach at the thought of that happening. But all it took was the reminder of how he had betrayed her in the worst possible way to keep any attraction between them from igniting into full-blown passion.

However, she felt the need to remind herself that her best efforts hadn't drummed up any opposition to him when they'd been alone in the lab earlier that day. He had stood close while she'd gone over the reports, and she'd inhaled his scent while all kinds of conflicting emotions rammed through her. And every time she glanced up into his too-handsome face and stared into his turn-you-on brown eyes she could barely think straight.

Okay, she was faced with a challenge, but it wouldn't be the first time nor did she figure it would be the last. She'd never been a person who was quick to jump into bed with a man just for the sake of doing so, and she had surprised herself with how quickly she had agreed to an affair with Micah two years ago. She had dated in college and had slept with a couple of the guys. The sex between them hadn't been anything to write home about. She had eventually reached the conclusion that she and sex didn't work well together, which had always been just fine and dandy to her. So when she'd felt the sparks fly between her and Micah in a way she'd never felt before, she'd believed the attraction was something worth exploring.

Kalina nibbled on her bottom lip, thinking that was then, this was now. She had learned her lesson regarding Micah. They shared a chemistry that hadn't faded with time. If he thought she had the cutest dimples then she could say the same about his lips. She could imagine her tongue gliding over them for a taste, and it wouldn't be a quick one.

She shook her head. Her thoughts were really getting out of hand, and it was time to rein them back in. Today had been a busy day, filled with numerous activities and a conference call with Washington that had lasted a couple of hours. More than once, she had glanced up from her notes to find Micah staring at her. And each time their gazes connected, a wild swirl of desire would try overtaking her senses.

"Have you found anything unusual, Kalina?"

Micah's deep, husky voice broke into her thoughts, reminding her he had entered the room. Not that she'd totally forgotten. She lifted her gaze from the microscope and wished she hadn't. He looked yummy enough to eat. Literally.

He had come to stand beside her. Glancing up at him,

she saw the intense concentration in his eyes seemed hot, near blazing. It only made her more aware of the deep physical chemistry radiating between them, which she was trying to ignore but finding almost impossible to do.

"I think you need to take a look at this," she said, moving aside so he could look through her microscope.

He moved in place and she studied him for a minute while he sat on the stool, absorbed in analyzing what she'd wanted him to see. Moments later, he glanced back up at her. "Granulated particles?"

"Yes, that's what they appear to be, and barely noticeable. I plan on separating them to see if I can pinpoint what they are. There's a possibility the substance entering the bloodstream wasn't a liquid like we first assumed."

He nodded, agreeing with her assumption. "Let me know what you find out."

"I will." God, she needed her head examined, but she couldn't shift her gaze away from his lips. Those oh-so-cute lips were making deep-seated feelings stir inside her and take center stage. His lips moved, and it was then she realized he had said something.

"Sorry, did you say something?" she asked, trying to regain her common sense, which seemed to have taken a tumble by the wayside.

"Yes, I said I dreamed about you last night."

She stared at him. Where had that come from? How on earth had they shifted from talking about the findings under her microscope to him having a dream about her?

"And in my dream, I touched you all over. I tasted you all over."

Her heart thudded painfully in her chest. His words left her momentarily speechless and breathless. And it didn't help matters that the tone he'd used was deep, husky and as masculine as any male voice could be. Instead of grating on her nerves, it was grating on other parts of her body. Stroking them into a sensual fever.

She drew in a deep breath and said, "I thought you were going to stay in your place, Micah."

He smiled that sexy, rich smile of his, and she felt something hot and achy take her over. Little pangs of sexual desire, and the need she'd tried ignoring for two years, expanded in full force.

"I *am* staying in my place, Kalina. But do you know what place I love most of all?"

Something told her not to ask but she did anyway. "What?"

"Deep inside you."

She wasn't sure how she remained standing. She was on wobbly legs with a heart rate that was higher than normal. She compressed her lips, shoving to the back of her mind all the things she'd like to do to his mouth. "You have no right to say something like that," she said, shaking off his words as if they were some unpleasant memory.

A crooked smile appeared on his face. "I have every right, especially since you've practically spoiled me for any other woman."

Yeah, right. Did he think she didn't remember the woman who'd picked him up yesterday at the CDC? "And what happened to your decision not to become involved with a woman who didn't trust you?"

He chuckled. "Nothing happened. I merely mentioned to you that I dreamed about you last night. No harm's done. No real involvement there."

She frowned. He was teasing her, and she didn't like it. A man didn't tell a woman he'd dreamed about her without there being a hint of his desire for an involvement. What kind of game was Micah playing?

"Theo has already made plans for dinner. What about you?"

She answered without thinking. "No, I haven't made any plans."

"Good, then have dinner with me."

She stared at him. He was smooth, but not smooth enough. "We agreed not to become involved."

He chuckled. "Eating is not an involvement, Kalina. It's a way to feed the urges of one's body."

She didn't say anything, but she knew too well about bodily urges. Food wasn't what her body was craving.

"Having dinner with me is not a prerequisite for an affair. It's where two friends, past lovers, colleagues… however you want to describe our relationship…sit down and eat. I know this nice café not far from here. It's one I used to frequent when I was here the last time. I'd like to take you there."

Don't go, an inner voice warned. *All it will take is for you to sit across from him at a table and watch him eat.* The man had a way of moving his mouth that was so downright sensual it was a crying shame. It had taken all she had just to get through breakfast this morning.

"I don't think going out to dinner with you is a good idea," she finally said.

"And why not?"

"Mainly because you forgot to add the word *enemy* to the list to describe our relationship. I don't like you."

He simply grinned. "Well, I happen to like you a lot. And I don't consider us enemies. Besides, you're not the injured party here, I am. I'm an innocent man, falsely accused of something he didn't do."

She turned back to the microscope as she spoke. "I see things differently."

"I know you do, so why can't you go out to eat with me since nothing I say or do will change your mind? I merely invited you to dinner because I noticed you worked through lunch. But if you're afraid to be with me then I—"

"I'm not afraid to be with you."

"So you say," he said, turning to leave. Before reaching the door, he shot her a smile over his shoulder. "If you change your mind about dinner, I'll be leaving here around seven and you can meet me downstairs in the lobby."

Kalina watched him leave. She disliked him, so she wasn't sure why her hormones could respond to him the way they did. The depth of desire she felt around him was unreal. And dangerous. It only heightened the tension between them, and the thought that he wanted them to share dinner filled her with a heat she could very well do without.

The best thing for her to do was to stay in and order room service. That was the safest choice. But then, why should she be a coward? She, of all people, knew that Micah did not have a place in her life anymore. So, despite his mild flirtation—and that's what it was whether he admitted to it or not—she would not succumb. Nor would she lock herself in her room because she couldn't control her attraction to him. It was time that she learned to control her response to him.

There would be other assignments when they would work together, and she needed to put their past involvement behind her once and for all.

She stood and checked her watch, deciding she would have dinner with Micah after all. But she would make sure that she was the one in control at all times.

Chapter 5

At precisely seven o'clock, Micah stepped out of the elevator hoping he hadn't overplayed his hand. When he glanced around the lobby and saw Kalina sitting on one of the sofas, he felt an incredible sense of relief. He had been prepared to dine alone if it had come to that, but he'd more than hoped that she was willing to dine with him.

He walked over to her. From the expression on her face, it was obvious she was apprehensive about them dining together, so he intended to make sure she enjoyed herself—even as he made sure she remembered what they'd once shared. A shiver of desire raced up his spine when she saw him and stood. She was wearing a dress that reminded him of what a nice pair of legs she had. And her curvy physique seemed made for that outfit.

He had gone over his strategy upstairs in case she

joined him. He wouldn't make a big deal of her accompanying him. However, he would let her know he appreciated her being there.

He stopped when he reached her. "Kalina. You look nice tonight."

"Thanks. I think we need to get a couple of things straight."

He figured she would say that. "Let's wait until we get to the restaurant. Then you can let go all you want," he replied, taking her arm and placing it in the crux of his.

He felt her initial resistance before she relaxed. "Fine, but we will have that conversation. I don't have a problem joining you for dinner, but I don't want you getting any ideas."

Too late. He had gotten plenty already. He smiled. "You worry too much. There's no need for me to ask if you trust me because I know you don't. But can you cut me a little slack?"

Kalina held his gaze for a moment longer than he thought necessary, before she released an exasperated breath. "Does it matter to you that I don't particularly like you anymore?"

He took her hand in his to lead her out of the villa. "I'm sorry to hear that because I definitely like you. Always have. From the first."

She rolled her eyes. "So you say."

He chuckled. "So I know."

She pulled her hand from his when they stepped outside. The air was cool, and he thought it was a smart thing that she'd brought along a shawl. He could visualize her wrapped up in it and wearing nothing else.

She had done that once, and he could still remember

her doing so. It had been a red one with fringes around the hem. He had shown up at the hotel where they were staying in Sydney with their take-out dinner, and she had emerged from the bedroom looking like a lush red morsel. She had ended up being his treat for the night.

"Micah?"

He glanced over when he realized she'd said something. "Yes?"

"Are we walking or taking a cab?"

"We'll take a cab and tell the driver not to hurry so we can enjoy the beautiful view. Unless, however, you prefer to walk. It's not far away, within walking distance."

"Makes no difference to me," she said, moving her gaze from his to glance around.

'In that case, we'll take the cab. I know how much you like a good ride."

Kalina's face flushed after she heard what Micah said. There was no way he could convince her he hadn't meant what she thought he'd meant. That innocent look on his face meant nothing. But then, he, of all people, knew how much she liked to be on top and he'd always accommodated her. She just loved the feel of being on top of a body so well built and fine it could make even an old woman weep in pleasure.

She decided that if he was waiting on a response to his comment, he would be disappointed because she didn't intend to give him one. She would say her piece at the restaurant.

"Here's our cab."

The bellman opened the door for her. Kalina slid in the back and Micah eased in right behind her. The cab was small but not small enough where they needed to be all but sitting in each other's lap. "You have plenty of space over there," she said, pointing to Micah's side.

Without any argument he slid over, but then he turned and flashed those pearly-white teeth as he smiled at her. Her gaze narrowed. "Any reason you find me amusing?"

He shrugged. "I don't. But I do find you sexy as hell."

That was a compliment she didn't need and opened her mouth to tell him so, then closed it, deciding to leave well enough alone. He would be getting an earful soon enough.

When he continued to sit there and stare at her, she found it annoying and asked, "I thought you said you were going to enjoy the view."

"I am."

God, how had she forgotten how much he considered seduction an art form? Of course, he should know that using that charm on her was a wasted effort. "Can I ask you something, Micah?"

"Baby, you can ask me anything."

She hated to admit that his term of endearment caused a whirling sensation in her stomach. "Why are you doing this? Saying those things? I'm sure you're well aware it's a waste of your time."

"Is it?"

"Yes."

He didn't say anything for a moment and then, "To answer your question, the reason I'm doing this and saying all these things is that I'm hoping you'll remember."

She didn't have to ask what he wanted her to remember. She knew. Things had been good between them. Every night. Every morning. He'd been the best lover a woman could have and she had appreciated those nights spent in his arms. And speaking of those arms…they were hidden in a nice shirt that showed off the wide breadth of his shoulders. She knew those shoulders well and used to hold on to him while she rode him mercilessly. And then there were his hands. Beautiful. Strong. Capable of delivering mindless pleasure. And they were hands that would travel all over her body, touching her in places no man had touched her before and leaving a trail of heat in their wake.

Her gaze traveled upward past his throat to his mouth. It lingered there while recalling the ways he would use that mouth to make her scream. Oh, how she would scream while he took care of that wild, primal craving deep within her.

Gradually, her gaze left his mouth to move upward and stared into the depth of his bedroom-brown eyes. They were staring straight at her, pinning her in place and almost snatching the air from her lungs with their intensity. She wished she could dismiss that stare. Instead she was ensnarled by it in a way that increased her heart rate. An all-too-familiar ache settled right between her thighs. He was making her want something she hadn't had since he'd given it to her.

"Do you remember all the things we used to do behind closed doors, Kalina?"

Yes, she remembered and doubted she could ever forget. Sex between them had been good. The best. But it had all been a lie. That memory of his betrayal cut through her desire and forced a laugh from deep within her throat. "I've got to hand it to you, Micah. You're good."

He shrugged and then said in a low, husky tone, "You always said I was."

Yes, she had and it had been the truth. "Yes, but you're not good enough to get me into bed ever again. If you'll recall, I know the reason you slept with me." She was grateful for the glass partition that kept the cabby from hearing their conversation.

"I know the reason, as well. I wanted you. Pure and simple. From the moment you walked into that ballroom on your father's arm, I knew I wanted you. And being with you in Sydney afforded me the opportunity to have you. I wanted those legs wrapped around me, while I stroked you inside out. I wanted to bury my head between your thighs, to know the taste of you, and I wanted you to know the taste of me."

Her traitorous body began responding to his words. Myriad sensations were rolling around in her stomach. "It was all about sex, then," she said, trying to once again destroy the heated moment.

He nodded. "Yes, in the beginning. That's why I gave you my ground rules. But then…"

She shouldn't ask but couldn't help doing so. "But then what?" she asked breathlessly.

"And then the hunter got captured by the prey."

She opened her mouth and then closed it when the cabdriver told them via a speaker that they'd arrived. She glanced out the window. It was a beautiful restaurant—quaint and romantic.

He opened the door and reached for her hand. The reaction to his touch instantly swept through her. The man could make her ache without even trying.

"You're going to like the food here," he said, helping her out of the cab and not releasing her hand. She wanted to pull it from his grasp, but the feel of that one lone finger stroking her palm kept her hand where it was.

"I'm sure I will."

They walked side by side into the restaurant and she couldn't recall the last time they'd done so. It had felt good, downright giddy, being the center of Micah Westmoreland's attention and he had lavished it on her abundantly.

She didn't know what game Micah was playing tonight or what he was trying to prove. The only thing she did know was that by the time they left this restaurant he would know where she stood, and he would discover that she didn't intend to be a part of his game playing.

"The food here is delicious, Micah."

He smiled. "Thanks. I was hoping you would join me since I knew you would love everything they had on the menu. The last time I was here, this was my favorite place to eat."

He recalled the last time he'd been in Bajadad. He'd felt guilty about being so far away from home, so far away from his family, especially when the younger Westmorelands, who'd taken his parents' and aunt's and uncle's deaths hard, had rebelled like hell. Getting a call from Dillon to let him know their youngest brother, Bane, had gotten into trouble again had become a common occurrence.

"We need to talk, Micah."

He glanced across the table at Kalina and saw the firm set of her jaw. He'd figured she would have a lot to say, so he'd asked that they be given a private room in the back. It was a nice room with a nice view, but nothing was nicer than looking at the woman he was with.

He now knew he had played right into her father's hands just as much as she had. The general had been certain that Micah would be so pissed that Kalina didn't believe him that he wouldn't waste his time trying to convince her of the truth. He hadn't. He had allowed two years to pass while the lie she believed festered.

But now he was back, seeking her forgiveness. Not for what he had done but for what he hadn't done, which was to fight for her and to prove his innocence. Dillon had urged him to do that as soon as Kalina had confronted him, but Micah had been too stubborn, too hurt that she could so easily believe the worst about him. Now he wished he had fought for her.

"Okay, you can talk and I'll listen," he said, pushing his plate aside and taking a sip of his wine.

She frowned and blew out a breath. "I want you to stop with the game playing."

"And that's what you think I'm doing?"

"Yes."

He had news for her, what he was doing was fighting for his survival the only way he knew how. He intended to make her trust him. He would lower his guard and include her in his world, which is something he hadn't done since Patrice. He would seduce her back into a relationship and then prove she was wrong. He would do things differently this time and show her he wasn't the man she believed him to be.

"What if I told you that you're wrong?"

"Then what do you call what you're doing?" she asked in a frustrated tone.

"Pursuing the woman I want," he said simply.

"To get me in your bed?"

"Or any other way I can get you. It's not all sexual."

She gave a ladylike snort. "And you expect me to believe that?"

He chuckled. "No, not really. You've told me numerous times that you don't believe a word I say."

"Then why are you doing this? Why would you want to run behind a woman who doesn't want you?"

"But you *do* want me."

She shook her head. "No, I don't."

He smiled. "Yes, you do. Even though you dislike me for what you think I did, there's a part of you that wants me as much as I want you. Should I prove it?"

She narrowed her gaze. "You can't prove anything."

He preferred to disagree but decided not to argue with her. "All right."

She lifted her brow. "So you agree with what I said?"

"No, but I'm not going to sit here and argue with you about it."

She inclined her head. "We are not arguing about it, we are discussing it. Things can't continue this way."

"So what do you suggest?"

"That you cease the flirtation and sexual innuendoes. I don't need them."

Micah was well acquainted with what she needed. It was the same thing he needed. A night together. But sharing one night would just be a start. Once he got her back in his bed he intended to keep her there. Forever. He drew in a deep breath. The thought of forever with any other woman was enough to send him into a panic. But not with her.

He placed his napkin on the table as he glanced over

at her. "Since you've brought them up, let's take a moment to talk about needs, shall we?"

She nodded. That meant she would at least listen, although he knew in the end she wouldn't agree to what he was about to suggest. "Although our relationship two years ago got off on a good start, it ended on a bad note. I'm not going to sit here and rehash all that happened, everything you've falsely accused me of. At first I was pretty pissed off that you would think so low of me. Then I realized the same thing you said a couple of nights ago at that party—you didn't know me. I never gave you the chance to know the real me. If you'd known the real *me* then you would not have believed the lie your father told you."

She didn't say anything, but he knew that didn't necessarily mean she was agreeing with him. In her eyes, he was guilty until proven innocent. "I want you to get to know the real me, Kalina."

She took a sip of her wine and held his gaze. "And how am I supposed to do that?"

At least she had asked. "You and I both have a thirty-day leave coming up as soon as we fly out of India. I'd like to invite you to go home with me."

Kalina sat up straight in her chair. "Go home with you?"

"Yes."

She stared at him across the lit candle in the middle of the table. "And where exactly is home?"

"Denver. Not in the city limits, though. My family and I own land in Colorado."

"Your family?"

"Yes, and I would love for you to meet them. I have

fourteen brothers and cousins, total, that live in Denver. And then there are those cousins living in Atlanta, Montana and Texas."

This was the first time he'd mentioned anything about his family to her, except for the day he had briefly spoken of his parents when she'd asked. "What a diverse family." She didn't have any siblings or cousins. He was blessed to have so many.

He leaned back in his chair with his gaze directly on her. "So, will you come?"

"No." She hadn't even needed to think about it. There was no reason for her to spend her vacation time with Micah and his family. What would it accomplish?

As if he had read her mind, he said, "It would help mend things between us."

She narrowed her gaze. "Why would I want them mended?"

"Because you are a fair person, and I believe deep down you want to know the truth as much as I want you to. For whatever reason—and I have my suspicions as to what they are—your father lied about me. I need to redeem myself."

"No, you don't."

"Yes, I do, Kalina. Whether there's ever anything between us again matters to me. Like I told you before, I truly did enjoy the time we spent together, and I think if you put aside that stubborn pride of yours, you'll admit that you did, too."

He was right, she had. But the pain of his betrayal was something she hadn't been able to get beyond. "What made you decide to invite me to your home, Micah?"

"I told you. I want you to get to know me."

She narrowed her gaze. "Could it be that you're also planning for us to sleep together again?"

His mouth eased into a smile, and he took another sip of his wine. "I won't lie to you. That thought had crossed my mind. But I have never forced myself on any woman and I don't ever plan to do so. I would love to share a bed with you, Kalina, but the purpose of this trip is for you to get to know me. And I also want you to meet my family."

She set down her glass. "Why do you want me to get to know your family now, Micah, when you didn't before?"

Kalina noted the serious expression that descended upon his features. Was she mistaken or had her question hit a raw nerve? Leaning back in her chair, she stared at him while waiting for an answer. Given that he'd invited her to his home to meet his family, she felt she deserved one.

He took another sip of wine and, for a moment, she thought he wasn't going to answer and then he said, "Her name was Patrice Nelson. I met her in my second year of college. I was nineteen at the time. We dated only a short while before I knew she was the one. I assumed she thought the same thing about me. We had been together a few months when a plane carrying my parents went down, killing everyone on board, including my father's brother and his wife."

She gasped, and a sharp pain hit her chest. She had known about his parents, but hadn't known other family members had been killed in that plane crash, as well. "You lost your parents and your aunt and uncle?"

"Yes. My father and his brother were close and so were my mother and my aunt. They did practically everything together, which was the reason they were on the same plane. They had gone away for the weekend. My parents had seven kids and my aunt and uncle had eight. That meant fifteen Westmorelands were left both motherless and fatherless. Nine of them were under the age of sixteen at the time."

"I'm sorry," she said, feeling a lump in her throat. She hadn't known him at the time, but she could still feel his pain. That had to have been an awful time for him.

"We all managed to stay together, though," he said, breaking into her thoughts.

"How?"

"The oldest of all the Westmorelands was my brother Dillon. He was twenty-one and had just graduated from the university and had been set to begin a professional basketball career. He gave it all up to come home. Dillon, and my cousin Ramsey, who was twenty, worked hard to keep us together, even when people were encouraging him to put the younger four in foster homes. He refused. Dil, with Ramsey's help, kept us all together."

In his voice, she could hear the admiration he had for his brother and cousin. She then recalled the woman in his life at the time. "And I'm sure this Patrice was there for you during that time, right?"

"Yes, so it seemed. I took a semester off to help with things at home since I'm the third oldest in the family, although there's only a month separating me from my cousin Zane."

He took a sip of wine and then said, "Patrice came to visit me several times while I was out that semester, and she got to know my family. Everyone liked her…

at least everyone but one. My cousin Bailey, who was the youngest of the Westmorelands, was barely seven, and she didn't take a liking to Patrice for reasons we couldn't understand."

He didn't say anything for a moment, as if getting his thoughts together, then he continued, "I returned to school that January, arriving a couple of days earlier than planned. I went straight to Patrice's apartment and…"

Kalina lifted a brow. "And what?"

"And I walked in on her in bed with one of her professors."

Of all the things Kalina had assumed he would say, that definitely wasn't one of them. She stared at him, and he stared back. She could see it, there, plain, right in his features—the strained look that came from remembered pain. He had been hurt deeply by the woman's deception.

"What happened after that?" she asked, curious.

"I left and went to my own apartment, and she followed me there. She told me how sorry she was. She said that she felt she needed to be honest with me, as well as with herself, so she also admitted it hadn't been the first time she'd done it with one of her professors, nor would it be the last. She said she needed her degree, wanted to graduate top of her class and saw nothing wrong with what she was doing. She said that if I loved her I would understand."

Kalina's mouth dropped. *The nerve of the hussy assuming something like that!* "And did you understand?"

"No." He didn't say anything for a moment. "Her actions not only hurt me, but they hurt my family. They had liked her and had become used to her being with me whenever I came home. It probably wouldn't have been so bad if Dillon's and Ramsey's girls hadn't betrayed them around the same time. We didn't set a good example for the others as far as knowing how to pick decent and honest women."

He paused a moment and then said in a low, disappointed voice, "I vowed then never to get involved with a woman to the extent that I'd bring her home to my family. And I've kept that promise...until now."

Kalina took a sip of her drink and held Micah's gaze, not knowing what to say. Why was he breaking his vow now, for her? Did it matter that much to him that she got to know him better than she had in Sydney?

Granted, she realized he was right. Other than being familiar with how well he performed in bed, she didn't know the simplest things about him, like his favorite color, his political affiliation or his religious beliefs. Those things might not be important for a short-term affair, but they were essential for a long-term relationship.

But then they'd never committed to a relationship. They had been merely enjoying each other's company and companionship. She hadn't expected "forever" and frankly hadn't been looking for it, either. But that didn't mean the thought hadn't crossed her mind once or twice during their two-month affair.

And she was very much aware that the reason he wanted her to get to know him now still didn't have anything to do with "forever." He assumed if she got to know him then she would see that she'd been wrong to accuse him of manipulating her for her father.

The lump in her throat thickened. What if she was wrong about him and her father had lied? What if she had begun to mean something to Micah the way he claimed? She frowned, feeling a tension headache coming on when so many what-ifs flooded her brain. Her father had never lied to her before, but there was a first time for everything. Perhaps he hadn't outright lied, but she knew how manipulative he could be where she was concerned.

"You don't have to give me your answer tonight, Kal, but please think about it."

She broke eye contact with him to study her wineglass for a moment, twirling the dark liquid around. Then she lifted her gaze to meet his again and said, "Okay, I will think about it."

A smile touched his lips. "Good. That's all I'm asking." He then checked his watch. "Ready to leave?"

"Yes."

Moments later, as they stood outside while a cab was hailed for them, she couldn't help remembering everything Micah had told her. She couldn't imagine any woman being unfaithful to him, and she could tell from the sound of his voice while he'd relayed the story that the pain had gone deep. That had been well over ten years ago. Was he one of those men, like her father, who could and would love only one woman?

She was aware of how her mother's death had affected her father. Although she'd known him to have lady friends over the years, she also knew he hadn't gotten serious about any of them. Her mother, he said, would always have his heart. Kalina couldn't help wondering if this Patrice character still claimed Micah's heart.

When they were settled in the cab, she glanced over at him and said, "I'm sorry."

He lifted a brow. "For what?"

"Your loss. Your parents. Your uncle and aunt." She wouldn't apologize for Patrice because she didn't see her being out of the picture as a loss. Whether he realized it or not, finding out how deceitful his girlfriend was had been a blessing.

His gaze held hers intensely, unflinchingly, when he said, "I didn't share my history with you for your pity or sympathy."

She nodded. "I know." And she did know. He had taken the first steps in allowing her to get beyond that guard he'd put up. For some reason, she felt that he truly wanted her to get to know him. The real Micah Westmoreland. Was he truly any different from the one she already knew?

She had to decide just how much of him, if any, she wanted to get to know. He had invited her to spend time with him and his family in Denver, and she had to think hard if that was something she really wanted to do.

A few hours later, back in his room at the villa, Micah turned off the lamp beside his bed and stared up at the ceiling in darkness. He had enjoyed sharing dinner with Kalina, and doing so had brought back memories of the time they'd spent together in Sydney. Tonight, more than ever, he had been aware of her as a woman. A woman he wanted. A woman he desired. A woman he intended to have.

He'd never wanted to be attracted to Kalina, even in the beginning. Mainly because he'd known she would hold his interest too much and for way too long. But there hadn't been any hope for him. The chemistry had been too strong. The desire too thick. He had been attracted to her in a way he had never been attracted to another woman.

And tonight she had been a good listener. She had asked the questions he had expected her to ask and hadn't asked ones that were irrelevant. The private room they'd been given had been perfect for such a conversation. But even the intense subject matter did nothing to lessen the heat that stirred in the air, or waylay the desire that simmered between them.

Very few people knew the real reason he and Patrice had ended things. He'd only told Dillon, Ramsey and Zane, the cousin he was closest to. Micah was certain the others probably assumed they knew the reason, but he knew their assumptions wouldn't even come close.

Walking in and finding the woman he loved in bed with another man had been traumatic for him, especially given that he'd been going through a very distressing time in his life already. The sad thing was that there hadn't been any remorse because Patrice had felt justified in doing what she'd done. She just hadn't been able to comprehend that normal men and women didn't share their partners.

He shifted in bed and thought about Kalina. He had enjoyed her company tonight and believed she'd enjoyed his. He'd even felt an emotional connection to her, something he hadn't felt with a woman in years. He didn't need to close his eyes to remember the stricken look on her face two years ago when she'd overheard words that had implicated him. And no matter how much he had proclaimed his innocence, she hadn't believed him.

For two years, they had gone their separate ways. At first, he'd been so angry he hadn't given a damn. But at night he would lie in bed awake. Wanting her and missing her. It was then that he'd realized just how much Kalina had worked her way into his bloodstream, how deeply she'd become embedded under his skin. He had traveled to several countries over the past two years. He had worked a ton of hours. But nothing had been able to eradicate Kalina from his mind.

Now she was back in his life, and he intended to use this opportunity to right a wrong. If only she would agree to go home to Denver with him. He wouldn't question why it was so important to him for her to do so, but it was. And although he hadn't told her, he wouldn't accept no for an answer.

So what are you going to do if she turns you down, Westmoreland? Kidnap her?

Kidnapping Kalina didn't sound like a bad idea, but he knew he wouldn't operate on the wrong side of the law. He hoped that she gave his invitation some serious consideration so it didn't come to that.

It had been hard being so close to her and having to keep his hands to himself when he'd wanted them all over her, touching her in places he'd been privy to before. But as he'd told her, it was important that they get to know each other, something they hadn't taken the time to do in Sydney.

On the cab ride back, he'd even discovered she knew how to ride a horse and that her grandparents had been farmers in Alabama. Her grandparents had even raised, among other things, sheep. His cousin Ramsey, who was the sheep rancher in the Westmoreland family, would appreciate knowing that. And Micah couldn't wait to show Kalina his ranch. He hoped she liked it as much as he did. And…

He drew in a deep breath, forcing himself to slow down and put a lid on his excitement. He had to face the possibility that she would decide not to go to Denver. He refused to let that happen. The woman had no idea just how much he wanted her and he intended to do whatever he had to to have her.

If he had to turn up the heat to start breaking down her defenses then that's what he would do.

Chapter 6

The next day, Kalina's body tensed when she entered the lab and immediately remembered that she and Micah would be working alone together today. Theo was in another area analyzing the granules taken from the bodies of the five victims.

She eased the door closed behind her and stood leaning against it while she looked over at Micah. He was standing with his head tilted back as he studied the solution in the flask he was holding up to the light. She figured he wasn't aware she had entered, which was just as well for the time being.

His request from last night was still on her mind, and even after a good night's sleep, she hadn't made a decision about what she would do. She had weighed the pros and cons of accompanying him to Denver, but even that hadn't helped. It had been late when she had returned from dinner, but she'd tried reaching her father. The person she'd talked to at the Pentagon wouldn't even tell her his whereabouts, saying that, at the moment, the general's location was confidential. She had wanted to hear her father tell her again how Micah had played a role in keeping her out of China. A part of her resented the fact that Micah was back in her life, but another part of her felt she deserved to know the truth.

She wrapped her arms around herself, feeling a slight damp in the air. Everyone had awakened to find it raining that morning. And although the showers only lasted for all of ten minutes, it had been enough to drench the mountainside pretty darn good.

Micah's back was to her, and her gaze lowered to his backside, thinking it was one part of his body she'd always admired. He certainly had a nice-looking butt. She'd heard from Theo that Micah had gotten up before five this morning to go to the villa's gym to work out. She would have loved to have been a fly on the wall, to watch him flex those masculine biceps of his.

Her thoughts drifted to the night before. On the cab ride back to the villa he'd told her more about his brothers and cousins. She wasn't sure if he was feeding her curiosity or deliberately enticing her to want to meet them all for herself. And she would admit that she'd become intrigued. But was that enough to make her want to spend an entire month with him in Denver?

"Are you going to just stand there or get to work? There's plenty of it to be done."

She frowned, wondering if he had eyes in the back of his head, as he'd yet to turn around. "How did you know it was me?"

"Your scent gave you away, like it always does."

Since she usually wore the same cologne every day, she would let that one slide. She moved away from the door at the same time as he turned around, and she really wished he hadn't when he latched those dark, intense eyes onto her. Evidently, this was going to be one of her "drool over Micah" days. She'd had a number of them before. He was looking extremely handsome today. He probably looked the same yesterday, but today her hormones were out in full force, reminding her just how much of a woman she was and reminding her of all those sexual needs she had ignored for two years.

"Have most of the tissues been analyzed?" she asked, sliding onto her stool in front of a table that contained skin samples taken during autopsies of the five victims.

"No, I left that for you to do."

"No problem."

She glanced over at Micah, who was still studying the flask while jotting down notes. He was definitely engrossed in his work. Last night, he'd been engrossed in her. Was this the same man whose gaze had filled her with heated lust last night during the cab rides to the restaurant and back? The same man who'd sat across from her at dinner with a look that said he wanted to eat her alive? The same man whose flirtation and sexual innuendoes had stirred her with X-rated sensations? The same man who exuded a virility that said he was all man, totally and completely?

"Are you going to get some work done or sit there and waste time daydreaming?"

She scowled, not appreciating his comment. Evidently, he wasn't in a good mood. She wondered who had stolen his favorite toy. Now he was sitting on a stool at the counter and hadn't glanced up.

"For your information, I get paid for the work I do and not the time it takes me to do it."

She shook her head. And to think that this was the same man who'd wanted her to spend thirty days with him and his family. She'd have thought he would be going out of his way to be nice to her.

"In other words…"

"In other words, Dr. Westmoreland," she said, placing her palms on the table and leaning forward, "I can handle my business."

He looked up at her and his mouth twitched in a grin. "Yes, Dr. Daniels, I know for a fact that you most certainly can."

She narrowed her eyes when it became obvious he'd been doing nothing more than teasing her. "I was beginning to wonder about you, Micah."

"In what respect?" he asked.

"Your sanity."

"Ouch."

"Hey, you had that coming," she said, and couldn't help the smile that touched her lips.

"I wish I had something else coming about now. My sanity as well as my body could definitely use it."

Her eyebrows lifted. The look in his eyes, the heated lust she saw in their dark depths told her they were discussing something that had no place in the lab. Deciding it was time to change the subject, she said, "How are things going? Found anything unusual?"

He shook his head. "Other than what you found yesterday, no, I could find nothing else. Theo's dissecting those tissue particles now. Maybe he'll come across something else in the breakdown."

She blew out a breath, feeling a degree of frustration. Granted, it was just the second day, but still, she was anxious about those samples Theo was analyzing. So far there hadn't been any more deaths and that was a good thing. But, at the same time, if they couldn't discover the cause, there was a chance the same type of deaths could occur again.

She glanced over at Micah at the exact moment that he raised his head from his microscope. "Come and take a look at this."

There was something in his voice that made her curious. Without thinking, she quickly moved across the room. When he slid off his stool, she slid onto it. She looked down into his microscope and frowned. She then looked up at him, confused. "I don't see anything."

"Then maybe you aren't looking in the right place."

Kalina wasn't sure exactly what she was expecting, but it wasn't Micah reaching out and gently pulling her from the stool to wrap his arms around her. His manly scent consumed her and his touch sent fire racing all through her body. She drew in a steadying breath and tilted her head back to look up at him. And when he brought her closer to his hard frame, she felt every inch of him against her.

Although her pulse was drumming erratically in response, she said, "I don't want this, Micah." She knew it was a lie the moment she said it and, from the heat of his gaze, he knew it was a lie, as well.

"Then maybe I need to convince you otherwise," he said, seconds before lowering his mouth to hers.

She had intended to shove him away…honestly she had, but the moment she parted her lips on an enraged sigh and he took the opportunity to slide his tongue in her mouth, she was a goner. Her stomach muscles quivered at the intensity and strength in the tongue that caught hold of hers and began sucking as if it had every right to do so. Sucking on her tongue as if it was the last female tongue on earth.

He was devouring her. Feasting on her. Driving her insane while tasting her with a sexual hunger she felt all the way to her toes. A strong concentration of that hunger settled in the juncture of her thighs.

And speaking of that spot, she felt his erection— right there—hard, rigid, pressing against her belly, making her remember a time when it had done more than nudge her, making her remember a time when it had actually slid inside her, between her legs, going all the way to the hilt, touching her womb. It had once triggered her inner muscles to give a possessive little squeeze, just seconds before they began milking his aroused body for everything they could get and forcing him to explode in an out-of-this-world orgasm. She remembered. She couldn't forget.

And then she began doing something she was driven to do because of the way he was making love to her mouth, as well as the memories overtaking her. Just like the last time he'd overstepped his boundaries in a kiss, she began kissing him back, taking the lead by escaping the captivity of his tongue and then capturing his tongue with hers. Ignoring the conflicting emotions swamping her, she kissed him in earnest, with a hunger only he could stir. She took possession of his mouth and he let her. He was allowing her to do whatever she wanted. Whatever pleased her. And when she heard a deep guttural moan, she wasn't sure if it had come from his throat or hers.

At the moment she really didn't care.

* * *

Micah deepened the kiss, deciding it was time for him to take over. Or else he would have Kalina stretched across the nearest table with her legs spread so fast neither of them would have a chance to think about the consequences. He doubted he would ever get tired of kissing her and was surprised this was just the second time their tongues had mingled since seeing each other again. But then, staying away from each other had been her decision, not his. If he had his way, their mouths would be locked together 24/7.

As usual, she fit perfectly in his arms, and she felt as if she belonged there. There was nothing like kissing a beautiful woman, especially one who could fill a man's head with steamy dreams at night and heated reality during the day. He found it simply amazing, the power a woman could wield over a man. Case in point, the power that this particular woman had over him.

It didn't matter when he kissed her, or how often, he always wanted more of her. There was nothing quite like having her mouth beneath his. And he liked playing the tongue game with her. He would insert his tongue into her mouth and deepen the kiss before withdrawing and then going back in. He could tell from her moans that she was enjoying the game as much as he was.

His aroused body was straining hard against his zipper, begging for release, pleading for that part of her it had gotten to know so well in Australia. Her feminine scent was in the air, feeding his mind and body with a heated lust that had blood rushing through his body.

A door slamming somewhere had them quickly pulling apart, and he watched as she licked her lips as if she could still taste him there. His guts clenched at the thought. He'd concluded from the first that she had a very sexy mouth, and from their initial kiss he'd discovered that not only was it sexy, it was damn tasty as sin. She took a step back and crossed her arms over her chest, pulling in quick breaths. "I can't believe you did that. What if someone had walked in on us?"

He shrugged while trying to catch his own breath. His mouth was filled with her taste, yet he wanted more. "Then I would have been pretty upset about the interruption," he said.

She glared. "We should be working."

He smiled smoothly. "We are. However, we are entitled to breaks." He leaned against the table. "I think you need to loosen up a little."

"And I think you need to get a grip. You've gotten your kiss, Micah. That's two now. If I were you, I wouldn't try for a third."

He had news for her, he would try for a third, fourth, fifth and plenty more beyond that. There was no way his mouth wouldn't be locking with hers again. She had sat back down on the stool and had picked up one of the vials as if to dismiss not only him but also what they'd just shared. He had no intention of letting her do that. "Why can't we kiss again? I'm sure there's plenty more where those two came from."

She lifted her gaze to his. "I beg to differ."

He chuckled. "Oh, I plan to have you begging, all right."

Her eyes narrowed, and he thought she looked absolutely adorable. Hot, saucy and totally delectable. "If you're trying to impress me then—"

"I'm not. I want you to get to know me and the one thing you'll discover about me is that I love the unexpected. I like being unpredictable, and when it comes to you, I happen to be addicted."

"Thanks for letting me know. I will take all that into consideration while deciding if I'm going home with you in a couple of weeks. You might as well know none of it works in your favor."

"I never took you for a coward."

She frowned. "Being a coward has nothing to do with it. It's using logical thinking and not giving in to whims. Maybe you should do the same."

He couldn't help the grin that spread across his lips. Lips that still carried her taste. "Oh, sweetheart, I *am* using logical thinking. If I got any more sensible I would have stripped you naked by now instead of just imagining doing it. In fact, I'm doing more than imagining it, I'm anticipating it happening. And when it does, I promise to make it worth every moan I get out of you."

Ignoring her full-fledged glare, he glanced at his watch. "I think I'll go grab some lunch. I've finished logging my findings on today's report, but if you need help with what you have to do then—"

"Thanks for the offer, but I can handle things myself."

"No problem. And just so we have a clear understanding… My invitation to go home with me to Denver has no bearing on my kissing you, touching you or wanting to make love to you. You have the last word."

She raised an eyebrow. "Do I really?"

"Absolutely. But I'd like to warn you not to say one thing while your body says another. I tend to listen more to body language."

"Thanks for the warning."

"And thanks for the kiss," he countered.

She frowned, and he smiled. If only she knew what he had in store for her... Hell, it was a good thing that she didn't know. His smile widened as he removed his lab jacket. "I'll be back later. Don't work too hard while I'm gone. You might want to start storing up your energy."

"Storing up my energy for what?"

He leaned in close, reached out, lightly stroked her cheek with his fingertips and whispered, "For when we make love again."

Seeing the immediate flash of fire in her gaze, he said, "Not that I plan on gloating, but when you find out the truth, that I've been falsely accused, I figure you'll want to be nice to me. And when you do, I'll be ready. I want you to be ready, as well. I can't wait to make love to you again, and I plan to make it worth the hell you've put me through, baby."

The heat in her gaze flared so hotly he had to struggle not to pull her back into his arms and go after that third kiss. He was definitely going to enjoy pushing her buttons.

As he moved to walk out of the lab, he thought that if that last kiss was anything to go by, he might as well start storing up some energy, as well. He turned back around before opening the door and his gaze traveled over her. He wanted her to feel the heat, feel his desire. He wanted her to want to make love to him as much as he wanted to make love to her.

She held his gaze with a defiant frown and said nothing. He smiled and gave her a wink before finally opening the door to leave.

* * *

"It's all his fault," Kalina muttered angrily as she tossed back her covers to ease out of bed. It had been almost a week since that kiss in the lab and she hadn't had a single good night's sleep since.

She was convinced he was deliberately trying to drive her loony. Although he hadn't taken any more liberties with her, he had his unique ways of making her privy to his lusty thoughts. His eye contact told her everything—regardless of whether it was his lazy perusal or his intense gaze—whenever she looked into his eyes there was no doubt about what was on his mind. More than once she'd looked up from her microscope to find those penetrating dark eyes trained directly on her.

It didn't take much to get her juices flowing, literally, and for the past week he'd been doing a pretty good job of it. She knew he enjoyed getting on her last nerve, and it seemed that particular nerve was a hot wire located right at the juncture of her thighs.

She had tried pouring her full concentration into her work. All the test results on the tissues had come back negative. Although they suspected that some deadly virus had killed those five people, as of yet the team hadn't been able to pinpoint a cause, or come up with conclusive data to support their hypothesis. The granules were still a mystery, and so far they had not been able to trace the source. The Indian government was determined not to make a big to-do about what they considered nothing and wouldn't let them test any others who'd gotten sick but had recovered. The team had reported their findings to Washington. The only thing left was to wrap things up. She knew that Micah was still concerned and had expressed as much in his report. A contagious virus was bad enough, but one that could not be traced was even worse.

Although it had been over a week since he'd issued his invitation, she still hadn't given Micah an answer regarding going with him to Denver. With only three days before they left India, he had to be wondering about her decision. Unfortunately, she still didn't have a clue how she would answer him. The smart thing would be to head for Florida for a month, especially since Micah hadn't made the past week easy for her. He deliberately tested her sanity every chance he got. And although he hadn't tried kissing her again, more than once he had intentionally gotten close to her, brushed against her for no reason at all or set up a situation where he was alone with her. Those were the times he would do nothing but stare at her with a heated gaze as potent as any caress.

Kalina drew in a deep breath, suddenly feeling hot and in need of cool air. After slipping into her robe, she crossed the room and pushed open the French doors to step out on the balcony. She appreciated the whisper of a breeze that swept across her face. The chill made her shiver but still didn't put out the fire raging inside her.

Over the past two years she'd gone each day without caring that she was denying her body's sexual needs. Now, being around Micah was reminding her of just what she'd gone without. Whenever she was around him, she was reminded of how it felt to have fingertips stroke her skin, hands touch her all over and arms pull her close to the warmth of a male body.

She missed the caress of a man's lips against hers, the graze of a male's knuckles across her breasts, the lick of a man's tongue and the soft stroke of masculine fingers between her legs.

There was nothing like the feel of a man's aroused body sliding inside, distended and engorged, ready to take her on one remarkable ride. Making her pleasure his own. And giving all of himself while she gave everything back to him.

Her breathing quickened and her pulse rate increased at what she could now admit she'd been missing. What she had given up. No other man had brought her abstinence more to the forefront of her thoughts than Micah. She felt hot, deliriously needy, and she stood there a moment in silence, fighting to get her bearings and control the turbulent, edgy desire thrumming through her.

Nothing like this had ever happened to her before. All it took was for her to close her eyes to recall how it felt for Micah's hands to glide over the curve of her backside, cup it in his large palms and bring her closer to his body and his throbbing erection.

The memories were scorching, hypnotic and almost more than she could handle. But she would handle them. She had no choice. She would not let Micah get the best of her. She had no qualms, however, about getting the best of him—in the area right below his belt.

She rubbed her hand down her face, not believing her thoughts. They had gotten downright racy lately, and she blamed Micah for it. She was just about to turn to go back inside when a movement below her balcony caught her attention. A man was out jogging and she couldn't help noticing what a fine specimen of a man he was.

The temperature outside had to be in the low thirties, yet he was wearing a T-shirt and a pair of shorts. In her opinion, he was pneumonia just waiting to happen. Who in their right mind would be out jogging at this hour of the night, half dressed?

She leaned against the railing and squinted her eyes in the moonlight. That's when she saw that the man who'd captured her attention was Micah. Evidently, she wasn't the only one who couldn't sleep. She found that interesting and couldn't help wondering if perhaps the same desire that was keeping her awake had him in its lusty clutches, as well.

Serves him right if it did. He had spent a lot of his time this week trying his best to tempt her into his bed, but apparently he was getting the backlash.

He was about to jog beneath her balcony, so she held her breath to keep him from detecting her presence. Except for the glow of the half moon, it was dark, and there was no reason for him to glance up…or so she reasoned. But it didn't stop him from doing so. In fact, as if he'd sensed she was there, he slowed to a stop and stared straight up at her, locking in on her gaze.

And he kept right on staring at her while her heart rate increased tenfold. Suddenly there was more than a breeze stirring the air around her, and it seemed as if her surroundings got extremely quiet. The only thing that was coming in clear was the sound of her irregular breathing.

She stared right back at him and saw that his gaze was devouring her in a way she felt clear beneath her robe. In fact, if she didn't know for certain she was wearing clothes, she would think that she was naked. Oh, why were the sensual lines of his lips so well-defined in the moonlight? Knowing she could be headed for serious trouble if their gazes continued to connect, she broke eye contact, only to be drawn back to his gaze seconds later.

He had to be cold, she thought, yet he was standing in that one spot, beneath her balcony, staring up at her. She licked her lips and felt his gaze shift to her mouth.

Then he spoke in a deep, husky voice, "Meet me in the staircase, Kalina."

His request flowed through her, touching her already aroused body in places it shouldn't have. Turbulent emotions swept through her, and from the look in his eyes it was obvious that he expected her to act on his demand. Should she? Could she? Why would she?

She was bright enough to know that he didn't want her to meet him so they could discuss the weather. Nor would they discuss their inability to pinpoint the origin of the deadly virus. There was no doubt in her mind as to why he wanted to meet her on the stairs, and she would be crazy, completely insane, to do what he asked.

Breaking eye contact with him, she moved away from the balcony's railing and slid open the French doors to go back inside. She moved toward her bed, tossed off her robe and was about to slide between the sheets, when she paused. Okay, she didn't like him anymore, but why was she denying herself a chance to have a good night's sleep? She had needs that hadn't been met in more than two years, and she knew for a fact that he was good at that sort of thing. She didn't love him, and he didn't love her. It would be all about needs and wants being satisfied, nothing more.

She drew in a deep breath, thinking she might be jumping the gun here. All he'd asked her to do was to meet him at the stairs. For all she knew, he might just want to talk. Or maybe he merely wanted to kiss her.

She gave herself a mental shake, knowing a kiss would only be the start. Any man who looked at her the way Micah had looked at her a few moments ago had more than kissing on his mind.

Deciding to take the guesswork out of it, she reached for the blouse and skirt she'd taken off earlier and quickly put them on. She knew what she wanted, and Micah better not be playing games with her, because she wasn't in the mood.

Heaven help her, but she was only in the mood for one thing, and at the moment, she didn't care whether she liked him or not just as long as he eased that ache within her.

As she grabbed her room key off the nightstand and shoved it into the pocket of her skirt, she headed toward the door.

Micah paced the stairway, trying to be optimistic. Kalina would come. Although he knew it would be a long shot if she did, he refused to give up hope. He had read that look in her eyes. It had been the same one he knew was in his. She wanted him as much as he wanted her. He had been playing cat-and-mouse games with her all week, to the point where Theo had finally pulled him aside and told him to do something about his attitude problem. He'd almost laughed in his friend's face. Nothing was wrong with his attitude; it was his body that had issues.

So here he was. Waiting. Hoping she wouldn't walk through the door just to tell him to go to hell. Well, he would have news for her. As far as he was concerned, he was already there. Going without a woman for two years hadn't been a picnic, but he hadn't wanted anyone except her and had denied himself because of it. It was unbelievable how a man's desire for one woman could rule his life, dictate his urges and serve as a thermostat for his constant craving. He was feeling the heat. It was flooding his insides and taking control of every part of his being.

Over the past several days, he'd thought about knocking on Kalina's door but had always talked himself out of it. He wouldn't have been so bold as to ask her to meet him on the staircase tonight if he hadn't seen that particular look in her eyes. He knew that look in a woman's eyes well enough: heated lust. He'd seen it in Kalina's eyes many times.

He turned when he heard footsteps. It was late. Most normal people were asleep. He should be asleep. Instead, he was up, wide awake, horny as hell and lusting after a woman. But not just any woman. He wanted Kalina. She still hadn't told him whether she'd made a decision about going home with him, and he hoped that no news was good news.

He heard the sound of the knob turning and his gaze stayed glued to the door. Most people used the elevator. He preferred the stairs when jogging, for the additional workout. He drew in a deep breath. Was it her? Had she really come after two years of separation and the misunderstanding that still existed between them?

The door slowly opened, and he gradually released his breath. It was Kalina, and at that moment, as his gaze held tight to hers, he couldn't stop looking at her. The more he looked at her, the more he wanted her. The more he needed to be with her.

Had to be with her.

But he needed her to want to be with him just as

much. Deciding not to take her appearance here for granted, he slowly moved toward her, his steps unhurried yet precise. His breathing was coming out just as hard as the erection he felt pressing against his shorts.

Micah reached her and lifted his hand to push a lock of hair from her face. Knowing what she thought was the truth about him, he understood that it had taken a lot for her to come to him. He intended to make sure she didn't regret it.

He opened his mouth to say something, but she placed a finger to his lips. "Please don't say anything, Micah. Just do it. Take me now and take me hard."

Her words fired his blood, and his immediate thought was that, given the degree of his need, he would have no problem doing that. He tightened his hand on hers. "Come on, let's go up to my room."

She pulled back and shook her head. "No. Do it here. Now."

He met her gaze, stared deep into her eyes. "I wouldn't suggest that if I were you," he warned. "You just might get what you ask for."

"I'm hoping."

He heard the quiver in her voice and saw the degree of urgency in her expression. There was a momentous need within her that was hitting him right in the gut and stirring his own need. He drew in a deep breath. There was no doubt in his mind that he was about to lose focus, but he also knew he was about to gain something more rewarding.

He then thought of something. *Damn, damn and triple damn.* "I don't have a condom on me."

His words didn't seem to faze her. She merely nodded and said, "I'm still on the pill and still in good health."

"I'm still in good health, as well," he said and thought there was no need to admit that he hadn't made love to another woman since her.

"Then do it, Micah."

He heard the urgency and need in her voice. "Whatever you want, baby."

Reaching behind her, he locked the entry door before lifting her off her feet to place her back against the wall. Raising her skirt, he spread her legs so they could wrap around him. His shaft began twitching, hardening even more as he lowered his zipper to release it. He skimmed his hands between Kalina's legs and smiled when he saw there were no panties he needed to dispense with. She was hot, and ready.

So was he.

He lowered his head to take her mouth, and at the same moment he aimed his erection straight for her center and began sliding in. Her hands on his shoulders were used to draw him closer into the fit of her.

She took in several deep breaths as he became more entrenched in her body. She felt tight, and her inner muscles clenched him. He broke off the kiss, closed his eyes and threw his head back as he clutched her hips and bottom in his hands and went deeper and deeper. There was nothing like having your manhood gripped, pulled and squeezed by feminine muscles intent on milking you dry.

His lips returned to hers in a deep, openmouthed kiss as he began thrusting hard inside her, tilting her body so he could hit her G-spot. He wanted to drive her wild, over the edge.

"Micah. Oh, Micah, don't stop. Please don't stop. I missed this."

She wasn't alone. He had missed this, as well. At that moment, something fierce and overpowering tore through him and like a jackhammer out of control, he thrust inside her hard, quick and deep. Being inside her this way was driving him over the edge, sending fire through his veins and rushing blood to all parts of his body, especially the part connected to her.

"Micah!"

Her orgasm triggered his as hard and hot desire raged through him. He plunged deeper into her body. The explosion mingled their juices as his release shot straight to her womb as if that's where it wanted to be, where it belonged. She shuddered uncontrollably, going over the edge. He followed her there.

Unable to resist, he used his free hand to push aside her blouse and bra and then latched his mouth to her nipple, sucking hard. At the same time, his body erupted into yet another orgasm and a second explosion rocketed him to heights he hadn't scaled in two years.

He now knew without a doubt what had been missing in his life. Kalina. Now more than ever he intended to make sure she never left him again.

Chapter 7

Kalina slowly opened her eyes. Immediately, she knew that although she was in her room at the villa, she was not in bed alone. Her backside was spooned against hard masculine muscles with an engorged erection against the center of her back.

She drew in a deep breath as memories of the night before consumed her. Micah had a way of making her feel feminine and womanly each and every time he kissed her, touched her or made love to her. And he had made love to her several times during the night. It was as if they were both trying to make up for the two years they'd been apart.

Considering the unfinished business between them, she wasn't sure their insatiable passion had been a good thing. But last night she hadn't cared. Her needs had overridden her common sense. Instead of concentrating on what he had done to betray her, she had been focused on what he could do to her body. What he had done last night had taken the edge off, and she had needed it as much as she'd needed to breathe. He had gone above and beyond the call of duty and had satisfied her more than she had imagined possible. Now all she wanted to do was stay in bed, be lazy and luxuriate in the afterglow.

"Hey, babe. You awake?" Micah asked while sliding a bare leg over her naked body.

If she hadn't been awake, she was now, she thought when the feel of his erection on her back stiffened even more. She drew in a deep breath, not sure she was ready to converse with him yet. With the sensation of him pressing against her, however, she had a feeling conversation was the last thing on Micah's mind.

"Kal?"

Knowing she had to answer him sometime, she slowly turned onto her back. "Yes, I'm awake."

He lifted up on his elbow to loom over her and smiled. "Good morning."

She opened her mouth to give him the same greeting, but that was as far as she got. He slid a hand up her hip just seconds before his lips swooped down and captured hers. The second his tongue entered her mouth she was a pathetic goner. No man kissed like Micah. He put everything he was into the kiss, and she could feel all kinds of sensations overtaking her and wrapping her in a sensual cocoon.

A part of her felt that maybe she should pull back. She didn't want to give him the wrong message, but another part of her was in a quandary as to what the wrong message could be, in light of what they'd shared the night before.

And as he kissed her, she remembered every moment of what they'd shared.

She recalled them making love on the stairwell twice before he'd carried her back to her room. Once inside, they had stripped off their clothes and showered together. They'd made out beneath the heated spray of water before lathering each other clean. He had dried her off, only to lick her all over and make her wet again.

Then they had made love in her bed several times. She had ridden him, and he had ridden her. Then they had ridden each other. The last thing she remembered was falling asleep totally exhausted in his arms.

It was Micah who finally pulled his mouth away, but not before using his tongue to lick her lips from corner to corner.

"You need to stop that," she said in a voice that lacked any real conviction.

"I will, when I'm finished with you," he said, nibbling at the corners of her mouth.

She knew that could very well be never. "You need to go to your room so I can get dressed for work, and you need to get dressed, too."

"Later."

And then he was kissing her again, more passionately than before. She tried to ignore the pleasure overtaking her, but she couldn't. So she became a willing recipient and took everything he was giving her. His kiss was so strong and potent that when he finally pulled his mouth away, she actually felt light-headed.

"I missed that," he murmured, close to her ear. "And I missed this, as well." He moved to slide his body over hers, lifted her hips and entered her in one smooth thrust.

He looked down at her and held her gaze in a breathless moment before moving his body in and out of her. "Being inside you feels so incredibly good, Kal," he whispered, and she thought a woman could get spoiled by this. She certainly had been spoiled during their time in Sydney. So much so that she had suffered through withdrawal for months afterward.

"Oh, baby, you're killing me," Micah growled out, increasing the intensity of his strokes. Kalina begged to differ. He was the one killing her. Her body was the one getting the workout of a lifetime. Blood was rushing through all parts of her, sending shock waves that escalated and touched her everywhere. Never had she been made love to so completely.

All further thought was forced from her mind when he hollered her name just seconds before his body bucked in a powerful orgasm. She felt the essence of his release shoot straight to her womb. The feel of it triggered a riot of sensations, which burst loose within her.

"Micah!"

"I'm here, baby. Let it go. Give yourself to me completely. Don't hold anything back."

She heard his words and tried closing her mind to them but found that she couldn't. She couldn't hold anything back, even if she tried. The strength of her need for him stunned her, but whether she wanted to admit it or not, she knew that what she and Micah were sharing was special. She wanted to believe it was meant just for them.

He continued to hold her, even when he eventually shifted his body off hers. He'd gotten quiet, and she wondered what he was thinking. As if he'd read her thoughts, he reached out and cupped her chin in his hand then tilted her head so she could look at him and he could look at her.

She felt the heat of his gaze in every part of her body. He brushed a kiss across her lips. "Have dinner with me tonight."

She quickly recalled that dinner after a night of passion was how their last affair had begun. They had slept together one night after work and the next evening he'd taken her out to eat. After dinner, they'd gone back to her place and had been intimately involved for two glorious months.

"We've done that already, Micah."

At his confused look, she added, "Dinner and all that goes with it. Remember Sydney? Different place. Same technique."

He frowned. "Are you trying to say I'm boring you?"

She couldn't help smiling. "Do I look bored? Have I acted bored?"

He laughed. "No to both."

"All right, then. All I meant was that I recall a casual dinner was how things started between us the last time."

"You have to eat."

"Yes, but you don't have to be the one who's always there to feed me. I'm a big girl. I can take care of myself."

"Okay, then," he said, leaning in close to run the tip of his tongue around her earlobe. "What do you want from me?"

She chuckled. "What I got last night and this morning was pretty darn good. I have no complaints."

He lifted his head and frowned down at her. "Shouldn't you want more?"

"Are you prepared to give me more?" she countered.

He seemed to sober with her question. He held her gaze a moment then said, "I want you to get to know the real me, Kal. You never did decide if you're willing to go home with me or not."

Mainly because she'd tried putting the invitation out of her mind. She hadn't wanted to talk about it or even think about it. "I need more time."

"You have only two days left," he reminded her.

Yes, she knew. And she wasn't any closer to making a decision than she had been a week ago. Sleeping together had only complicated things. But she had no regrets. She had needed a sexual release.

She had needed him.

"Well, that's it," Micah told Kalina and Theo several hours later, at the end of the workday. "There haven't been any more reported deaths, and with the case of the few survivors, the Indian government won't let us get close enough to do an examination since we have no proof it's linked and the people did survive."

"The initial symptoms were the same. They could have survived for a number of reasons," Kalina said in frustration.

The only way to assure the U.S. military had a preventative mechanism in place if the virus popped up again was to come up with a vaccine. Micah and his team hadn't been able to do that. The chemicals that had been used were not traceable in the human body after death. And the only sign of abnormality they'd been able to find was the enlargement of the tongue.

Other than that, all they had was an unexplained virus that presented as death by natural causes.

She, Theo and Micah knew there was nothing natural about it, but there was nothing they could do in this instance except report their findings to Washington and hope this type of "mysterious illness" didn't pop up again. Before the Indian government had pulled the plug on any further examinations of the survivors, Kalina had managed to obtain blood samples, which she had shipped off to Washington for further study.

"I'm flying out tonight," Theo said, standing. "I'm meeting Renee in Paris for one of her shows. Where are you two headed now?"

"I'm headed home to Denver," Micah said. He then glanced over at Kalina expectantly.

Without looking at Micah, she said, "I'm not sure where I'm going yet."

"Well, you two take care of yourselves. I'm going up to my room to pack. It's been a lot of fun, but I'm ready to leave."

Micah was ready to leave as well and looked forward to going home to chill for a while. He glanced over at Kalina, deciding he wouldn't ask her about her decision again. He'd made it pretty clear he wanted her to spend her time off with him.

He glanced over at her while she stood to gather up her belongings. He couldn't stop his gaze from warming with pleasure as he watched her. Kalina Daniels had the ability to turn him on without even trying. His response to her had set off warning bells inside his head in Sydney, and those same bells were going off now. He hadn't taken heed then, and he wouldn't be taking heed now.

He wanted her. Yes, she had hurt him by believing

the worst, but he was willing to overlook that hurt because he had been partially to blame. He hadn't given her the opportunity to really get to know him. Now, he was offering her that chance, but it was something she had to want to do. So far, she didn't appear to know if she wanted to make that effort.

"I'm glad I was able to draw that blood and have it shipped to Washington before the Indian government stepped in," he heard her say.

He nodded as he stood. "I'm glad, as well. Hopefully, they'll be able to find something we couldn't."

"I hope so."

He studied her for a moment. "So, what are your plans for the evening?" Because of what she'd said that morning, he didn't want to ask specifically about dinner.

She drew in a deep breath. "Not sure. I just might decide to stay in with a good book."

"All right."

He fought back the desire to suggest they stay in together. Regardless of what they'd shared last night and this morning, Kalina would have to invite him to share any more time with her. The decision had to be hers…but there was nothing wrong with making sure she made the right one.

"I'm renting a car and going for a drive later," he offered.

She glanced over at him. "Really? Where?"

"No place in particular. I just need to get away from the villa for a while." He felt that they both did. Although they would be leaving India in a couple of days, they had pretty much stayed on the premises during the entire investigation. "You're invited to come with me if you'd like."

He could tell by her expression that she wanted to but was hesitant to accept his invitation. He wouldn't push. "Well, I'll see you later."

He had almost made it to the door, when she called after him. "Micah, if you're sure you don't mind having company, I'll tag alone."

Inwardly, he released a sigh of relief. He slowly turned to her. "No, I wouldn't mind. I would love having you with me. And there's a club I plan to check out, so put on your dancing shoes." Then without saying anything else, he walked out of the room.

Dancing shoes?

She shook her head recalling Micah's suggestion as she moved around her room at the villa. She loved dancing, but she'd never known him to dance. At least he'd never danced with her during those two months they'd been together. Even the night they'd met, at the ball. Other guys had asked her to dance, but Micah had not.

Micah had a lean, muscular physique, and she could imagine his body moving around on anyone's dance floor. So far, that had been something she hadn't seen. But she had been more than satisfied with all his moves in the bedroom and couldn't have cared less if any of those moves ever made it to the dance floor.

She heard a knock at the door, and her breath caught. Even with the distance separating them, she could feel the impact of his presence. After making love that morning, he had left her room to go to his and dress. They had met downstairs for breakfast with Theo. Today had been their last day at the lab. Tomorrow was a free day to do whatever they wanted, and then on Friday they would be flying out.

Major Harris had already called twice, asking where she wanted to go after she returned to Washington, and Kalina still wasn't certain she wanted to join Micah in Denver.

She knew she'd have to decide soon.

She quickly moved toward the door and opened it. Micah's slow perusal of her outfit let her know she'd done the right thing in wearing this particular dress. She had purchased it sometime last year at a boutique in Atlanta while visiting a college friend.

"You look nice," he said, giving her an appreciative smile.

She let her gaze roam over him and chuckled. "So do you. Come in for a moment. You're a little early, and I haven't switched out purses."

"No problem. Take your time."

Micah followed her into a sitting area and took the wingback chair she offered. When she left the room, he glanced around at the pictures on the wall. They were different from the ones in his room. His cousin Gemma was an interior decorator, and while taking classes at the university, she had decorated most of her family members' homes for practice. He would be the first to admit she'd done a good job. No one had been disappointed. He had been home for a short visit while she'd decorated his place, and she had educated him about what to look for in a painting when judging if it would fit the decor.

He was sure these same paintings had been on the wall when he'd carried Kalina through here in his arms last night. But his mind had been so preoccupied with getting her to bed, he hadn't paid any attention.

"I'm ready. Sorry to make you wait."

He glanced around, smiled and came to his feet. "No problem."

For a moment, neither of them said anything, but just stood there and stared at each other. Then finally he said, "I'm not going to pretend last night and this morning didn't happen, Kal."

She nodded slowly. "I don't recall asking you to."

She was right, she hadn't. "Good, then I guess it's safe for me to do this, since I've been dying to all day."

He reached out, tugged her closer to him and lowered his mouth to hers.

The arms that encompassed Kalina in an embrace were warm and protective. And the hand that rubbed up and down her spine was gentle.

But nothing could compare to the mouth that was taking her over with slow, deep, measured strokes. Already, desire was racing through her, and she couldn't do anything but moan her pleasure. No other two tongues could mate like theirs could, and she enjoyed the feel of his tongue in her mouth.

He shifted his stance to bring them closer, and she felt his hard erection pressing into her. It wouldn't bother her in the least if he were to suggest they stay in for the evening.

Instead, he finally broke contact, but immediately placed a quick kiss on her lips. "I love your taste," he whispered hotly.

She smiled up at him. "And I love yours, too."

The grin he shot her was naughty. "I'm going to have to keep that in mind."

She chuckled as she saw the glint of mischief in his gaze. "Yes, you do that."

Kalina always thought she could handle just about

anything or anyone, but an hour or so after they'd left her room, she wasn't sure. She was seeing a side of Micah she had never seen before. It had started with the drive around the countryside. There had been just enough daylight left to enjoy the beauty of the section of town they hadn't yet seen, especially the shops situated at the foot of the Himalayas.

They had dined at a restaurant in the shopping district, and the food had been delicious. Now they were at the nightclub the restaurant manager had recommended.

She was in Micah's arms on the dance floor. The music was slow, and he was holding her while their bodies moved together in perfect rhythm. She was vaguely aware of their surroundings. The inside of the club was dark and crowded. Evidently this was a popular hangout. The servers were moving at a hurried pace to fill mixed-drink orders. And the live band rotated periodically with a deejay.

"I like this place, Micah. Thanks for bringing me here."

"You're welcome."

"And this is our first dance," she added.

He glanced down at her, tightened his arms around her and smiled. "I hope it's not our last."

She hoped that, as well. She liked the feel of being held by him in a place other than the bedroom. It felt good. But she could tell he wanted her from the hard bulge pressing against her whenever their bodies moved together. She liked the feel of it. She liked knowing she was desired. She especially appreciated knowing she could do that to him—even here in a crowded nightclub in the middle of a dance floor.

"Excalibur."

She glanced up at him. "Excuse me."

"My middle name is Excalibur."

She blinked, wondering why he was telling her that. "Oh, okay."

He chuckled. "You didn't know that, did you?"

She shrugged. "Was I supposed to?"

"I wish you had. I should have told you. We were involved for two months."

Yes, they had been involved, but their affair had been more about sex than conversation. He interrupted her thoughts by saying, "I know more about you than you know about me, Kalina."

She tilted her head to the side and looked at him. "You think so?"

"Yes."

"Well, then, tell me what you know," she said.

He tightened his arms around her waist as they swayed their bodies in time with the music. "You're twenty-seven. Your middle name is Marie. Your birthday is June fifteenth. Your favorite color is red. You hate eating beets. Your mother's name was Yvonne, and she died of cancer when you were ten."

He grinned as if proud of himself. "So what does that tell you?"

She stared at him for a few moments as if collecting her thoughts and then said, "I did more pillow talk than you did."

He laughed at that. "Sort of. What it tells me is that you shared more of yourself with me than I did with you."

They had already concluded there were a lot of things they didn't know about each other. So, okay, he had a heads-up on her information. That was fine. What they'd shared for those two months was a bed and not much else.

"It should not have been just sex between us, Kalina. I can see that now."

Now, *that's* where she disagreed. Their affair was never intended to be about anything but sex. For those two months, they had gotten to know each other intimately but not intellectually, and that's the way they'd wanted it. "If what you say is true, Micah, nobody told me. I distinctly recall you laying down the rules for a no-strings affair. And I remember agreeing to those rules. Your career was your life, and so was mine."

Evidently, she'd given him something to think about, because he didn't say anything to that. The music stopped, and he led her back to their table. A server was there, ready to take their drink order. One thing she'd noticed, two years ago and today, was that Micah was always a gentleman. He was a man who held doors open for ladies, who stood when women entered the room and who pulled out chairs for his date...the way he was doing now. "Thanks."

"You're welcome."

She glanced across the table at him. "You have impeccable manners."

He chuckled. "I wouldn't go that far, but I do my best."

"Do your brothers and cousins all have good manners like you?"

He winked. "Come home to Denver with me and find out."

Kalina rolled her eyes in exasperation. "You won't give up, will you?"

"No. I think you owe me the chance to clear my name."

He didn't say anything for a moment, allowing the server to place their drinks in front of them. Then she took a sip of her wine and asked, "Is clearing your name important to you, Micah?"

Leaning back, he stared over at her before saying, "If you really knew me the way I want you to know me, you wouldn't be asking me that."

She didn't say anything for a while. A part of her wanted to believe him, to believe that he truly did want her to get to know him better, to believe that he hadn't done what her father had said. But what if she went home with him, got to know him and, in the end, still felt he was capable of doing what she had accused him of doing?

"Micah—"

"You owe me that, Kalina. I think I've been more than fair, considering I am innocent of everything you've accused me of. Some men wouldn't give a damn about what you believed, but I do. Like I said, you owe me the chance to prove your father lied."

She drew in a deep breath. Did she owe him? She didn't have much time to think about it. He reached across the table and captured her small hand in his bigger one. Just a touch from him did things to her, made her feel what she didn't want to feel.

"I hadn't wanted to make love to you again until we resolved things between us," he said in a low tone.

She gave a cynical laugh. "So now you're going to claim making love last night and this morning was my idea?"

"No. I wanted you, and I knew that you wanted me."

He was right, and there was no need to ask how he'd known that. She had wanted him, and she'd been fully aware that he had wanted her.

"Would it make you feel more comfortable about going home with me if I promise not to touch you while you're there?"

She narrowed her gaze. "No, because all you'll do is find ways to tempt me to the point where I'll end up being the one seeking you out. I'm well aware of those games you play, Micah."

He didn't deny it. "Okay, then. We are adults," he said. "With needs. But the purpose of you going to Denver with me is not to continue our sexual interactions. I want to make that clear up front."

He had made that clear more times than she cared to count. Her stomach knotted, and she wondered when she would finally admit that the real reason she was reluctant to go to Denver was that she might end up getting too attached to him, to his family, to her surroundings…

Her heart hammered at the mere thought of that happening. For years, especially after her grandparents' deaths, she had felt like a loner. She'd had her father— whenever he managed to stay in one place long enough to be with her. But their relationship wasn't like most parent-child relationships. She believed deep down that he loved her, but she also knew that he expressed that love by trying to control her. As long as she followed his orders like one of his soldiers, she remained in his good graces. But if she rebelled, there was hell to pay. The only reason he had apologized for his actions regarding her canceled trip to Beijing was that, for the first time in his life, he saw that he could make her angry enough that he could lose her. She had been just that upset with him, and he knew it. Although he had never admitted it, her father was just as much of a maverick as she was.

She glanced down at the table and saw that Micah was still holding her hand. It felt good. Too good. Too right. She thought about pulling her hand away, but decided to let it stay put since he seemed content holding it. Her breathing quickened when he began stroking her palm in a light caress. His touch was so stimulating it played on her nerve endings as if they were the strings of a well-tuned guitar.

She glanced up and met his gaze. He stopped stroking her skin and curved his hand over hers to entwine their fingers. "No matter what you believe, Kal, I would never intentionally hurt you."

She nodded and then he slowly withdrew his hand from hers. She instantly felt the loss of that contact.

He glanced around the club and then at the dance floor. The deejay was playing another slow song. "Come on, I want to hold you in my arms again," he said, reaching out and taking her hand one more time.

He led her to the dance floor, and she placed her head on his chest. He wrapped his arms around her, encompassing her in his embrace. His heart was beating fast against her cheek, and his erection pressed hard against her middle again. She smiled. Did he really think they could go to Denver together and not share a bed?

She chuckled. Now she was beginning to wonder if he really knew *her* that well.

He touched her chin and tipped her head back to meet his gaze. "You okay?"

She nodded, deciding not to tell him what she'd

found so comical, especially since he was wearing such a serious expression on his face.

She saw something in the depths of his dark eyes that she didn't understand at first glance. But then she knew what she saw. It was a tenderness that was reaching out to her, making her feel both vulnerable and needed at the same time. At that moment she knew the truth.

"Kalina?"

The release of her name from his lips sent a shiver racing up her spine. Drawing in much-needed air, she said, "Yes, I'm fine. And I've reached a decision, Micah. I'm going to Denver with you."

Chapter 8

"Welcome to Micah's Manor, Kalina."

Micah stood aside as Kalina entered his home and looked around. He saw both awe and admiration reflected in her features. He hadn't told her what to expect and now he was glad that he hadn't. This was the first official visit to his place by any woman other than one of his relatives. What Kalina thought mattered to him.

In his great-grandfather's will, it had been declared that every Westmoreland heir would receive one hundred acres of land at the age of twenty-five. As the oldest, Dillon got the family homestead, which included the huge family house that sat on over three hundred acres.

Micah had already established a career as an epidemiologist and was living in Washington by the time his twenty-fifth birthday came around. For years, he'd kept the land undeveloped and whenever he came home he would crash at Dillon's place. But when Dillon got married and had a family of his own, Micah felt it was time to build his own house.

He had taken off six months to supervise the project. That had been the six months following the end of his affair with the very woman now standing in his living room. He had needed something to occupy his time, and his thoughts, and having this house built seemed the perfect project.

He could count on one finger the number of times he had actually spent the night here, since he rarely came home. The last time had been when he'd come to Denver for his brother Jason's wedding reception in August. It had been nice to stay at his own place, and the logistics had worked out fine since he, his siblings and cousins all had houses in proximity to each other.

"So, what do you think?" he asked, placing Kalina's luggage by the front door.

"This place is for one person?"

He couldn't help laughing. He knew why she was asking. Located at the south end of the rural area that the locals referred to as Westmoreland Country, Micah's Manor sat on Gemma Lake, the huge body of water his great-grandfather had named in honor of his wife when he'd settled here all those years ago. Micah's huge ranch-style house was three stories high with over six thousand square feet of living space.

"Yes. I admit I let Gemma talk me into getting carried away, but—"

"Gemma?"

"One of my cousins. She's an interior designer. To take full advantage of the lake, she figured I needed the third floor, and as for the size, I figured when my time ended with the feds, I would want to settle down, marry and raise a family. It was easier to build that dream house now instead of adding on later."

"Good planning."

"I thought so at the time. I picked the plan I liked best, hired a builder and hung around for six months to make sure things got off to a good start," he added.

"Oh, I see."

He knew she really didn't. She had no idea that when he'd selected this particular floor plan he had envisioned her sharing it with him, even though the last thing she had uttered to him was that she hated his guts. For some reason, he hadn't been able to push away the fantasy that one day she would come here and see this place. He had even envisioned them making love in his bedroom while seeing the beauty of the lake. Having Kalina here now was a dream come true.

"I had to leave on assignment to Peru for a few months and when I returned, the house was nearly finished. I took more time off and was here when Gemma began decorating it."

"It is beautiful, Micah."

He was glad she liked it. "Thanks. I practically gave Gemma an open checkbook, and she did her thing. Of course, since it wasn't her money, she decided to splurge a little."

Kalina raised a dubious brow. "A little?"

He shrugged and grinned. "Okay, maybe a lot. Up until a year ago she used this place as a model home to showcase her work whenever she was trying to impress new clients. As you can see, her work speaks for itself."

Kalina glanced around. "Yes, it sure does. Your cousin is very gifted. Is she no longer in the business?"

"She's still in it."

"But she no longer needs your house as a model?" Kalina asked.

"No, mainly because she's living in Australia now that she and Callum are married. That's where he's from. They have a two-month-old son. You'll get to meet them sometime next week. She's coming home for a visit."

He had given his family strict orders to stay away from his place to give him time to get settled in with his houseguest. Of course, everyone was anxious to meet the woman he'd brought home with him.

"This should be an interesting thirty days," she said, admiring a huge painting on the wall.

"Why do you say that?"

She shrugged. "Well, all those markers I saw getting here. Jason's Place. Zane's Hideout. Canyon's Bluff. Ramsey's Web. Derringer's Dungeon. Stern's Stronghold… Need I go on?"

He chuckled. "No, and you have my cousin Bailey to thank for that. We give her the honor of naming everyone's parcel of land, and she's come up with some doozies." He picked up her luggage. "Come on, I'll show you to your room. If you aren't in the mood to climb the stairs, I do have an elevator."

"No, the stairs are fine. Besides, it gives me the chance to work the kinks out of my body from our long flight."

She followed him to one of the guest rooms on the third floor. They hadn't slept together since that one night he'd spent with her after they'd met on the staircase. Even after he'd taken her dancing, he had returned her to her room at the villa, planted a kiss on her cheek and left. The next day had been extremely busy with them packing up the lab's equipment and finalizing reports.

They had been too busy to spend time getting naked on silken sheets. But that hadn't meant the thought hadn't run through his mind a few times. Yesterday they'd taken the plane here, and sat beside each other for the flight. The twelve hours from India to Washington, and then the six hours from Washington to Denver had given him time to reflect on what he hoped she would get from her thirty days with him and his family.

"Wow!" Kalina walked into Micah's guest bedroom and couldn't do anything but stare, turn around and stare some more.

The room was done in chocolate, white and lime green. Everything—from the four-poster, white, queen-size bed, to the curtains and throw pillows—was perfectly matched. The walls of the room were painted white, which made the space look light and airy. Outside her huge window was a panoramic view of the lake she'd seen when they arrived. There was a private bath that was triple the size of the one she had in her home in Virginia. It had both a Jacuzzi tub and a walk-in shower.

She wasn't surprised Micah had given her one of his guest rooms to use. He wanted to shift their relationship from the physical to the mental. She just wasn't so sure she agreed with his logic. She could still get to know him while they shared a bed, and she didn't understand why he assumed differently. She watched him place the luggage by her bed. He said nothing as she continued to check out other interesting aspects of the room.

"I can see why Gemma used your house as a model home," Kalina said, coming to stand in front of him.

"Your house should be featured in one of those magazines."

He chuckled. "It was. Last year. I have a copy downstairs. You can read the article if you like."

"All right."

"I'll leave you to rest up and relax. I plan on preparing dinner later."

She raised a surprised brow. "You can cook?"

He laughed. "Of course I can cook. And I'm pretty good at it, you'll see." He reached out and softly kissed her on the lips. "Now, get some rest."

He turned to leave, but she stopped him. "Where's your room?"

He smiled down at her as if he had an idea why she was asking. "It's on the second floor. I'll give you a tour of my bedroom anytime you want it."

She nodded, fully aware that a tour of his bedroom wasn't what she was really interested in. She wanted to try out his bed.

A few hours later, Kalina closed her eyes as she savored the food in her mouth. "Mmm, this is delicious," she said, slowly opening her eyes and glancing across the dinner table at Micah.

After indulging in a bath in the Jacuzzi, she had taken a nap, only to awaken hours later to the smell of something good cooking in the kitchen downstairs. She had slipped into a T-shirt and a pair of capris, and, not bothering to put shoes on, she had headed downstairs to find Micah at the stove. In his bare feet, shirtless, with jeans riding low on his hips, he'd looked the epitome of sexy as he moved around his spacious kitchen. She had watched him and had seen for herself just how at home he was while making a meal. She couldn't help admiring him. Some men couldn't even boil water.

He had told her he could cook, but she hadn't taken him at his word. Now, after tasting what he'd prepared, she was forced to believe him. *Almost.* She glanced around the kitchen.

"What are you looking for?" he asked her.

She looked back at him and smiled. "Your chef."

Micah chuckled. "You won't find one here. I did all this myself. I don't particularly like cooking, but I won't starve if I have to do it for myself."

No, he wouldn't starve. In fact, he had enough cooking skills to keep himself well fed. He had prepared meat loaf, rice and gravy, green beans and iced tea. He'd explained that he'd called ahead and had gotten his cousin Megan to go grocery shopping for him. She'd picked up everything he'd asked her to get and a few things he hadn't asked her for…like the three flavors of ice cream now in the freezer.

"Do you ever get lonely out here, Micah?"

He glanced across the table at her and laughed. "Are you kidding? I have relatives all around me. I try to catch up on my rest whenever I'm home, but they don't make it easy. Although I'm not here the majority of the time, I'm involved in the family business. I have a share in my brother's and cousins' horse-breeding business, in my cousin Ramsey's sheep business and I'm on the board of Blue Ridge Land Management." He then told her how his father and uncle had founded the company years ago and how his brother Dillon was now CEO.

Kalina immediately recognized the name of the company. It had made the Forbes Top 50 just this year. She could only sit and stare at him. She'd had no idea he was one of *those* Westmorelands.

Not that having a lot of money was everything, but it told her more about his character than he realized. He worked because he wanted to work, not because he had to. Yet he always worked just as hard as any member of his team—sometimes even harder. She couldn't help wondering how he'd chosen his field of work and why he was so committed and dedicated to it.

Over dinner he told her more about his family, his brothers and cousins, especially the escapades of the younger Westmorelands. Although she tried not to laugh, she found some of their antics downright comical and could only imagine how his brother Dillon and cousin Ramsey had survived it all while still managing to keep the family together.

"And you say there are fifteen of you?" she asked, pushing her plate away.

"Yes, of the Denver clan. Everyone is here except Gemma, who now lives in Sydney, and the few who are still away at college. Needless to say, the holidays are fun times for us when everyone comes home."

Getting up to take their plates to the sink, he asked, "Do you feel like going horseback riding later? I thought I'd give you a tour of the rest of the house and then we can ride around my property."

Excitement spread through her. "I'd like that."

He returned to the seat next to her. "But first I think we need to have a talk."

She lifted an eyebrow. "About what?"

"About whose bed you'll be sleeping in while you're here."

And before she could respond, he had swept her out

of her chair and into his arms. He carried her from the kitchen into the living room where he settled down on the sofa with her in his lap.

Micah smiled at the confused look on Kalina's face. She brushed back a handful of hair and then pinned him with one of her famous glares. "I didn't know there was a question about where I'd be sleeping."

She wasn't fooling him one bit. "Isn't there? I put you in the guest room for a reason."

She waved off his words. "Then maybe we do need to talk about that foolishness regarding your no-sex policy again."

He'd figured she would want to discuss it, which was why he'd brought up the subject. "It will be less complicated if we don't share the same bed for a while."

"Until I really get to know you?"

"Yes."

"I disagree with your logic on taking that approach, especially since you want me. Do you deny it?"

How could he deny it when he had an erection he knew she could feel since she was practically sitting on it. "No, I don't deny it, but like I said when I invited you here, I want you to—"

"Get to know you," she muttered. "I heard you. More times than I care to. And I don't think us sharing a bed has anything to do with what we do outside the bedroom."

"Well, I do. Last time we had an affair it was strictly sexual. Now I want to change the way you think about me, about us."

Now she really looked confused. "To what?"

He wished he could tell her the truth, that she was the

woman he wanted above all others. That he wanted to
marry her. He wanted her to have his babies. He wanted
her to wear his name. But all the things he wanted meant
nothing until she could trust him. They would never
come into existence until she could believe he was not
the man her father had made him out to be. This time
around, Micah refused to allow sex to push those wants
to the side.

"I want you to think of things other than sex when
it comes to us, Kalina," he said.

She frowned. "Why?"

He could come clean and tell her how he felt about
her, but he didn't think she would believe him, just as
she still didn't believe he had not betrayed her two years
ago. "Because we've been there before. Even you said
that our relationship was starting with the same technique. I want you to feel that it's different this time."

He could tell she still didn't know where he was coming from, but the important thing was that *he* knew. A
dawning awareness suddenly appeared on her features,
but he had a feeling, even before she opened her mouth,
that whatever she was thinking was all wrong.

"Okay, I think I get it," she said, nodding.

He was afraid to ask, but knew he had to. "And just
what do you get?"

"You're one of the older Westmorelands and you feel
you should set an example for the others." She nodded
her head as if her assumption made perfect sense.

"Set an example for them in what way?" he asked.

"By presenting me as a friend and not a lover. You
did say your cousin Bailey was young and impressionable."

He had to keep a straight face. He forced his eyes to

stay focused even though he was tempted to roll them. Once she met Bailey she would see how absurd her assumption was. First of all, although she was twenty-three years old, Bailey probably didn't have much of a love life, thanks to all her older, overbearing and protective brothers and male cousins. And she had gone past being impressionable. Bailey could curse worse than any sailor when she put her mind to it. He and his brothers and cousins had already decided that the man who fell for Bailey would have to be admired... as well as pitied.

"The key word where Bailey is concerned is *was*. Trust me. I don't have to hide my affairs from anyone. Everyone around here is an adult and understands what grown-ups do."

"In that case, what other reason could you have for not wanting us to sleep together? Unless..."

He stared at her for several long moments, and when she didn't finish what she was about to say, he prompted her. "Unless what?"

She looked down at her hands in her lap. "Nothing."

He had a feeling that again, whatever was bothering her, she'd figured wrong. He reached out, lifted her chin up and brought his face closer to hers. "And I know good and well you aren't thinking what I think you're thinking, not when my desire for you is about to burst through my zipper. There's no way you can deny that you feel it."

She nodded slowly. "Yes, I can feel it," she said softly.

So could he, and he was aware, even more than he'd been before, of just how much he wanted her. Unfortunately, pointing out his body's reaction made her aware of how much he wanted her, as well.

She stuck her tongue out and slowly licked the corner of his lips. "Then why are you denying me what I want? Why are you denying yourself what you want?"

Good question. He had to think hard to recall the reason he was denying them both. He had a plan. A little sacrifice now would pay off plenty of dividends in the years to come. Remembering his goals wouldn't have been so hard if she hadn't decided at that very moment to play the vixen. She purposely twisted that little behind of hers in his lap, against his zipper, making him mindful of just how good his erection felt against her backside. And what the hell was she doing with her tongue, using the tip of it to lick his mouth? She was deliberately boggling his mind.

"Kalina?"

"Mmm?"

"Stop it," he said in a tone he knew was not really strong on persuasion. It wasn't helping matters that he'd once fantasized about them making love in this very room and on this very sofa.

"No, I don't want to stop and you can't make me," she said in that stubborn voice of hers.

Hell, okay, he silently agreed. *Maybe I can't make her stop.* And he figured that reasoning with her would be a waste of time....

At that moment she moved her tongue lower to lick the area around his jaw and he groaned.

"Oh, I so love the way you taste, Micah."

Those were the wrong words for her to say. Hearing them made him recall just how much he loved how she tasted, as well. He drew in a deep breath, hoping to find resistance. Instead, he inhaled her feminine scent, a telltale sign of how much she wanted him. He could just imagine the sweetness of her nectar.

He thought of everything…counting sheep, the pictures on the wall, the fact that he hadn't yet cleaned off the kitchen table…but nothing could clear his mind of her scent, or the way she was using her tongue. Now she had moved even lower to lick around his shoulder blades. Hell, why hadn't he put on a shirt?

"Baby, you've got to stop," he urged her in a strained voice.

She ignored him and kept right on doing what she was doing. He tried giving himself a mental shake and found it did not work. She was using her secret weapon, that blasted tongue of hers, to break him down. Hell, he would give anything for something—even a visit from one of his kin—to interrupt what she was doing, because he was losing the willpower to put a stop to it.

Hot, achy sensations swirled in his gut when she scooted off his lap. By the time he had figured out what she was about to do, it was too late. She had slid down his zipper and reached inside his jeans to get just what she wanted. He tightened his arms on her, planning to pull her up, but again he was too late. She lowered her head and took him into her mouth.

Kalina ignored the tug on her hair and kept her mouth firmly planted on Micah. By the time she was finished with him, he would think twice about resisting her, not giving her what she wanted or acting on foolish thoughts like them not sharing a bed now that she'd come all the way to Denver with him. He had a lot of nerve.

And he had a lot of this, she thought, fitting her

mouth firmly on him, barely able to do so because he was so large. He was the only man she'd ever done this to. The first time she hadn't been sure she had done it correctly. But he had assured her that she had, and he'd also assured her he had enjoyed it immensely. So she might as well provide him with more enjoyment, maybe then he would start thinking the way she wanted him to. Or, for the moment, stop thinking at all.

"Damn, Kalina, please stop."

She heard his plea, but thought it didn't sound all that convincing, so she continued doing what she was doing, and pretty soon the tug on her hair stopped. Now he was twirling her locks around his fingers to hold her mouth in place. No need. She didn't intend to go anywhere.

At least she thought she wouldn't be. Suddenly, he pulled her up and tossed her down on the sofa. The moment her back hit the cushions he was there, lifting her T-shirt over her head and sliding her capris and panties down her legs, leaving her totally naked.

The heat of his gaze raked over her, and she felt it everywhere, especially in her feminine core. "No need to let a good erection go to waste, Micah," she said saucily.

He evidently agreed with her. Tugging his jeans and briefs down over his muscular hips, he didn't waste any time slipping out of the clothes before moving to take his place between her open legs.

She lifted her arms to receive him and whispered, "Just think of this as giving me a much-deserved treat."

Kalina would have laughed at his snort if he hadn't captured her mouth in his the moment he slid inside her, not stopping until he went all the way to the hilt. And then he began moving inside her, stroking her desire to the point of raging out of control. She lifted her hips off the sofa to receive every hard thrust. The wall of his chest touched hers, brushing against her breasts in a rhythm that sent sensations rushing through her bloodstream.

Then he pulled away from her mouth, looked down at her and asked in a guttural voice, "Why?"

She knew what he was asking. "Because it makes no sense to deny us this pleasure."

He didn't say whether he agreed with her or not. Instead, he placed his hands against her backside and lifted her hips so they would be ready to meet his downward plunge. She figured he probably wasn't happy with her. He wouldn't appreciate how she had tempted him and pushed him over the edge. She figured he would stew for a while, but that was fine. Eventually he would get over it.

But apparently not before he put one sensuous whipping on her, she thought, loving the feel of how he was moving inside her. It was as if he wanted to use his body to give her a message, but she wasn't sure just what point he was trying to make. She reached up and cupped his face in her hands, forcing him to look at her. "What?" she asked breathlessly.

He started to move his lips in reply, but then, instead, leaned down and captured her mouth in his, leaving her wondering what he had been about to say. Probably just another scolding. All thoughts left her mind when she got caught up in his kiss and the way he was stroking inside her body.

She dropped her hands to his shoulders and then wrapped her arms around his neck as every sensation

intensified. Then her body exploded, and simultaneously, so did his. They cried out each other's names.

This, she concluded, as a rush swept over her, was
pleasure beyond anything they'd shared before. This
was worth his irritation once everything was over. For
now, she was fueled by this. She was stroked, claimed
and overpowered by the most sensuous lovemaking
she had ever known. By Micah's hands and his body.

This had been better than any fantasy, and she
couldn't think of a better way to be welcomed to
Micah's Manor.

Chapter 9

Okay, so she hadn't held a gun to his head or forced him to make love to her, but he was still pissed. Not only at her but at himself, Micah concluded the next morning as he walked out of the house toward the barn.

After they'd made love yesterday, Kalina had passed out. He had gathered her in his arms and taken her up the stairs to the guest room. After placing her naked body beneath the covers, he had left, closing the door behind him. He'd even thought about locking it. The woman was dangerous. She had not been so rebellious the last time.

Cursing and calling himself all kinds of names— including whipped, weakling and fickle—he had cleaned up the kitchen, unpacked his luggage and done some laundry. By the time he'd finished all his chores, it had gotten dark outside. He'd then gone into his office and made calls to his family to let them know he'd returned. Most had figured as much when they'd seen lights burning over at his place. He had again warned them that he didn't want to be disturbed. He'd assured them that he and his houseguest would make an appearance when they got good and ready. He ended up agreeing to bring her to dinner tomorrow night at the big house.

By the time he'd hung up the phone after talking to everyone, it was close to nine o'clock and he was surprised that he hadn't heard a peep out of Kalina. He checked on her and found her still sleeping. He had left her that way, figuring that when she'd caught up on her rest she would wake up. Still angry with himself for giving in to temptation and momentarily forgetting his plan, he'd gone to bed.

He'd awakened around midnight to the sound of footsteps coming down the stairs. He was very much aware when the footsteps paused in front of his closed bedroom door before finally progressing to the first floor. He had flipped onto his back and listened to the sound of Kalina moving around downstairs, knowing she was raiding his refrigerator—probably getting into those three flavors of ice cream.

When he had woken up this morning he had checked on her again. Sometime during the night she had changed into a pair of pajamas and was now sleeping on top of the covers. It had taken everything within him not to shed his own clothes and slide into that bed beside her.

Then he'd gotten mad at himself for thinking he should not have let her sleep alone. He should have made love to her all through the night. He should have let her go to sleep in his arms. He should have woken her up with his lovemaking this morning.

He had quickly forced those thoughts from his mind, considering them foolish, and had gone into the kitchen. He had prepared breakfast and kept it warming on the stove for her while he headed to the barn. He preferred not to be around when she woke up. The woman was pure temptation and making love to her every chance he got was not what he had in mind for this trip.

He had thought about getting into his truck and going to visit his family, but knew it wouldn't be a good idea to be off the property when Kalina finally woke up. He glanced at his watch. It was nine o'clock already. Was she planning to sleep until noon? His family probably figured he was keeping them away because he didn't want them to invade his private time with her. Boy, were they wrong.

"Good morning, Micah. I'm ready to go riding now."

He spun around and stared straight into Kalina's face. "Where did you come from?"

She smiled and looked at him as if he'd asked a silly question. "From inside the house. Where else would I have been?"

He frowned. "I didn't hear you approach."

She used her hand to wave off his words. "Whatever. You promised to take me riding yesterday, but we didn't get around to it since we were indulging in other things. I'm ready now."

His frown deepened, knowing just what those "other things" were. She was dressed in a pair of well-worn jeans, boots and a button-down shirt. He tried not to stare so hard at how the jeans fit her body, making him want to caress each of her curves. She looked good, and it took everything he had to keep his eyes from popping out of their sockets.

"Are we going riding or not?"

He glanced up at her face and saw her chin had risen a fraction. She expected a fight and was evidently ready for one. Just as she had been ready for them to make love yesterday. Well, he had news for her. Unlike yesterday, he wouldn't be accommodating her.

"Fine," he said, grabbing his Stetson off a rack on the barn wall. "Let's ride."

Kalina couldn't believe Micah was in a bad mood just because she had tempted him into making love to her. But here they were, riding side by side, and he was all but ignoring her.

She glanced over at him when he brought the horses to a stop along a ridge so she could look down over the valley. His Stetson was pulled low on his brow, and the shadow on his chin denoted he hadn't shaved that morning. He wore a dark brooding look, but, in her opinion, he appeared so sexy, so devastatingly handsome, that it was a total turn-on. It had taken all she had not to suggest they return to his place and make love. With his present mood, she knew better than to push her luck.

"Any reason you're staring at me, Kal?"

She inwardly smiled. So…he'd known she was looking. "No reason. I was just thinking."

He glanced over at her, tipped his hat back and those bedroom-brown eyes sent sensations floating around in her stomach. "Thinking about what?"

"Your mood. Are you typically a moody person?"

He frowned and looked back at the valley. "I'm not moody," he muttered.

"Yes, you are. Sex puts most men in a good mood. I see it does the opposite for you. I find that pretty interesting."

He glanced back at her. A tremor coursed through her with the look he was giving her. It was hot, regardless of the reason. "You just don't get it, do you?"

She shrugged. "Evidently not, so how about enlightening me on what I just don't get."

He inhaled deeply and then muttered, "Nothing."

"Evidently there is something, Micah."

He looked away again and moments later looked back at her. "There is nothing."

He then glanced at his watch. "I promised everyone I would bring you to dinner at the big house. They can hardly wait to meet you."

"And I'm looking forward to meeting them, too."

He watched her for a long moment. Too long. "What?" she asked, wondering why he kept staring at her.

He shook his head. "Nothing. I promised you a tour of the place. Come on. Let's go back home."

It was only moments later, as they rode side by side, that it dawned on her what he'd said.

"Let's go back home..."

Although she knew Micah hadn't meant it the way it had sounded, he'd said it as if they were a married couple and Micah's Manor was theirs. Something pricked inside her. Why was she suddenly feeling disappointed at the thought that Micah's home would never be hers?

"I like Kalina, Micah, and she's nothing like I expected."

Micah took a sip of his drink as he stood with Zane

on the sidelines, watching how his female cousins and cousins-in-law had taken Kalina into their midst and were making her feel right at home. He could tell from the smile on Kalina's face that she was comfortable around them.

Micah glanced up at his cousin. "What were you expecting?"

Zane chuckled. "Another mad scientist like you. Someone who was going to bore us with all that scientific mumbo jumbo. I definitely wasn't expecting a sexy doctor. Hell, if she didn't belong to you, I would hit on her myself."

Micah couldn't help smiling. He, of all people, knew about his cousin's womanizing ways. "I'm sure you would, and I'm glad you're not. I appreciate the loyalty."

"No problem. But you might want to lay down the law to the twins when they arrive next week."

He thought about his twin cousins, Aidan and Adrian, and the trouble they used to get into—the trouble they could still get into at times although both were away at college and doing well. It was something about being in Westmoreland Country that made them want to revert to being hellions—especially when it came to women.

"You haven't brought a woman home for us to meet since Patrice. Does this mean anything?"

Micah took another sip of his drink before deciding to be completely honest. "I plan to marry Kalina one day."

A smooth smile touched Zane's features. "Figured as much. Does she know it?"

"Not yet. I'm trying to give her the chance to get to know me."

If Zane found that comment strange he didn't let on. Instead, he changed the subject and brought Micah up to date on how things were going in the community. Micah listened, knowing that if anyone knew what was going on it would be Zane.

Micah was well aware that Westmoreland Country would become a madhouse in a few weeks, when everyone began arriving for the christening of Gemma's baby. They were expecting all those other Westmorelands from Atlanta, Texas and Montana. And his brothers and cousins attending college had planned to return for the event, as well.

"I hadn't heard Dillon say whether Bane is coming home."

Zane shrugged. "Not sure since he might be in training someplace."

Micah nodded. Everyone knew of his baby brother's quest to become a Navy SEAL, as well as Bane's mission to one day find the woman he'd given up a few years ago. And knowing his brother as he did, Micah knew Brisbane would eventually succeed in doing both.

"I like Kalina, Micah."

Micah turned when his brother Jason walked up. The most recent member of the family to marry, Jason and his wife, Bella, were expecting twins. From the look of Bella, the babies would definitely arrive any day now.

"I'm glad you do since you might as well get used to seeing her around," Micah said.

"Does that mean you're thinking of retiring as the Westmoreland mad scientist and returning home to start a family?" Jason asked.

Micah chuckled. "No, it doesn't mean any of that. I love my career, and Kalina loves hers. It just means we'll be working together more, and whenever I come home we'll come together."

He took a sip of his drink, thinking that what he'd just said sounded really good. Now all he had to do was convince Kalina. She had to get to know the real him, believe in him, trust him and then they could move on in their lives together.

He still wasn't happy about the stunt she'd pulled on him yesterday. He was determined to keep his distance until she realized the truth about him.

Kalina glanced across the room at Micah before turning her attention back to the women surrounding her. All of them had gone out of their way to make her feel at home. She hadn't known what to expect from this family dinner, but the one thing she hadn't expected was to find a group of women who were so warm and friendly.

Even Bailey, who Micah had said had been standoffish to Patrice, was more than friendly, and Kalina felt the warm hospitality was genuine. She readily accepted the women's invitation to go shopping with them later this week and to do other things like take in a couple of chick flicks, visit the spa and get their hair done. They wanted to have a "fun" week. Given Micah's present mood, she figured spending time away from him wouldn't be a bad idea.

After they'd returned to the ranch from riding, he had taken her on a quick tour of his home. Just like yesterday, she had been more than impressed with what she'd seen. His bedroom had left her speechless, and she couldn't imagine him sleeping in that huge bed alone. She planned to remedy that. It made no sense for them to be sleeping in separate beds. He wouldn't be happy about it, but he would just have to get over it.

"Um, I wonder what has Micah frowning," Pam Westmoreland, Dillon's wife, leaned over to whisper to her. "He keeps looking over this way, and I recognize that look. It's one of those Westmoreland 'you're not doing as I say' looks."

Kalina couldn't help smiling. The woman who was married to the oldest Westmoreland here had pegged her brother-in-law perfectly. "He's stewing over something I did, but he'll get over it."

Pam chuckled. "Yes, eventually he will. Once in a while they like to have their way but don't think we should have ours. There's nothing wrong with showing them that 'their way' isn't always the best way."

Hours later, while sitting beside Micah as he drove them back to Micah's Manor, Kalina recalled the conversation she'd had with Pam. Maybe continuing to defy his expectations—showing him that his way wasn't the best way—was how she should continue to handle Micah.

"Did you enjoy yourself, Kalina?"

She glanced over at him. He hadn't said much to her all evening, although the only time he'd left her side was when the women had come to claim her. If this was his way of letting her get to know him then he was way off the mark.

"Yes, I had a wonderful time. I enjoyed conversing with the women in your family. They're all nice. I like them."

"They like you, too. I could tell."

"What about you, Micah? Do you like me?"

He seemed surprised by her question. "Yes, of course. Why do you ask?"

"Um, no reason."

She looked straight ahead at the scenery flying by the car's windshield, and felt a warm sensation ignite within her every time she was aware that he was looking at her.

She surprised him when she caught him staring one of those times. Just so he wouldn't know she was on to what he was doing, she smiled and asked, "Was your grandfather Raphel really married to all those women? Bailey told me the story of how he became the black sheep of the family after running off in the early 1900s with the preacher's wife and about all the other wives he supposedly collected along the way."

Micah made a turn into Micah's Manor. "That's what everyone wants to find out. We need to know if there are any more Westmorelands out there that we don't know about. That's how we found out about our cousins living in Atlanta, Montana and Texas. Until a few years ago, we were unaware that Raphel had a twin by the name of Reginald Westmoreland. He's the great-grandfather for those other Westmorelands. Megan is hiring a private detective to help solve the puzzle about Raphel's other wives. We've eliminated two as having given birth to heirs, and now we have two more to check out."

He paused a moment and said, "The investigator, a guy by the name of Rico Claiborne, was to start work on the case months ago, but his involvement in another case has delayed things for a while. We're hoping he can start the search soon. Megan is determined to see how many more Westmorelands she can dig up."

Kalina chuckled. "There are so many of you now. I can't imagine there being others."

Micah smiled. "Well, there are, trust me. You'll get to meet them in a few weeks when they arrive for Gemma and Callum's son's christening."

"Must be nice," she said softly.

He glanced over at her. "What must be?"

"To be part of a big family where everyone is close and looks out for each other. I like that. I've never experienced anything like that before. Other than my grandparents, there has only been me and Dad…and well, you know how my relationship with him is most of the time."

Micah didn't say anything, and maybe it was just as well. It didn't take much for Kalina to recall what had kept them apart for the past two years. Although he was probably hoping otherwise, by getting to know him better, all she'd seen so far was his moody side.

When he brought the car to a stop, she said, "You like having your way, don't you, Micah?"

He didn't say anything at first and then he pushed his Stetson back out of his face. "Is that what you think?"

"Yes. But maybe you should consider something?"

"What?"

"Whatever it is you're trying to prove to me, there's a possibility that your way isn't the best way to prove it. You brought me here so I could get to know you better. It's day two and already we're at odds with each other, and only because I tempted you into doing something that I knew we both wanted to do anyway. But if you prefer that it not happen again, then it won't. In other words, I will give you just what you want…which is practically nothing."

Without saying anything else, she opened the door, got out of the truck and walked toward the house.

Be careful what you ask for, Micah thought over his cup of coffee a few mornings later as he watched Kalina enter the kitchen. She'd been here for five days. Things between them weren't bad, but they could be better. It wasn't that they were mad at each other. In fact, they were always pleasant to each other. Too pleasant.

She had no idea that beneath all his pleasantry was a man who was horny as hell. A man whose body ached to make love to her, hold her at night. He wished she could sleep with him instead of sleeping alone in his guest bedroom. But his mind knew his decision that he and Kalina not make love for a while was the right one to make. It was his body wishing things could be different.

They would see each other in the mornings, and then usually, during the day, they went their separate ways. It wasn't uncommon for one of his female cousins or cousins-in-laws to come pick her up. On those days, he wouldn't see her till much later. So much for them spending time together.

"Good morning, Micah."

He put down his cup and pushed the newspaper aside. "Good morning, Kalina. Did you enjoy going shopping yesterday?"

She sat down at the table across from him and smiled. "I didn't go shopping yesterday. We did that two days ago. Yesterday, we went into town and watched a movie. One of those chick flicks."

He nodded. She could have asked him, and he would have taken her to the movies, chick flick or not. He got up to pour himself another cup of coffee, trying not to notice what she was wearing. Most days she would be wearing jeans and a top. Today she had put on a simple dress. Seeing her in it reminded him once again of what a nice pair of legs she owned.

"Are you and the ladies going someplace again today?" he decided to ask her.

She shook her head. "No. I plan to hang around here today. But I promise not to get in your way."

"You won't get in my way." He came back to the table and sat down. "Other than that day we went riding, I haven't shown you the rest of my property."

She lifted an eyebrow in surprise. "You mean there's more?"

He chuckled. "Yes, there's a part that I lease out to Ramsey for his sheep, and then another part I lease out to my brother Jason and my cousins Zane and Derringer for their horse-breeding business."

He took a sip of his coffee. "So how about us spending the day together?"

She smiled brightly. "I'd love to."

Hours later when Micah and Kalina returned to Micah's Manor, she dropped down in the first chair she came to, which was a leather recliner in the living room. When Micah had suggested they spend time together, she hadn't expected that they would be gone for most of the day.

First, after she had changed clothes, they had gone riding and he'd shown her the rest of his property. Then he had come back so they could change clothes, and they had taken the truck into town. He had driven to the nursing home to visit a man by the name of Henry Ryan. Henry, Micah had explained, had been the town's doctor for years and had delivered every Westmoreland born in Denver, including his parents. The old man, who was in his late nineties, was suffering from a severe case of Alzheimer's.

It had been obvious to Kalina from the first that the old man had been glad to see Micah and vice versa. Today, Henry's mind appeared sharp, and he had shared a lot with her, including some stories from Micah's childhood years. On the drive home, Micah had explained that things weren't always that way. There would be days when he visited Henry and the old man hadn't known who he was. Micah had credited Henry with being the one to influence him to go into the medical field.

Today, Kalina had seen another side of Micah. She'd known he was a dedicated doctor, but she'd seen him interact with people on a personal level. Not only had he visited with Henry, but he had dropped by the rooms of others at the nursing home that he'd gotten to know over the years. He remembered them, and they remembered him. Before arriving at the home, he had stopped by a market and purchased fresh fruit for everyone, which they all seemed to enjoy.

Seeing them, especially the older men, made her realize that her father would one day get old and she would be his caretaker. He was in the best of health now, but he wasn't getting any younger. It also made her realize, more so than ever, just what a caring person Micah was.

She turned to Micah, who'd come to sit on the sofa across from her. "I'll prepare dinner tonight."

He raised an eyebrow. "You can cook?"

Kalina laughed. "Yes. I lived on my grandparents'

farm in Alabama for a while, remember. They were big cooks and taught me my way around any kitchen. I just don't usually have a lot of time to do it when I'm working."

She glanced at her watch. "I think I'll cook a pot of spaghetti with a salad. Mind if I borrow the truck and go to that Walmart we passed on the way back to get some fresh ingredients?"

"No, I don't mind," he said, standing and pulling the truck keys from his pocket. His cousins had stocked his kitchen, but only with nonperishables. "Although you might want to check with Chloe or Pam. They probably have what you'll need since they like to cook."

"I'm sure they do, but I need to get a prescription filled anyway. I didn't think about it earlier while we were out."

"No problem. Do you want me to drive you?"

"No, I'll be fine." She stood. "And I won't be gone long."

"Glad to see that you're out of your foul mood, Micah," Derringer Westmoreland said with a grin as he fed one of the horses he kept in Micah's barn.

Micah shot him a dirty look, which any other man would have known meant he should zip it, but Derringer wasn't worried. He knew his cousin was not the hostile type. "I don't know what brought it on, but you need to chill. Save your frown for those contagious diseases."

Micah folded his arms across his chest. "And when did you become an expert on domestic matters, Derringer?"

Derringer chuckled. "On the day I married Lucia. I

tell you, my life hasn't been the same since. Being married is good. You ought to try it."

Micah dropped his hands to his sides and shrugged. "I plan on it. I just have to get Kalina to trust me. She's got to get to know me better."

Derringer frowned, which didn't surprise Micah. Whereas Zane hadn't seen anything strange by that comment, Derringer would. "Doesn't she know you already?"

"Not the way I want her to. She thinks I betrayed her a couple of years ago, and I believe that once she gets to know me she'll see I'm not capable of doing anything like that."

Now it was Derringer who crossed his arms over his chest. "Wouldn't it be easier just to tell her that you didn't do it?"

"I tried that. It's her father's word against mine, and she chose to believe her father."

Derringer rubbed his chin in a thoughtful way. "You can always confront her old man and beat the truth out of him." He then glanced around. "And speaking of Kalina, where is she? I know the ladies decided not to do anything today since both Lucia and Chloe had to take the babies in for their regular pediatric visits."

"She's preparing dinner and needed to pick up a few items from the store." Micah checked his watch. "She's been gone longer than I figured she would be."

Concern touched Derringer's features. "You think she's gotten lost?"

"She shouldn't be lost since she was only going to that Walmart a few miles away. If she's not back in a few more minutes, I'll call her on her cell phone to make sure she's okay."

The two men had walked out of the barn when Micah's phone rang. He didn't recognize the number. "Yes?"

"Mr. Westmoreland, this is Nurse Nelson at Denver Memorial. There was a car accident involving Kalina Daniels, and she was brought into the emergency room. Your number was listed in her phone directory as one of those to call in case of an emergency. Since you're local we thought we would call you first."

Micah's heart stopped beating. "She was in an accident?"

"Yes."

"How is she?" he asked in a frantic tone.

"Not sure. The doctor is checking her out now."

Absently, Micah ended the call and looked at Derringer. "Kalina was in an accident, and she's been taken to Denver Memorial."

Derringer quickly tied the horse to the nearest post. "Come on. Let's go."

"Do you know an E.R. doctor's biggest nightmare?"

Kalina glanced over at the doctor who was checking out the bruise on her arm. "What?"

"Having to treat another doctor."

Kalina laughed. "Hey, I wasn't *that* bad, Dr. Parker."

"No." The older doctor nodded while grinning. "I understand you were worse. According to the paramedics, you wouldn't let them work on you until they'd checked out the person who was driving the other car. The one who ran the red light and caused the accident."

"Only because I knew I was fine. She's the one whose air bag deployed," Kalina said.

"Yes, but still, you deserved to be checked out as much as she did."

Kalina didn't say anything as she remembered the accident. She hadn't seen it coming. She had picked up all the things she needed from the store and was on her way back to Micah's Manor when out of nowhere, a car plowed into her from the side. She could only be thankful that she'd been driving Micah's heavy-duty truck and not a small car. Otherwise, her injuries would have been more severe.

"I don't like the look of this knot on your head. I should keep you overnight for observation."

Kalina shook her head. "Don't waste a bed. I'll be fine."

"Maybe. Maybe not. I don't have to tell you about head injuries, do I, Dr. Daniels?"

She rolled her eyes. "No, sir, you don't."

"Are you living alone?"

"No, I'm visiting someone in this area. I think your nurse has already called Micah."

The doctor looked at her. "Micah? Micah Westmoreland?"

Kalina smiled. "Yes. You know him?"

The doctor nodded. "Yes, I went to high school with his father. I know those Westmorelands well. It was tragic how they lost their parents, aunt and uncle in that plane crash."

"Yes, it was."

"The folks around here can't help admiring how they all stuck together in light of that devastation, and now all of them have made something of themselves, even Bane. God knows we'd almost given up on him, but now I understand that he's—"

Suddenly the privacy curtain was snatched aside, and Micah stood there with a terrified look on his face. "Kalina!"

And before she could draw her next breath, he had crossed the floor and pulled her into his arms.

Chapter 10

Back at Micah's Manor, Kalina, who was sitting comfortably on the sofa, rolled her eyes. "If you ask me one more time if I'm okay, I'm going to scream. Read my lips, Micah. I'm fine."

Micah drew in a deep breath. He knew he was being anal, but he couldn't help it. When he'd received a call from that nurse about Kalina's accident, he'd lost it. It was a good thing Derringer had been there. There was probably no way he could have driven to the hospital without causing his own accident. He'd been that much of a basket case.

"Don't fall asleep, Kalina. If you do, I'm only going to wake you up," he warned.

She shook her head. "Micah, have you forgotten I'm a doctor, as well. I'm familiar with the do's and don'ts following a head injury. But, like I told Dr. Parker at the hospital, I'm fine."

"And I intend to make sure you stay that way." Micah crossed the room to her, leaned down and placed a kiss on her lips.

He straightened and glanced down at her. "I don't think you know how I felt when I received that call, Kal. It reminded me so much of the call I got that day from Dillon, telling me about Mom, Dad, Uncle Thomas and Aunt Susan. I was at the university, in between classes, and it seemed that everything went black."

She nodded slowly, hearing the pain in his voice. "I can imagine."

He shook his head. "No, honestly, you can't." He sat down beside her. "It was the kind of emotional pain and fear I'd hoped never to experience again. But I did today, when I got that call about you."

She stared at him for a few moments and then reached over and took his hand in hers. "Sorry. I didn't mean to do that to you."

He sighed deeply. "It wasn't your fault. Accidents happen. But if I didn't know before, I know now."

She lifted a brow. "You know what?"

"How much I care for you." He gently pulled her onto his lap. "I know you've been thinking that I've been acting moody and out of sorts for the past couple of days, but I wanted so much for you to believe I'm not the person you think I am."

She wrapped her arms around him, as well. "I know. And I also know that's why you didn't want to make love to me."

She twisted around in his arms to face him. "You were wasting both our time by doing that, you know. I realized even before leaving India that you hadn't lied to me about our affair in Sydney."

He pulled back, surprised. "You had?"

"Yes. I had accepted what you said as the truth before I agreed to come here to Denver with you."

She smiled. "I figured that you *had* to be telling the truth, otherwise, you were taking a big risk in bringing me here to meet your family. But then I knew for a fact that you had been telling the truth once you got me here and wanted to put a hold on our lovemaking. You were willing to do without something I knew you really wanted just to prove yourself to me. You really didn't have to."

He covered her hand with his. "I felt that I did have to do it. Someone once told me that sacrifices today will result in dividends tomorrow, and I wanted you for my dividend. I love you, Kalina."

"And I love you, too. I realized that before coming here, as well. That night you took me dancing and I felt something in the way you held me, in the way you were talking to me. That night, I knew the truth in what you had been trying to tell me. And I knew the truth about what my feelings were for you."

She quieted for a moment and then said, "Although there's not an excuse for my father's actions, I believe I know why he did what he did. He's always been controlling, but I never thought he would go that far. I was wrong. And I was wrong for not believing you in the first place."

He shook his head. "No, like I said, you didn't know me. We had an affair that was purely sexual. The only commitment we'd made was to share a bed. It didn't take me long to figure out that I wanted more from you.

That night you ended things was the night I had planned on telling you how I felt. Afterward, I was angry that you didn't believe in me, that you actually thought I didn't care, that I would go along with your father about something like that."

He paused. "When I came home, I told Dillon everything and he suggested that I straighten things out. But my pride wouldn't let me. I wasted two years being angry, but the night I saw you again I knew that no matter what, I would make you mine."

"No worries then," Kalina said, reaching up and cupping his chin. "I am yours."

He inhaled sharply when her fingers slid beneath his T-shirt to touch his naked skin over his heart. It seemed the moment she touched him that heat consumed him and spread to every part of his body. Although he tried playing it down, his desire for her was magnified to a level he hadn't thought possible.

All he could think about was that he'd almost lost her and the fear that had lodged in his throat had made it difficult to breathe. And now she was here, back at his manor, where she belonged. He knew then that he would always protect her. Not control her like her old man tended to do, but to protect her.

"Make love to me, Micah."

Her whispered request swept across his lips. "I need you inside me."

Micah studied her thoughtfully. He saw the heat in her eyes and felt the feverishness of her skin. Other than that one time on the sofa, he hadn't touched her since coming to Denver, wanting her to get to know the real him. Well, at that moment, the real him wanted her with a passion that he felt even in the tips of his fingers. She knew him, and she loved him, just as he loved her.

"What about your head?" he whispered, standing, sweeping her into his arms and moving toward the stairs.

She wrapped her arms around him and chuckled against his neck. "My head is fine, but there is another ache that's bothering me. To be quite honest with you, it was bothering me a long time before the accident. It's the way my body is aching to be touched by you. Loved by you. Needed by you."

Just how he made it up the stairs to his bedroom, he wasn't sure. All he knew was that he had placed her in the middle of his bed, stripped off her clothes and taken off his own clothes in no time at all. He stood at the foot of the bed, gazing at her. He let his eyes roam all over her and knew there was nothing subtle about how he was doing it.

This was the first time she had been in his bed, but he had fantasized about her being here plenty of times. Even during the last five days, when he'd known she was sleeping in the bedroom above his, he had wanted her here, with him. More than once, he had been tempted to get up during the night and go to her, to forget about the promise of not touching her until she had gotten to know him. It had been hard wanting her and vowing not to touch her.

And she hadn't made it easy. At times she had deliberately tried tempting him again. She would go shopping with his cousins and then parade around in some of the sexiest outfits a store could sell. But he had resisted temptation.

But not now. He didn't plan on resisting anything,

especially not the naked woman stretched out in the middle of his huge bed looking as if she belonged there. He intended to keep her there.

"I love you," he said in a low, gravelly voice filled with so much emotion he had to fight from getting choked. "I knew I did, but I didn't know just how much until I got that phone call, Kalina. You are my heart. My soul. My very reason for existing."

He slowly moved toward the bed. "I never knew how much I cherished this part of our relationship until it was gone. I can't go back and see it as 'just sex' anymore. Not when I can distinctively hear, in the back of my mind, all your moans of pleasure, the way you groan to let me know how much you want me. Not when I remember that little smile that lets me know just how much you are satisfied. No, we never had sex. We've always made love."

Kalina breathed in Micah's scent as he moved closer to her. Not wanting to wait any longer, she rose up in the bed and met him. When he placed his knee on the bed, they tumbled back into the bedcovers together. At that moment, everything ceased to exist except them.

As if she needed to make sure this moment was real, she reached out and touched his face, using her fingertips to caress the strong lines of his features. But she didn't stop there, she trailed her fingers down to his chest, feeling the hard muscles of his stomach. Her hands moved even lower, to the hardest part of him, cupping him. She thought, for someone to be so hard, there were certain parts of him that were smooth as a baby's behind.

"What are you doing to me?" he asked in a tortured groan when she continued to stroke him.

She met his gaze. "Staking my claim."

He chuckled softly. "Baby, trust me. You staked your claim two years ago. I haven't been able to make love to another woman since."

Micah knew the moment she realized the truth of what he'd said. The smile that touched her features warmed him all over, made him appreciate that he was a man, the man who had *this* woman.

Not being able to wait any longer, he leaned over and brushed a kiss against her lips. Then he moved his mouth lower to capture a nipple in his mouth and suck on it.

She arched against him, and he appreciated her doing so. He increased the suction of his mouth, relishing the taste of her while thinking of all the hours he'd lain in this bed awake and aroused, knowing she'd been only one floor away.

"Micah."

The tone of her voice alerted him that she needed him inside that part of her that was aching. Releasing her nipple, he eased her down in the bed. Before he moved in place between her legs, he had to taste her. He shifted his body to bury his head between her legs.

Kalina screamed the moment Micah's tongue swept inside her. The tip of it was hot and determined. And the way it swirled inside her had her senses swirling in unison. She was convinced that no other man could do things with their tongue the way he could. He was devouring her senseless, and she couldn't do anything but lie there and moan.

And then she felt it, an early sign that a quake was about to happen. The way her toes began tingling while her head crested with sensations that moved through every part of her.

She sucked in a deep breath, and it was then that she saw he had sensed what was about to happen and had moved in place over her. The hardness of him slid through her wetness, filling her and going beyond.

She was well aware of the moment when their bodies locked. He gazed down at her, and their eyes connected. He was about to give her the ride of her life, and she needed it. She wanted it.

He began moving, thrusting in and out of her while holding her gaze. She felt it. She felt him. There was nothing like the feeling of being made love to by the one man who had your heart. Your soul.

He kept moving, thrusting, pounding into her as if making up for lost time, for misunderstandings and disagreements. She wouldn't delude herself into thinking those things wouldn't happen again, but now they would have love to cushion the blows.

At that moment, he deliberately curved his body to hit her at an angle that made her G-spot weep. It triggered her scream, and she exploded at the same time as he did. They clung to each other, limbs entwined, bodies united. She sucked up air along with his scent. And moments later, when the last remnants of the blast flittered away from her, she collapsed against Micah, moaning his name and knowing she had finally christened his bed.

Their bed.

The next two weeks flowed smoothly, although they were busy ones for the Westmoreland family. Gemma and Callum were returning to christen their firstborn. Ramsey and Chloe had consented to be godparents.

All the out-of-towners were scheduled to arrive by Thursday. Most had made plans to stay at nearby hotels, but others were staying with family members. Jason and his wife, Bella, had turned what had been the home she'd inherited from her grandfather into a private inn just for family when they came to visit.

Pam had solicited Kalina's help in planning activities for everyone, and Kalina appreciated being included. Her days were kept busy, but her nights remained exclusively for Micah. They rode horses around the property every evening, cooked dinner together, took their shower, once in a while watched a movie. But every night they shared a bed. She thought there was nothing like waking up each morning in his arms.

Like this morning.

She glanced over at him and frowned. "Just look what you did to me. What if I wanted to wear a low-cut dress?"

Micah glanced over at the passion mark he'd left on Kalina. Right there on her breast. There was not even a hint of remorse in his voice when he said, "Then I guess you'd be changing outfits."

"Oh, you!" she said, snatching the pillow and throwing it at him. "You probably did it deliberately. You like branding me."

He couldn't deny her charge because it was true. But what he liked most of all was tasting her. Unfortunately, he had a tendency to leave a mark whenever he did. Hell, he couldn't help that she tasted so damn good.

He reached out and grabbed her before she could

toss another pillow his way. "Come here, sweetheart. Let me kiss it away."

"All you're going to do is make another mark. Stay away from me."

He rolled his eyes. "Yeah. Right."

When she tried scooting away, he grabbed her foot to bring her back. He then lowered his mouth to lick her calf. When she moaned, he said, "See, you know you like it."

"Yes, but we don't have the time. Everyone starts arriving today."

"Let them. They can wait."

When he released his hold on her to grab her around the waist, she used that opportunity to scoot away from him and quickly made a move to get out of bed. But she wasn't quick enough. He grabbed her arm and pulled her back. "Did you think you would get away, Dr. Daniels?"

She couldn't help laughing, and she threw herself into his arms. "It's not like I'm ready to get out of bed anyway," she said, before pressing her lips to his. He kissed her the way she liked, in a way that sent sensations escalating all through her.

When he released her lips she felt a tug on her left hand and looked down. She sucked in a deep breath at the beautiful diamond ring Micah had just slid on her finger. She threw her hand to her chest to stop the rapid beating of her heart. "Oh, my God!"

Micah chuckled as he brought her ringed hand to his lips and kissed it. "Will you, Kalina Marie Daniels, marry me? Will you live here with me at Micah's Manor? Have my babies? Make me the happiest man on earth?"

Tears streamed down her face, and she tried swiping them away, but more kept coming. "Oh, Micah, yes! Yes! I'll marry you, live here and have your babies."

Micah laughed and pulled her into his arms, sealing her promise with another kiss.

It was much later when they left Micah's Manor to head over to Dillon's place. Dillon had called to say the Atlanta Westmorelands had begun arriving already. Micah had put his brother on the speakerphone and Kalina could hear the excitement in Dillon's voice. It didn't take long, when around the Westmorelands, to know that family meant everything to them. They enjoyed the times they were able to get together.

Micah had explained that all the Westmorelands were making up for the years they hadn't shared when they hadn't known about each other. Their dedication to family was the reason it was important to make sure there weren't any other Westmorelands out there they didn't know about.

Kalina walked into Dillon and Pam's house with Micah by her side and a ring on her finger. Several family members noticed her diamond and congratulated them and asked when the big day would be. She and Micah both wanted a June wedding, which was less than a couple of months away.

Once they walked into the living room, Kalina suddenly came to a stop. Several people were standing around talking. Micah's arm tightened around her shoulders and he glanced down at her. "What's wrong, baby?"

Instead of answering, she stared across the room

and he followed her gaze. Immediately, he knew what was bothering her.

"That woman is here," was all Kalina would say.

Micah couldn't help fighting back a smile as he gazed over at Olivia. "Yes, she's here, and I think it's time for you to meet her."

Kalina began backing up slowly. "I'd rather not do that."

"And if you don't, my cousin Senator Reggie Westmoreland will wonder why you're deliberately being rude to his wife."

Kalina jerked her head up and looked at Micah. "His wife?"

Micah couldn't hold back his smile any longer. "Yes, his wife. That's Olivia Jeffries Westmoreland."

"But you had me thinking that—"

Micah reached out and quickly kissed the words from Kalina's lips. "Don't place the blame on me, sweetheart. You assumed Olivia and I had something going on. I never told you that. In fact, I recall telling you that there was nothing going on with us. Olivia and Reggie had invited me to lunch while I was in D.C., but it was Olivia who came to pick me up that day. I couldn't help that you got jealous."

She glared. "I didn't get jealous."

"Didn't you?"

He stared at her, and she stared back. Then a slow smile spread across her face, and she shrugged her shoulders. "Okay, maybe I did. But just a little."

He raised a dubious eyebrow. "Um, just a little."

"Don't press it, Micah."

He laughed and tightened his hand on hers. "Okay, I won't. Come on and meet Reggie, Olivia and their twin sons, as well as the rest of my cousins. And I think we should announce our good news."

The christening for Callum Austell II was a beautiful ceremony, and Kalina got to meet Micah's cousin Gemma. She couldn't wait to tell her just how gifted she was as an interior designer, which prompted Gemma to share how her husband had whisked her off to Australia in the first place.

It was obvious to anyone around them that Gemma and her husband were in love and that they shared a happy marriage. But then, Kalina thought, the same thing could be said for all of Micah's cousins' marriages. All the men favored each other, and the women they'd selected as their mates complemented them.

After the church service, dinner was served at the big house with all the women pitching in and cooking. Kalina felt good knowing the games she had organized for everyone, especially the kids, had been a big hit.

It was late when she and Micah finally made it back to Micah's Manor. After a full day of being around the Westmorelands, she should have been exhausted, ready to fall on her face, but she felt wired and had Micah telling her the story about Raphel all over again. She was even more fascinated with it the second time.

"That's how Dillon and Pam met," Micah said as they headed up the stairs. An hour or so later, he and Kalina had showered together and were settling down to watch a movie in bed, when the phone rang.

He glanced over at the clock. "I wonder who's calling this late," he said, reaching for the phone. "Probably Megan wanting to know if we still have any of that ice cream she bought."

He picked up the phone. "Hello."

"Are you watching television, Micah?"

He heard the urgency in Dillon's voice. "I just turned it on to watch a DVD, why?"

"I think you ought to switch to CNN. There's something going on in Oregon."

Micah raised a brow. "Oregon?"

"Yes. It's like people are falling dead in the streets for no reason."

Micah was out of the bed in a flash. He looked at Kalina, who had the remote in her hand. "Switch to CNN."

She did so, and Anderson Cooper's face flared to life on the screen as he said, "No one is sure what is happening here, but it's like a scene out of *Contagion*. So far, more than ten people have died. The Centers for Disease Control has…"

At that moment Micah's phone on his dresser, the one with a direct line to Washington, rang. He moved quickly to pick it up. "Yes?"

He looked over at Kalina and nodded. Her gaze held his, knowing whenever that particular phone rang it was urgent. "All right, we're on our way."

He clicked off. "They're calling the entire team in. We're needed in Oregon."

Chapter 11

Micah looked around the huge room. His team was reunited. Kalina, Theo and Beau. They had all read the report and knew what they were up against. The Centers for Disease Control had called in an international team and the three of them were just a part of it. But in his mind they were a major part. All the evidence collected pointed to a possible terrorist attack. If they didn't get a grip on what was happening and stop it, the effect could make 9/11 look small in comparison.

It didn't take long to see, from the tissue taken from some of the victims, that they were dealing with the same kind of virus that he, Kalina and Theo had investigated in India just weeks ago. How did it get to the States? And, more important, who was responsible for spreading it?

He felt his phone vibrating in his pocket and didn't

have to pull it out to see who was calling. It was the same person who'd been blowing up his phone for the past two days. General Daniels. He was demanding that Kalina be sent home, out of harm's way. Like two years ago, a part of Micah understood the man's concern for his daughter's safety. He, of all people, didn't want a single hair on Kalina's head hurt in any way. But as much as he loved Kalina and wanted to keep her safe, he also respected her profession and her choices in life. That's how he and the old man differed.

But still…

"That's all for now. I'll give everyone an update when I get one from Washington. Stay safe." Micah then glanced over at Kalina. "Dr. Daniels, can you remain a few moments, please? I'd like to talk to you."

He moved behind his desk as the others filed out. Beau, being the last one, closed the door behind him. But not before giving Micah the eye, communicating to him, for his own benefit and safety, to move the vase off the desk. Micah smiled. Beau knew of Kalina's need to throw things when she was angry. He had tried telling his best friend that the vase throwing had been limited to that one episode. It hadn't happened again.

"Yes, Micah? What is it?"

He pulled his still-vibrating phone out of his pocket and placed it in the middle of his desk. "Your father."

He then reached into his desk and pulled out a sealed, official-looking envelope and handed it to her. "Your father, as well."

She opened the envelope and began reading the documents. Moments later, she lifted her head and met his gaze. "Orders for me to be reassigned to another project?"

"Yes."

She held his gaze for a long time as she placed the documents back in the envelope. He saw the defeated shift of her shoulders. "So when do I leave?"

He leaned back in his chair. "I, of all people, don't want anything to happen to you, Kalina," he said in a low voice. "I love you more than life itself, and I know how dangerous it is for you to be here. The death toll has gone up to fifteen. Already a domestic terrorist group is claiming victory and vows more people will lose their lives here before it's over, before we can find a way to stop it. I don't want you in that number."

There was an intensity, a desperation, in his tone that even he heard. It was also one that he felt. He drew in a deep breath and continued, "You are the other half that makes me whole. The sunshine I wake up to each morning, and the rock I hold near me when I go to bed at night. I don't want to lose you. If anything happens to you, I die, as well."

He could see she was fighting the tears in her eyes, as if she already knew the verdict. She was getting used to it. She lifted her chin defiantly. "So, you're sending me away?"

He held his gaze as he shook his head. "No, I'm keeping you safe. Your father doesn't call the shots anymore in your personal or professional life. I'm denying his orders on the grounds that you're needed here. You worked on this virus just weeks ago. You're familiar with it. That alone should override his request at the CDC."

She released an appreciative sigh. "Thank you."

"Don't thank me. The next days are going to be rough. Whoever did this is out there and waiting around for their attack to be successful. There have been few survivors and those who have survived are quarantined and in critical condition."

She sat down on the edge of his desk. "We're working against time, Micah. People want to leave Portland, but everyone is being forced to stay because the virus is contagious."

Already the level of fear among citizens had been raised. People were naturally afraid of the unknown… and this was definitely an unknown. Each victim had presented the same symptoms they'd found in India.

"I wish the CDC hadn't just put that blood sample I sent to them on the shelf," she added. "It was the one thing I was able to get from the surviving—"

Micah sat up in his seat. "Hey, that might be it. We need someone to analyze the contents of those vials, immediately. I don't give a damn about how behind they are. This is urgent." He picked up the phone that was a direct line to Washington and the Department of Health and Human Services.

Four more people died over a two-day period, but Micah put the fire under the CDC to study the contents of those vials that Kalina had sent to them weeks ago. He had assembled his team in the lab to apprise them of what was going on.

"And you think we might be able to come up with a serum that can stop the virus?" Beau asked.

"We hope so," Micah said, rubbing a hand down his face. "It might be a shot in the dark, but it's the only one we have."

At that moment, the phone—his direct line to the

CDC—rang, and he quickly picked it up. "Dr. Westmoreland."

He nodded a few times and then he felt a relieved expression touch his features. "Great! You get it here, and we'll dispense it."

He looked over at his team. "Based on what they analyzed in those vials, they think they've come up with an antidote. They're flying it here via military aircraft. We are to work with the local teams and make sure every man, woman and child is inoculated immediately." He stood. "Let's go!"

Five days later, a military aircraft carrying Micah and his team arrived at Andrews Air Force Base. The antidote had worked, and millions of lives were saved. Homeland Security had arrested those involved.

Micah and every member of his team had worked nonstop to save lives and thanks to their hard work, and the work of all the others, there hadn't been any more deaths.

He drew in a deep breath as he glanced over at Kalina. He knew how exhausted she was, though she didn't show it. All of them had kept long hours, and he was looking forward to a hotel room with a big bed…and his woman. They would rest up, and then they would ease into much-needed lovemaking.

They had barely departed the plane when an official government vehicle pulled up. They paused, and Micah really wasn't surprised when Kalina's father got out of the car. General Daniels frowned at them. All military personnel there saluted and stood at attention as he moved toward them.

As much as Micah wanted to hate the man, he

couldn't. After all, he was Kalina's father and without the man his daughter would not have been born. So Micah figured that he owed the older man something. That was all he could find to like about him. At the moment, he couldn't think of a single other thing.

General Daniels came to a stop in front of them. "Dr. Westmoreland. I need to congratulate you and your team for a job well done."

"Thank you, sir." Micah decided to give the man the respect he had earned. Considering the lie the man had told, whether he really deserved it was another matter.

The general's gaze shifted to Kalina, and Micah knew where she had gotten her stubbornness. She lifted her chin and glared at her father, general or not. Micah noticed something else, as well. It was there in the older man's eyes as he looked at Kalina. He loved his daughter and was scared to death of losing her. Kalina had told him how her mother had died when she was ten and how hard her father had taken her mother's death.

"Kalina Marie."

"General."

"You look well."

"Thank you."

The general spoke to all the others and then officially dismissed them to leave. He then said to Kalina when the three of them were alone, "I'm here to take you and Dr. Westmoreland to your hotel."

Kalina's glare deepened. "I'll walk first. Sir."

Micah saw the pain from Kalina's words settle in the old man's eyes. He decided to extend something to General Daniels that the old man would never extend to him: empathy.

He then turned to Kalina and said in a joking tone,

"No, you aren't walking to the hotel because that means I'll have to walk with you. We're a team, remember? And if I take another step, I'm going to drop. I think we should take your father up on his offer. Besides, there're a couple things we need to talk to him about, don't you think? Like our wedding plans."

The general blinked. "The two of you are back together? And getting married?"

Kalina turned on her father. "Yes, with no thanks to you."

The man did have the decency to look chagrined. Micah had a feeling the man truly felt regret for his actions two years ago. "And there's something else I think you should tell your father, Kalina."

She glanced up at Micah. "What?"

Micah smiled. "That he's going to be a grandfather."

Both Kalina and her father gasped in shock, but for different reasons. Kalina turned to Micah. "You knew?"

He nodded as his smile widened. "Yes, I'm a doctor, remember."

"And you still let me stay on the team? You didn't send me away, knowing my condition?"

He reached out and gently caressed her cheek. "You were under my love and protection, but not my control."

He then looked over at her father when he added, "There is a difference, General, and one day I'll be happy to sit down and explain it to you."

The old man nodded appreciatively and held Micah's gaze as a deep understanding and acceptance passed between them.

"But right now, I'd like to be taken to the nearest hotel. I plan on sleeping for the next five days," Micah said, moving toward the government car.

"With me right beside you," Kalina added as she walked with him. She figured she'd gotten pregnant during the time the doctor had placed her on antibiotics after the auto accident. Even as a medical professional, it hadn't crossed her mind that the prescribed medicine would have a negative effect on her birth control pills. There had been too much going on for her emotionally at the time. Since she'd found out, she had been waiting for the perfect time to tell Micah that he would be a father. And to think, he'd suspected all the time.

Micah took Kalina's hand in his, immediately feeling the heat that always seemed to generate between them. This was his woman, soon to be his wife and the mother of his child. Life couldn't be better.

Epilogue

Two months later, on a hot June day, Micah and Kalina stood before a minister on the grounds of Micah's Manor and listened when a minister proclaimed, "I now pronounce you man and wife."

All the Westmorelands had returned to help celebrate on their beautiful day.

"You may now kiss your bride."

Micah pulled Kalina into his arms and gave her a kiss she had come to know, love and expect. He released her from the kiss only when a couple of his brothers and cousins began clearing their throats.

With the help of Pam, Lucia, Bella, Megan, Bailey and Chloe, Kalina had found the perfect wedding dress. She'd also formed relationships with the women she now considered sisters. Kalina and Micah's honeymoon to Paris was a nice wedding gift—compliments of her father.

And Bella had taken time to give birth to beautiful identical twin daughters. And Ramsey and Chloe now had a son who was the spitting image of his father. Already, the fathers, uncles and cousins were spoiling them rotten. Kalina had to admit she was in that number, and couldn't wait to hold her own baby in her arms.

A short while later, at the reception, Kalina glanced over at her husband. He was such a handsome man, dashing as ever in his tux. More than one person had said that they made a beautiful couple.

She had been pulled to the side and was talking to the ladies when suddenly the group got quiet. Everyone turned when an extremely handsome man got out of a car. The first thing Kalina thought, with his dashing good looks, was that perhaps he was some Hollywood celebrity who was a friend of one of Micah's cousins, especially since it seemed all the male Westmorelands knew who he was.

When Micah approached and touched her hand she glanced up at him and smiled. She hadn't been aware he had returned to her side. "Who's that?" she asked curiously.

He followed her gaze and chuckled. "That's Rico Claiborne. Savannah and Jessica's brother."

Kalina nodded. Savannah and Jessica were sisters who'd married the Westmoreland cousins Durango and Chase. "He's handsome," she couldn't help saying. Then she quickly looked up at her husband and added sheepishly, "But not as handsome as you, of course."

Micah laughed. "Of course. Here, I brought this for you," he said, placing a cold glass of ice water in her hand. "And although Megan is hiring Rico, they are meeting for the first time today," he added. "But from the expression on Megan's face, maybe she needs this cold drink of water instead of you."

Kalina understood exactly what Micah meant when she, like everyone else, watched as the man turned to stare over at Megan, who'd been pointed out to him by some of the Westmoreland cousins. If the look on Megan's face, and the look on the man's face when he saw Megan, was anything to go by, then everyone was feeling the heat.

Kalina took a sip of her seltzer water thinking that Micah was right. Megan should be the one drinking the cooling beverage instead of her.

"Are you ready for our honeymoon, sweetheart?"

Micah's question reclaimed her attention and she smiled up at him, Megan and the hottie private investigator forgotten already. "Yes, I'm ready."

And she was. She was more than ready to start sharing her life with the man she loved.

* * * * *

The first two stories in the *Love in the Limelight* series, where four unstoppable women find fame, fortune and ultimately... true love.

LOVE IN THE LIMELIGHT

New York Times bestselling author
BRENDA JACKSON
&
A.C. ARTHUR

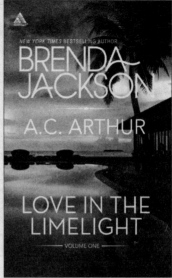

In *Star of His Heart,* Ethan Chambers is Hollywood's most eligible bachelor. But when he meets his costar Rachel Wellesley, he suddenly finds himself thinking twice about staying single.

In *Sing Your Pleasure,* Charlene Quinn has just landed a major contract with L.A.'s hottest record label, working with none other than Akil Hutton. Despite his gruff attitude, she finds herself powerfully attracted to the driven music producer.

Available now wherever books are sold!

www.Harlequin.com

KPLIM11631014R

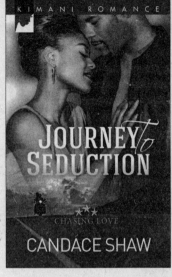